Sally Murrer is a journalist who has written for national magazines and local newspapers for more than 30 years. Years of crime reporting and working with local police led to the ideas for this, her first novel.

Sally has three children and lives in a rambling cottage in Bedfordshire. In 2007 Sally was arrested and charged with obtaining police information illegally – a charge that could potentially threaten the rights of every journalist in the country. The case against her was thrown out of court in November 2008 and 'the Murrer case' became a landmark triumph for press freedom.

ACCORDING TO BELLA

Sally Murrer

Book Guild Publishing
Sussex, England

First published in Great Britain in 2010 by
The Book Guild Ltd
Pavilion View
19 New Road
Brighton, BN1 1UF

Typesetting in Baskerville by
Keyboard Services, Luton, Bedfordshire

Printed in Great Britain by
CPI Antony Rowe

A catalogue record for this book is available from
The British Library

ISBN 978 1 84624 403 2

To Daphne Albertella,
with much love from afar

Prologue

The girl did not flinch as the beetle picked its way cautiously across her cheek and stopped, tiny legs quivering, at the bridge of her nose.

There it hesitated, waiting for the prostrate body to fling out the inevitable hand and brush it aside in irritation, sending it spinning into beetle orbit before plummeting softly onto the dank, dark earth littering the floor of the wooden hut.

But the hand did not come. It did not move. It gleamed coldly against the black earth, its fingers stiffly curled as if in silent plea ... help me, find me, catch my killer...

The beetle, bored of its journey, scuttled outside. The body remained. Waiting.

Chapter One

Bella knew it was going to be a bad Monday when her first phone call was from a deceased person. She may have been moaning that the newsdesk was a little dead lately but she didn't expect to be called by a corpse – and an extremely distressed corpse at that.

'So ... er... you're actually alive then?' she asked, somewhat inanely, of the loudly sobbing Mrs Gladys Worthing, who, according to the current issue of the *Haybridge Gazette*, in an obituary report prepared by Bella's fair hand, had only last week died peacefully at home after a short illness, bravely born. She had been eighty-two. A loving mother and devoted grandmother. Sadly missed by all who'd known her.

Oh bugger, cursed Bella silently. How could she have forgotten the number one Golden Rule for Journalists: never accept an obituary report from anyone other than an authorised Funeral Director? But the politely spoken woman had sounded so sincere when she had called, begging her to pop in just a 'teeny little tribute' to her poor departed mum, who'd been such a stalwart of the Haybridge WI for so many years. She had reminded Bella of her own mum, actually. Oh bugger, bloody, damn, bugger... It was at times like this when Bella wished she had a nice, safe little job in a hairdressing salon.

'Mrs Worthing, I am so terribly sorry. There has obviously been some dreadful mistake and I will put it right, I promise.' She clutched the phone tighter, her eyes darting round the office to check whether her news editor was within earshot. 'We'll print a front page apology,' she whispered.

Front page apology. The three little words guaranteed to cause the beads of sweat to break out on the brow of the most hardened journalist. Three little words synonymous with sackings, disgrace and humiliating grovels at the local benefit office. She would be an unemployed, single mum. Oh God! Emily would be singled out for free school meals. Bella's hands began to tremble.

'It was the shock of seeing my own death report in the paper, you see, my dear,' the quavering voice was explaining. 'It's made me feel right poorly. It's brought on them pains in my chest. I'm having real trouble getting my breath.' To prove the point, the once-departed Mrs Worthing wheezed loudly and gave an ominous splutter.

Now the panic was palpable, dancing a quickstep up Bella's spine and shuddering down her arms. The back of her neck began to prickle. 'Oh dear. Wait! Don't die! I'll call an ambulance,' she squeaked.

There was another splutter. Then a gurgle. Finally there came a most unladylike snort and a sickeningly familiar cackle – of *laughter*.

Bella's eyes shot to the other end of the office, where her colleague Suzy was doubled up in the photographer's chair, her shoulders shaking with laughter and the telephone receiver dangling limply from one hand. Clustered around her, two reporters and a photographer were joining in the merriment, flapping their hands and making 'nee naw, nee naw' ambulance noises.

The cool rush of relief started in Bella's fingertips and spread right down to her toes. 'You ... you bastards!' she yelled, sinking her head into her hands and grinning despite herself.

Sean the news editor looked up from his computer and

shot her a scowl. 'Could we possibly get some work done this morning, children?' He stressed the last word.

Suzy blew him a defiant kiss as she flounced across the office and plonked herself down, still grinning, at her desk opposite Bella's. 'All this excitement will bring on them pains in me chest,' she announced in a falsetto whisper, flicking back her long blonde hair dramatically.

The resulting fit of giggles brought Sean striding officiously across with a pile of papers. 'Press releases. Now WORK! As you are hell-bent on behaving like infants in a kindergarten then you can start with the junior school's Halloween apple bobbing and the Bumbles playgroup fancy dress – that is providing either of you is capable of stringing a sentence together this morning.'

Oh shut up, you pompous old prat, thought Bella, flashing him her most dazzling smile. 'OK – and you can check our spelling afterwards if you like,' she offered.

Everyone knew that Sean Wycroft, in his too tight trousers and carefully ironed shirts, was a chronic anal retentive, probably held over a potty at the age of six months by the formidable Mrs Wycroft with whom, at the age of forty-five, he still lived in a spotless three-bedroom terrace at the posher end of town. He even read *Essential Law for Journalists* in bed.

Not that Bella had been in his bedroom of course. But she couldn't resist that little peek round the door, on the pretext of looking for the bathroom, that time she took some copy round to Sean when he had flu. There it was – the journalists' bible – neatly stacked between the *Oxford English Dictionary* and *Roget's Thesaurus* on his little bedside table, next to his ironed and folded pyjamas on his hospital-cornered bed. That little snoop won her £1 from Mick the sports editor, who'd bet her Sean did *The Times* crossword in bed every night.

Bella was strictly a chick lit girl herself, though she

made the occasional foray into grisly murder mystery novels, particularly when the hero was a handsome chisel-jawed detective with ice-blue eyes, muscles of iron and a heart of steel just waiting to be melted by a tumble-haired local newspaper reporter who could, on a good day, squeeze into size 10 jeans.

Oh, and Mr Flint Eyes would also, of course, fall in love with the journalist's utterly adorable six-year-old daughter and the three of them would live happily ever after, solving grisly murders in a country cottage with honeysuckle round the door. And free-range chickens. And an orchard.

A nudge from Suzy broke Bella's reverie: 'Have you made Em's Halloween party costume yet?' she whispered.

'No. I wanted her to be a witch but she says she absolutely must go as a pumpkin. God knows how I'm going to make it though,' said Bella gloomily, running her hand through her already wild curls, which famous artists might have described decades ago as a shade of Titian but she thought of as irritatingly carrot.

'Mind you, it will make a change to see her in anything else but grubby football shirts and jeans,' she mused, thinking fondly of her freckle-faced tomboy daughter who named her Barbies after her favourite Arsenal players. 'Five more and I'll have the whole team,' Em had announced that morning as she ruthlessly cropped the hair of the latest Princess Barbie handed down by the family of girlie girls next door.

'I'll help with the costume,' said Suzy. 'I owe you one after that obit trick.'

'Thanks,' grinned Bella, switching on her computer. 'But I'll still get you back.'

An hour later she had polished off the apple-bobbing press release, a warning from Trading Standards about dodgy market stall toys and a 200-word story about two people stuck in a lift at an old folks' home. She had also polished off one and a half doughnuts and two cups of coffee.

'Eat the rest of my doughnut, Suze. I'm on a diet,' she begged her friend, one of those infuriatingly stick-thin people who could eat whatever they liked without putting on an ounce.

'But you've eaten all the jam. That's the best bit.'

'Yes. But the jam's less fattening than the doughy bit. There's no fat in jam.'

Bella was still licking the sugar off her fingers when Sean shoved a yellow Post-It note under her nose. 'Police Station. 11.30am. Press conference re crackdown on burglaries.'

'Ask for DS Jonathan Wright. He's a new guy, sent down from the Met to sharpen the local CID guys up a bit apparently. Do try to make a good impression.'

Bella felt Sean eyeing up her best black skirt, which had gone just slightly bobbly in the wash, and the little frayed bits on the cuffs of her only decent white shirt. At least she had washed her hair this morning though, and she was sure she had some lipstick somewhere in the car.

Shrugging her bag onto her shoulder she ran down the stairs of the *Haybridge Gazette* office, almost bumping into Ron, the caretaker and odd-job man who had worked at the small town local paper for as long as anyone could remember, in the reception lobby at the bottom.

'Hi Ron. How's the lumbago?'

'Playing me up something dreadful today, Miss Bella. We're in for some rain I reckon – it's better than them fancy weather reports, is my old back.'

'You poor thing, Ron. Are you using those stick-on heat pad things?'

'Oh aye. They help and you're a good girl for getting

7

them for me, Miss Bella. You're not like some of those reporters up there – don't care about no one expect themselves.' Ron sniffed disdainfully, running his gnarled old hand across his nose.

Bella felt a surge of sympathy for the old man, who lived alone in a stone cottage next to the Common. When he was not pottering about the *Haybridge Gazette* with a screwdriver in his hand, he devoted himself to his allotment, growing copious amounts of huge, rather misshapen vegetables, which he entered religiously each year in the Haybridge horticultural show.

'Tell Miss Emily her pumpkin's coming on a treat. That'll be ready to cut any day now,' he said, showing his stumpy brown teeth in a rare grin.

'Thank you, Ron. We'll pop round and get it. You're a star,' said Bella, bestowing a quick kiss on the old man's leathery brown cheek.

Rubbing his cheek, he watched her fondly as she ran out of the door to her battered Mini Cooper, which she insisted upon calling Daisy. She was a good girl, that Miss Bella. Heart of gold, she had. It was just a crying shame she couldn't find herself a good man.

Chapter Two

Manoeuvring Daisy triumphantly into a space right outside the police station doors, Bella checked her watch – 11.25am. Perfect. Now, what was this press conference about? Ah, burglaries. She tried to remember the statistics she had dredged up to make a somewhat sensationalist page three story two weeks ago. She had interviewed the latest victim, an elderly lady who'd been robbed of her late husband's treasured possessions.

'They took his wedding ring out of my bedroom drawer. We'd bought it together fifty years ago. It cost twelve guineas, I remember. But it's not the money is it, my dear? It's the sentimental value,' the lady had said, wiping away a tear with a delicate lace hanky.

Bella had made the widow a cup of tea in the cosy little kitchen and promised to write a strong witness appeal to help the police catch the crooks. Thinking of the poor old lady, she poured her heart into that burglary story. 'Burglaries rocket out of control in Haybridge' she'd written, going on to give dire warnings about dark nights and local shops selling out of security locks.

Afterwards the police press officer, Chris Cox, had ribbed her about the words 'rocket' and 'out of control' and Bella had argued that, in her mind, a twenty-five per cent increase in burglaries over a 12-month period was most definitely worthy of a rocket, if not a soar or even an incredible escalation.

'We only had two hundred break-ins. That's low compared to other forces,' said Chris.

'But last year it was one hundred and fifty. That's a twenty-five per cent increase – as I said in my story,' said Bella, frantically wondering if she had got her percentages right. Chris pointed out that the largest increase was in burglaries of shops and businesses yet Bella had inferred it was in burglaries in people's houses.

'Our readers live in houses, Chris – that's the bit they want to read about,' she had countered.

Today the press officer was there to meet her in the police reception area, together with Jed Cummings, the local radio reporter, and Ann Clarke, an infuriating, smart and efficient freelance who covered Haybridge stories for the regional television news. Gosh, we're honoured – it must be a quiet day for TV, thought Bella, eyeing the other woman's perfectly cut and obviously expensive black trouser suit.

The trio was led through the white-painted corridors to a small office off the CID room, where a row of chairs was set out before a Formica table, behind which a dark-haired, rumpled looking man was scowling at an open copy of the *Haybridge Gazette*. Next to him was DC Jerry Boswell, an affable, fair-haired young officer who could always be relied upon for an extra detail or two to liven up a dull story. Bella had found the winning formula with Boz over the years – a cup of coffee, a bit of flattery, a spiel about press/public relations and he would come up with a few welcome off-the-record quotes. And, when Boz needed help tracking down a witness or asking readers to identify a CCTV pic of a suspect, Bella would move heaven and earth to get him a good spread in the paper.

The young policeman's love life was also an entertainment in itself, thought Bella, who frequently acted as agony aunt when Boz got in a tangle by dating two women at once. She shot him a smile and a surreptitious wink as she sat down on the end chair, crossing her legs carefully to hide a small ladder in her tights.

The dark, dishevelled head beside Boz lifted and scanned its audience. Suddenly Bella found herself looking into a pair of the bluest eyes she had ever seen. There was a flash of something... Irritation? Recognition? Maybe even anger? Then the eyebrows drew together in a frown and the blue eyes looked away, giving Bella a chance to take in the rest of the craggy features and the broad shoulders straining the fabric of a plain white shirt. Bloody hell, it's Mr Flint Eyes' not-so-handsome older brother, she thought, suppressing a sudden urge to giggle. No chance of anyone seducing *him*, the moody old devil.

Mr Not-So-Handsome cleared his throat and introduced himself: 'I am Detective Sergeant Jonathan Wright and I will be working in this area, with the aim of reducing the burglary statistics, for the next few months.'

Bella scrabbled in the handbag on her knee for her notebook and pen. Damn, surely she had a pen somewhere? Tissues, sweet papers, Emily's football bootlace, lipgloss ... she really *must* sort this bag out. There was a soft plop as something small and cylindrical fell onto the linoleum floor. Oh no, please God, don't let it, *don't* let it be a tampon.

'I believe you have dropped something Miss ... er?' said the DS, raising one dark eyebrow very slowly.

I am not going to blush. I am not going to blush, thought Bella. Quick as a flash she arranged her features in a wicked grin and, kicking the offending object under her chair, said: 'No, it can't be mine. I only smoke filter tips... And I'm Miss Smart – from the *Haybridge Gazette*.'

A corner of the police officer's mouth twitched, almost imperceptibly, into an almost smile while Boz tried in vain to smother a snort of laughter and Ann Clarke rolled her eyes to heaven.

'Perhaps then, Miss Smart, you could use your obvious talent for entertainment to explain to us why the *Haybridge Gazette* employs such scaremongering and inaccurate tactics to report the fact that there was an increase in burglaries this year?' he said smoothly.

He reached for the *Gazette* and read aloud: 'Burglaries have increased by a staggering twenty-five per cent ... Heartless crooks are targeting Haybridge as a soft-touch town ... Local stores are selling out of locks as people flock to make their homes more secure.'

Oh dear, perhaps she *had* gone a bit over the top on that one, thought Bella but she took a deep breath regardless and adopted her silkiest voice.

'The *Gazette* does not use scaremongering tactics but we do pride ourselves on carrying out our public duty to inform our readers of precisely what is happening as regards public safety. And we are highly trained to be accurate.' Hmm, was that too much? Did the 'as regards' bit make her sound like a trade union leader at a seaside conference? She tried to ignore Boz's slight warning frown and continued:

'And, quite frankly, DS Wright, if my report of the rise was so "inaccurate" as you put it, then it was very good of our local force to go to all the trouble of bringing you in specially to reduce it.'

That tight-lipped mouth twitched again, this time more noticeably.

'I see your verbal agility is fine, Miss Smart, but your mathematics is atrocious. When the figure of one hundred and fifty rises to two hundred it is actually an increase of thirty-three and a third per cent – one third as much again – *not* twenty-five per cent, as you reported. That was the inaccuracy to which I referred.'

Oh shit, thought Bella.

'So the problem is actually *worse* than Bella wrote?' chipped in Jed.

'Exactly! Which is why the Metropolitan police agreed to loan me to Haybridge for six months, so that we can tackle this problem calmly and effectively – *without* scaremongering.'

Bella, having finally located a pen, scribbled notes furiously as the DS outlined his plans: regular police patrols of residential areas after dark, more Neighbourhood Watch schemes and an intelligence-led campaign to catch the culprits.

'We will set up a confidential phone line to encourage people to shop the offenders. We will scour second-hand shops, car boot sales and newspaper ads for stolen goods ... we will leave no stone unturned. We aim to reduce burglaries by well over *one third* by the end of six months,' he said, aiming his blue eyes directly at Bella.

She was grateful for once when, as soon as the press conference was over, immaculate Ann sidled up to DS Wright to arrange for him to be interviewed later on camera. Jed too was hanging around clutching his tape recorder hopefully. 'Er, I'll be off then,' Bella said, shoving her notebook in her bag and heading for the door.

'I'll see you out,' said Boz, springing to attention. 'Christ, Bella, you really went for him! And what's with the Tampax thing? I can't wait to tell the boys about that!' he chortled as soon as they were out of earshot.

Bella knew it was no good being coy with the CID crowd. Or cool and sophisticated, come to that. She felt a giggle bubble up inside her.

'Of all the things to drop out of my bag. And just when I wanted to be really impressive...'

'And that filter tip joke!' guffawed Boz.

'Well, what else was I meant to say? That it's a padded pen or something?'

The giggles finally erupted and Bella leaned weakly against the wall, her shoulders shaking with laughter.

'Come on, Bel. I'll buy you a coffee in the canteen. You can tell me what to do about this new bird I'm seeing,' said Boz, flinging an arm around her.

Later, after relating his tale of woe about how his new girlfriend had caught him out sending flirty text messages to his old girlfriend, Boz assumed a serious expression.

'Why do you want to impress him, Bel?'

'Who?'

'Jonny. DS Wright. He's not a bad guy, you know. His bark's worse than his bite.'

'He makes me feel ... um ... sort of inferior somehow. He looked at me like I was a silly young girl – like I'd done something wrong. And that was *before* I dropped my tampon clanger!'

'Aw, that really is silly, Bel. Mind you, I did notice him give you the once-over. Perhaps he fancied you!' joked Boz, spooning sugar into his coffee.

'Now who's being silly? He's got to be at least forty and he's probably married. Though goodness knows who'd have him.'

'He's thirty-five. Told me the other day. And he's not married but he's got a girlfriend – bit of a stunner by all accounts. Chopper, one of the uniform guys, saw them in the Red Lion together. She had amazing –'

'OK Boz,' interrupted Bella. 'Let's change the subject, shall we? Have you any stories for me?'

'Hmm... There was another break-in at the off-licence, but the press office will give that out. Couple more thefts from a washing line, but you did that knicker nicker story for me last week, didn't you? Oh, and the missing au pair girl, of course.'

'Missing au pair?' Bella was all ears.

'Yeah, a Polish girl. But we're not worried about it – she was a bit flighty by all accounts. Probably found herself a fella and took off with him. She worked for a family in Trent Drive.'

'Have you a name?' Bella asked.

'No. The job's still with uniform at the moment. She's only been gone three days – probably took off for a long weekend. It'll probably come to CID tomorrow or the next day if she still hasn't turned up.'

Bella made a mental note to put in a call to Chris Cox in the morning, before the *Gazette* went to press, to check whether the girl had been found. And, talking of the *Gazette*, she'd better get back to work before Sean started his irate boss routine.

'I've got to dash, Boz. Will you see me out?'

The DC walked her to the foyer. 'Take care, Bel. And keep that bag zipped up!' he grinned.

Back at the office Suzy was tucking into a bacon roll with relish, dripping brown sauce onto her desk.

'You missed the snack van. I didn't know whether to get you anything,' she told Bella.

'It's OK. I'm on a diet, I told you. I had to lie on the floor to get the zip on my jeans done up last night.'

'Had you just washed them?'

'Yes, I had actually.'

'Well, you'd probably shrunk them.'

'Oh yes. I never thought of that. I'll have a bite of your bacon roll then,' grinned Bella, suddenly starving.

Bella, despite constant teasing from her colleagues, started a new diet most Monday mornings. She broke the diet most Monday lunchtimes – or sooner if someone had bought doughnuts. Her willpower waged a constant war against Pam's Van, a mobile food service which called at the *Gazette* offices twice daily, proffering everything from steaming hot steak and onion pies to home-made fruit buns dripping snowy white icing. Then there was chocolate... Bella was a real chocolate girl, savouring every sweet sticky mouthful and almost groaning aloud with pleasure. Her idea of bliss was a double portion of chunky chocolate chip ice cream with hot chocolate fudge sauce. When the local chip shop invited her to the launch of their Deep Fried Mars Bar special she thought she had died and gone to heaven. Nevertheless, every evening she cooked healthy, wholesome meals for her and Em and chewed determinedly on her steamed carrots and chopped cabbage before she crept guiltily to the Kit Kat tin for her daily chocolate fix. Thus Bella's weight remained at a resolute nine stone and, naively oblivious to the male admiration prompted by her softly curving frame, she continued her impossible battle to be a willowy size eight with a concave stomach and protruding collar bones.

That afternoon the lunch-less Bella felt virtuous as she bashed out the details of the press conference, making sure DS Wright's quotes were word-perfect. Sean allowed her to go on time for once, and she arrived at Emily's after-school club on the dot of 5.30pm.

Em came rushing towards her, pigtails flying and socks round her ankles. 'I was picked for the team, Mum! Mr Irons says I can play in the tournament!'

Bella hugged her daughter. ' Well done, darling. You'll have to ring Uncle Toby and tell him. He'll be really proud. And how did you do in your spelling test?'

'I got five ticks but I didn't get a housepoint. Megan did though. She got *loads* of ticks.'

'How many spellings were there, Emily?'

'Um ... I dunno. Can't remember. Mum, will Uncle Toby come and watch me at the football tournament, do you think?'

Bella sighed, wishing her daughter would put as much effort into her school work as she did on the football field. She blamed her brother entirely for the child's obsession with the game. He'd bought Emily her first mini Arsenal strip at the age of twelve months and had her kicking a ball into a makeshift goal in the family garden by the age of two.

'We'll see. But I'll definitely be there,' she promised.

Emily rushed straight to the telephone as soon as they got home, scattering her schoolbag, lunch box and dirty PE kit all over the tiny hall. She chattered away to her uncle while Bella peeled the potatoes, put two lamb chops under the grill, fed the cat and shoved the contents of the washing machine into the tumble dryer. This was her favourite time of day, just her and Em – no fussy news editors, no stressful deadlines and certainly no moody coppers with sardonic expressions and raised eyebrows. She wondered what DS Wright was doing right then, picturing him returning to an immaculate house – or perhaps a hotel room if he was only here for a few months – and sipping gin and tonic with his equally immaculate girlfriend. Or maybe he would be getting changed to go out, unbuttoning that formal shirt and pulling a casual T-shirt over that broad, broad chest... God, why on earth was she thinking about that dreadful man's chest? Pull yourself together, girl. Get a grip. Chop a carrot or something. Damn, the chops were burning...

DS Jonathan Wright was, in fact, engaged in expanding that broad chest at that very moment, pumping away at the weights machine in the gym until rivulets of sweat were running down his impressive torso. He paused occasionally to grin at the memory of that sparring match with the flame-haired reporter who had blushed so cutely when he finally caught her out. She had taken it well though – kept her dignity. Not like that television woman,

Ann somebody, who had patted his arm and made a great show of giving him her personal telephone number. 'Call me any time if you have a story; I'm available twenty-four hours a day,' she had said suggestively.

He had imagined, briefly, taking her up on the obvious offer, inviting her out to dinner, feigning an interest in her career and listening to her tales about previous relationships and disastrous loves. It never ceased to amaze him what women came out with on the first date. Why did they think men wanted to hear all that stuff? He would assume an attentive expression and murmur his sympathy or encouragement in the right places; he would lean across the table and then he would move in for the kill, placing his hand gently over hers and telling her she was a very attractive woman...

But he wouldn't do any of this of course. Because he wouldn't be unfaithful to Madeleine; beautiful, blonde-haired, poised and elegant Madeleine, who was probably right now draped with her cat-like grace across the bed of their hotel room waiting for him to return. She was 'resting' between modelling assignments at the moment and she had suggested finding a house to rent together in Haybridge for the duration of this job.

Jonathan felt a vague unease at this plan but, uncharacteristically, could not figure out why. Any man would be flattered to have a woman like Madeleine on his arm. She only had to walk into a room – all toned, tanned 5ft 10ins of her – and every pair of male eyes would be upon her. Sure, she could be a little high maintenance sometimes and refused to go anywhere unless her hair, her nails and her clothes were perfect, but her first love was her career and she made few emotional demands on Jonathan. What more could a man want?

While he was soaping himself under the shower,

wondering whether Madeleine would be wearing her wispy little black lace thingy, a frowning Bella was crouched over the edge of her dingy-looking bath, staring a huge, ferocious looking and extremely hairy spider in the face.

'Don't kill it Mummy, please don't kill it. It's probably a mummy spider with lots of little spiders waiting for it at home,' pleaded Em.

'Er, what shall we do with it then? How about we give it a nice little ride up the nozzle of the vacuum cleaner? Spiders like vacuum cleaners.'

'No. You can't suck it up. It won't be able to breathe. Spiders have to breathe, Mummy.'

'Well, we can't leave it here! Mind you, you could always get in the bath with it and shampoo its hair.'

Em's bottom lip trembled ominously and, taking a deep breath, Bella reached for the tooth mug and a copy of the *UK Press Gazette* she'd left by the loo.

'Don't worry, darling, I'll put it outside. Then she'll be able to find her babies all snuggled up in their nice little nest.'

She glared at the spider, which seemed to be growing bigger and hairier by the second. 'OK you – let's go. And you are *not* going to crawl up my arm.'

She gritted her teeth and gingerly laid the mug next to the angry-looking arachnid, then, with a flick of the *UK Press Gazette*, she knocked it inside. 'Argh!' she screamed, slamming the paper over the top of the mug and dancing a little jig of horror.

'Argh ... Ugh ... Help!' Bella danced out of the bathroom, hopping from foot to foot as she held the mug as far away from her as possible. 'Em, quick – open the back door!'

Her daughter sped nimbly to oblige and, screwing her eyes shut, Bella hurled the mug, the spider and the *UK Press Gazette* with all her might into the darkness, hearing them land with a satisfying plop in the rhododendron bush at the bottom of the garden.

'Good shot, Mum! Awesome!' said Em, holding her hand up for a high five.

'Thanks, baby,' said Bella, clapping the hand weakly.

Less than half a mile away in The Royal Oak Hotel, Jonathan drummed his fingers impatiently on the polished mahogany table in the bar. Madeleine had had all day to get ready – what the hell was keeping her? He'd returned from the gym to find her perched naked on the bed, painting her toenails a bright, sugary pink while some God-awful American chat show blared out from the television. Bizarrely, her face was covered in a glossy seaweed-green coating of goo, with two white circles around her eyes making her look like an alien panda bear.

'Ugh,' he had said instinctively. 'What on earth are you doing?'

'Face pack,' mumbled Madeleine without moving her lips.

'Right,' said Jonathan.

'I thought we'd go out to eat – I found a vegetarian restaurant.' She sounded like a ventriloquist's dummy.

'Right,' repeated Jonathan, who could have murdered a huge, juicy steak. 'Er, shall I meet you down in the bar then?'

Nursing a glass of malt whisky, he flicked idly through the sheaf of papers he had been given by his Detective Inspector. Burglary statistics, burglary analyses, burglary methods ... he was bored with burglaries already. After six years on CID with the Met he yearned to get his teeth into something more substantial but his boss had given him no choice about the secondment to sleepy Haybridge. 'It's a good career move, Jonny – it will look good on your record,' he had told him, drawing deeply on his umpteenth cigarette of the day. Jonathan actually couldn't care less about his record. He was an old-style copper with a dogged tenacity to solve a crime and a quick wit that allowed him frequently to bypass the more bureaucratic police procedures to get his results. He would never be a career cop. But he was also a caring man and he hated letting people down. If Haybridge needed help then he would give it – and he would do his damnedest to catch those bloody burglars.

'Are you ready, honey?' Madeleine was standing over him, looking a dream in a clinging red dress that ended halfway up her bare thighs.

Jonathan wondered fleetingly whether his faded jeans and black T-shirt would be smart enough for this undoubtedly posh veggie place. But then his stomach growled loudly. Sod it, the social elite of Haybridge could take him as they found him – a hungry burglar hunter.

'Let's go. Feed me,' he said.

Chapter Three

Ron was not a happy man when Bella breezed through the *Gazette* doors on Tuesday morning. His thin shoulders drooped as he polished the desk in reception and his normally cheery face was set in a rigid frown.

'Are you OK?' asked Bella immediately, putting her hand on the old man's shoulder. She was already five minutes late for work because Em had lost her school reading book at the last minute, but she could not bear to see the caretaker so miserable.

'I had this letter, Miss Bella. I don't understand why they're doing it.'

'Doing what, Ron?'

'Taking our allotments away. I've only just put in me winter greens and now they want to build a bloomin' supermarket on them. Said they're going to the council for permission.'

'Who is?'

'BestBuys – those big supermarket people. They've got one just outside Weatherford, where my sister lives. She said their fruit and veg are 'orrible – they look like something out of one of them posh magazines but they don't taste of anything at all. They grow them abroad, you know, and they spray them with those preservative things. They have strawberries bang in the middle of winter, my sister says, great big red strawberries, and they have new potatoes all year round, she says. What's the point of eating new potatoes if they're not new, I say? Me, I never set a new potato before –'

Bella interrupted the old man mid-flow, 'But the allotments are public land. Surely the council can't sell it off for development? And they're really popular, aren't they?'

'Well, they were but there's a fair few lying empty now. You get them flash folks moving up from London, fancying themselves as gardeners. They pay a fortune for plants and posh shiny spades and dig like hell for a few weeks. But the first drop of rain and they're letting all the weeds grow and then the slugs come and before you know it they're driving off to BestBuys to buy their veg like the rest of 'em.'

'I'll put in an enquiry to the council and see what's happening. I'm sure the planning application won't go through,' said Bella soothingly. 'Can I pop round after work and have a look at the letter? I'm picking Emily up at four today and we could collect her pumpkin if that's OK?'

'That'd be champion. Thanks, Miss Bella,' said Ron, his face wrinkling into his first smile of the day.

Doug Blakemore, the Haybridge and District Council press officer, was a taciturn, grey-faced man in his fifties and, despite his job title, did not welcome reporters ringing up to disrupt his routines by asking questions.

'If you would care to wait until I send you the monthly list of planning applications on November 16th then you could see for yourself whether there is such a submission,' he told Bella.

'That's two weeks away, Doug. And the allotment holders have already received a letter so the story is now. BestBuys wouldn't just pick a council-owned site out of the blue – they must have been in negotiation with the planning office for ages. Could you check for me, please?'

'Any negotiations are confidential before they are officially lodged. I cannot possibly confirm anything,' said Doug firmly.

Sod you then, thought Bella, plonking down the phone and reaching for her dog-eared contacts book. P for planning... Ah yes, Tim Booth, that nice young planning worker she interviewed last year at the opening of the council's new sheltered housing scheme in Vale Road.

Tim was the antithesis of Doug. Flattered to be approached 'strictly off the record' by the attractive reporter, whom he remembered had such a cute smattering of freckles across her nose, he told her far more than his job actually permitted.

BestBuys, he said, were keen to move into Haybridge and the company had originally pinned its hopes on the site of the old animal feeds factory. But Westfield Homes, a massive firm of developers, had approached the council at the last minute with plans to build a mini estate of 200 starter homes and low cost family houses. It was exactly what the steadily growing town needed and, several months later, the deal was swung with Westfield's pledge to give the council letting rights on thirty of the homes. The first foundations were now being laid on the site – as reported in the *Gazette* a few weeks ago.

'So BestBuys were miffed, understandably really, and promptly offered a huge sum for the old allotments and that patch of scrub land next to them,' said Tim. 'We were dead against at first – it's against all our policies on preserving the environment and all that. But the rent for allotments we get is peanuts, so some of the councillors are really keen. They reckon a decent supermarket is just what Haybridge needs – particularly with all the new people who'll live on the Westfields' development.'

'But won't it kill trade in the town?' asked Bella.

'It will have an effect, yes. We expect the traders to

moan like hell when this goes public. Councillor Ted Hanson's said he'll organise public meetings and formal consultations so they can have their say. You'd think he'd object because he's got a shop himself.'

'He runs the newsagents at the end of the High Street, doesn't he?' Bella asked.

'Yes. But he's still all for the supermarket – apparently he told the head of planning he's willing to sacrifice a few bob from his own business if it's for the good of the town.'

Bella said nothing, recalling the large, exuberant man with a booming voice and a ruddy complexion who was a frequent visitor to the *Gazette* offices – usually to hand over a press release about his latest good deed or charity donation. As chairman of the planning committee, leader of the dominant Conservative group, and vice-chair of the Chamber of Commerce, Councillor Hanson, still only in his late forties, was an influential figure in the small town and the editor always treated him with respect. But, personally, Bella thought he was a somewhat egotistical publicity-seeker. True do-gooders, in her experience, preferred to keep quiet about what they did and avoided publicity like the plague.

She wondered if the Mr Nice Guy councillor would care so much about Ron's cabbages.

'Thanks, Tim. That's really helpful,' she said, putting down the phone thoughtfully.

She would do a story, she decided: 'Haybridge Allotments Under Threat' and she would get Dave the photographer to take an atmospheric picture of Ron and his cronies leaning on their spades surveying their winter vegetables.

But first she made another call – to the police press office. 'Has the missing Polish au pair girl been found?' she asked Chris Cox.

Chris, like his council counterpart, was evasive. 'This

one's not for public release, Bella – at least not yet. The family she works for is fairly sure she's met some bloke and will turn up in a few days. She may even be planning to go back to Poland, they reckon.'

'How come they reported her missing then?' asked Bella, quick as a flash.

'They did it as a formality – just in case. But we're not seriously worried about her welfare.'

'Why not?'

'God, Bella, you're persistent. She took some stuff, that's why. Clothes and things were gone from her room.'

'Passport?'

'Bella – I am not saying another word.'

'Can you give me a name?'

'No.'

'An age?'

'No.'

'Can you tell me anything?'

'Yes, there's been a break-in at the hardware shop – tools and a bit of cash taken. We need a witness appeal.'

Bella fought back an urge to tell Chris to stuff it but, remembering her professionalism, she took down the details obediently. Suzy noticed her scowl though.

'Bad morning? Chocolate biscuit?' she said, shoving an open packet across the desk.

'Bloody press officers,' moaned Bella, taking two Hob Nobs. Well, she'd only had half a slice of toast for breakfast.

After a short reflection – and one more Hob Nob – she decided it was time to call in a favour with Boz. She had done two appeals for information on quite a routine criminal damage job for him recently and she had listened to endless stories about his women troubles. He owed her one about the au pair. She dialled his direct line number.

'CID,' said a clipped voice at the other end.

'DC Jerry Boswell please.'

'Who's speaking?' The tone was suspicious.

'It's a personal call.'

'DC Boswell is out on a job at the moment. Can I take a message.'

The voice sounded familiar to Bella. Oh no – it couldn't be that arrogant DS Wright, could it? She'd better not give a name, just in case. He was the type who wouldn't appreciate her making off the record calls to his young officers.

'Yes, could you ask him to call, er, Julie on...' She gave her mobile number, trying to disguise her voice with a slightly nasal drawl.

'I'll give him the message, Miss Smart. And I hope your cold gets better,' grinned Jonathan.

'Oh,' squeaked Bella.

'Bad throat too?' Really, thought Jonathan, this girl was *easy* today.

Bella's eyes blazed and her chin jutted out. 'Uh oh,' murmured Suzy from the opposite desk.

'I am fine, thank you DS Wright, despite your diagnosis. I was calling my contact DC Boswell about a particularly important job, which needs a sensitive approach.' She stressed the word sensitive. 'I realised it would not be suitable to question you about it as you only deal with burglaries.' She stressed 'burglaries' too, allowing a disdainful note to creep into her voice.

To her amazement DS Wright burst out laughing. 'What's the job?' he said. Actually, he was the temporary sergeant in charge of every major Haybridge CID job but burglaries were the only thing happening in this godforsaken town.

'I do not feel it is appropriate to tell you.' God, she was sounding like a prissy schoolmistress now.

'Would it have anything to do with the missing girl?'

'How did you know that?' The words slipped out of Bella's mouth before she had a chance to control it.

'Because Chris Cox just called to see if there was any update and said you were pestering him about it.'

'I do *not* pester!' said Bella.

'Good. I'm glad about that. Then you will accept my advice to leave this alone then. If we need your help we will contact you. Goodbye, Bella.'

Jonathan replaced the handset and leaned back in his chair, chortling. Round Two to him, he thought, picturing the reporter slamming down her phone, her cheeks flushed and her sexy, rather full lips pursed in outrage. She looked such a kittenish little thing, with that heart-shaped face and that little button of a freckled nose and those big grey eyes. But she had resilience and a stubborn streak that both impressed and annoyed the hardened detective, who preferred his women cool and elegant. Like Madeleine.

His highly trained, observant gaze had taken in the dark circles under Bella's eyes, where the milky skin took on a faint, bluish hue, and the small frown line between her eyebrows. Too many late nights, he thought. She probably lived life to the full, lording it up in the pubs and clubs with a string of willing admirers like DC Jerry Boswell. He had heard about Boz's reputation with women and wondered idly if there was anything between him and Bella. Maybe not, he decided – a young policeman's salary wouldn't be impressive enough for a girl like her. Flash playboys were probably more her type.

Jonathan snorted and picked up his pen. *Julie* indeed! What a little madam. Well, she needn't think she could twist him round her spoilt little finger. She could stick to her city blokes with their big fat wallets. Chinless wonders, the lot of them.

Hugo may have had a big fat wallet but he had a perfectly sculpted chin, complete with perfect Michael Douglas dimple. The only son of wealthy Haybridge factory owner Charles Copeland, Hugo had been given every advantage in his spoilt young life – the best private schools and the fastest, sportiest cars to take him to a succession of top nightclubs and parties.

Bella, studying hard at the local college on her media studies course, had been literally bowled over when she bumped into him at a disco in the church hall, spilling her half-pint of lager down his Yves St Laurent shirtfront.

Bored with her surburban semi lifestyle, she was instantly impressed with his poised sophistication, while Hugo, who had strolled down to the church disco out of boredom, noticed the mass of red hair and the interesting curves under the cheap shiny top and made a mental note to investigate this slightly ungainly 'village girl' further.

When he called, a week later, to invite Bella to a party at his grand house on Lanark's Hill, she could not believe her luck. Her best friend Kate Spencer loaned her a slinky black dress and helped her stuff tissue paper down her bra. 'Be careful, Bel,' she warned. 'He'll only be after one thing...'

'Rugger buggers, the lot of 'em,' said her brother Toby a few days later, when a glowing Bella announced that she had been invited to stay for the weekend with Hugo and his public school friends at a 'huge, posh country house' in Gloucestershire.

'Gosh – how many outfits are you planning to wear each day?' said Bella's younger sister Sophie, watching her frantically pack and repack her old Adidas school bag.

But the strappy tops and chiffon dresses proved to be totally unsuitable for the Gloucestershire mansion, which was probably the coldest place Bella had ever experienced. Her overriding memory of the weekend was shivering helplessly while the rest of the guests – two braying men called Rupert and Tarquin and several willowy model girl types – strode around confidently in thick woollens and corduroy trousers cracking 'in' jokes about the season in St Tropez.

When Hugo, having ignored her during most of the first long, bewildering evening, finally grabbed her by the hand and pulled her into his bedroom she responded obligingly, deciding that two bodies would be warmer than one.

Afterwards, cuddled up against Hugo's tanned chest, she listened to his plans to work at a ski resort for six months then go travelling around Europe and then perhaps settle in France, where his parents were buying a chateau for their retirement. Bella fought back the tears stinging her eyes.

So this was obviously a one-off then. So much for the man of her dreams. But even in her disappointment she noticed that Hugo never asked her one question about herself. It was as though he simply was not interested in her as a person. Sod it, she'd tell him anyway.

'I'm going to be a journalist,' she announced proudly.

'That's nice sweetheart... Shall we go and see what Rupes and co are doing? I could murder a drink,' said Hugo, giving her an absent-minded peck on the cheek.

Later, at home, after three weeks of blindly hoping Hugo would call, Bella let the tears flow, sobbing out her woes in her flowery wallpapered bedroom to the kind-hearted Kate, who hugged her friend fiercely and told her she was worth far more than that selfish upper-class prat.

'Th-there's another thing worrying me, Kate ... m-my period's late. It's never late...'

'Christ Bella! Surely you used something?'

'No. Hugo said it was too c-cold to get out of bed and get one. He ... he said he'd be c-careful.'

Kate hugged her friend even tighter. 'We'll do a test, Bella. Don't worry, I'm sure it's a false alarm.'

Bella would never forget the shock of seeing the two blue lines appear on the little white stick, nor the subsequent humiliation of the call to Hugo's mobile – the call she had summoned every ounce of her courage to make.

'Who? Oh, Bella. How are you, sweetie? I'm in Switzerland – the skiing's fantastic! What? Oh God. Are you sure it's mine? ... OK, don't worry. I'll send you a hundred quid to get it sorted... Sorted – you know ... an abortion. Well, you're not going to keep the damn thing, are you?'

Today the memory of that conversation still made Bella shudder. But it also made her grey eyes blaze with defiance. 'Sod you, Hugo Copeland,' she had said, ripping up the cheque for £100 when it arrived.

Seven subsequent years of battling, battling against the disappointment of her parents, against the trials of pregnancy and birth, against the exhaustion of coping with a tiny baby and against the stigma of being a single mum in a small town, had made her into what she was today – a stronger, more determined person.

The staff at the college had been wonderful when she told them of her pregnancy, arranging a creche place for Emily so Bella could continue her studies part-time, and David Ryan, the editor of the *Haybridge Gazette*, found himself surprisingly impressed with the young mum who duly applied for her first job. He watched her eyes light up as she spoke about how much she wanted to be a journalist and he listened to her ideas, tumbling enthusiastically from her lips, for features and interviews that would enhance his paper. David, an old-fashioned and meticulous editor with a chain-smoking habit and soaring blood pressure, thought of his own two pampered daughters at home with not an ounce of ambition between them and wished they could be more like the plucky little lass who stood before him.

'And your daughter, Bella?' he had asked gently. Everyone

in Haybridge knew about her little bit of trouble after all. The Copelands had moved to France before the baby was born and rumour had it Bella had never asked Hugo for a penny for the child.

'My daughter is the best thing that ever happened to me. But I have excellent childcare and there is no way she will stand in the way of me being a journalist. I am doing this for both of us,' declared Bella, jutting out her chin in a defiant gesture that was to become so familiar to David.

With the support of her parents and by saving every spare penny of her wages, she finally managed to scrape together a deposit to buy her own tiny two-bedroomed ground floor flat four years ago, on her twenty-third birthday.

'We've done it, Em! We have our own place,' she had cried, whirling her daughter round and round in the bare living room until the toddler shrieked with delight.

A year later, after months of driving lessons from her ever patient dad, Bella passed her driving test and bought Daisy, her pride and joy. Now she and Em had made it – they were finally self-sufficient. To celebrate, Bella bought a cat, a purring ball of ginger fluff called Thomas. Friends could rave about men and dates and fiancés and marriage but Bella was not going down that route. No way. She would be a single-parent spinster with a cat. She had accepted the odd evening out with an admiring male or two but always made it quite clear that she was not interested in any repeat performance. She had learned her lesson and in future she would stick to her nice little fantasies about Mr Right and honeysuckle-strewn cottages. Fantasies were fine. They were safe. Every girl had daydreams – but Bella had no intention of ever making hers a reality.

Chapter Four

Tuesday was press day. By 4pm the copies of the *Haybridge Gazette* were rolling off the giant presses on an industrial estate twenty miles away and fair-minded David Ryan allowed his staff to go home early. He invariably stayed in his editor's office though, sifting through papers, reading letters and stubbing out cigarette after cigarette in his big brass ashtray. Anything to avoid going home to his tight-lipped wife and his two spoilt daughters...

Bella enjoyed the luxury of being able to pick her daughter up early. It meant Emily had time to have a friend round to tea, or play in the park with her mum or even, if Bella was feeling flush, to drive into Weatherford to see a film at the cinema. Sometimes they popped round to see Bella's parents, who cooked the little girl her favourite meal and invariably presented her with a new colouring book, a comic or some little knick-knack that had caught their eye.

This Tuesday though, Bella told Emily, was a special day. They were going to see Ron to collect Emily's pumpkin which later they would scoop out into a Halloween lantern.

'Yes!' said Em, jumping up and down.

Bella smoothed her daughter's flyaway hair and wiped a smudge of dirt from her cheek. 'And,' she said, 'I have a packet of wine gums in my bag.'

'Yes!' said Em again, jumping even higher.

She demolished the wine gums and chattered non-stop as they drove across town to Ron's house. The old man was waiting for them at the front door, a smile on his face, as they pulled up. 'Wait 'til you see this pumpkin, young lady – it's a big 'un.'

'I can see it from here,' cried Emily, as they crossed the road to the allotments. 'I can see a huge orange thing!'

Ron puffed his chest out with pride. 'I've bin feeding it best fertiliser all summer,' he said.

The pumpkin was indeed a good one and Emily declared it twice as big as Megan's and a much brighter orange than Lauren's. The old gardener and the little girl were equally delighted.

'Play for a moment, Em, while I have a chat with Ron,' said Bella, patting her daughter's skinny rump.

She filled the old man in on her conversation with the council press officer. 'Nothing is certain yet, Ron. Planning permission is going to be sticky and it's months away. I can't help thinking the traders will object like fury and the council has to take their views into account. You have rights too,' she continued. 'You pay rent for this allotment and therefore they have to listen to you. I'll help you write a letter, if you like.'

Ron looked at her with his rheumy eyes. 'That would be grand. We won't let these people walk all over us, will we? We'll dig for victory – just like in the war!'

Bella was explaining the council's planning processes and consultation procedures when she was interrupted by Emily tugging at her sleeve.

'I found a handbag, Mum. Can I keep it? Please?'

'No, of course not, Em. We have to find who it belongs to and give it back to them,' said Bella automatically, reaching down for the tiny black leather bag which sported a trendy silver chain handle.

'That'll be a courting couple dropped it. We gets loads of those smooching round by the old sheds,' declared Ron.

The bag was completely empty at first glance but inside a tiny zipped pocket were two neatly folded, crisp-looking £10 notes – and nothing else. Odd, thought Bella, perhaps the other stuff had fallen out.

'Show me where you found it, Em. There may be something with ID on which fell out. Then we can give it back to the lady who lost it.'

Emily pointed to a shabby-looking hut on the next door allotment. 'By that shed. I'll help you look.'

'No, you stay here and help Ron cut that great big pumpkin – otherwise it will be too dark to see,' said Bella, already striding across the muddy soil, silently cursing the fact that she had worn her one decent pair of black shoes. She would bet that Em's school shoes were in a state too if she'd been grubbing around in this lot.

The dusk was indeed gathering and slight drizzle was descending. This allotment was nothing like Ron's meticulously cultivated patch, where rows of seedlings were planted with a military precision and even the dark green cabbages stood to attention as if reporting for army inspection. This was a wilderness of wilted, untended plants, rotting cabbage stumps and clusters of vicious-looking thistles, shedding their down over an assortment of dented cans, beer bottles and faded old carrier bags. Maybe Ron's right about the amorous kids, thought Bella, neatly side-stepping a plastic cider bottle and a used condom.

She pictured the young couple giggling as they picked their way, hand in hand, over the allotment, the boy gallantly brushing the thistles aside for the girl. They would make their way to that old tree stump by the hut and the boy would sit down, pulling the girl on to his lap. Alone at last... Much later the girl would shriek 'My bag! My bag!' and together they would search in vain in the pitch darkness, panicking because their parents expected them home.

The £20 was probably a fortune to her, thought Bella, who, more than anyone, knew the value of hard-earned cash.

The ground outside the hut was flat and firm and, apart from a smattering of coarse grass, free of weeds and overgrowth. Bella's eyes scanned the surrounding area for a purse, a lipstick, any one of the dozen pieces of paraphernalia that a woman would carry in her handbag – no, there was nothing. How strange. God, it was really quite shadowy now. Those great big thistles looked creepy the way they were waving in the breeze. This allotment really was a dump – you could almost smell the decay. It was. It was *palpable*, yes, that was the word.

The door of the hut had a stout and rusty nail driven into it instead of a handle. Ah, of course, the couple would go in there and nestle among the old plant pots and empty compost sacks, thought Bella. Although, her quick brain reasoned, there was unlikely to be any identification in there if the bag had been dropped outside. But she'd better check anyway.

The door would not budge, although there was no evidence of a lock. Bella, remembering how the door of her dad's old shed used to swell and stick in damp weather, grasped the nail with both hands and leaned back to give it an almighty tug.

It flew open with a huge creak, throwing Bella backwards. She teetered once, twice, then landed heftily on her bottom on the old tree stump. 'Ouch!' she cried, feeling her spine jolt in protest. 'Yuk!' she shrieked as her hands encountered the soft muddy earth as she heaved herself up.

'Are you all right?' called Ron.

'Yeah – just tripped,' shouted Bella, rubbing her backside as she peered in to the hut.

How bizarre. Someone had left an old shop dummy in here. One of those mannequin things wearing a long dark

36

wig. It looked almost real the way it was laid out on its back at a slight angle across the floor, one leg bent inwards at the knee. It was wearing quite nice stiletto shoes too – and a pale pink sweater and short denim skirt. What a waste of good clothes, she thought.

The realisation dawned in small waves, sending ripples of shock reverberating through Bella's body. At the same time the smell hit her – a pungent, sweetly sinister smell, which filled her nostrils and crept thickly into her mouth until she could almost taste it, causing her stomach to lurch in protest. She let out a cry, an almost animal-like moan, and fought a ridiculous urge to cram her fist into her mouth, like a small child seeking comfort.

She had heard the expression 'rooted to the spot' but never realised what it truly meant before. She wanted to move, to run blindly back through the thistles – which seemed almost friendly now in comparison to the horror before her – inhaling great lungfuls of clean, crisp air to force out that smell, that dreadful smell. But it was as though someone had severed the tiny nerve endings between her brain and her legs. Her feet were numb – useless. Her hands had flown up to her cheeks and were fixed in that position. Her eyes would not move either. They were fixed on the poor, dead, stinking body and defiantly devouring every detail – the white, marbled legs, the claw-like hand reaching out in a silent plea for help and, worse of all, the bulging eyes that glowed almost luminously in the dimness.

Bella realised she was holding her breath. Her lungs were burning. Somewhere, in the frozen recesses of her mind, she remembered Emily. She was just yards away – she must *not* see this body.

She let out a great lungful of air and breathed in again slowly, trying to control a great rush of nausea. It took every ounce of strength not to let out a long, primeval scream. Instead she concentrated on her breathing ... in ... out ... in ... out ... as she picked her way rigidly back across the allotment.

'Ron, could you take Emily into your house, do you think? I'm worried she might catch cold,' she asked, her voice coming out as a high-pitched waver.

The old man and the little girl both jerked their heads up in surprise from the purple sprouting broccoli they were examining. 'I *never* get colds, Mum – they're for *girls*,' said Em.

'Please, Ron,' Bella urged, meeting his eyes imploringly. 'I'll be with you in a moment.'

'Come on, little 'un – I'll find you a biscuit,' said Ron, scooping the pumpkin up with difficulty under his arm and taking the child's hand, frowning with puzzlement as he ambled off.

As soon as they were out of earshot Bella fumbled in her bag for her mobile phone, her fingers feeling peculiarly numb and stiff. She hit the 9 button three times – then promptly burst into tears. 'Fire, police or ambulance?' a voice asked.

'Everything,' sobbed Bella. 'Everything. I've found a body – a dead body,' she wailed to a calm-sounding woman a second later. Somehow Bella managed to blurt out the details, though when the woman asked for the name of the road her mind went a complete blank. 'The allotments – in Haybridge – by the Common. You know the allotments...'

'We'll find them, dear,' said the woman kindly. 'Is there somewhere you can go and sit down and wait for the police to arrive. Somewhere you can get a nice cup of tea?'

Bella gave Ron's address, hoping the old bachelor would cope with the invasion. She rang off, then immediately clicked on Suzy's number.

'Suze – I'm so sorry. Something terrible's happened – I found a b-body... Can you come and collect Emily? She's at Ron's house – 2 Wheelwrights Row, by the Common. I can't let her get involved in this, Suze,' she gabbled.

'Very funny,' drawled Suzy. 'Don't tell me – the late Mrs Worthing has come back from the grave to haunt us after my little joke.'

Bella gave a strangled moan then a sob. 'Suze ... please. I'm serious.'

There was a silence.

'Bloody hell,' gasped Suzy. 'I do believe you are.' She grabbed her car keys. 'Stay there. I'm on my way.'

Bella took a calming deep breath and walked over the road to Ron's house where Emily was playing happily with a fat tabby cat in the corner of the kitchen. Bella quietly took the old man aside to explain what had happened, watching his face go pale with shock.

'The police will be here soon. Em's being collected – we have to act normal in front of her,' she whispered through chattering teeth. Why was she so cold? And she was trembling from head to toe – it must be the shock.

'Why are you whispering, Mummy?' said Emily, looking up. 'Gosh, you look a right mess. Have you been playing in the mud?'

Bella glanced down at her muddy hands and grubby black trousers. 'Yes – silly me,' she answered automatically.

Ron was just filling the kettle when Suzy arrived. Her hand flew to her mouth as she saw her friend's dishevelled state and pale face but she quickly collected herself and fought back the urge to ask questions.

'Emily, would you like to come to my house for tea? I've got some fish fingers,' she asked the little girl. The child's face broke out in a smile and she looked questioningly at her mother.

'Mummy's a bit busy at the moment, darling. You go with Auntie Suzy and I'll collect you soon,' said Bella.

As soon as Emily had gone she sank down weakly onto Ron's rush-seated kitchen chair, sinking her head into her arms on the cool, smooth surface of the old pine table and allowing the tremors to rush through her body.

Ron had just set a cup of steaming tea in front of her and launched into a tirade about what a rum old thing it was to find a body in an allotment hut when there was an authoritative knock at the door. 'Police – can we come in?' Two dark-suited figures walked into the room.

Bella looked up briefly then sank her head down again. Oh no, not him. This was exactly what she didn't need.

Jonathan looked from the old man to the crumpled little figure at the kitchen table with a jolt of recognition. He would know that red hair anywhere – what the hell was *she* doing here?

Slowly Bella raised her head and Jonathon took in her chalk-white face, the red-rimmed eyes and the streaks of mud down either cheek and instinctively he strode over to her.

'Can you tell me where the body is?' he said surprisingly gently, fighting a ridiculous urge to gather her in his arms and rock her like a small child. God, man, you must be getting soft in your old age, he thought.

PC Henderson, a plump, rosy-cheeked man with ears that stuck out at almost a 90-degree angle beneath his regulation crew cut, silently scribbled down notes as Bella stammered out the exact location and sipped the hot, sweet tea.

'I didn't touch it; I knew it could interfere with forensics,' she declared, a trace of her former resilience returning as she looked Jonathan in the eye.

The detective smiled and turned his head to murmur

a few words to PC Henderson, who nodded and disappeared outside.

'We are going to call Scene of Crime now. And a doctor, and a few other officers. I'm going over to take a quick look but I'd like you to stay here. Then I will need you to come back to the station with me for a couple of hours to give me a statement.'

'I can't,' said Bella automatically, thinking of Em's bedtime.

Jonathan's face clouded. 'Why can't you?'

Bella's brain was still muddled but for some reason she did not want to blurt out to this police officer about her childcare problems. It wasn't that she was ashamed of being a single mum, of course, it was just that it didn't seem ... well ... professional somehow. It suddenly dawned on her that she was a journalist and this was the best story of her career. But she couldn't drag a six-year-old child into it – God, it would be Em's bedtime in an hour.

'I'm, er, busy tonight. Could I possibly do it tomorrow? Surely you'll be busy with the body tonight?'

Jesus, thought Jonathan. You'd think she'd realise the importance of a bloody murder enquiry. She probably had a hot date or something. Well, she'd just have to miss it.

'I'm afraid there's no choice. A suspicious death must take priority,' he said firmly, heading towards the door. 'I will be back for you in twenty minutes.'

Suzy, summoned shakily once again to the phone, promised to bath Emily and tuck her up in her mum's big feather bed. Bella could collect her whenever she was ready. 'But you've simply *got* to tell me what's happened! We're worried sick,' she insisted.

Weakly Bella recounted her find, picturing her friend's

41

eyes growing wide with disbelief at the other end of the phone.

'Wow! What a brilliant story! I mean, not for the poor dead girl, but for us. And you found the body! Who was she? Do they know? You'll have a picture by-line on the front page for this, Bel.'

Yes, thought Bella, suddenly feeling her brain click into focus. It is one hell of a story. Who was this poor girl, just a few years younger than she was? How exactly did she ended up lifeless in an allotment hut? Was she killed there or was her body dumped? How did she die? There was no visible blood or wounds. It must have been strangulation, or an invisible blow to the back of the head, or even poison... Bella's imagination ran wild. In her journalist mode she found she could be far more detached and cool about it all – and she could certainly ask that DS Wright a few questions tonight.

At the police station it was pretty hard to be cool – not when you were standing with sopping wet hair wearing nothing but a cotton bathrobe facing some arrogant detective who wanted to take away your knickers in a brown paper bag.

'What the hell do you want my knickers for?' Bella had demanded, eyes blazing. You big pervert, she added silently.

Jonathan sighed. It had been a long evening. First there was Bella's protest about driving with him in his car, despite the fact that her old Mini was wedged in between several police cars, the doctor's Rover and two SOCO vans behind a cordon of yellow and white police tape. Then there was all the fuss about handing over her clothes for forensic tests – vital in case she had contaminated the crime scene. She hadn't seemed to care about her clothes but for some reason she didn't want him to call by her house and collect fresh ones on the way to the station, even though it had seemed like a sensible idea to him. Probably had some bloke waiting there... Now she was probably going to kick up about wearing the faded old jogging bottoms, T-shirt and paper knickers he had unearthed in the spare clothes drawer in the Rape Suite. She had liked the suite though – especially when he had told her she could take advantage of the newly fitted shower to wash all that mud off. She had seemed impressed when he explained that police tried to make things as homely as possible for rape victims and traumatised female witnesses.

'We need to examine *every* item of clothing you were wearing. Put each item separately in a bag and hand them to me,' he told her, handing her the clean outfit and wishing with all his heart there was a WPC on duty to deal with all this girlie stuff. God knows what she'll say about those paper pants, he thought.

Bella did not say a word when she emerged a few minutes later. She was too busy clutching the pile of brown paper bags to her chest, desperately trying to hide the fact that she had no bra on and that this stupid T-shirt was far too tight and made her breasts look droopy. It had better be bloody warm in that interview room, she thought.

'I'll take those,' said Jonathan, holding out his arms for the bags.

'No. I'm fine.' Bella scowled and clutched them tighter to her chest.

'Well, with all due respect you can't cuddle them all night. They have to go to forensics.'

Bella was sure his eyes were twinkling an even more iridescent blue than usual. She handed over the bags then crossed her arms firmly across her chest in one swift movement.

Nice tits, thought Jonathan, who was far too quick to miss a thing.

The statement taking was laborious and Bella shuddered as she recounted her story. When she got to the part about the mottled white legs her head went fuzzy and the room started to swim slightly. 'Would you like a cup of tea?' asked Jonathan, seeing the colour drain out of her face.

'Actually, I don't suppose you have any chocolate, do you?' she said. Jonathan nodded to the PC sitting beside him, who promptly left the room and headed for the vending machine outside the canteen. Strange request, he thought. He was used to dishing out tea and endless cigarettes – but *chocolate*?

Bella pounced on the Cadbury's Wholenut like she hadn't eaten for weeks, forgetting her arms were meant to be folded across her chest. She paused only to offer a square to each of the officers. They shook their heads politely, trying not to look at her nipples.

'That's better,' she said, licking her fingers. 'Now – have you any idea of the identity of the poor girl? Who do you think murdered her? Was it a crime of passion? Do you think she is the missing Polish au pair? It seems an obvious choice.'

Oh dear, thought Jonathan, she's gone from flaky witness to pushy journalist in just a few mouthfuls of Dairy Milk. Thank God she hadn't scoffed a king-size bar.

'I'll ask the questions if you don't mind. It is far too early to speculate,' he said, thinking of the uniformed officers he had only an hour ago dispatched to Trent Drive to interview the au pair's employers. The body had indeed matched the description exactly, right down to the cheap pink jumper and skirt she was wearing. As soon as he had a positive ID he could contact the girl's parents in Poland – might need an interpreter for that one, he thought.

Bella tried a few more questions then, realising she was fighting a losing battle and thinking of Em, she decided to cooperate. She rattled through the statement and promised to return at 11am the next morning for fingerprinting because, as DS Wright had pointed out so irritatingly, she had touched the little black handbag, which could be a vital clue.

'Anyone would think I was the murderer,' she grumbled to the obliging PC Henderson, who offered to run her back to her car.

A white van and three police cars still remained at the scene and Ron was standing gloomily in his porch surveying the ghostly white tent erected on the allotment and the almost surreal, bustling figures dressed in white plastic spacesuits. Bella waved at him, urging him to try to get some sleep, before sliding gratefully into Daisy's sagging cloth seat.

Emily was, obligingly, fast asleep and did not stir as Bella carried her out wrapped in a fluffy blue blanket. Suzy's mum, Sheila, followed them to the car, triumphantly brandishing a strange-shaped orange bundle.

'We made her pumpkin suit – out of an old throw over, some upholstery foam and an orange bobble hat. We made the stalk from a green sock and Emily sewed it on herself!'

'Mrs Mapleton – you are a miracle maker!' said Bella, bestowing a kiss on her plump cheek. 'And I promise I will tell you both every single word about the body tomorrow, but I must go now and put Em to bed.'

Suzy tried very hard to smother her excitement with sympathy. A true journalist, excitement won.

'I'll hold the front page!' she said.

Chapter Five

It was a tired and tatty-looking Bella who plonked herself down at her desk at 9.10am to find the entire editorial office hovering to hear her story. She had tossed and turned most of the night, seeing the mannequin body every time she closed her eyelids, before finally succumbing to a fitful sleep seemingly only minutes before her alarm shrilled. Then she had scrabbled frantically through her meagre wardrobe looking for something passable to wear, cursing the fact that she'd had no time to do the ironing the night before. She had settled for an ancient high-waisted pair of grey trousers which she knew made her bum look huge and a pale green shirt with a very faint spaghetti hoops stain down the front. She just knew she looked fat and frumpy. Then Em had been unusually truculent, demanding to wear her pumpkin suit to school and hiding her grey uniform skirt when Bella, quite naturally, refused. Em objected to her usual cornflakes for breakfast too, whining that Megan had chocolate crispies or fruity loops every morning. Bella hoped the child wasn't getting spoiled; she usually had such a sunny nature.

The petty delays meant she had no time to sort out her hair, which bushed out in a frizzy halo round her head because she had let it dry naturally after the police station shower. And make-up was out of the question too in the rush to get Em through the school gate just as the bell was sounding. But, thought Bella, she shouldn't even be worrying about how she looked when that poor girl was dead, lying in a cold mortuary by now, never to wield a mascara brush again...

Even so, she couldn't help hamming it up just a little when she told her colleagues about the body, and she watched with satisfaction as Sean's face went a bit pale. 'Still, it's not every day we get an eyewitness account of an unsolved murder, well, an eyewitness account of finding a body, anyway,' she concluded.

'It's gone out on local radio already,' said Pete, a skinny twenty-one-year-old fresh from college and bubbling over with enthusiasm at the prospect of something other than fetes, WI's and burglaries. 'They said police were definitely treating it as murder and that Councillor Hanson bloke was on air, offering a five hundred quid reward for information leading to a conviction.'

'Typical!' grunted Suze.

'It's very good of him,' said Sean. 'But we've got a better angle than that, hey Bella? You'd better start writing, girl. Pete and Suzy, you start door knocking round the Common – see if anyone saw anything. Get some quotes about how shocked people are and stuff.'

That's tame, thought Bella, as she began her eyewitness story. The words tumbled from her brain and her fingers flew over the keypad as she painted a picture of the overgrown allotment, the rickety hut and the shock she felt when she saw the body. 'Never write a news story in the first person,' she remembered her old tutor at college saying. Well, she bet he'd never had a journalist who stumbled across a body before.

She was annoyed when Suze nudged her and reminded her she had to be at the police station by 11am. The morning had flown past and she hadn't even had time for a coffee, let alone a doughnut. Good job really – these trousers could not take any more strain, she thought.

* * *

DS Wright, for someone who had been up half the night dealing with a murder, looked surprisingly dapper. His dark navy suit was expensively tailored and the crisp blue shirt and striped tie made his eyes look very blue indeed. Bella picked up a sharp citrus scent of aftershave as he opened the door of the interview room for her.

'We'll do the fingerprints first and then the DNA mouth swab.'

'Mouth swab? Bloody hell – I didn't kiss her!'

Bella watched as one eyebrow shot up and a tiny muscle twitched at the side of his jaw. Oh good, she was getting to him. How dare he be all polished and sweet-smelling when she was looking so rough?

But despite her pique she was interested as the DS laid out two sheets of white paper, one marked with ten small squares, and a pad of black ink. Sitting her down on a chair he stood behind her and gently picked up her hand. 'I'll press each finger down on the ink and then onto the paper. We'll start with the right thumb,' he explained.

His hand felt warm and dry and surprisingly big, almost engulfing Bella's much smaller one as he gently pressed down on the pad. By the tenth time they'd got quite a soothing little rhythm going – pad, roll, paper, press, pad, roll, paper, press – and she was almost disappointed when it was over.

'Just a palm print now,' he murmured, pressing her whole hand down on the ink and then transferring it gently to the second sheet of paper. How delicate her hands were, he thought, taking in the faint blue veins meandering underneath against the white skin, the slim fingers and the neatly trimmed nails. She smelled good too – a light, delicate, soapy sort of smell. It made a change to get this close to a woman who wasn't wearing heavy perfume that made his nose tickle and his throat feel all closed up.

'Do I have to spit in something now?' said Bella, shattering any illusions he had about delicate femininity.

'What? Oh, the DNA swab. No, I have to scrape this thing along the inside of your mouth. It won't hurt,' he said, sitting down beside her and producing from the drawer a slender white stick topped with toothbrush-like plastic bristles. Bella opened her mouth compliantly, thanking her lucky stars that she did not have bits of doughnut in her teeth that morning.

'There. All done,' he said, popping the end of the stick into a plastic test tube.

'Good. Can I go then? I have my story to finish – the scoop of the century!' she grinned.

Jonathan blinked. The woman wasn't seriously intending to write every single detail of her find in that blasted newspaper? It would ruin his investigation, giving away all those little details, letting the murderer know exactly what the police knew, allowing him to twist and turn and wriggle out of any possible arrest... A man who normally maintained his control and calm at all cost, Jonathan felt something snap. He let rip. He even raised his voice and made Bella jump slightly. She watched wide-eyed as he ranted on about public responsibility, moral obligations and breach of confidentiality. When he got to Press Council codes of conduct, Bella snapped too and leapt up from her chair, almost knocking it backwards.

'How dare you tell me how to do my job?' she shouted. 'I am simply reporting what I saw and I can't possibly be breaching any confidentiality or responsibility because, so far, you have refused to tell me a damn thing about this investigation! In fact, you have treated me like some know-nothing kid who can't be trusted with any information at all!' she blazed, the words snapping out of her mouth like bullets from a machine gun.

She tossed back her hair and stomped to the door, high

heels clicking on the tiled floor. 'I'll see myself out, thank you,' she hissed.

Jonathan passed one hand across his brow and then rubbed his eyes. He felt weary.

'You can't,' he sighed. 'There's a security pass system on the door into the foyer.'

'Oh,' said Bella, feeling suddenly deflated and tired of all these extreme emotions. Her shoulders sagged. 'Look, I'm sorry. I think I'm still a bit shocked from all that's happened. I didn't mean to shout.' She paused. 'But you did shout at me first.'

'I did not shout,' said Jonathan.

'You definitely raised your voice!'

'I...' Jonathan bit back another denial, realising he had indeed acted somewhat unprofessionally in front of someone who was a shocked witness as well as a journalist. Anyway, this whole exchange was starting to sound like something out of a school playground. 'I'm sorry too. Look, why don't I buy you lunch?'

He was surprised when that came out. He hadn't meant to say the lunch bit at all – it just sprang from nowhere. He watched Bella's eyes widen slightly, her mouth drop open a tiny fraction and a small frown appear on her brow as she seemed to weigh up the suggestion.

'Okay,' she said simply.

The King's Arms was almost empty, but the log fire was burning and sunshine streamed in through the leaded glass windows, highlighting the tiny particles of dust dancing over the old oak tables and comfortable sofas. My kind of pub, thought Jonathan, sniffing appreciatively the aroma of stale beer, furniture polish and wood fires. He was surprised Bella had suggested it – he would have thought that trendy wine bar off Drovers Street would have been far more her cup of tea. Bet she'd ask for a glass of dry white wine though.

'Dry white wine please,' said Bella, who actually hated the taste of the stuff but thought it made her seem sophisticated. 'They do the best home-made steak and kidney pies in town here!' she added.

Jonathan groaned. 'I've got to go to the dead girl's post-mortem this afternoon. Maybe kidney is not such a good idea.' His stomach gave a little lurch as he pictured the PMs he had attended in the past, when he had stood stiffly trying not to breathe in that awful smell while the invariably cheery-faced pathologist kept up a running commentary of body parts.

'That means,' mused Bella, 'that you'll find out how she died.'

'Funnily enough, that's what post-mortems are for.'

'I think she was strangled – I couldn't see any other marks or anything.'

'I think you're probably right,' said Jonathan slowly.

Wow, thought Bella. He's actually imparted some information! Breakthrough! Perhaps we can work up a bit of trust here.

'Look,' she said, 'I really don't want to hinder the investigation in any way and I'm as keen as you are for this murderer to be caught. I'm quite prepared to work *with* you on this – you tell me what you *don't* want to come out in the *Gazette* and I won't print it. And don't forget how I can help you with witness appeals. Somebody somewhere must have seen something. You need the people of Haybridge to help. The *Gazette*'s been their oracle for fifty years; they trust us – and we're your mouthpiece. Radio and television are five-minute wonders – you'll get a couple of minutes coverage maximum with them but a local newspaper will never tire of a murder on its patch.'

It was a long speech and Bella was impressed with herself. She met Jonathan's gaze steadily as he considered.

Finally, after a swig of his beer, he spoke. 'I *don't* want you to go into detail about how the body was positioned or exactly which hut it was in. I *don't* want you to mention the handbag or what was or was not in it. And I particularly don't want you to go haring off on your own talking to people who have not yet been interviewed by my officers. I *will* keep you informed with snippets of what is happening but you will *not* publish them unless I specifically tell you.'

'Deal!' grinned Bella, taking a gulp of her wine to celebrate. Jonathan noticed her slight grimace. 'Is your wine okay? Don't you like it?'

'Oh yes, it's fine. I drink it all the time.'

You do not, he thought.

She obviously ate steak and kidney pies all the time though, he mused, watching her tuck in a few minutes later, dabbing with a napkin at the gravy on her chin. It made a change from watching Madeleine pick like a bird at lettuce leaves and cottage cheese. Madeleine wasn't too happy with him at the moment. She had invited her agent down to dinner last night and had expected Jonathan to accompany them to some new-fangled restaurant where everything came in a puddle of strange tasting coulis stuff and the vegetables were ornaments rather than food. 'I'm in the middle of a murder hunt,' he had explained when she called his mobile. 'I'll be working for hours.'

'But that means I'll have to entertain Quentin on my own,' Madeleine had whined. At that moment Jonathan was standing in the middle of the freezing allotment supervising the Scene of Crime officers. He couldn't give a toss about Quentin. 'Got to go,' he snapped, shoving the phone back in his pocket.

He had returned at 3am to find Madeleine lying pointedly on the furthermost side of the bed, feigning sleep under her fuchsia pink eye mask. At one point, just as he was drifting off, she had made a move towards him, curling one long, tanned leg over his thigh and putting one manicured hand on his shoulder. He'd grunted and rolled away.

That morning, conversation had been strained as he showered and dressed and Madeleine seemed miffed that he couldn't tell her what time he would finish work. What the hell had happened to the cool, independent woman he had been dating in London for the past twelve months? Maybe Quentin could swing that job for the new collection she had been rattling on about. She could do with something to occupy her, he thought, picturing her, with a rush of pride, gliding down the catwalk, her lips pursed provocatively and her long, long hair, cascading down her back...

Bella swept her own frizzy mop away from her face and laid down her knife and fork, 'So,' she said, 'do you think it is that Polish girl?'

'It seems like it,' said Jonathan. 'Her name is Carla, Carla Kapochkin, and she is – or was – twenty-two. But you can't release anything until the official ID. Her employer is seeing the body later today and Interpol will be contacting the parents afterwards.'

Five years younger than me, thought Bella, biting her lip. She didn't like the body suddenly becoming a real person, a flesh and blood girl who laughed and cried and played with the children in her care and had dreams for the future... She tried to compose herself.

'Do you have a suspect yet?'

'No. The family thinks she may have had a boyfriend. She had a couple of nights off a week and she always dressed up and went out. Sometimes she didn't return until the early hours but they didn't mind as long as she was there in time to get the kids up for school.'

'Do you know the boyfriend's name? I bet she would have mentioned it to the children at least – women can never resist talking about their boyfriends.'

'No,' said Jonathan shortly, thinking it was actually rather a good point and he should send a WPC round to talk to the kids.

Bella suddenly changed tack. 'What's going to happen to all your burglaries while you're investigating the murder?'

Jonathan sighed. 'That's a real problem. We're trying to persuade headquarters to draft in a couple of extra officers to take over the burglary side. We can't afford to lose any time on that investigation. Things are really hotting up. There was another one last night; came in this morning. While police were swarming everywhere on the Common someone broke into the video shop and stole a load of computer games – put a brick through the window at the back.'

'We'll get that from the press office. We'll put in an appeal. Although I'm afraid the murder will take priority in the next issue,' said Bella.

'Yes, but we really need to concentrate on these burglaries too. There's something odd about it all ... I can't put my finger on it.' Jonathan's eyes clouded into a faraway expression and he rubbed his chin thoughtfully.

He looks almost handsome when he relaxes his guard, thought Bella. 'Why?' she couldn't resist asking.

'There's an abnormally high percentage of burglaries of shops and businesses. There's no previous history of this and quite honestly it's not what you'd expect in a place like Haybridge. Though I suppose the place was ripe for the plucking – half the traders hadn't even bothered to have alarms or CCTV installed.'

'So are you linking them all? Do you think it's a professional gang that's suddenly moved into the town?' asked Bella eagerly.

'Probably. It's all quite slick. They wear gloves and we haven't managed to find a single print. But...' Jonathan paused.

'What?'

'The stuff they take is not consistent with a professional gang. These guys are going for a quick fix – a bit of petty cash and a few sellable items. Often they'll leave behind a whole rake of other high value stuff. In a lot of cases the damage to the premises adds up to more than the value of the stolen goods.'

'Do you think they're responsible for the house burglaries too?' asked Bella, wide-eyed.

'Some of them, without a doubt, bear all the hallmarks of this gang. Again they're keen to get cash and easy to sell goods. They leave behind chequebooks and credit cards potentially worth thousands, whereas a true professional would pocket those immediately.'

Bella felt a glow of pleasure that this hardened detective was taking her into his confidence. She decided to stop prodding him while the going was good. 'So you're going to be pretty busy then? Burning the midnight oil and all that?'

'Yeah. Just when I was desperate to discover the delights of Haybridge nightlife!' quipped Jonathan, his eyes suddenly twinkling. 'Actually, the only thing that bothers me is that the uniformed guys were running a coach down to see Arsenal tonight and I'd managed to get a ticket. Had to give it to one of the traffic blokes now though.'

'Arsenal?' cried Bella. 'My ... my brother is mad about Arsenal!' God, she'd almost told him about Emily. Though why she was being so unusually secretive about her daughter she could not understand. 'It's the quarter-final tonight isn't it – Barcelona? Isn't Walcott still off with his hamstring injury?' she added, thinking of her promise to Em that she could stay up and watch the first half of the match.

'Yes,' said Jonathan, with an impressed little smile. 'Your brother could have had my ticket if I'd known – anything rather than give it to traffic! He could probably get one another time though – they're often looking for people to fill the coach and they get a special rate apparently.'

'Oh, he's ... he's a bit ... a bit young to go on his own,' lied Bella, lowering her eyes. 'But it was a nice thought,' she added, flushing.

She's hiding something, thought Jonathan. What is it with this girl? He stood up, pushing aside the remains of his cheese sandwich. 'We'd better go. I don't want to be late for the post-mortem and you have your scoop of the century to write.'

'I'll fax you the copy if you like,' said Bella almost shyly. 'I don't usually, but...'

'That would be great. And I'll let you know the PM results in the morning – although –'

'They're *not* for publication yet!' finished Bella, with a grin.

A wicked look stole across Jonathan's face: 'I'll call you on your mobile shall I, *Julie*? I mean, Bella?'

Bella made her exit before her blushes showed. Well, she thought, driving Daisy back to the office, that hadn't been too bad after all. Now she'd better set to and delete a few adjectives on her masterpiece – and chop that detailed description of the little black bag. She couldn't afford to upset old Flint Eyes now. Not when she'd got him practically eating out of her hand.

Chapter Six

'What did she die of then, Bel?' asked Suzy the following evening, shoving a bottle of wine and a king size bar of Cadbury's into her friend's hand as soon as she opened the door.

'God, Suze, get in the door first!' laughed Bella, who had a blob of something that looked suspiciously like chocolate cake mix on the side of her nose. The angelic-looking Suzy had a bloodthirsty appetite for gory detail, and Bella had spent many an evening next to her on the sofa, burying her own head in a cushion while her friend calmly watched a grisly horror movie, her blue eyes staring unblinking at the screen.

In the office that morning Suze had been furious when Sean sent her to cover the usual Thursday session at the magistrates' court. 'But how can I write about people not having a TV licence when there's a murder hunt on?' she had wailed. Bella had smiled soothingly: 'Nothing much is going to happen today – police might release a name later, that's all. I'll fill you in tonight,' she'd whispered.

Suzy had nipped home to change after court and looked, as usual, like something out of a glossy magazine in a casual pale blue designer sweater, leather boots and new skinny jeans, which must have cost a fortune. But she didn't bat an eyelid when a tiny tornado swept through the kitchen door and wrapped itself round her legs with very chocolatey hands.

'Auntie Suzy! It's girls' night in and I'm a girl tonight

and Auntie Kate's coming and we're making a cake and Mummy says I can stay up till eight-thirty!'

'Eight, actually Em. But nice try,' said Bella.

Suzy scooped Em up in her arms and showered her head with kisses. 'Is it a chocolate cake?'

'Yep. Do you want to help me lick the bowl out?'

'You bet,' said Suzy. 'Lead the way.'

Bella watched the two heads bent solemnly over the bowl on her kitchen table, taking alternate licks of the wooden spoon, and she wondered again why someone as fundamentally uncomplicated and *nice* as Suzy had so many problems with men. She fell head over heels in love, on average, every three or four months, showering her chosen man with text messages, emails and phone calls until he backed falteringly away with that unerring male instinct for avoiding a needy woman.

Yet, had they bothered to get to know her, Suze wasn't needy at all. When not in love, she was one of the most grounded people Bella knew. But at twenty-eight, she simply wanted to be married with a tribe of children and she tried desperately to tailor each new man to fit in with this dream, convincing herself that this time it was Mr Right. But the handsome, brayingly-confident young men about town she attracted ran a mile at the thought of domestic bliss and the talk about children's middle names. Ironically, thought Bella, if her friend had been born less stunning and didn't scare away all the Mr Average guys, she probably would have achieved her dream by now. She was the only woman Bella knew whose good looks got in the way of her ambition.

Looks had not deterred Kate Spencer at all. A solid, ruddy-cheeked girl with wiry dark hair, her ambition from the time she had met Bella at secondary school was to be a social worker and help the needy or troubled families of Haybridge. This task she performed daily now, using the same tact and calm sympathy she had shown Bella that day she first sobbed her heart out about Hugo and blurted out the possibility of her pregnancy. Her dedication was rewarded and she shot up the social work ladder until she was now Head of Children's and Young Persons' Services.

Serious-minded Kate had, somewhat surprisingly, taken instantly to Suzy when Bella introduced her to the frivolous fellow journalist a few years ago and the trio had enjoyed regular mid-week girlie evenings ever since. These usually took place at Bella's flat, to avoid the need for a babysitter, and the tried and tested formula was pasta, cake, a DVD – and of course chocolate.

Kate, when she breezed through the door, was wearing a voluminous brown hand-knitted jumper, a long brown skirt sagging slightly at the hem and a flowing green and gold scarf draped artily round her neck.

'I'm a girl tonight, Auntie Kate. I can stay up,' Em announced again.

'Sweetheart, there's no need for gender confusion yet. You can be a girl and stay up with us but you are still a girl when you play football. Girls can be as empowered as boys – you don't have to assume the masculine persona just to achieve success.'

Bella blinked. 'Shall I put the pasta on?' she said.

'So,' said Suzy, the minute a chocolate cake-stuffed Emily had been tucked up in bed, kissed goodnight by all three women, read a politically correct bedtime story by Kate and stopped twice from trying to smuggle Thomas the cat under her duvet. 'So, what did she die of?'

'Asphyxiation,' said Bella. 'She was strangled, probably with bare hands, some time between eight pm and midnight on Saturday night. But I think he's hiding something else.'

'Who is?'

'Flint Eyes ... oh, sorry, Jonathan ... DS Wright, I mean.'

Kate and Suzy exchanged significant glances; *Jonathan* now, was it?

'He rang this morning. He sounded evasive when I asked if the PM had revealed anything more,' said Bella.

'The police always hold something back from the post-mortem – so they can lull the killer into a false sense of security,' said Suzy knowingly. 'They've officially ID'd her though?'

'Yes, an au pair girl. Came over from Poland nine months ago and worked for a family in Trent Drive. Carla someone ... can't pronounce the surname.'

'Kapochkin,' interjected Kate, pronouncing it perfectly.

'How do you know?' said Bella and Suzy simultaneously.

'Well,' drawled Kate, 'I heard it on the local radio news at five o'clock...'

Bella and Suzy groaned.

'And then, just as I was leaving the office, Jane Grimsby – you know, the case worker I took on last year – well, she recognised the name. She thought one of the young people she deals with on the Hilltops estate Young Offenders' Scheme was this girl's boyfriend... Oh dear, I hope I'm not breaching confidentiality by telling you this.'

'Of course you're not,' said Suzy hastily. 'We wouldn't dream of asking details about the case. We'd just like this little crook's ... this *young person's* name, if possible.'

'Ricky. Ricky Thomas... But it may not be right. He just told Jane at the last anger management session that he was seeing this girl from Poland called Carla,' said Kate nervously.

Anger management! This was looking more promising by the second. Suzy and Bella exchanged an excited glance.

Bella moved across to hug her old school friend. 'Kate,

we wouldn't publish anything without checking ... but Jane must tell the police about this. It could be important. Get her to pop in to the station tomorrow.'

But first, she thought, she and Suze would be fast-footing it to Hilltops the minute she got in to the office. Gosh, she'd better be on time for once.

With the prospect of a lead on the murder, Bella and Suzy became more and more exuberant as the evening wore on. Or it may have been a sugar high from all the chocolate. Either way, they shrieked with laughter as they mimicked Sean the news editor at his anal retentive worst, reducing poor Kate to a quivering mass of giggles, and then re-enacted, with much embellishment, Bella's dropped tampon story. When she got to the bit about the filter tips Suzy snorted so loudly that the cat leapt off the sofa in horror and Roger from upstairs came down and knocked on the door.

'Are you all right in there, Bella? I heard a strange noise,' he said, his kind, round face crinkled with concern.

Roger was a staid young man and far more at home with computers than with people. He really couldn't understand why his innocent remark should prompt quite such shrieks of merriment from these three rather wild-eyed women.

'Roger, Roger, come and have a drink; don't be a party pooper!' cried the fair one, who looked like a blonde version of Lara Croft. With smaller breasts. But they were still very nice. Definitely out of his league though.

Roger felt the blood rush to his cheeks and the tips of his ears flushed bright red as he automatically took two steps backwards. 'Er, no. I'd better go,' he muttered, diving for the door.

Bella clutched her stomach, which ached from laughing. How good it felt not to think about dead bodies for once. 'Right girls – you've crucified Roger – now it's time for

Hugh Grant,' she said, popping *Four Weddings and a Funeral* into the DVD player.

At 9.05am the next morning, after a quick check on the electoral register, a slightly hung-over Suzy and a still buoyant Bella were about to sneak off to 92 Crispin Drive on the Hilltops estate when Bella's mobile rang.

'DS Jonathan Wright here,' said the crisp voice. 'Can you talk?'

'Yes, of course,' squeaked Bella.

'I've copied a photograph of Carla for you to print with the appeal and I've set up an incident room with a phone number for you to print also.'

'Thank you!' said Bella, hardly believing her luck

'The reason I have done this is that I need you to appeal for anyone who was in the Swan pub between 7.30pm and 8.30pm last Saturday evening and anyone who was outside the pub, in College Road, immediately after that time. Before you ask why,' continued Jonathan, 'we've had someone call in saying a girl answering Carla's description was seen in the pub arguing with a young, slim man of ethnic origin.'

'Do you know who the man is?' asked Bella immediately, frowning at Suzy.

'Not yet. Someone thought his first name might be Richard or Ricky. We'll find him though,' said Jonathan grimly.

Bella's brain buzzed and she began an almighty wrestle with her conscience. Should she tell this detective what she knew about the possible boyfriend or should she dash round there before the police caught up with him and grab an exclusive? Suzy was waiting, hopping from foot to foot and swinging her car keys. It would be so easy. But he would be *furious...*

'Um, I think I may know who he is. He's a boyfriend,' she ventured. Suzy's mouth dropped open and she waved both hands frantically at her colleague.

'It could be Ricky Thomas. He lives at 92 Crispin Drive, Hilltops, with a Maria Louise Thomas. You'll find he's known to Social Services.' She had blown her exclusive but boy, she'd felt good telling this cop something he didn't know.

But the ungrateful sod did not even say thank you. Just clicked the phone down without a word. How dare he?

'That was your copper, wasn't it?' Suzy's eyes stared accusingly.

'Suze – I had to tell him. You don't know what he's like. And he ... he *trusted* me. They would have found out soon anyway – from Kate's colleague.'

'Yeah. But so much for our head start,' moaned Suzy, plonking herself down at her desk and staring gloomily at her computer. 'They'll probably arrest him now and it'll be all over by lunchtime.'

'But that's good isn't it? If they catch the murderer?' said Bella, wondering why she felt so deflated herself.

DC Jerry 'Boz' Boswell clung on to the side of his seat for dear life as his boss drove the regulation issue Ford Mondeo like a Formula One racing car through the winding streets of Haybridge, overshooting two red lights and narrowly missing a row of bollards marking the new traffic calming scheme.

Someone got out of bed the wrong side this morning, thought Boz, who had, in fact, got out of the right side of the wrong *bed* himself, having fallen for the charms of a young WPC in the singles quarters and failed completely to return home to his current girlfriend. As usual, he'd solved the problem of a potential row by keeping his mobile firmly switched off.

Jonathan's black brows were drawn together in an angry frown and his lips were pinched tight together.

'Anything wrong, boss?' ventured Boz.

'That bloody Bella woman... If she's been meddling around with this suspect... Why can't the woman back off? She's a local hack – not a bloody detective.'

'Bella? She's okay, boss. What's the problem?'

Jonathan explained tersely. 'I warned her to stop nosing around – this is a crucial time for us,' he concluded.

'Look, Bella knows a lot of people in this town. She was born and bred here and she's a cracking journalist with loads of contacts. People like her and trust her. They talk to her,' reasoned Boz. 'And,' he continued, 'she hasn't got much time to nose around, as you put it, what with bringing up that kid on her own and everything.'

'Kid?'

'Yeah, she's a single mum. Got caught by some flash git who legged it afterwards apparently.'

'Boy or girl?'

'Girl. Right little tomboy though – mad on football.'

Hmm, thought Jonathan. He felt a pang of a something unfamiliar, maybe even guilt at being a little harsh on a single mother. But he shoved it aside as he noticed the signpost to Crispin Drive. 'Number ninety-two – and you'd better be in, Ricky Thomas,' he murmured.

'My Ricky wouldn't do it. He's a good boy. He wouldn't harm a fly,' sobbed an incredibly large Jamaican lady, who had been sweeping her kitchen floor when Jonathan and Boz rapped on the door.

'Were you aware Miss Kapochkin was dead, Mrs Thomas?' asked Jonathan. 'It's been reported on local radio and TV.'

'No!' The wails grew louder and she wiped her eyes on the corner of her lurid-coloured flowery apron. 'I only watch my soaps … but my Ricky wouldn't hurt her… He's a good boy.'

'Let's go and get this good boy out of bed,' muttered Jonathan, thinking of the swift conversation he'd had with the social worker about Ricky's Anger Management classes. He motioned for Boz to follow him up the uncarpeted stairs.

Ricky Lester Thomas was lying on his back under a faded blue duvet in a cramped but clean bedroom, one arm slung casually out of bed as small, bubbling snores erupted rhythmically from his mouth. He was dreaming about driving a brand new gleaming back BMW convertible along a country road, rap music blaring from the stereo and a nubile, smiling girl at his side, her hair flying in the wind. He was not at all pleased to be rudely awoken by two poker-faced police officers asking him questions about that crazy bird Carla.

'Did you know she was dead?' asked Jonathan for the third time.

'No,' Ricky shook his head violently as if to chase away the sleep. 'It's, like, a real shock. I thought she was okay, cool, like.'

'When did you think she was okay? When did you last see her?'

'In the pub. We had a row, didn't we? She got stroppy, didn't she? Walked out.'

'Did you follow her?'

'Nah. I finished me pint, didn't I?' Ricky paused indignantly from zipping up a pair of baggy jeans that hung in limp folds around his skinny crotch.

'What did you do then?'

'I … um… I can't remember.' The gangster speech was suddenly dropped and Ricky looked down at the floor.

'I think you should try very hard indeed to remember where you were between 8pm and midnight on Saturday night, Ricky.'

'I came home and watched telly.'

'Was your mother home?'

'She was at Bingo.'

'Was anyone home?'

'No. But I was here. I was, like, just chilling out.'

'What did you watch on television, Ricky?'

'Uh... Football. I watched the football.'

'Who was playing?'

'Some team in red. I fell asleep. I was knackered, wasn't I?'

Jonathan did a quick mental assessment. He had an admission of a row, no alibi and an obvious pack of lies about watching television. This was almost too easy. 'Ricky, we are going to have to ask you to come with us to the police station...'

'Bugger it, damn it, bugger, bugger, bugger!' said Bella when the statement came at 4pm from the police press office. 'A twenty-three-year-old man is being questioned in connection with the murder of Polish au pair girl Carla Kapochkin. No charges have yet been made. There will be no further comment.'

That was it then. Ricky Thomas would doubtless be charged in a couple of days; the murder hunt would be over and all press coverage would be severely restricted under the sub judice laws until the case went to Crown Court in around nine months' time. And all because she handed that name on a plate to bloody Jonathan Wright, who incidentally had not even bothered to call her and say thank you. She had irrationally forgotten that the determined detective was hot on the trail anyway as she sat and smouldered silently at a press release about speed humps. Bloody speed humps! It hadn't helped at all when she and Suzy had shot out to the Swan pub as soon as it opened at lunchtime, planning to charm the landlord into telling them all about the lovers' tiff that probably led to grisly murder.

'You talk and I'll flutter my eyelashes,' whispered Suze as they walked into the pub, taking in the new laminate floor, brightly-coloured tables and massive plasma TV screens. In a chiller cabinet behind the bar were dozens of bottles of alcopops, the lurid colours glistening temptingly under the fluorescent lights and, even at this hour, loud hip hop music was blaring. Bella felt the stirrings of a headache start to creep around her temples.

'Yes?' barked a hefty sandy-haired woman who had muscular wrestler's forearms folded impatiently across her chest.

'Hello!' chirped Bella. 'Would it be possible to speak to the landlord please?'

'I *am* the licensee.' The forearms bulged as they worked a pump, splashing toffee-coloured beer into a pint glass.

'Ah... We're reporters from the *Haybridge Gazette*. We –'

'The police have told me not to comment. I have nothing to say.'

'Er, could we buy two halves of lager then? And one for you?' asked Bella. There was still a chance this Amazonian landlady might just thaw out over a beer or two.

'No.' The answer was short but definite and two reporters crept shame-faced out of the pub.

They hoped for better luck in Trent Drive where they planned to chat to Carla's employers and find out what the young Polish girl was really like – get a human interest twist to the story. Maybe they could arrange a photograph of the bewildered couple cuddling their sad-eyed children, all missing their beloved au pair. Perhaps they could borrow some pictures of Carla, smiling into the sunshine as she pushed the kids on the swings in the park...

Thirty-six Trent Drive was a solid, three-storey red brick house which looked as though it could easily house five or six inhabitants. But that lunchtime there was not a single sign of life and the imitation Victorian brass bell rang hollowly around the terracotta-tiled hallway, which, after a quick peep through the letterbox, Bella could see was cluttered with shoes, coats and toddler toys. 'We'll come back later,' she sighed.

But ever since then Sean had piled on the stories relentlessly. 'You may want to gad about on this murder but we still have a paper to fill,' he admonished, handing Bella an inch-thick wad of council agendas. Childishly, she poked her tongue out behind his retreating back and Ron, pottering about emptying the bins in editorial, had spotted the gesture and winked. Good to see Miss Bella was getting her spirit back again...

But now, mused Bella, it was almost time to go home and another vital murder reporting day had been wasted – and still no phone call from measly Mr Flint Eyes.

As if on cue the phone on her desk shrilled. She snatched it eagerly.

'Bella?' asked an agitated and familiar voice.

'Hello Mum,' she sighed.

There was no preamble. 'Mrs Heathcliffe from the post office said she saw Mrs Mapleton at the church wine and cheese evening and Mrs Mapleton said you'd found ... found a *body*! What are you doing finding bodies, Bella? We didn't bring you up to find *bodies*! What were you doing rooting about those allotments after dark? And where was Emily? Please tell me Emily didn't see a *body*! You can't be a mum and do these things, Bella. Why can't you write about *nice* stories? The vicar was only saying to me the other day...'

Luckily Mrs Smart paused for breath. Bella, imagining her father hovering anxiously in the background, his hand placed reassuringly on his wife's shoulder, tried to explain as briefly and as calmly as she could. 'Emily knew nothing about it, Mum, I promise. Look, how about I bring her round tomorrow, after her Halloween party, and you can see we're both fine? She can trick and treat you.'

'I'll get some tea,' said Mrs Smart automatically, 'I'll bake some of those witch's hat biscuits you used to love when you were small.' She tailed off and the anxious note crept back into her voice 'But *bodies*, Bella ... why *bodies?*'

'Only one, Mum. And I have to write about it. It's my job.'

'It's my job,' snapped DS Jonathan Wright when Ricky Thomas stared at him challengingly, his dark young face creased with anger, and demanded to know why the hell the Old Bill were questioning him about a murder he did not commit.

'We are here to solve a murder,' he told the young man, who for the past three hours had failed to admit, despite the most vigorous questioning from Jonathan and Boz, that he had strangled his girlfriend to death.

He had also failed spectacularly to give a true account of what he did or where he went after he left the Swan, just five minutes after Carla stormed out.

'I didn't go after her, I promise. I wasn't that bothered, you see. She'd given me a hard time, like, and I didn't see why I should go after her and get another mouthful. It wasn't even like she was my proper bird or anything. She was just a ... a...'

'Sexual partner?' offered DC Boswell helpfully.

Ricky nodded. He had already told the officers that he had met the buxom, black-haired Polish girl three months previously, while she was pushing a young kid across the Common in a buggy. Ricky saw her stop as a stick got tangled up in a wheel and watched her bend over and struggle to remove it, her skimpy cropped jeans straining across a pair of round buttocks. 'Here, let me help,' he had said gruffly, seizing the stick and straightening up the buggy. She smiled up at him with very white teeth and moved so close he could see the faint, dark moustache on her upper lip. Then she started prattling on about how kind he was in this funny but quite sexy accent. He thought she was French or something but then she said she was from Poland and she didn't know many people here. Before he knew it he had invited her out for a drink the following Tuesday – his dole cheque came on Tuesdays – and after that he had seen her two or three times a week, if she could get the nights off.

He didn't take her out much, though; he didn't like his mates seeing him with her. She wasn't his usual type – not much of a looker really – and they might have taken the piss out of that moustache. Usually they went back to his house and up to his room while his mum sat watching *EastEnders* downstairs. Afterwards Carla would want to cuddle and stuff and she would try to stroke his hair and tell him that she loved him in that funny accent. He had felt trapped then. He wanted her gone. He wanted to go down the pub and meet his mates. He hated it when birds got all clingy. He'd never promised her any more than a shag anyway, had he?

She was good though, old Carla – bit more adventurous than Haybridge girls, who always worried about what time their mum expected them home or what their mates would say. She could stay out all night if she wanted too, could Carla. He hated it when she got pushy though. 'You must come to Poland – meet my parents and my brothers and my sister,' she would say, kissing him wetly on the lips.

When he pushed her away she would look cross; sometimes she looked like she was going to cry and he hated girls howling. But she usually cheered up in the end.

Man, she was in a foul mood on Saturday night, though. Made him jump the way she had stormed into the pub and started laying into him while he was with all his mates, banging on about how he had said he would take her back to Poland and that he'd let her down. He had grabbed her arm and tried to get her outside – anything to stop his mates hearing – but she wouldn't budge. Made a right idiot of him, she did. He felt like shaking her, he was so angry. Stupid bitch...

'So, despite feeling so angry, you finished your drink then walked home and watched the television alone?' Jonathan had interrupted, watching Ricky's face carefully.

'Yes,' he replied, rubbing his eyes with both hands.

'I put it to you that you followed Carla out of the pub. The row continued and you lost your temper, put your hands around her neck and started shaking her –'

'I did NOT!' shouted Ricky.

The young, wispy-bearded duty solicitor at his side put a hand on his shoulder. 'You don't have to answer any more questions if you don't wish to, Ricky,' he said.

'One more question,' said Jonathan firmly. 'Was Carla pregnant?'

'Pregnant?' Ricky looked genuinely surprised. 'Up the duff? No! Well, if she was it wasn't mine – I'm always really careful, like.'

Jonathan clicked off the tape machine. 'OK, we will release you on police bail for one week – you must return here on Friday November sixth at 12 noon,' he sighed. By then, he thought, the preliminary forensic results would be back from the lab. All he needed was one match from any one of the dozens of skin, dust and hair samples taken from the girl's body – one tiny molecule showing

Ricky Thomas's DNA – and he would have his guilty conviction. A fingerprint would be nice, of course – judges like fingerprint evidence.

Luckily there had been no need to fingerprint or mouth swab Ricky today though. Two convictions for stealing cars, one theft from a petrol station, one shoplifting and an actual bodily harm after a fight outside a pub had placed his details firmly on the police computerised system. It was just a shame these damn forensic labs took so long – even for an urgent murder enquiry.

'What do you reckon, boss?' said Boz, when the young West Indian had been led away by his solicitor.

'I think,' said Jonathan thoughtfully, 'that we have a lot of work to do.'

One aspect was bugging him. All the evidence pointed to the fact that Carla was killed elsewhere and her body had been taken to the hut. How had slightly built Ricky Thomas dragged a 10-stone dead-weight girl to the allotments – without any witnesses so far reporting they'd seen him? Had he used a car? Early results from tapings of the clothes indicated there were short grey fibres present, possibly consistent with a carpet. Had she been in a car boot? But Ricky had no access to a car; he didn't own one. But he *did* have convictions for car theft. Why hadn't any cars been reported stolen in Haybridge on Saturday night then?

Jonathan's mind was spinning. Suddenly the prospect of Madeleine waiting for him in the hotel room, pouring him a drink and wanting to talk about nothing more demanding than the shade of her nail varnish, was an extremely tempting one. But there was no chance. He had reports to write, statements to read and evidence to sort. It was going to be another long night. A long weekend, in fact.

Chapter Seven

Bella crammed a Jammie Dodger in her mouth and surveyed the three dozen assorted little witches, devils, vampires and ghosts – and one fat orange pumpkin – dancing like maniacs all around her, fake blood and chocolate cake icing smeared in clashing stripes across many of their faces. Do I actually like other people's kids? she pondered, watching one small boy whack his plastic devil's pitchfork solidly across the head of a wailing red-faced little ghoul. Em was having a ball though. She'd spotted her friend Megan as soon as they arrived at the Church Hall and ran off to give her a hug, her wobbly orange tummy banging against Meg's witch costume like a Mr Blobby doll.

It was good of the Sunday school teachers to organise this party though and lucky for Emily – who, despite her grandma's protests had never been to Sunday school in her life – that she had managed to wangle an invitation through Megan's mum, the do-gooding Sharon.

The lady in question, flushed from organising a rowdy game of musical ghost bumps, approached with a beaming smile. Bella swallowed hastily; it wouldn't do to be caught stealing the kids' party tea.

'How lovely to see you here, Bella. Are you staying to help us?'

'Yes, of course. Absolutely! Er, if you really need me, that is.' Damn, she had been hoping to have a wander around the High Street shops. Not that she had any money to spend but an hour or two alone would have been bliss.

'We always appreciate help, Bella. Now, if you could start by taking the clingfilm off the egg sandwiches.'

Sharon looked so *happy* to be stuck in a hall with thirty-six shrieking children. And she was so damn enthusiastic, prancing around in those dreadful leggings, clapping her hands with glee and gushing 'oh gosh' and 'golly' and 'dearie me' like something out of a Famous Five book.

'They're getting thirsty now. Could you get the fizzy pop ready, Bella?' she trilled at that moment.

See, thought Bella, pure Enid Blyton. They would be having lashings of ginger ale next. She was opening a lemonade bottle when she felt a timid tug on her sleeve. A very small girl with big brown eyes and curly blonde hair was staring solemnly up at her. 'Could I have a drink please, Miss? I'm very thirsty.' she asked politely.

You, thought Bella, are the cutest thing I've ever seen. 'Yes darling,' she said, crouching down to the child's level. 'Would you like orange squash, blackcurrant or lemonade?'

The little girl, who, Bella noticed, had only a hastily modelled black bin bag for a costume, cocked her head on one side and considered carefully. 'Could I have water please? Squash is bad for my teeth,' she finally replied sadly.

Bella looked at the serious little face. Poor little mite. She wanted to take her home and let her have all the squash she wanted and see that solemn little mouth break out into a great big smile. 'What's your name?' she asked gently.

But before the child could answer Sharon appeared in a flurry of flowery leggings and seized her by her tiny little arm. 'Amelia!' she cried. 'Your mummy was looking for you! Now, why don't you go and play Throw The Witch's Hat with Matthew and Thomas – over there, where Mummy can see you.' She twirled Amelia round and gave her a firm shove in the direction of the two rather over-excited little boys.

'Amelia's mummy has *problems*, at the moment,' she hissed in a stage whisper, gesturing with her head to a smartly dressed woman sitting on a chair in the corner, rocking a grizzling toddler in a pushchair.

'Oh. Is it man trouble?' asked Bella sympathetically.

'Oh gosh no! Amelia's mummy is happily married. But she's had a very nasty shock. She's the lady who employed that –' Sharon cast a furtive glance around the room and cupped her hand in front of her mouth, 'that poor au pair girl.'

Bella felt her heart suddenly skip a beat. Yes! Now, how could she get this woman to talk?

'Of course, you'd know all about it, you working for the *Gazette* and all that,' Sharon was saying.

Bella considered her options swiftly. 'Actually,' she said, 'I was the person who found the body – quite by chance. She looked ... she looked very *peaceful*.' Well, she did look quite peaceful lying there – as long as you didn't look at those bulging eyes. Ugh.

'Oh Bella!' Sharon was clutching her by the arm and gazing at her with misty eyes. 'Do you think you could go and have a little chat with Amelia's mummy and tell her the girl looked *peaceful*? I'm sure it would be a great comfort to her.'

'Oh dear. I don't know. Well, if you think it will help,' dithered Bella, trying to hide her excitement. Lead me there!

'It's just such a nuisance,' confided Amelia's mum, who turned out to be called Caroline Williams.

'I mean, you go to all the trouble of contacting the agencies and flying over an au pair and getting her settled in and used to your ways and then she gets killed. Now I'm left with no help at all. I've had to take all this week off work and they reckon they can't get me another girl until next Thursday. We've had policemen traipsing all over the house with their muddy boots – we'd only just had the new carpet laid in the lounge – and we've had to spend hours answering questions. And,' she added, almost as an afterthought, 'the children are really upset.'

I don't like you, thought Bella instinctively. You don't deserve a gorgeous little girl like Amelia. But she forced herself to smile sympathetically and relayed her story about finding the oh-so-peaceful body.

'Yuk!' said Caroline, unimpressed. 'It was the boyfriend that killed her, wasn't it?'

News travels fast in Haybridge, thought Bella. Even though Ricky Thomas had been neither named nor charged by police, the whole town knew he was the murderer. He won't dare show his face, even though he's still legally innocent and out on bail.

It took hardly any prodding at all to get Caroline to relate her story. Still rocking the fractious toddler, she described how Carla had come to them last February, speaking excellent English and willing to cook and clean as well as care for Amelia and her brother George. The Williamses considered themselves really lucky; honestly, one heard such ghastly tales about au pair girls these days – neglecting the children, eating all the food and flirting outrageously with the husbands. Carla, for the first few months, was not much trouble at all. She did all her chores efficiently, she was sweet with the children and, when the Williamses wanted a bit of peace and quiet in the evenings, she was quite happy to stay in her room watching the little black and white portable TV they had put in there for her. Sometimes Carla would earn extra cash by babysitting in the evenings for the Williamses' friends. It got her out of the house and it did the friends a favour because Carla only charged £3 an hour instead of £5 like the local girls. She didn't need much money. The £50 a week the Williamses paid her was a fortune to her. She didn't even spend it all and sent some home to her parents each month. She came from quite a poor family apparently but you wouldn't know – she was quite well mannered.

'But then, two or three months ago – in the summer – she started to change.' Caroline wrinkled her nose. 'She started going out more at night and even refused the odd babysitting job. She bought some new clothes from the market – tarty little outfits, really – and she would spend longer in the bathroom fiddling with her hair and make-up. She wasn't quite as ... as obliging somehow.'

I bet that's when she met Ricky, thought Bella.

'I asked if she'd found a boyfriend,' said Caroline, as if reading Bella's thoughts. 'But she just laughed and shook her head. To be honest, it didn't really make much difference to us whether she was seeing anyone or not – as long as she didn't see him in work time.'

'She never brought anyone home?' asked Bella.

'Goodness no! It was in her contract that no friends could visit.'

Over the past few weeks, Caroline continued, Carla had became more withdrawn, even quite surly at times. A girl who had always eaten anything put in front of her, she started being fussy with food, pushing it around on her plate. It really wasn't a good example for the children. Some nights she obviously stayed out until the early hours and looked totally wrung out when she did the children's breakfast. The Williamses had been forced to have a few sharp words with her but she had just stared at them with that surly expression. So it was no great surprise at first when she failed to come home on Saturday night.

77

They thought she was sulking – just a spot of rebellion. A friend advised them to report her missing, just in case, you know. But they hadn't really thought she was in any danger or anything – until the police suddenly knocked on the door on Tuesday night … and trod mud all over the new carpet.

Suddenly tired of the self-centred monologue, Bella asked Caroline if she could use some of her quotes in the *Gazette*.

'Yes, if you wish,' was the reply. 'Will you need a photograph?' she asked, patting her blonde bobbed hair.

Bella looked up. The children had devoured the party tea and were clutching Halloween balloons, ready to go. Swiftly she found Em, grabbed her hand and led her over to thank the helpers.

'I think Amelia's mummy feels better now,' she whispered to a beaming Sharon.

Jonathan grimaced as he took a swig of tepid orange-coloured tea and tried to remember when he had last eaten. Judging by the hollow feeling in his stomach it had been a long time ago and he would even welcome one of Madeleine's slimy vegetable salads right now. But a steaming steak pie would be better he thought, suddenly picturing Bella's laughing mouth closing around a forkful of golden flaky pastry soaked with thick, beefy gravy. His stomach growled and, pushing aside a pile of papers, he reached for the phone.

'Hi, it's me. I'm going to take a break for a couple of hours. Do you fancy meeting me in the King's Arms for a pie and pint?'

'A *pie*?' The voice was incredulous.

'Well, they probably do other stuff too. Come on, I'll buy you a salad.'

'Couldn't we go somewhere a bit smarter? It's just that I bought this new top today – it's amazing really what you can find if you persevere in these poky little High Street shops – and I wanted to wear it with that beige skirt. You know the one with the Versace bias cut. But I think that may be just a teensy bit overdressed for a pub, don't you?'

'Madeleine, just sling on a pair of jeans and meet me in the pub, will you?' groaned Jonathan.

Fifteen minutes later, standing at the bar in the King's Arms lounge, which had seemed to welcome him like an old friend into its faded rustic charms, he eyed Madeleine's long demin-cladded legs appreciatively. It didn't matter what this woman wore; she looked stunning in anything. But she looked even more stunning without anything on at all. Well, perhaps just that little black wispy lace thing...

Her petulant mood had passed, thank God, and she greeted him with a 'Hello Honey' and a lingering kiss, which he interrupted, totally unintentionally, by a rather violent sneeze as his nostrils were assaulted by a blast of Chanel perfume.

One hand resting in the small of her back, he steered her to a sagging velvet sofa in front of the fire, watching as she lowered herself gracefully down and crossed one elegant leg over the other. 'So, sweetheart, how's it going?' she asked.

'OK I think,' said Jonathan. 'The post-mortem has revealed some very interesting –'

'Oh darling. Please don't talk about horrid things like post-mortems. You know how squeamish I am. Remember that photo shoot in Thailand where I saw that poor dead dog, with all those horrible flies?' Madeleine gave a delicate shudder, then, almost instantly, a tinkling laugh. 'Anyway, you're looking very dishevelled and sexy so you must be working very hard to catch your murderer. I quite like you with a bit of stubble – it's the bad boy about town look and all the magazines are raving about it at the moment, you know.'

Jonathan rubbed his jaw. She was right. He shouldn't burden her with the details of a murder. He had to learn to switch off. It was Saturday night; he was out with a beautiful woman and, he remembered with a surge of pleasure, he had a steak pie on its way right now. He leaned forward, cupping Madeleine's face in both his strong, tanned hands. 'How do you fancy a bit of stubble rash later?' he growled.

The lipsticked lips formed a perfect, provocative pout. 'Only if you don't work too late.'

Toby Smart was an uncomplicated man. Give him an undemanding day at work, a bit of sport on television and a decent meal and he was happy. He breezed though life with an easy smile, avoided all confrontation and accepted other people's idiosyncrasies, seldom troubling his brain about the complexities of human nature. So when his sister came flying into their parents' kitchen and dragged him off for an 'urgent word' without even giving him time to do his high five routine with young Emily, he simply shrugged his shoulders and followed her outside. She hissed that it was 'absolutely imperative' that he suggested popping out to the pub after supper and it was 'vital' that he asked Bella to accompany him.

Mum and Dad would look after Emily for an hour or so, Bella had said, her eyes shining just the way they used to when she was a small child scheming some exciting adventure game for her less imaginative small brother. Toby had only popped over to spend a quiet couple of hours with his parents and exchange a bit of football banter with his niece – but if Bella insisted…

Rita and Paul Smart had indeed been only too happy to babysit and by 7pm were happily ensconced on their green Draylon sofa, their granddaughter snuggled between them, watching *Family Fortunes* on television.

'But why the Swan, Bel?' asked Toby, his smooth young face looking unusually perplexed as they walked across town. 'It's a bit rough, isn't it? Don't all the teenagers drink there? What's wrong with the King's Arms?'

Bella swiftly filled her brother in on her plan. Toby would pretend to be her boyfriend and they would manoeuvre their way into a conversation with a certain group of lads. Perhaps Toby could pretend he was new to the area and ask about the local football league or something. Then Bella would start talking about the murder, all shocked and horrified and feminine, and she would flutter her eyelashes and ask the lads if they had known the murdered girl. Toby shrugged his shoulders for the second time that evening – if this was the way reporters worked then of course he would help his big sister.

Ms Amazonian was, thank goodness, nowhere to be seen and instead two trendy-looking young men were serving at the bar, swirling glasses with professional flourish and bustling between the pumps and the till. Bella's eyes fixed on the oldest looking one, a muscular youth with dark, gel-spiked hair, and she gave him her very best smile while Toby ordered a pint of best bitter and a Coca Cola with ice. Sipping the drink, she surveyed her fellow customers. That group to the left looked promising but perhaps they were a bit too young. And the group huddled round that big table, clutching half-pint glasses and puffing rather nervously on Benson and Hedges – now they looked barely old enough to be out of school. Those guys chatting up the two girls were definitely businessmen; you could tell by the confident way they leaned back against the bar and sipped their gin and tonics, surveying the giggling, mini-skirted pair through slightly narrowed eyes.

But those half a dozen young men playing darts – *they* looked perfect. They were in their early twenties, casually but trendily dressed in baggy jeans and T-shirts, and they all had a slight swagger in their step. Bella nudged Toby heavily, causing him to slop his beer down his checked shirt. 'Over there!' she hissed.

Toby, familiar with the all-male bonhomie of the sporting world, was a natural. 'Hi mate,' he greeted the obvious ringleader, a handsome, broad-chested black lad engaged in keeping the score and showering his team mates with friendly but expletive-littered abuse. 'Do you know if they're showing the football in here tonight?'

'Yeah. Man United and Everton. Only the highlights though.'

'Well I hope Man U pull their finger out. That penalty last week...'

Soon the darts were forgotten in an animated bout of player bitching, score predicting and managerial tactic slamming. So this is male bonding, thought Bella, feeling rather bored. She waited for a tiny gap in a conversation about a weak midfield and dived straight in: 'So does anything happen in Haybridge apart from football? It seems really quiet here.' Oh dear, she hoped her voice didn't sound too squeaky.

The black lad looked straight at her, almost challengingly. 'Yeah. We had a murder last week.'

'Gosh!' said Bella, this time with a deliberate squeak. 'Did you know the person who was killed?'

'Not really. But we know the poor bastard who's meant to have done it. But the Old Bill can't prove a thing – let him out on bail already they have.'

'You mean you know a *murderer?*' Bella tried to make her tone both incredulous and impressed.

'Ricky didn't do it, sugar, and don't you go thinking he did. Yeah, he had a temper on him but he wouldn't go killing a *girl*. He might shag 'em half to death but he wouldn't hurt 'em! He's a right one for the women, Ricky is.'

A sudden surge of questions flew into Bella's brain, each one jostling for space to make the short journey to her lips. She took a deep breath and exhaled slowly. Time to dig about Ricky and Carla's relationship. What had they argued about last Saturday night? Had these guys been there? She rested her eyes on the handsome black face – only to see it suddenly jerk sharply upwards, the dark eyes widening slightly with surprise. A split second later Bella almost jumped out of her skin as a heavy hand gripped her shoulder from behind. Ouch! What the hell was happening? She turned her head sharply.

'Miss Smart. How nice to see you. May I buy you a drink?' The tone was honey smooth and impassive but Bella was not fooled. Those blue eyes were alight with pure, flashing anger.

She had a choice. She could tell this pig-headed interfering Jonathan Wright to sod off now and leave her to enjoy her quiet Saturday night drink. Or she could look a right prat and confess that she had been trying to play amateur detective and poke her nose in where she shouldn't. Or, maybe, just maybe, there was an alternative...

'Yes, please,' she said, looking up with a particularly sweet smile, 'I'd love a drink.'

Jonathan wrestled to change his expression from sardonic to friendly in one swift second. Two can play at this game, he thought. He'd called into the Swan on a sudden impulse after saying goodbye to Madeleine in the King's Arms. It was this time last week – almost to the minute – that Carla and Ricky Thomas were seen rowing in the pub. Obviously his officers had made their enquiries, speaking to the landlady and tracing customers to give statements, but there was bound to be a witness or two who had given them the slip. Perhaps some of Ricky's slippery little mates had gathered, seven days later, to talk about what had really happened. Perhaps the beer would loosen their tongues enough for a sharp-eyed, off-duty detective, sitting at a table and sipping an innocent pint, to see or hear something that might just help along a guilty conviction.

What he *hadn't* expected to see was a redheaded young woman thrusting her button nose firmly into police business once again. 'You mean, you know a *murderer?*' he had heard her squeal, playing the Little Miss Innocent. God, she deserved an Oscar for that one! His instincts had been right about this woman; she was certainly far from innocent.

Nevertheless he was the epitome of charm and he invited Bella to join him at the bar. The pleasant-looking chap in a blue checked shirt followed, rather protectively, he thought. Obviously one of her blokes then.

Bella gestured to him. 'This is my –'

'Boyfriend,' the chap interjected firmly.

Jonathan noticed Bella shoot her companion an odd glance, her eyebrows raised a fraction. The chap gave a tiny, quizzical frown. She's up to something again, he thought.

'So,' he said, 'what brings you here tonight?'

'We were just passing and we thought we'd call in for a quick drink. I suppose I wanted to see what the place was like before I did your witness appeal.' Bella gave a tinkly little laugh. God, she sounded like Madeleine now, thought Jonathan.

'I'm sorry I dragged you away from your friends,' he said, motioning to the group around the darts board.

'Oh goodness me! Gosh!' Shit – this Enid Blyton stuff

must be contagious. 'They're not my friends! Toby just got talking to them about football, didn't you ... *darling*? Bella let out another little laugh – more of a trill this time. Sounds like a canary now, thought Jonathan. A canary lying through its teeth. Or beak.

'Actually darling, we ought to be making a move. We'll be late for the film. Perhaps we could have that drink another time, DS Wright? It was *very* nice to bump into you like this though!' Bella grabbed her bewildered-looking escort by the hand and towed him towards the door. 'Byeee!' she trilled, waggling her fingers at him when she reached it.

Jonathan reached for his pint and took several long, soothing mouthfuls. He plonked down his glass, wiped his mouth and took a slow, deep breath. That was one crazy, crazy woman...

Chapter Eight

Emily was twiddling a long sandy-coloured strand of hair with one hand while absent-mindedly picking her nose with the other. Her cropped-headed Barbies lay in a naked clutter on the living-room floor and her grey-green eyes stared rather vacantly into space.

'What's up, Em?' asked Bella, breezing through the room with her usual Sunday morning heap of ironing.

'Megan's daddy is taking her swimming today. And Chloe's daddy is taking her to the wild animal park where you see real lions and things. Why haven't I got a daddy?'

Uh oh, thought Bella. She'd waited six years for this question and had been amazed that it had never, so far, been asked. Kind-hearted Kate had prepared her with a stock-pile of suitable answers, just in case, but Bella had always thanked her lucky stars that her happy-go-lucky little daughter had seemed more than satisfied to have Uncle Toby and her granddad as the role-model men in her life. And, she thought, people like dear old childless Ron and geeky Roger from upstairs, both of whom never failed to treat the little girl like some precious princess. Not that Em was the type to want to be treated like a princess by some doting daddy; it was more the rough and tumble in the park and the strong capable hands constructing her a Barbie goalpost that she really craved. Bella swallowed hard, and felt a hot rush of tears prick her eyes. Her instinct was to scoop up her daughter, who looked so small and defenceless at that very moment, and sob her heart out on her skinny little shoulder, apologising profusely for so badly letting her down.

But don't be silly, she reasoned. *She* hadn't let Emily down. That bastard Hugo Copeland had. Or had he? How could he be expected to take an interest in a child he clearly had not wanted to have? A baby Bella had defiantly insisted on bringing up alone. Had it been an act of extreme selfishness on her part? She took a deep breath and rummaged in the recesses of her brain for Kate's words of advice.

'You do have a daddy, Em. All children have a daddy. But your daddy never lived with Mummy and he moved a long way away before you were born. He never got to know you and to see what a lovely little girl you are. But he couldn't help it – he was ... he was busy.'

'Don't poison the child against her father.' 'Boost her self esteem.' 'Make it quite clear it is not Emily's fault.' Kate's professional phrases swam in Bella's head. Em stared up at her with wide, wide eyes. Now hit me with the six million dollar question, Bella thought: Can I see my daddy?

The few seconds of silence seemed to last for ever and Bella swore her heart stopped beating. Emily finally cocked her head on one side and looked her straight in the eye...

'Will you play football with me in the park today?' she asked her mum.

Yes! thought Bella, stooping down to shower the freckled face with kisses. Yes! I will play football with you for ever, my beautiful, tough little daughter. I detest kicking a ball around and I hate the cold and the mud and pretending to be ecstatic every time you score a goal. But for you – anything. Anything in the world.

'Ugh, get off, Mum!' said Em, dragging the back of her hand across her face. 'Shall we go now?'

* * *

It was, indeed, bloody freezing in the park and Bella was not the only parent hopping from foot to foot and feigning enthusiasm at their offspring's achievements while casting surreptitious glances at their watches. But Bella's heart was still glowing with emotion, matching the end of her nose, which had turned an unflattering puce in the bitter wind and was probably, she thought, sporting at least one glistening dewdrop. The ball landed neatly at her feet and, jumping slightly, she gave it a little kick.

'*Feeble!*' cried Em, running up with a huge grin and rugby tackling her mum's legs.

'Brr. Aren't you cold, darling?' Bella asked, trying to keep her balance.

'No.' Em looked up in surprise, as if anything as trivial as the weather was worth bothering her busy little six-year-old brain about.

'How about,' said Bella, 'how about we give Auntie Suzy a ring and see if she wants to come round this afternoon?'

'Can we make some cakes?'

'Absolutely. You can try out that new yellow squirty icing we bought...'

'It's a deal,' declared Em, grabbing her mum's hand.

The pair walked companionably out of the park and down the street of terraced houses to the flat. I'm a lucky, lucky woman, thought Bella – even if I do have a pile of ironing as high as Vesuvius.

Bella and Suzy were mopping up the yellow squirty icing, which, despite any amount of Mr Muscle spray, persisted in leaving a dull sticky patina on the green plastic table cloth covering the rather cheap and wobbly kitchen table. Em, as usual, had become bored at the clearing up stage and had slipped craftily out to the living room, where she was currently lying on her tummy, tongue poking out in concentration, creating more mess with paper, scissors and felt-tipped pens. Thomas sat squarely on her back, purring loudly.

'Oh Suze, I felt such a fool,' groaned Bella, who had recounted the tale of her unexpected Saturday night rendezvous with Mr Flint Eyes. 'I'm sure he knew I was lying through my teeth. He just looks at you with this arrogant expression and those bloody eyes bore right through you.'

'But you had every right to be there, Bel! It's a public place and there's nothing to stop you talking to whoever you like. That Ricky bloke hasn't even been charged yet so it's not as though you're interfering with the trial or anything. And,' Suzy continued, 'you are a *reporter* for God's sake. Reporters are meant to ask questions... If you ask me you're letting this jumped-up detective walk all over you.'

Perhaps I am, thought Bella, an image of the dark, brooding face suddenly springing into her mind. I don't know why I care so much about what this man thinks of me. I'm nothing to him. But he just makes me feel so ... *stupid*.

She changed the subject, and soon Suze was chattering happily away about how she was planning to have her hair cut in that new sharp, geometric fashion and how she intended to blow half a month's wages on a black designer skirt suit.

'I need to sharpen up my image. Look more businesslike. Men don't want women slobbing around in jeans and baggy jumpers any more –' Suzy suddenly stopped and looked at her friend, who was wearing faded, somewhat sagging Levis and an ancient black roll-necked sweater she had 'borrowed' from Toby years ago.

'Well, it's all right for you, Bel. You don't need to worry. You're lucky – you've got what you want, with Em and everything...' Suzy, a kind-hearted girl, felt dreadful gabbling on about how much money she had to spend while poor Bel stood there, looking wistful.

But Bella smiled. 'Yes,' she said, 'I have got what I want. And the *last* thing I want is a man! God, imagine having to shave your legs every other day and paint your toenails all the time. Imagine not being able to cuddle up at night with your old fleecy pyjamas and a good book! And I bet you can't eat biscuits in bed either!'

There's something to be said for all that, thought Suze. But I want to find a man who loves me for my stubbly legs and cuddles up alongside me in fleecy pyjamas to eat biscuits in bed together. I want someone who'll give the kids piggyback rides in the garden while I cook the shepherd's pie. I want someone who'll gaze at our son and daughter sleeping peacefully at night, put his arm around me and positively glow with pride...

Her thoughts were interrupted by a timid knock at the door. Bella dashed to answer it. 'That's probably Roger from upstairs,' she said. 'He sometimes comes to see us on Sunday afternoons.'

'Oh,' said Suzy, swiftly adding an addendum to her daydream. But I want a *real* man. Not a nervous little computer geek, she thought, eyeing Roger's flushed cheeks and hesitant smile as he realised Bella had a guest.

Oh dear, it's Lara Croft, thought the young man, plucking nervously at his patterned sweater. He was wondering whether he should offer to leave when Em bombed into the kitchen, a purple felt-tip pen mark across one cheek, and threw her arms around his rather paunchy middle. 'Roger! Are you staying for tea ... pleeese?'

'Hello gorgeous,' said Roger, ruffling the sandy head and momentarily forgetting his shyness. 'I'd love to – if it's OK with your mum, that is?' He looked anxiously at Bella.

'You know you're always welcome, Roger. But I don't suppose you could do me a huge favour could you? Em has these sums for homework and, well, she's always better when you do it with her...'

'Emily May Smart – go and get your homework book. We'll have you top of the class again!' said Roger, his face lighting up in a rather attractive smile.

He was the picture of patience as he sat with Emily at the kitchen table, their heads bent together over a photocopied sheet of questions.

'Now, if you have ten apples and you eat four of them, how many would you have left?' he asked slowly.

'Fourteen!' piped up Em.

'No, gorgeous. You've *eaten* four. Four are gone and you started with ten. How many would there be still to eat?'

Em screwed up her face and considered carefully. 'Eight!' she announced triumphantly.

Roger took her hand gently and looked her in the eyes. 'Em, Arsenal have scored ten goals and Manchester United have scored four. What is the goal difference?'

'Six,' said Em, as quick as a flash. 'But you'd never get ten scored in one match, that would be silly. Not unless they were playing a second division team, perhaps.'

Cool, thought Suze. What a nice bloke. Shame he looks such a mummy's boy though.

The four of them had a pleasant time that afternoon around the kitchen table, eating lurid yellow cakes and chatting aimlessly. Suzy stayed to help put Em to bed, reading *Miss Tiggywinkle* three times, but managing to miss out at least four pages each time, and Bella pottered around, ironing school shirts, finding PE shorts and doing those endless other little Sunday evening chores.

It was only after she had bid her friend goodbye and was preparing to go to bed herself that she spotted Em's card, a badly folded sheet of A4 left by a pile of children's books on the coffee table. On the front was a beautifully drawn picture of a round-faced woman with wild poppy-red hair, extending her stick-like fingers to a little girl at her side.

'Mummy I love you very muck. You are the best in the wurld. Lost and lost of love from Emily Smart. xxx' it proclaimed.

Bella finally succumbed to the tears that had been burning behind her eyelids all day. She put her head down and let them flow, scalding hot, down her cheeks. To be absolutely honest, she didn't really know what she was crying about but it felt good anyway to let out all the pent-up emotion of the past week. Afterwards, when the sobs had slowed to a few desultory hiccups, Bella padded slowly to the kitchen in her pink fluffy slippers. She needed a companion in bed tonight – now where had she hidden that king-size bar of Cadbury's?

I wish I hadn't eaten all that chocolate, she thought, as struggled to make the button meet on her faithful black skirt the following morning. Why couldn't she just nibble daintily at a couple of squares and then put it away again? She poked at the little roll of flesh which hung defiantly over the top of her waistband once the skirt was done up. Better leave her shirt untucked today. And she'd keep her jacket on.

Bella did have time to do her hair though, even though Em had insisted on having her own shoulder-length hair done in two plaits, which took ages because she would not stop wriggling throughout. 'Yuk, not pink bobbles, Mum,' she groaned. Why was she the only little girl in the world who did not like pink? And the two of them had been forced to perform this funny little two-step dance, Bella holding onto one unsecured plait, while they sashayed around the flat for blue bobbles. That made them get the giggles and Bella's mascara had run so she had to wipe it off and start again. That explained why she was ten minutes late for work – again.

No sooner had she sat at her desk than the editor, David Ryan, buzzed through to ask Bella to come to his office.

'Oh my God – I bet your copper's complained about you!' cried Suze, with her usual lack of tact.

Bella's mouth dropped open. Then it snapped shut into a determined scowl.

'Bel, let me come in with you. I'll stand up for you – tell him what a bastard this guy is!' begged Suzy.

Hang on, thought Bella, as the pair walked to David's office. You don't even know him. You've never met him. But you're right about the bastard bit though.

David was sitting behind his untidy mahogany desk, in animated conversation with Councillor Ted Hanson. The editor looked slightly surprised to see two young ladies instead of one but pulled up another chair politely. 'Oh, I suppose you're working on this story together, are you?'

'The murder?' asked Bella, trying rapidly to swing her brain from prickly defensive mode to local dignitary greeting mode 'Hello Councillor Hanson. How are you?' she said, extending a hand. Surely the council didn't get involved in police complaints?

'I'm fine thank you … well, apart from this dreadful business about this murdered lass.' The broad face sagged. 'It's a sad state of affairs. You don't expect this kind of thing in Haybridge.'

If I had a pound for the amount of times I've heard that in the past week, thought Bella. But she felt a wave of sympathy for the councillor – he did look upset. Perhaps she had misjudged him and he wasn't so self-centred after all.

Mr Hanson, explained David, had kindly agreed last week to put up a reward for information which helped catch the murderer. But, with a man already on police bail and, according to the local grapevine, likely to be charged as soon as the forensic results were through, a reward was perhaps not appropriate any more.

'But I still want to help,' said the councillor. 'I wondered if I could set up a fund for Carla's family – maybe help them pay her funeral expenses or the cost of flying the body back. I don't know their financial situation, of course – money might not be a problem for them. But it would be a nice gesture from the folk of Haybridge and it would show that we care.'

'The family is quite poor,' said Bella, thinking back to her conversation with Carla's employer. 'In fact, I'm told she saved a lot of her wages and sent money home each month.'

'Oh,' said Ted Hanson, and frowned. David Ryan looked across his desk questioningly.

'It's just that the girl babysat for us occasionally.'

Bella pricked up her ears.

'Only a couple of times really,' continued the councillor. 'The woman she worked for – Mrs Williams – is a friend of my wife's and she recommended her. But she told us to only pay her £3 an hour – the going rate is usually more apparently – because she didn't need much spending money ... I wish I'd given her more now. She was a nice girl too. My youngest, Maisy, really took to her and she's normally a timid little thing. Not like my eldest, Matthew – he's a real lad!' he added proudly.

How nice, thought Bella, to see a man speak so enthusiastically about his children.

'So,' concluded Councillor Hanson, 'that's all the more reason to set up this fund. Now, I'll start it off with a donation of £1,000 and I'll ask all the other traders to stump up some cash. You can whip up your readers to do coffee mornings and bring and buy sales and all that malarkey. What do you think, David?'

The editor nodded. 'The *Gazette* prides itself on its community spirit and this is just the sort of thing we like to get involved in. Bella and Suzy – you'll give it your best, won't you?

'We certainly will!' vowed Suzy. 'And thank you, Councillor Hanson. We'll give the appeal a good spread and we'll print your picture.'

'Aw lass, please not another picture! I get sick of seeing myself in the paper all the time. That's the trouble with being a councillor you see – sometimes I wish I'd just stuck to running a paper shop! But,' he added hastily, 'I can't give up now. We can't afford to let that Labour lot in, can we?'

Unlikely, thought Bella. Haybridge Council had been under Conservative rule for as long as anyone could remember and the *Gazette*, whether she liked it or not, was essentially a Tory paper.

The councillor was smiling broadly at her and Suzy now. 'I'll tell you what, ladies. How about you represent the *Gazette* at the ball at the civic centre next Saturday, seeing as you're making such an effort for this appeal? I bought a batch of twelve tickets and I've been so distracted by all this business I haven't got round to inviting many people yet. Would you like to go?'

Bella's lips were automatically starting to form the word no. Then she felt a resounding kick on her ankle and winced.

'We would absolutely love to,' gushed Suzy. 'And it will give us a chance to meet all the people at the council that we write about!'

'Oh – it's not a council ball, lass. It's the Haybridge police ball. I'm friends with the Superintendent, Ray Nixon, and I get him a little bit of a discount at the civic centre!' Councillor Hanson winked amicably then stood up and extended a friendly hand to the two reporters.

'I'll see you two next Saturday. You can bring your partners. I'll send you four tickets.'

'Suze!' groaned Bella the second they got out of the door. 'What the hell am I going to wear to a ball – and a *police* ball at that? And what if that Jonathan Wright is there?'

'Bella!' admonished her friend. 'How often do you get a chance to go to a *ball*, for God's sake? It won't hurt you at all to get out and enjoy yourself for once. We'll find you something to wear and you will look stunning. And if that bloody detective is there you will simply ignore him!'

'OK,' said Bella weakly. 'But ... our "partners"? Who will we take?'

'We have five days to sort out that one. Come on, let's write that story,' said Suzy, marching purposefully to her desk.

Chapter Nine

Jonathan had ploughed methodically through his pile of reports and statements once and now he was re-reading them, waiting for a vital clue to jump out and hit him between the eyes. But the officious words stayed firmly on the page, giving him no real understanding of exactly why Ricky Thomas had killed Carla Kapochkin and how he got her body to the allotment hut.

Maybe he needed a break, a quick bacon sandwich in the canteen, and he could return with fresh eyes and a fresh brain. Or maybe, he groaned, he ought to sort out this pile of burglary reports that had been shoved to the side of his desk ever since the murder broke and were lying there gathering dust and tea stains. A fresh report had joined them today: a break-in at a small general store, where thieves had broken a tiny toilet window to gain access and stolen £200 worth of cigarettes. The newly fitted alarm had, apparently, failed to go off.

Jonathan frowned. The problem was he needed a blast of publicity to get a lead on these burglars. He needed help from people in the town and the only way to get that help was through the town's newspaper. But the town's newspaper meant Bella Smart, the girl with those intriguing grey eyes and that infuriating nosy nature. Surely they could be professional about this though? Surely they could have *one* conversation without it ending in all-out war? He picked up the phone.

If Bella was surprised to hear from Jonathan she was certainly not going to show it and she greeted him with what she hoped was a cool and professional tone.

'Burglaries? Yes of course. Tell me the points you wish to get across and any contact details for readers to ring and I'll try to give it some prominence. I think we have a slot for about 400 words as a page three lead.' Bella knew that for a fact because young Pete was, at the moment, loudly bewailing the fact that his 'wacky wedding' story had fallen through when the heavily pregnant bride turned out to be thirty-nine and not fifty-nine. 'Well she *looks* fifty-nine!' he protested, clutching the photograph. She must have had a hard life, thought Bella, wondering if she would look as haggard and grey in twelve years' time.

She scrawled down Jonathan's quotes about a possible link between the burglaries and his theory about professional gangs, then, just to make doubly sure, she read them back to him. She also gave him a quick blast of the proposed intro she had already formed in her head. 'Sharp-eyed Haybridge residents could unwittingly hold the key to solving a spate of business burglaries which police say bear all the hallmarks of a professional gang.'

That's good, thought Jonathan. Boz had said she was quick. 'I've had burglary analysis statistics done and they show that forty-one per cent of them have happened overnight on a Wednesday. That's a high percentage. We've organised extra patrols of course but we need people to rack their brains about anything suspicious they may have seen on a Wednesday. Your paper comes out that morning, doesn't it?'

'Yes. No problem,' said Bella obligingly.

This is going well, thought Jonathan. Now to find out what the little minx intended to write about the murder...

'Well,' Bella took a big breath. 'We're planning to have my eyewitness report on the front page – nicely amended as you requested – together with a short piece about a twenty-two-year-old man being questioned. We can't name him at this stage of course. Then there'll be a double-page spread inside with the public reaction, background stuff on Carla, your appeal for witnesses at the Swan and pictures of the allotments and Carla's employers. Oh – and there's the Carla Fund piece too,' related Bella proudly.

'That sounds fine,' said Jonathan. She's done well for a local hack, he thought.

Bella thought hard about her next move. A question had been bubbling away in her brain for two days now and it wouldn't go away. She knew it would probably send Jonathan off into another strop – just when she felt she had gained a bit of ground – but sod it, she had to know.

'Was Carla pregnant?' she blurted out.

Jonathan's reply was uncharacteristically instinctive: 'How the hell did you know that?'

Ah, thought Bella. I was right! She had been wondering ever since she heard Caroline Williams moaning that the au pair had gone off her food and started getting fussy about what she ate. She had looked wretched in the mornings too, Caroline had said, and Bella remembered the miserable nausea-ridden days of her own early pregnancy, when the mere sight of fried food or healthy vegetables would make her stomach heave.

'Just something her employer said. So was it Ricky's baby?'

'We assume so,' said Jonathan steadily.

'But surely you can tell by DNA these days. I would have thought –'

'There *was* no baby, Bella.'

'But...'

'The post-mortem picked up signs of a very recent pregnancy but...'

'She'd miscarried? Oh no, that's awful...' interrupted Bella, suddenly letting her professional tone slip.

SALLY MURRER

'She'd had a termination, Bella. A very recent termination.
There was still a trace of a general anaesthetic in her
blood. But I don't want this revealed just yet. It will all
come out at the inquest but we want to keep it to ourselves
for a bit.'

'Oh no, I wouldn't print anything. Oh dear, an abortion.
How terrible...' Bella's voice cracked and with a hurried
goodbye, she put the phone down. God, she surely wasn't
going to cry again, was she? What was wrong with her?

Probably touched a raw nerve there, thought Jonathan.
She was obviously anti-abortion because she had decided
to bring up her kid alone. Plucky really, he supposed.
Must be hard work.

Jonathan knew very little about bringing up babies and
children. And he wasn't terribly interested either. He knew
from reading police statistics that children from broken
homes stood a greater chance of getting involved in crime
and he hoped Bella would keep her kid on the rails.

But, of course, kids from perfect, albeit sterile, middle-
class homes were just as capable of offending too, he
thought suddenly, remembering his own brief debut as a
gawky fifteen-year-old shoplifter. It was a model aeroplane
kit of all things. The young Jonny had seen it in Woolworth's
and liked it because it reminded him of a rare
companionable moment when his workaholic parents, both
accountants, had sat down beside him and helped him
glue together a tiny grey Spitfire. So he had lifted the
box off the shelf, put it under his coat and walked out.
It had been as simple as that. Then there had been a
heavy hand on his shoulder...

'So did you mean to pay for it?' the grey-haired Sergeant
had asked, sitting facing Jonny in the store manager's tidy
little office.

'No,' admitted Jonny, hanging his head. The boy was
honest at least – even if he was a thief, mused the

experienced officer, making an instant decision not to take the case any further.

Instead he had laid into the young Jonny with a passionate lecture about honesty and integrity, describing the drudgery of prison and the downward spiral of a life of crime. It may have been a somewhat drastic tirade for someone who had only stolen a plastic aeroplane – but it worked.

From that day Jonny kept his nose clean and studied dutifully for his exams. And when his parents invited him to join their starchy family firm he politely declined – and revealed his ambition to be a police officer – just like the wise Sergeant.

The instant camaraderie of the police force was like a breath of fresh air and Jonny's confidence and popularity grew as he moved quickly up the ranks to CID. There his slightly quirky crime-solving methods came into their own. Colleagues knew to leave the DS alone to go off on some weird tangent when he was on a difficult case; he always got his result.

Women never learned to leave Jonathan alone though. Something about his broad shoulders and arrogant stance appealed to the opposite sex, particularly the young WPCs who would lay bets with each other on whether they could crack his cool. He was always charming, flirtatious even, but they went away disappointed, he always kept them at arm's length.

Instead Jonathan chose women who could be as emotionally detached as he was – generally confident career-minded women who clicked open their personal organisers to schedule in a date. Soon though the theatre trips, the dinners and the familiar seduction routines would lose their appeal and a jaded Jonathan would politely, but firmly, move on.

His relationship with Madeleine was the longest so far. She was a slight deviation from his norm but far more beautiful. Lately she seemed to be around much more than the others had been but he could cope with that – as long as she didn't get too demanding. God, that reminded him, he'd promised to look at a couple of rented houses with her this week.

But first he had to organise the extra burglary patrols. And pester the forensic boys to speed up the results on the murder – again.

Hmm, Wednesday nights, thought Bella, another plan bubbling in her brain. How brilliant would it be if the good old public-spirited *Gazette* launched its own little surveillance operation and caught these crooks red-handed? She'd read enough detective novels to know what to do – well, you just hid yourself away with a Thermos flask and a pair of binoculars really, didn't you? And perhaps a bar of chocolate or two in case you got peckish. Oh and she could take Em's little Barbie sleeping bag to keep out the cold; it had been freezing at night lately. But what if she did spot two burly crooks, creeping around by torchlight in black balaclava masks, about to hurl a brick through some innocent trader's window? Ah, of course – she'd dial 999 on her mobile. She wouldn't have to tackle them, would she?

But what about Em? She couldn't ask her parents to babysit – her mother would have a fit if she knew what she was up to. Ah... Suzy. She'd oblige.

Suzy looked across at her friend who was deep in thought and absent-mindedly chewing the end of her pen. She's up to something again, she thought. Bella suddenly shot her that very sweet smile, the one that made her nose crinkle. She wants a favour, thought Suze.

Now, I need a place to hide – a stake-out, thought Bella, wallowing in the image of herself as the intrepid sleuth, impervious to danger or cold, hell-bent on fighting for freedom for Haybridge residents.

It had better be indoors as she wasn't *that* impervious to cold, actually. How about Rose Turner's hair salon? That was nice and central to the High Street shops. No, dear old Rose, with her endless capacity for gossip, would have the secret surveillance plan spread about the whole of Haybridge before you could say swag bag. The butcher's shop? No, you wouldn't see much stuck out on that far corner. And besides, all that dead meat would put Bella off her chocolate.

She pictured the row of small-town shops. The greengrocers, the knitting shop – God knows how that made a living – then the bakery with its yummy chocolate eclairs, the clothes shop, the cheap shop where everything cost a pound, the newsagent's . . . Yes! Hanson's newsagents! It was in a perfect position to see the rest of the street. And she was in his good books now, wasn't she?

'Suze,' she said slowly. 'Have you got Councillor Hanson's number in your contacts book?'

'Why? Are you going to ask him to cough up for a ball gown?' grinned her friend.

Briefly Bella explained her plan, watching Suzy's eyes grow wide with disbelief: 'You will *never* get this one past Sean! Even for you Bel, this is crazy. And the chances are you'll sit there all night and never catch anyone anyway.'

There's a forty-one per cent chance that I will, though, thought Bella, forgetting that this was not quite the way that police crime analysis figures work and that actually the break-ins were spread over many weeks.

'I hadn't actually planned to tell Sean,' said Bella, imagining herself triumphantly handing in the story on Thursday morning. '*Gazette* reporter cracks gang of crooks. Have-a-go hero Bella Smart single-handedly launched a secret surveillance to solve the mystery of the Haybridge burglaries.'

'Well, I'll babysit, of course. I'll stay the night. But I still think you're mad,' said Suzy.

'Thank you! And I'll be back well before it's time to get Em up for school, I promise. Now – have you got that phone number?'

Councillor Hanson took some convincing but, after a couple of reinforcing bites of a jam doughnut, Bella was in full charm mode.

'Oh yes, of course I have my editor's permission,' she lied. 'He's more than happy that I can look after myself and naturally I would call the police immediately if I saw anything.'

'Well, if you insist, lass. It's not something I'd be happy about my own daughter doing, but I suppose you reporters have a job to do... If you sit behind the counter and keep your head down low no one should spot you.'

The councillor arranged to meet Bella at the back of his shop at 8pm on Wednesday to hand over his spare keys. He'd show her how to lock up and she could drop the keys through the letterbox when she'd finished.

Bella thanked him profusely and switched on her computer. She rattled through her stories with a vengeance that day, even prompting a few reluctant words of praise from Sean. But he did point out that she'd spelt accommodation wrong twice on a housing story though and thieves wrong three times in the burglary copy.

'These are pretty basic words for a journalist. What's happened to your spell check?'

Oh bugger off, thought Bella. I'm a super sleuth – who cares about spelling?

* * *

104

Even super sleuths have to eat though, and nothing brings them down to earth more than mashing potatoes and stirring mince for their daughter's supper, particularly when the daughter in question is asking a string of very difficult questions about planets, of all things.

'So if the sun is so hot, how come it doesn't burn the planets then?'

'Um, they look close but they're actually a long way away,' answered Bella, frantically trying to remember whether she learned about the solar system at school.

'Mrs Ellison said planets are made of liquid stuff. How come they don't drip on us? Or is that what rain is – drippy planets?'

'Um, I don't think so,' said Bella, wishing it would rain Mars bars occasionally. She gathered her thoughts and forced herself to turn away from the cooker and give her daughter some quality attention.

'Rain comes from clouds, darling. The water in the atmosphere collects and forms into cloud and then when the cloud gets too heavy it –'

'Mum. Thomas is eating the mince. And the potatoes are smoking.'

'Oh shit!' cried Bella, shoving the greedy cat down from the worktop and snatching the potato pan off the stove in one swift movement.

'You shouldn't say that word. Matthew Boyden said it at school and Mrs Ellison sent him to Mr Warner. He had to stand in the library and miss playtime.'

'Sorry,' said Bella. 'It just popped out.'

She was relieved when, seconds later, there was a tentative tap at the door. Roger! He probably knew everything about planets. 'Come on in,' she called.

'I'm popping out to get some milk, Bella. I just wondered if you needed anything.'

Bella noticed Roger's slightly wistful glance at the pots

and pans on the worktop. 'No, I'm fine thanks. But why don't you stay and have some supper while you're here? It's only mince and potatoes and vegetables but I've cooked loads.'

Roger's chubby face broke out into a smile. He'd been planning to heat up a can of ravioli and eat it in front of his computer. Bella's nursery cooking was always a real treat. 'If you're sure it's not too much trouble,' he said, his mouth watering.

'Sit down, Roger. You can sit next to me,' said Emily bossily. 'Thomas licked the mince but there's plenty left.'

'Er, I did scoop out the bit he licked,' said Bella, plonking some sliced carrots and broccoli florets into boiling water.

Roger gave what he hoped was a manly chortle. 'Oh, cat lick's fine. What's a bit of cat lick between friends?' he quipped, privately resolving to go onto Google and research Toxoplasmosis the minute he got home.

It tasted fine anyway, he thought several minutes later as he shovelled enthusiastically. 'Eat your carrots, Emily, or you'll never see in the dark,' he told the little girl, gently holding her fork to her mouth.

You are such a nice man, thought Bella for the umpteenth time. 'Roger,' she said wheedlingly. 'I don't suppose you could do me a favour?'

'More homework?'

'No. I need someone to come to the police ball with me on Friday.'

Now, Roger was an obliging man and liked nothing better than to help his pretty but slightly scatty neighbour, on whom he had secretly nursed a bit of a crush for the past two years. Sometimes he even lay in bed at night imagining him and Bella ensconced together in domestic bliss bringing up little Em between them, the mother and child allowing him to introduce calm and order to their chaotic life. He could start with a computerised school

106

run rota to make things easier for poor Bella in the mornings. He would, without a doubt, do anything to make her happy. But a *ball*? The very prospect made his stout heart flutter and beads of perspiration stand out on his brow.

'B – but I've nothing to wear,' he wailed.

Isn't that my line? thought Bella. She flashed her most dazzling smile, slightly impaired by a sliver of broccoli between her front teeth. 'We could hire you a dinner suit. Suzy will help make you look really cool. And it will be fun, Roger. Please come … pleeese.'

Oh dear, she sounds just like Em, thought Roger. How could he let her down? 'All right. But you'll have to help me with this dinner suit thing.'

Bella dropped her knife and fork on her plate, scattering carrots across the table, and rushed round to give Roger a huge, rather wet, kiss on his cheek. 'Thank you! We'll have a ball! Oh … yes … well, we literally will, won't we?'

Chapter Eleven

Standing shivering in the cold at the back of the newsagent's shop clutching a Barbie sleeping bag and a pair of Teletubby binoculars, Bella wondered if her super sleuth surveillance plan was quite such a good one after all. She didn't feel very professional somehow – in fact she felt a bit jittery. And she was starving hungry because she'd been trying not to eat all week so she would look slim for the ball. Not that she'd sorted out a dress to look slim in yet, she realised with a flash of panic. But Councillor Hanson oozed reassurance when he swept up in his dark green BMW, placing a solid hand on her shoulder and telling her she was a very public-spirited lass indeed.

'Now, the police are aware of this little plan, aren't they?' he asked as he let her into the tiny but meticulously tidy back office.

'Absolutely!' lied Bella.

The councillor must have asked her half a dozen times if she was sure she would be all right and fussed around showing her the kettle, the coffee and urging her to make herself at home. Bella was quite glad when he finally left, hastening away to be on time for a meeting.

Pulling a tiny little key-ring torch out of her pocket, she pushed open the door leading to the pitch dark shop floor and sank to her hands and knees to crawl to the wooden counter. It wouldn't do for a sleuth to be spotted, would it? Squinting in the pinprick torch light, she made a comfy little nest of her sleeping bag on the floor.

Now, if she sat with her back against the cigarette

cabinet she was out of view of anyone passing the huge window. Perfect. Cautiously Bella peeped round the corner of the counter. Ah, there was a problem. She couldn't actually see much at all – only a dim view of the hardware store opposite, bathed in the orange glow of the street lamps. She shifted impatiently to the other side of the counter and peered again. Ah, that was better, she could see the knitting shop and the little computer games store now. Oh dear, but there must be thirty or forty-shops in the High Street – how did she know the burglars would pick one of her paltry three? Perhaps she should have thought this surveillance thing out a bit better, she thought, squinting through the Teletubby binoculars to see if that helped at all.

There were an awful lot of people about too, couples strolling along clutching blue and white carrier bags from the video shop a few doors down, people striding purposefully to their local pub and teenagers eating chips out of a bag from Tony's Golden Fry bar on the corner, laughing and shoving into each other as they walked. I guess the burglars won't come for hours, thought Bella ruefully.

Nevertheless she stayed staunchly at her surveillance post, shifting from one end of the wooden counter to the other until her bottom was cold and numb from the cold tiled floor and she had pins and needles in both legs.

She looked at her watch. 8.25pm. It was going to be a long night.

At 8.30pm Bella decided she could murder a coffee and crawled out on her hands and knees into the little office, where she closed the door firmly behind her and thankfully turned on the light. She filled the kettle at a tiny stainless steel sink and plonked herself down on Ted Hanson's expensive-looking leather swivel chair.

By 8.40pm, Bella had finished her coffee, carefully

washed up the mug, and was leaning back in the chair, her feet on the pine desk, humming aimlessly to herself and wondering if she dare switch his computer on to play Solitaire. Better not, she thought. He probably has a password anyway.

The councillor clearly spent a lot of time working in his office though, she thought, eyeing the shelves of neatly marked black files. Income Tax, VAT, Wholesaler's Receipts, Newspapers, Wages, Insurance – God, it must be hard work running a newsagent's. There was council stuff too – a whole section of blue files marked Draft Town Plan, Policy Documents, Housing Committee and Planning Applications as well as, on the corner of the desk, a neat pile of papers Bella recognised as council meeting agendas.

I wonder if he has the agenda for the next planning committee meeting, thought Bella, suddenly remembering old Ron and his concern about the BestBuys application. Agendas are for public release anyway, she reasoned, although councillors probably get them just a little bit in advance. It wouldn't hurt to use all this spare time to swot up on that application. She'd just have a look.

The planning agenda was not in the pile. Bella eyed the desk drawer. Would it be rude just to have a very quick little peep? If there was anything private in there, surely he'd put a lock on it?

The drawer slid open easily and Bella stared inside, disappointed. Nothing but a stapler, a large grey and white calculator and a few red bills. God, £750 for electricity – and she thought her own £60 a quarter was extravagant! A bill from a security alarm company and a £2,000 demand from Costrite Wholesale Confectionery– that was a lot of bars of chocolate.

Bella wished she hadn't thought of chocolate. Her stomach gave a growl and her throat tightened with an almost physical rush of yearning. To distract herself she rifled through the bills again. Boring. At the bottom of the small pile were a few sheets of blank paper, on one of which was written, in neat, slightly sloping handwriting, a short list of fellow traders. Ah, these must be the people he's asked to donate to the Carla Kapochkin Fund, thought Bella. Four so far – a promising start. Ryan Estate Agents, Perry & Sons Butchers, Bessie's Bargain Basement – good old Bessie – thought Bella fondly, and finally Greens & Co Greengrocer, a name which always made her titter.

She replaced the papers, shut the drawer, and stretched her arms behind her head. God, this was boring. Then her eyes fell on a large pile of glossy magazines on a wire rack marked 'Returns' at the other side of the office. Yes!

The next two hours were probably the most blissful Bella had experienced for months. Leaning back in the comfortable chair she greedily devoured the contents of *Cosmopolitan*, *She*, *Fashion Monthly* and all the other magazines she had gazed at wistfully on newsagents' shelves but rarely been able to afford to buy. She memorised beauty treatments, drank in hair care tips and craved every single pair of shoes that was pink and sparkly and every £200 cashmere cardigan that adorned every bronzed, leggy model. Bella was in girlie heaven.

Until, that was, she read a feature called 'Chocolate – The Ultimate Pleasure', which described in perfect prose the ecstasy of unwrapping the golden foil, the sweet, clinging sensation on your tongue and the rush of pleasure afterwards. A strange, almost animal-like noise – something between a yelp and a groan – escaped from Bella's lips. She wanted chocolate – and she wanted it *now*.

She checked her watch. 10.40pm. Time to return to her post. She checked her jeans pocket. Fifty pence in loose change. Surely Ted Hanson would understand if she took just one little bar of Cadbury's Dairy Milk off his shelves and left the money by the till? Sod it, he would have to not mind – this was the ultimate chocolate craving.

Carefully holding her pin light torch, Bella switched off the office light, opened the door and sank once again to her hands and knees. She crawled carefully past the counter and along the floor. God, she could almost smell that chocolate getting closer.

There was a resounding whack as she thumped into the soft drinks cabinet. 'Ouch!' she yelled, instinctively jumping to her feet and rubbing her forehead. Oops, better get down again, she thought, feeling momentarily dizzy. But she could see the chocolate now – just an arm's reach away. She made one swift lunge for a Dairy Milk then legged it back to behind the counter, where she flopped down on the Barbie sleeping bag with a thudding heart and throbbing head.

As Bella was sinking her teeth restoratively into the first chocolatey chunk, a balding, middle-aged man walking his dog along the pavement outside was scratching his head and looking very worried. He could have sworn he'd seen a dark figure, brandishing a small beam of light, just grab something from Hanson's Newsagents shelves. Bloody hell, it couldn't have been one of those burglars he'd read about in the *Gazette*, could it? He remembered the headline he had read with his baked haddock supper only a few hours ago: 'Sharp-eyed Haybridge residents could unwittingly hold the key...'

Without hesitation he reached into his tweed jacket pocket and pulled out the little-used mobile telephone his children had clubbed together to buy for his birthday. Pressing the buttons carefully, the loyal, public-spirited *Gazette* reader, for the first time in his life, pressed the nine key three times.

* * *

'We have action guv!' yelled a young uniformed PC as he pelted into the CID office. 'Burglary in progress in the High Street. Hanson's newsagents.'

Jonathan sprang out of his chair and shoved aside the paperwork that had once again forced him to clock up several hours of overtime.

'Then what the bloody hell are we waiting for? Let's GO!' he ordered, snatching two pair of handcuffs from his desk drawer.

'Shouldn't we call the shop owner, guv?' asked the very correct PC.

'No time,' snapped Jonathan, inserting a nifty little gadget – not official police issue – into the back-door lock. It clicked open almost immediately. Right, you bastards, I'm coming to get you, he thought as he took three massive, silent strides through the office and into the shop.

'Aaaargh!' screamed Bella as the huge, black shape flew at her from nowhere.

'Fuck!' yelled Jonathan as he almost tripped over the Barbie sleeping bag.

'Help!' squawked Bella, shooting into the far corner of the counter and pulling the sleeping bag firmly over her head. 'Someone call the police – help!' It came out very muffled.

'Officer,' said Jonathan, very slowly indeed. 'Would you please switch on the light?'

'Oh ... my ... God,' thought Bella. 'Please make this a terrible dream after too much chocolate.'

'*Bella?*' said Jonathan. 'Are you all right?'

'Yes,' came a muffled squeak.

'Could you remove that pink thing from your head so that I can see you are all right?'

'No.' This time the squeak was even more muffled, and slightly tearful.

Jonathan strode behind the counter and yanked off the sleeping bag. A very pale face with tears streaming from a pair of terrified grey eyes stared up at him. He bent down until his nose was approximately six inches away from Bella's own rather pink one, which was currently performing a loud sniff. For the first time in his eventful life, he was truly lost for words.

'Before you say a word,' said Bella, 'I was helping you catch your burglars. I was doing surveillance.' With that she burst into noisy sobs.

Jonathan took in the plastic Teletubby binoculars slung around her neck, the lurid pink Barbie sleeping bag and the empty chocolate wrapper still clutched in her hand. Suddenly he felt an emotion he had not felt for as long as he could remember. It swept through his legs then rumbled up to his stomach, gradually rippling its way up his chest, into his throat ... unable to control it, he let out a surprised chuckle, followed by a deep chest-rippling laugh.

Standing up and leaning back against the counter, he gave way to great, relentless guffaws, his shoulders shaking helplessly and his eyes starting to stream. The young PC watched in amazement as the detective continued to laugh like the proverbial drain. He had heard this new chap was a bit unconventional but this took the biscuit.

Bella's tearful eyes moved slowly from one officer to the other from her squatting post in the corner. Suddenly she felt her mouth begin to twitch and a tiny bubble of laughter lodge in her throat, right in the middle of a sob. It came out as a titter, then a sob, then another, stronger titter. Finally it settled into one of the worst attacks of the giggles she had had for ages; the helpless, stomach-clutching kind that are silent excect for the occasional resounding pig-like snort.

At each snort, Jonathan banged his hand on the counter and guffawed even louder. Somewhere in the dark recesses of his brain a little voice said 'control yourself, man', but he couldn't. God, she looked so funny sitting there...

'I think,' he gasped finally, 'I think, Miss Smart, you have been hoisted by your own petard.'

'Uh?' she looked up, mid-giggle.

'The intrepid reporter asks her readers to keep an eye out for burglars then promptly gets reported as a burglar herself – probably by a reader!' The laughter was threatening to erupt again.

'Oh dear. When you put it like that...'

'Bella?' The tone was more sober. Oh God, here comes the telling off, she thought.

'Yes?' she said tentatively, wiping her eyes.

'How well do you know the landlord at the King's Arms?'

'Er, quite well actually... It's our local at work.'

'Well, if you can persuade the landlord to come up with a hot steak and kidney pie for each of us at this ungodly hour, I'll forget all about this little ... little episode. Is that a deal?'

'You bet,' said Bella, jumping up. 'All this drama has made me bloody starving.'

'So,' said Jonathan, his mouth full of delectably flaky pastry. 'What did you plan to do when you spotted your burglar? Choke him with your chocolate? Smother him with your sleeping bag?'

'I planned,' said Bella, with as much dignity as she could muster, 'to call the police of course, to come and arrest him.'

'Right,' said Jonathan, his mouth starting to twitch again at the memory of the huddled little figure behind the

115

counter. It was those blue plastic binoculars that did it, he thought.

He polished off the rest of his pie and leaned back contentedly on the sofa, stretching his arms behind his head, a huge yawn escaping from his mouth.

Nice chest, thought Bella, watching his pectorals bulge against the front of his shirt. Good teeth too, she thought, catching a glimpse of the inside of his mouth. Bloody hell, I'm assessing him like a racehorse – I'll be feeling his legs next. Another little giggle threatened to bubble up at the thought of her hands moving swiftly up and down those substantial-looking thigh muscles. She swallowed it hastily. He looked good tonight though in those faded jeans and that tight-fitting grey and red rugby shirt. His rugged features suited the casual look. That shirt looks expensive too, she mused, looking down ruefully at her own faded blue sweatshirt.

'How are the investigations going?' she asked. Anything to keep her mind off those pecs.

'Not bad actually. We've had a couple of little breakthroughs today.' Jonathan's tone was, for once, unguarded. He was full of pie, had a pint in his hand, he'd had the best laugh he remembered for years and this crazy redhead sitting beside him was proving to be surprisingly easy company.

'Tell me one and I won't pester you for the rest,' she said, quick as a flash.

Jonathan smiled. 'OK. There was a break-in at the little Spar shop on Green Street. Booze and cigarettes taken.' He counted to three in his head.

'But that's not a very exciting breakthrough,' wailed Bella. I was spot on, thought Jonathan.

'No, but for the first time the burglar may have left a clue. We found a couple of hairs caught in the jagged edge of the glass.'

'So when he stuck his head through to climb in...? Wow. That's good. And you've sent them off for DNA testing?' Bella's quick brain was racing ahead.

'Yes. Now we have to wait a week or so for a result and just hope that the burglar is known to us and the computer comes up with a match ... then he can lead us to the rest of his gang.' Then I can get these damn burglaries out of the way and concentrate on the murder, thought Jonathan.

'And the other breakthrough?'

'Bella! You promised.'

'I had my fingers crossed.'

Despite himself Jonathan laughed. 'A team did another fingertip search of the allotments and came up with a lipstick, a library card in Carla's name and a front-door key to her employers' house in Trent Drive.'

'I *knew* there would have been something else in that little black bag,' said Bella triumphantly. 'That's what I was looking for when I found the body. But how will they help the investigation?'

'Well, they were behind the hedge, some three metres away from the hut. Almost like they'd been thrown. Now a girl wouldn't throw her own lipstick away, would she?' Jonathan's eyes were teasing.

'No – but a murderer might empty out the contents of her bag and chuck it over the hedge in a moment of panic. Perhaps to delay the body being identified? And that means his fingerprints would be on them!' Bella wriggled with excitement.

Good answer. She's quicker than some of my DCs, thought Jonathan. 'You're spot on,' he said. 'And now, once again, we have to wait for the experts to scan for prints –'

'Then match the prints up to Ricky Thomas! Then the job's done,' interrupted Bella.

'Hopefully,' said Jonathan, with a slight frown.

The burst of brain power had tired Bella. It had been a long evening and she'd got up at six that morning to prepare a hearty casserole for Suze and Em's supper. Her body sagged slightly, moulding itself into the comfortable sofa. She yawned widely.

Jonathan felt her relax and he too allowed his shoulders to drop and his head to rest comfortably on the back of the sofa. He could feel the warmth from Bella's shoulder, just half an inch away. He glanced sideways at the pale face with the freckles standing out faintly across her nose and dark, bruised-looking circles under her eyes and he felt a sudden ridiculous urge to put his arm round her, snuggle her head against his chest and stroke those soft, red curls.

Bella felt her breathing slow and her eyelids droop. It was warm in front of the flickering fire. Her half pint of lager was coursing slowly through her veins and her tummy was pleasantly full. She gave a small sigh of contentment. She felt incredibly ... *safe* somehow. Safe and cosy next to that broad, broad shoulder. Jonathan's body was emitting an almost animal-like heat next to hers and she breathed in the faintest musky scent, overlaid with that slight tang of citrus. Wouldn't it be bliss to let her head drop onto that shoulder, then perhaps slide down onto his chest, nestling in that inviting little space just between his pecs? She gave herself a mental shake. Don't be stupid, woman. This is arrogant old Flint Eyes you're fantasising about. God, she was tired though.

Bella's eyelids drooped even further. Jonathan watched them flutter open, then fall again. Flutter, fall, flutter, fall. Her head dropped very slightly towards his shoulder and her mouth drooped open just a tiny fraction. It was quite a pretty mouth when it wasn't engaged in answering him back, thought Jonathan, studying the perfect arc her lashes made on her cheek.

Poor kid is exhausted, he thought, sliding one arm comfortably across the back of the sofa. I'll let her have a little nap. He felt unusually tired himself, come to think of it. It had been a strange old evening. He yawned.

Ten minutes later, when the smattering of customers had left the pub and Ed the landlord was collecting the empty glasses, he was not at all surprised to find the slumbering couple all snuggled up on his sofa. The King's Arms was that kind of pub. 'Wakey, wakey. Time to go home,' he said gently.

Bella was in the middle of a beautiful dream where she was lying on a sun-drenched beach, her head resting in a perfectly sculpted hollow in the soft sand. A dark-skinned, muscular waiter, wearing nothing but a loincloth, was hovering over her, bearing a long, cool drink on a tray. 'Wakey, wakey,' he was saying. Her eyes opened slowly – and she found herself gazing into the gnarled, grinning old ex-boxer's face of Ed Tripp. Bugger, I was looking forward to that Pina Colada, was her first thought.

Her second was that she had fallen asleep in someone's arms... Oh my God – she had fallen asleep in *Jonathan's* arms! And the owner of those arms was hastily shoving her head away from his chest and looking at her with a very bewildered, almost sleepy-eyed expression.

'You fell asleep!' she said accusingly, determined to get in first.

'I did not!' I am a macho police officer, I do not nod off in pubs, thought Jonathan.

'You did. I saw you,' lied Bella.

'How did you see me if you were asleep too?'

'Too? Ah, so you admit you were asleep?'

Bugger me, thought old Ed. They were all over each other one minute then fighting like cat or dog the next. 'Look,' he said, 'you both looked pretty asleep to me and

119

if you don't mind I'd quite like to go to bed and get some shut-eye myself now.'

Bella and Jonathan stood up, avoiding each other's eyes, and walked sheepishly to the door. Thank God I followed him here in my car, thought Bella, shuddering at the prospect of having to make embarrassed conversation while he drove her home.

Jonathan held open Daisy's door for her and Bella sank with relief onto the sagging seat.

'Goodnight, Sleeping Beauty,' he said sarcastically.

'Sod off, Prince Charming,' replied Bella, slamming the door firmly.

Chapter Eleven

A huge explosion assaulted Bella's eardrums and a thousand thunderbolts seemed to shoot across the sky. Instinctively she drew Emily closer to her, pulling the little girl's face safely to her chest.

'Get off, Mum, I can't see the fireworks,' she cried. 'Wow! Look – a rocket!'

Bella winced as she waited for the bang then smiled as the shower of silver sparks illuminated Emily's excited, flushed face. It had been so kind of Roger to turn up with a box of fireworks after work on Thursday. Bella had planned to quietly postpone bonfire night until Saturday when the Haybridge cricket club was holding its annual public do. Quite honestly, she felt she'd had enough sparks flying with a certain detective in the past few days to voluntarily watch any more.

But Roger was as excited as Emily and she couldn't spoil their fun. 'It's November the fifth – we need Catherine Wheels and bangers!' he had said, leading the way out into Bella's small garden with uncharacteristic authority. When the last firework finally lay in a charred black heap on the lawn and even Em had had enough of waving sparklers in the air, Bella rummaged through her fridge to find bangers of a different kind for a sausage and bean supper.

'So, it's the grand try-on, tonight,' she said, turning the sausages slowly and wishing she could feel a bit more enthusiastic about this damn police ball.

'I've got everything laid out ready upstairs. I've hired

the suit and one of those funny collared shirts and I bought new shoes and a bow tie. I need you to tell me how to tie it though,' said Roger almost proudly.

And I, thought Bella, have nipped over to my mum's at lunchtime and borrowed her ancient and slightly dusty ball gown, which has been stored in the attic for the past thirty years. I also rummaged through my sister's wardrobe and grabbed her old school prom dress – which is a very skimpy size ten and will show all my bulges. She was going to be second-hand Rose dressed in the lesser of two evils. But at least Roger seemed to be working up some excitement about the ball. All she felt was a vague, apathetic weariness at the prospect of having to glam herself up and make polite social chit-chat for hours. I'm blowed if I'm going to shave my legs, she vowed defiantly.

'Suzy will know how to tie bow ties. She's coming over later for a dress rehearsal,' she told Roger, trying to sound enthusiastic as she dished the sausages and beans onto plates.

Suzy had enough enthusiasm for at least two as she burst into the flat after supper in a flurry of blonde hair and Diorissimo perfume. Over her arm were three white, zippered, plastic clothes carriers. 'Come on, Cinders, get a smile on that face – your fairy godmother has arrived,' she cried.

'The red dress is mine because it would look bloody awful with your hair! I bought it from that discount fashion warehouse place. It fits like a dream and it was only £49.99! You can choose between that pale blue one and that gorgeous, gorgeous slinky black one. My cousin Sarah lent them to me – you know, the one who works for that posh recruitment agency in London. She earns a fortune so I bet they cost *hundreds*!' she continued breathlessly.

Bella hugged her, her spirits suddenly lifting. 'Suze, they're beautiful! What are we waiting for? Roger, you stay in the living room and we'll start the fashion parade! Get ready for the Babes of the Ball...'

'And me,' said a plaintive voice.

Bella turned in surprise to her daughter. 'You want to dress up too, Em?' This was the child who shunned anything pink and frilly and whose favourite item of clothing was a boy's rugby shirt

Suzy scooped up the little girl. 'Come on then, darling. You can be an honorary Babe. Your carriage awaits, Madam,' she said, throwing the giggling little body over her shoulder in a fireman's lift.

Roger settled himself down in the armchair and picked up 'Snuggle's Secret Adventure' to read, blushing at the thought of the state of undress going on behind the bedroom door.

Did women always make such strange noises when they tried on clothes, he wondered, listening to the high-pitched squeals and giggles and groans, interspersed with the occasional 'Oh my God!'.

The door swung open and Suzy strode out, head held high, looking ravishing in the simple, low cut red dress, which clung to her slender body like a second skin. Tossing her hair and throwing out one arm in a theatrical flourish she announced: 'Ladies and gentlemen, I present ... the Babes of the Ball!'

An anxious-looking pink face peeped around the door. 'I warn you, Roger – my saddlebags look awful,' it squeaked. What on earth were saddlebags? wondered Roger. Were they something Snuggles packed his adventure kit in?

'Muuum – go on!' said Em, with a shove. Bella lurched forward and staggered into the room, arms across her chest and looking decidedly uncomfortable in a straight-cut pale blue dress, which clung to her like an even tighter second skin.

'God!' she declared. 'My visible panty line is atrocious.'
Too much information, thought Roger.

Suzy grabbed her friend by the shoulders and surveyed
her critically. 'It's not too bad,' she pronounced. 'Hold
your stomach in for a minute.'

'I am,' said Bella mournfully. In fact, if she let it out
this bloody zip would probably explode.

'OK,' said Suzy hastily. She turned to the bedroom
door. 'And now, ladies and gentlemen, I present Miss
Emily Absolutely Gorgeous Smart!'

Em swaggered in on three-inch-heeled evening sandals
at least eight sizes too big, her Auntie Sophie's old prom
dress dropping off her shoulders and trailing a couple of
feet on the floor behind her. Her hair was swept up in
a bright blue scrunchie and her mouth was adorned with
a cupid's bow of red lipstick. She attempted a pirouette,
wobbled and then fell into a giggling heap onto Roger's
lap, one shoe flying off and almost hitting an astonished
Thomas the cat on the head.

'Well, ladies,' said Roger gallantly, 'I think you all look
beautiful but I think Emily looks the most beautiful of all.'

Five minutes later Suzy emerged in the blue dress, Bella
in the slinky black and Emily in the dashing red. She
must be a nice person to pay nearly £50 for a dress then
let a kid dress up in it, thought Roger.

Bella looked happier this time and even performed a
twirl. But Suzy, hand on hips, surveyed her friend with
a slight frown. 'It's not quite right, Bel. It's not hanging
right on the hips.'

'You mean it makes my bum look big?'

'Ginormous,' said Em helpfully.

Looks fine to me, thought Roger, feeling another blush
coming on.

'No. You look lovely and curvy,' said Suzy. 'But it still
doesn't hang right. Try on the green one.'

'Suze, that's my mum's old dance dress from the days before she had me! It's positively antique.'

'It's got an Audrey Hepburn feel to it. And vintage is in these days. Go on – just try it.'

Bella stomped back into the bedroom and reappeared within minutes. Roger, glancing up from Snuggles and his adventures, gave a gasp. Suzy took a step backwards.

'God, you look beautiful!' they said simultaneously.

Em stuck two fingers in her mouth and gave a piercing whistle, a trick of which her mum was slightly envious. 'You look cool,' she said.

Bella ran her hands over the emerald green satin, which nipped into a narrow V at her waist and flared out in flattering folds over her hips. 'Isn't it a bit tight on my boobs?' she asked, looking down at her pale cleavage spilling out over the sweetheart neckline.

'Bel, you look *fantastic*. That's the one. You have to wear it,' said Suzy.

'But it smells a bit of mothballs,' Bella wrinkled her nose.

'We'll hang it on the line tomorrow to air it. Now, Roger, it's your turn,' said Suzy bossily.

Roger scuttled upstairs, reappearing rather sheepishly several minutes later in his dinner suit, clutching a black bow tie.

'OK,' Suzy deftly knotted the tie. 'Now stand up straight.'

'I am,' bleated Roger.

'No – *straight*. Head up, shoulders back, chest out and tummy in.'

I don't think I can do all that at once, thought Roger, wincing as Suzy stuck a fist in his solar plexus and yanked his torso into position.

'And don't let your arms flap down at your sides like that. Put one hand in your pocket. That's it. Now,' Suzy squinted at him critically, 'we need to do something about your hair – that fringe has to go! Bella, bring me some scissors and your mousse.'

Oh my God, I'm going to look like Wurzel Gummidge, thought Roger as he sat down meekly to let Suzy chop at his fringe.

She squirted the white fluffy mousse, smoothed it with her fingers through Roger's limp mousy hair and stood back to assess the result. 'Wow! You've metamorphosed from a toad into Prince Charming,' she declared.

'You look really handsome, Roger,' agreed Bella, a note of surprise in her voice. 'But maybe we could do something about that little monobrow, Suze?'

Suzy dashed into the bedroom and emerged with a pair of tweezers. 'This won't hurt a bit,' she said, zooming in on her erstwhile toad.

Roger was a compliant chap and quite happy to let these young ladies pull him, prod him and boss him about unmercifully. But the sight of those flashing, silver tweezers just inches away from his eyes was too much. He jumped up from the sofa, brushing cat hairs from his suit.

'Ladies, I think we all need our beauty sleep. I will bid you goodnight.' With that he was off like a shot.

'Hmm,' pondered Suzy, 'maybe I should have tried Immac.'

As soon as Emily had been cajoled into bed, Bella returned to the subject that had been a burning issue all that day – the man that Suzy was taking to the ball.

'So you met him in that new wine bar? Didn't he think it was all a bit sudden when you asked him to a ball?'

'No, I was terribly businesslike about it. I said I was representing my company there and the colleague from work that was meant to accompany me had 'flu and couldn't go. He seemed totally cool about it. Said he'd love to come.'

'And he really is drop, dead gorgeous?'

'Absolutely. Six feet tall, blond hair, blue eyes and great body,' said Suzy, her eyes glazing over.

'So why is he on his own then?'

'He's just split up with a long-term girlfriend – which shows he has staying power at least – and he said he's not the type for one-night stands.'

'But you *are* a one-night stand. I mean, because you've invited him to the ball for one night – not that you're going to leap into bed with him or anything, of course,' said Bella hastily.

Suzy raised her eyebrows and grinned. 'Who says I won't? No, seriously, Bel, he is gorgeous and there's a definite spark there. I really think this one could be The One.'

Oh no, not again, thought Bella. She tried to keep it light. 'OK, but you simply must tell me his name now. I can't understand why you've been refusing all day. Is it something awful like Wilfred? Or Harold? Or Reginald?'

'No!' giggled Suzy.

'Archibald?'

'No – though actually I quite like the name Archie.'

'Umm … Herbert?'

'No!'

'OK Suze, I'm going to count to three and then you're going to spit it out. One … two.. –'

'CECIL!' shouted Suzy, then covered her head with a cushion.

Oh dear, thought Bella with a snort of laughter. Roger and Cecil. It sounds like we're going to a ball with a pair of pensioners. 'You'll just have to call him darling all night,' she giggled. 'Fancy a cup of hot chocolate?'

Madeleine was pacing the floor of her hotel room pondering a very difficult problem. Should she wear her pink Donna

Karan dress or the cheeky, cream, floaty number she'd picked up from that obscure little dress designer in Paris? Would the people of Haybridge really appreciate a Donna Karan label or did they think French Connection was the cutting edge of fashion? If she wore the cream then she could wear her new Jimmy Choo shoes; they were a perfect match.

'What do you think, honey?' she asked for the third time. 'The cream or the pink?'

'Pink,' said Jonathan briefly, without looking up from *The Times* sports pages.

'But if I wear the pink it would clash with that new nail varnish the manicurist has ordered for me. Really, you have to be so careful with pinks.'

'Cream then.' Jonathan sighed.

'But if I wear the cream I really need my silk and lace evening shawl and that's still in London. God, it's such a *nuisance* not having half my clothes here. I'm just wondering whether I ought to shoot into town tomorrow and buy something new – the winter collections will be in the shops now.'

Jonathan slammed down his paper. 'Madeleine, wear the bloody pink! Wear the bloody cream. Or buy something new. Or wear all three bloody dresses at once. Quite honestly I don't give a toss what you wear to the ball!'

Madeleine's eyes widened in surprise. It was not like Jonathan to lose his steely self-control and shout in such a ... *common* fashion. She knew he wasn't terribly interested in clothes but goodness, he wanted her to look *nice*, didn't he? He'd been tetchy all week, ever since he'd told her about this silly little police ball.

'Darling, don't you want to go tomorrow night? I thought you would be pleased the Superintendent had given you the tickets and wanted you on his table. It's quite a compliment, you know, and I'm sure it will be terribly good for your career prospects.' She planted a kiss on his brow, which Jonathan wiped away irritably.

'I don't care about my career prospects. I just want to nail a murderer,' he snapped.

'And you will, my darling. You will. Now, do you think I'll have time to get into town and back tomorrow and be back in time for my hair appointment at four? And should we give your dinner jacket a nice little brush down while we have a minute tonight?'

Jonathan stood up. 'You, Madeleine, can do what you like. I'm going down the pub with the boys.' With that he grabbed his coat and walked out.

Jerry Boswell and a couple of his fellow detective constables had bagged their favourite table in the trendy wine bar off Drovers Street and were happily engaged in discussing which one of the two new female CID recruits had the best body.

'Lou's tits are okay but the size of that backside! She bent over today and it was like a total eclipse,' said Paul Hayes, a dark, smooth-faced officer in his mid-thirties who had so far achieved the CID record of leaving three wives in fifteen years. Thus he was nicknamed 'Bolter'.

'Jen has a good body – plays tennis for the county apparently. I wouldn't mind serving her a couple myself if it wasn't for her face. She looks like she's sucking a lemon!' chipped in Gary 'Gazza' Potter.

Boz, who had already secretly explored the charms of both the young WDCs in question, kept quiet. He might be immoral but at least he was a gentleman – of sorts.

'I reckon Lou's got a bit of a thing for Jonny boy though,' said Bolter. 'Did you notice she kept standing by his desk today and asking him if he wanted a cup of tea?'

'Christ, he wouldn't give her a look-in. Have you seen

his bird? She's out of the top drawer,' said Gazza. 'Got some fancy name – Maryanne or something.'

'Madeleine,' supplied Boz helpfully. 'Quite a goer too.'

'God, Boz you haven't ... not already?' Gazza, who struggled in the women stakes, was impressed.

'Nah. But you can tell. When I went to pick up Jonny the other morning she came out, dressed in this little silky thing, and she gave me a right once-over. If she wasn't the boss's bird I'd be right in there.'

'Well, if she's that good, why's Jonny in such a bad mood lately? He's had a face like thunder the past couple of days,' said Bolter.

'I dunno,' shrugged Boz. 'He's under pressure from headquarters to get this murder sewn up. And he's having trouble getting those extra officers we need for the burglary patrols. I guess he's just stressed.'

'A good old session at the ball tomorrow will sort him out,' said Gazza. 'You got your dinner suit sorted, Boz?'

'Yeah. I can't decide whether to wear a black bow tie or a red one though. What do you reckon?'

'It says black tie on the ticket.'

'Yeah, but that doesn't mean black tie, you pillock. You can wear any colour you like.'

'Oh,' said Gazza. 'I might wear a blue one then.'

'I just can't decide,' said Boz. 'Black and sophisticated or red and dashing.'

It was at that moment, unfortunately, that Jonathan strode over to join them. For Christ's sake, not you lot too, he thought. Why is the whole world dithering about what it is going to wear to this bloody ball?

'Can I buy you a drink, ladies?' he said.

Chapter Twelve

Dr Peter Marsh, a forensic scientist and DNA expert of many years standing, was accustomed to dealing with irate coppers who had set their hearts on a result that would neatly tie up their case but that science simply could not provide. Some of them shouted, some of them demanded a re-test and some of them even challenged him personally, as if it was his fault that their victim was not liberally splattered with their suspect's DNA profile.

So when this new guy, Jonathan Wright, took the news with a calm nod and a series of intelligent questions, Dr Marsh was pleasantly surprised.

'So there was no saliva, no semen, no hairs – nothing on the body from which the killer's DNA could be gained?' Jonathan reiterated.

'Unfortunately not,' said Dr Marsh. 'And the scrapings from underneath the fingernails were not sufficient to tell us anything either.'

'But that, of course, does tell us that the girl didn't put up much of a fight – or didn't have a chance to?'

'That's correct.'

'And all you can say about the grey fibres at this stage is that they are consistent with a carpet, possibly a short fibre industrial carpet with a high percentage of acrylic? Could it be a carpet from a vehicle – a car boot for instance?'

'Possibly,' said Dr Marsh.

'But you can provide me with a more detailed analysis of these fibres so that I can make enquiries with manufacturers?'

'I certainly can.'

'Thank you, Dr Marsh. And I take it you're still working on the hair samples discovered in the broken window from the Spar shop burglary?

'I am and I can confirm we have just obtained a full DNA profile from one of the hairs. I have sent that profile to the database and we will hopefully get a result within three weeks – if, indeed, there is a match.'

What a charming man, thought Dr Marsh as Jonathan shook his hand and bade him goodbye. I wish they were all so level-headed, he sighed, reaching for his test tubes.

Jonathan's calm, analytical mind refused to panic. A defeat only made him more determined than ever to solve this case – if only through old-fashioned legwork. He picked up the now well-thumbed post-mortem report and glanced at this watch. Time to turn up the pressure up, he thought.

'Boz, Ricky Thomas should be downstairs, answering his bail. Could you bring him up please?'

The dark eyes once again stared challengingly across the table. 'Why are you asking all these questions about my jewellery?' Ricky demanded as Jonathan continued to fix his gaze on the bling bling gold chain around his neck.

'Just interested in these modern fashions,' said Jonathan. 'Show me your rings.'

Frowning, Ricky held out both hands, the right one adorned with a gold signet ring on the little finger and the left with a chunky, square cut silver ring.

'Do you always wear those?'

'Yeah. You don't have a problem with that, do you?'

'Yes, actually.'

'Listen mate, I don't know what the bleedin' hell you're

on about but I can tell you these rings aren't nicked. I bought them myself and I can prove it.'

'I'm sure you can,' said Jonathan calmly. 'But I can prove that you *did* follow Carla out of the pub and you did have another row with her. You lost your temper and slapped her with the palm of your hand around the face – so hard that your silver ring left a mark on her skin. Forensic analysis, with all its high tech advances, could analyse that mark and prove that it was made by your ring,' he continued. He wasn't actually lying. The PM report *had* detailed bruising on the dead girl's cheek, consistent with a medium-force slap. And it had mentioned that there was a small, centralised area of slightly deeper bruising just below the cheekbone. That bruising could well have been caused by a ring. And one day – but certainly not at the moment – forensic science *might* find a way to prove contact by metal against skin.

Jonathan continued to look steadily at Ricky, who was now visibly panicking, tapping his brown-booted foot on the floor and fiddling with the ring in question. He would stay silent now – wait for the boy to crack.

It came in a defiant gush. 'I didn't hit her hard. I just lost my rag, didn't I. The silly cow was going on and on at me and wouldn't stop. She was crazy, man. She just lost it. She was screaming and crying all over the place like a bloody mad woman. I was scared someone would hear and think I was mugging her or something. I didn't slap her to hurt her – I did it to calm her down.'

'So you admit you followed her out of the pub, Ricky.'

'Yeah – only to the corner of the street. I was only with her a couple of minutes.'

'And after you hit her?'

She kicked me – right here on the shin.' Ricky rubbed his leg. 'Then she ran off. Down that dark street, the one that goes to the swimming pool.'

'Queen Street?' interrupted Boz.

'Yeah. And I didn't see her after that. I swear I didn't see her, man.'

'OK Ricky,' said Jonathan abruptly. 'You may go now. I will ask for your bail to be extended for a further two weeks. We'll speak again then.'

Boz, a few seconds later, started at his boss in surprise. 'Christ, guv – you could have charged him. He's admitted he hit her and admitted he lied in his first statement. He's as guilty as hell!'

'Is he?' said Jonathan, handing the young officer a sheaf of papers. 'Could you make a start on these carpet manufacturers please?'

Madeleine had compromised and driven twenty miles to the much larger town of Weatherford, where she bought a new shawl for the cream dress in the most upmarket department store she could find. She was currently lying almost naked, face down on a padded table while a pretty young masseuse called Tracey pummelled and prodded her slender body.

'Mmm, that's bliss,' said Madeleine. 'Will you be able to fit me in for a sunbed session afterwards – before my facial?'

'No problem,' said Tracey, thinking it wasn't often a customer came in off the street and tried practically every single treatment.

'So, let me see,' said the girl on the till three hours later. 'That's a massage, sunbed, facial, eyelash perm, leg wax, bikini wax and eyebrow wax ... oh, and the new non-invasive, non-surgical facelift treatment of course. Plus two black coffees and one sparkling water. That will be £320 please.'

Worth every penny, thought Madeleine, who was

determined, by 8pm, to be utterly irresistible to Jonathan and his funny little colleagues.

She checked her watch. Just time to make it to the hairdressers by 4pm, where it would take at least half an hour to pin her hair up into a sophisticated chignon. By the time she got back to the hotel she would have less than two hours for her bath and make-up. Hmm, that was cutting it a bit fine. Thank God she'd had her manicure and pedicure first thing.

Part of her, accustomed to the glitz and glamour of the international fashion set, wondered why she was going to quite so much trouble over a poxy little small-town ball, which would doubtless be full of red-faced dignitaries in ill-fitting dinner suits and their frumpy little wives wearing dresses they'd bought off the shelf years ago. And there would be all those police officers, of course, talking shop while pouring pints down their throats and flapping their arms about inanely on the dance floor. Cheeky young devils they were too if that one who came to collect Jonathan the other day was anything to go by. Why, he looked Madeleine up and down so many times she thought his eyes would pop out, she remembered with a self-satisfied smile.

If the truth be known, Madeleine, normally cool and self-contained to the point of arrogance, was having a mini crisis of insecurity over Jonathan's increasingly withdrawn behaviour. It was an alien feeling to her, having to work to gain a man's attention. Normally all her efforts went into keeping them at an emotional arm's distance and dreaming up polite excuses not to go out with them every night of the week when she needed at least three clear evenings for her beauty routines. She found it annoying when they presented her with huge bunches of flowers – which inevitably clashed with the colour scheme in her chic London apartment – and when they came clutching boxes of chocolates, well that was truly pathetic. Surely any intelligent person knew that models couldn't eat *chocolate*? How the hell did they think she kept herself looking so good?

But Madeleine would have gone into raptures over a petrol station bunch of chrysanthemums at that moment and she might even have nibbled a coffee cream or two had Jonathan walked in with a box of chocolates under his arm. She would even agree to go out to that horrible little pub he liked so much if it meant he would look at her adoringly again, she thought, remembering with a smile the consequences of their last visit there.

What on earth was wrong with the man? For the first time in her life Madeleine had found someone she could not wrap around her little finger – someone who refused to be a devoted slave. And it was just her luck it had happened at this time of her life too, when her modelling assignments seemed to be drying up and she was thrown into a panic almost daily when she noticed yet another little sign of deterioration in her beautiful body. It was nothing major: a tiny wrinkle here, just the saggiest bit of skin there; nothing that couldn't be corrected by hours in the gym and twice weekly facials. But, at the age of thirty-one, Madeleine knew these changes were all part of a downward spiral, which could only end in enforced retirement from the ruthless world of perfection she had chosen to pursue.

So when she had met Jonathan – such a refreshing change from the string of image-conscious and self-indulgent young studs she'd previously dated – she had thought, for the first time in her life, about settling down, maybe even getting married, and starting a new life in readiness for the day that her body finally failed her. She could picture them sharing a large country home and shopping together for antique furniture to fill it. They would ski a couple of times a year, maybe buy a villa in the sun for the winter months, but they would spend most of their time enjoying the company of the country set, whom Madeleine would invite to frequent dinner parties, regaling the well-groomed couples with tales and photographs from her modelling days.

They would have a cook, maybe a gardener. Oh and a cleaner. But no children of course. She was lucky in that neither she nor Jonathan had the slightest interest in children. Goodness, it was bad enough getting wrinkles – she certainly didn't want stretch marks and saggy breasts too!

But it wasn't going to plan. It had all seemed so certain when Jonathan asked her to move to this temporary job in Haybridge with him. Why, she had even started flicking through bridal magazines and wondering about honeymoon destinations. But they had barely been here a month and his interest seemed to have waned with every day that passed until now he alternated between a distant politeness or a mild tetchiness every time she tried to get his attention.

As for that little outburst last night – well, that was quite disgraceful. And so was his lack of apology afterwards, thought Madeleine, recalling with a flush of anger how she had dressed in her best negligee and sat up waiting for him to come home, a carefully-rehearsed expression of wounded hurt on her glossy lips. But he had come in clearly drunk, stinking of cigarettes and beer, and flopped down on the bed with hardly a goodnight. What was wrong with the man?

Tonight, though, she would hook him back in. She would shine. She would dazzle. She would be vivacious, intelligent, supportive and incredibly sexy all at the same time. He would be so proud of her. She would be the Belle of the Ball.

*　*　*

'Em! Will you get out of that bath?' shouted Bella, hopping from foot to foot and shivering with just a skimpy bath towel wrapped round her.

'One minute, Mum. I'm just sinking the submarine.'

'Em, if you are not out by the time I count to three I'm coming in with you. One ... two..–'

'I *want* you to come in. That would be fun.'

Bella quickly checked the bathroom clock. 6.45pm. She had to dry Em's hair, get the little girl in her pyjamas, pack her Tweenies overnight bag and drive her to her grandparents' house. And in between she had to transform her own frazzled self into a dazzling beauty and be at the ball by 8pm. With a sigh she dropped her towel and lowered herself into the tepid water.

'Hey Mum. I'll help you wash your hair,' said Emily, pouring a red plastic bucketful of water over her head. 'Close your eyes. This is fun!'

She insisted on liberally dousing her mother's head with shampoo and rinsing it off, inadequately, with the little red bucket.

'You're such a help, Em,' lied Bella, feeling guilty because she'd been chivvying her small daughter along all evening when she clearly did not want to be hurried. It was not her fault her mum was going to a ball and needed at least two hours these days to make herself look even passable.

But it had been an exceptionally slow evening. First Bella had been forced to stand on a freezing playing field for half an hour because Em's football practice was late finishing. Then she rushed home and cooked the quickest pasta supper ever, only for her daughter to take what seemed like hours chewing every mouthful. And now the child was refusing to get out of the bath – despite the fact that only last night she had protested loudly about getting in it at all.

Still shivering and still sporting stubbly legs and arm-pits – she didn't want Em copying her with a razor – Bella climbed out of the bath and examined her face ruefully in the mirror. Ten minutes to do her make-up, when she clearly needed an hour and a cement mixer.

Wrapping her towel around her, she sat down on the stool before her dressing table mirror only to feel a little bottom hitching up next to hers. 'Can I have some of that stuff on my eyes, Mummy? Oh look – I've given myself big red lips now.'

Bella smothered a terribly unmaternal instinct to shove her young daughter off the stool and snatch the make-up away from her. 'Why don't you go and find your pyjamas to wear to Nanny and Grandad's, Em?'

'Because I don't want to,' she replied with an air of surprise. Why didn't Bella ever remember not to turn a request into a question?

Bella gritted her teeth and quickly swept green eyeshadow across her lids and a mascara brush across her lashes. She flung a pale pink lipstick into her little evening bag and rummaged through the drawer for her only pair of decent sexy knickers, wondering vaguely why she was bothering if nobody was going to see them. Then she fished out a lacy white bra. 'Please hold them in when I bend over tonight,' she told it sternly.

Em, by now bouncing naked on the bed, hooted with laughter. 'I'm going to tell my teacher you talk to your bra, Mummy!'

As long as you don't write it in your news book though, Em. Like you did that time I slipped on Thomas's cat sick in the kitchen and bruised my backside.

Fifteen minutes later Bella's ballgown was on, her hair was up, with only a few damp tendrils escaping from the sides, and Em was dressed, packed and ready to leave with only a trace of lipstick smudges on her face. We'll do it if we hurry, thought Bella, hitching up her voluminous skirts and legging it to the car.

'You look beautiful, darling. Dad! Come here! Come and see how lovely that old dress I wore when we were courting looks on our Bella.'

'Thanks Mum,' said Bella, desperate to hand over Emily and flee.

'Just wait here a minute. I've got just the thing to set that dress off. Now, where did I put it?'

'No Mum, honestly. Don't worry. I have to meet Suzy and Roger at the civic centre in five minutes...' But it was too late. Rita Smart's broad backside was already disappearing up the stairs.

Paul Smart stepped into the hallway to survey his daughter with pride. She looked a real picture. 'Now, you're not going to drink and drive are you, my love?' he asked gently.

'No Dad. I'll leave my car at the centre and share a cab home with the others. But I'm not planning to drink much at all,' lied Bella. Well, the first part was true. But there was only one way she was going to get through this evening – particularly if old Flint Eyes was about with his Sleeping Beauty quips and probably some glamorous girlfriend in tow. That way was alcohol – and a lot of it.

Her mum came bustling down the stairs holding out an old-fashioned silver necklace, an emerald held in a tiny filigree heart, which she fastened around Bella's throat. 'This was my mother's – she would have loved you to wear it. You can't go to a ball with a bare neck, darling.'

'Thank you, Mum. It's beautiful,' said Bella. And she meant it.

Her parents insisted upon coming out into the street

to wave her off, Em standing between them. 'Have a wonderful time!' they shouted in unison.

'I'll try,' said Bella with a very fixed smile.

Chapter Thirteen

If Bella had not been wearing such a feminine dress she would probably have let forth a volley of very rude words indeed when she looked at the seating plan in the reception area of the ball. Instead she made do with a very quiet but satisfying expletive under her breath, a fact that was not missed by Suzy's handsome but badly named Cecil.

'Is everything OK?' he asked. 'We're all seated together, aren't we?'

'No! I mean, yes! We are all together. And that's lovely!' chirped Bella, looking up at his chiselled features. God, he's handsome. He reminds me of Hugo, though. Another stupid name.

Suzy clearly thought everything about Cecil was wonderful and was clinging onto his arm and talking in a very fast, vivacious monologue. She'll have a sore throat by the end of the night if she doesn't calm down, thought Bella. Perhaps it was the two gin and tonics she had downed so quickly at the bar. She was glad someone was happy, though.

The organisers of the Haybridge annual police ball had thought long and hard about their guests' feelings when designing the seating plan this year and decided it would be an interesting and fun touch to mix their officers with ordinary people – outsiders. It would avoid shop talk, they decided, and encourage folk to mingle nicely. Bella, staring once again at the seating plan, thought it was the worst idea she had heard of in her entire life.

She felt Roger's tentative hand on the small of her back

and smiled gratefully at him. 'Shall we go in?' she murmured. 'Like lambs to the slaughter,' he replied.

Bella tried frantically to manoeuvre a semi-masticated piece of boeuf bourguignon to the side of her mouth in response to the weasel-faced councillor's question.

'Yes, I'm the reporter who found the body,' she agreed. 'It seems to be my claim to local fame!'

'Or notoriety,' growled a voice from across the table.

Bella ignored it. 'Tell me, Councillor Howard, how do you manage to chair the housing committee and do all that voluntary work with the homeless hostel? It must be exhausting.'

'I bet you find it hard to keep your eyes open sometimes, don't you?' came the voice again, deceptively polite this time.

'Well, it *is* hard work,' said the councillor. 'But then you chaps must be used to hard work with this murder to contend with. And all those burglaries as well. How are all your public appeals going, incidentally? I'm sure the people of Haybridge are helping you – we have a fine community spirit here.'

'Most people have been extremely helpful,' said Jonathan, whose name card, Bella could not help noticing, was misspelled as 'Mr J Right'. That was a joke, she thought.

'One or two people, though, have proved rather a hindrance,' he continued. ' But I can deal with people like that. They're easy.'

It was the sarcastic little smile aimed straight at her that did it for Bella. That and the three glasses of red wine she had glugged down during this interminable dinner – despite the fact that the stuff tasted foul. He thought he was so damned clever... She shot him a warning glance and shot one foot out petulantly under the table, aiming straight for his ankle.

'Ouch!' cried the blonde bombshell next to him.

Oops. Hope I haven't dented a Jimmy Choo, thought Bella, watching Jonathon stroke his companion's manicured hand. 'Did you catch your leg on the chair, darling?' he said.

God, he'll be kissing her foot next. Two can play at that game. She turned to Roger beside her. She had no intention of kissing his foot – she had smelt his socks, for God's sake – but she could certainly flirt a bit. She ran her hand tenderly down his cheek. 'Could you pour me some more wine, *darling*?'

Roger blushed scarlet and reached for the wine so fast he almost knocked over the water jug. Suzy, two seats down, stopped flirting with Cecil for the first time that evening and gave her friend a puzzled stare. What on earth was Bella doing to poor Roger? And why was she knocking back the booze when everyone knew she hated wine and started talking gibberish after two glasses?

Jonathan simply raised one eyebrow and shovelled in a forkful of beef. 'Bella, you haven't introduced me to your friends,' he said charmingly. He leaned across and picked up Suzy's name card. 'Miss S Mapleton. Are you a colleague?'

'Suzy ish a reporter too,' said Bella. Ooops, better watch that letter s. 'And these,' she enunciated carefully, with a dramatic sweep of her arm, 'these are our friendth, Roger and ... Th ... Roger and...'

Jonathan waited patiently.

'Roger and ... Sh...'

The eyebrow shot up.

'THESHHIL!' said Bella triumphantly.

'Hello Theshhil,' said Jonathan, deadpan. 'I am very pleased to meet you.'

Bella popped a baby roast potato in her mouth and chewed very hard. Her head felt peculiarly swimmy and that bloody detective's face kept going out of focus. She knew from bitter experience that she had to eat something and she had to eat it fast. Councillor Weasel was telling her he liked seeing young ladies with a healthy appetite. Oh dear, that wasn't his name, was it? Better be careful there. She popped in the last roast potato and felt tempted to reach over and steal a couple from Bombshell's plate. She had hardly touched her food, even though she had made a great big fuss about having a nut cutlet instead of the beef. No wonder she was so skinny. Bloody beautiful though.

I'd tell her that dress is stunning if I could rely on the s coming out right, thought Bella. Oh dear, I think I made a right cock-up of Cecil. Why does my tongue feel too big when I've had too much wine? Everyone else seems okay – they're talking normally. Weasel's talking to Roger about computers and Mrs Weasel is joining in. Cecil's talking to the bombshell – flirting a bit by the look of it – and Suzy's talking to that bloody Jonathan. Why on earth does she want to talk to *him*?

Suzy was actually answering Jonathan's enquiry about whether she thought her friend was just a little bit drunk.

'Legless,' she replied cheerfully, raising her glass. 'But then Bel's a real lightweight with wine. I don't know why she's drinking it – she can't stand the stuff. But she'll sober up in a bit when she's got enough food down her. I know Bella of old!'

And I'm getting to know her pretty well too, thought Jonathan. 'She probably needs chocolate now,' he remarked.

'How did you know that?' asked Suzy, gazing at him in amazement. God, he had lovely blue eyes. How could Bella say he was ugly? It was a shame he was attached. Mind you, his stunning blonde really seemed to be hitting it off with her Cecil, she thought, her heart suddenly sinking as she looked at the two fair heads nodding in animated conversation. Jonathan kept shooting them

145

sideways glances too – maybe it was time for Suzy to interrupt. She leaned across the table, making sure she gave Cecil a tempting flash of her cleavage. 'So, what do you do for a living?' she asked the blonde.

'I'm a model,' said Madeleine proudly.

Shit, thought Bella, who was now chomping the watercress garnish.

'I do a bit of magazine work – you may have seen me in the latest Clairol ad in some of the glossies this month. But mainly I do catwalk stuff in Europe for the big labels.'

Double shit, thought Bella. Bet she didn't buy her dress in Top Shop. Bet she's not wearing her mum's old ballgown either, she thought ruefully, glancing down at the satin folds.

Jonathan too was surveying Bella's dress, thinking how tiny it made her waist look and how the colour looked so striking against her hair and brought out that faint flush in her cheeks. It makes her eyes look really sparkly too, he thought. Oh actually, the waitress has just handed her a dish of chocolate mousse – that was why her eyes were twinkling. That was a pretty little necklace she was wearing too. Mind you, he preferred her in those Teletubby binoculars, they were the best! He suppressed a tiny smile.

What are you smirking at? thought Bella. 'Have I got chocolate round my mouth?' she whispered to Roger, grateful that her powers of pronunciation seemed to be returning.

'Your mouth is fine,' butted in Jonathan, before Roger could say a word. God, that man had ears like a bloodhound. No – that was wrong. Ears like an elephant maybe? Oh, she couldn't remember, but he actually had quite nice ears now she came to look at them. She liked the way his dark hair curled round them. But he was still a nosy sod.

Determinedly, Bella leaned across the table, turning her

back on Jonathan, and began an animated conversation with Mrs Weasel about what it was like being the wife of an eminent councillor. She was glad when, in the middle of a lengthy recital about dinner party recipes used for entertaining 'hubby's colleagues', people started finishing their puddings and swapping tables.

'Hello, gorgeous,' said Boz, plonking himself down in Roger's chair and planting a kiss on Bella's cheek. Roger, bless him, had plucked up courage to sit next to Suzy, who, he thought, looked even more beautiful than Lara Croft tonight. Cecil, meanwhile, had wandered off to the bar.

'Boz! You look so handsome in your DJ. And is this your girlfriend? I've heard so much about you!' gushed Bella, turning to the buxom young girl hovering at the officer's side.

'Have you?' said the girl in surprise. 'I only met 'im last night.'

Jonathan let out a snort from across the table, causing Madeleine to shoot him a look of surprise. Boz, who had hastily trawled the late-night bars for a partner after a blazing row with his girlfriend, did not bat an eyelid. 'See, angel – you're making such an impression on me that I just had to tell my friends about you,' he drawled charmingly. 'This is Kayleigh, everyone. And, as you can see, she is lovely.'

Kayleigh simpered. 'Are you Old Bill too, then?' she asked Bella.

Oh dear, thought Madeleine, wrinkling her nose. She sounded a little bit *council estate* to her.

Bella noticed the gesture and felt a surge of sympathy for the poor young girl, who would doubtless be cast aside just as soon as Boz reconciled with his girlfriend – which he always did in the end, despite his dramatic misdemeanours.

147

'No,' she said gently, 'I work for the local paper. My name's Bella – Bella Smart.'

Kayleigh's eyes widened immediately. 'Ooh. You're the one what found –'

'Found the body, yes.' Bella sighed. Really she was getting sick of this subject.

'Found Carla,' finished Kayleigh.

There was something about the familiar way she used the name. Bella did not hesitate: 'Did you know her?'

'Yeah. Well, not really. She came in the golf club a few weeks before she was killed. I recognised her picture when I saw it in the *Gazette*. I work there – behind the bar. And they let me help with the buffets and stuff sometimes,' she said proudly.

The golf club? That's an odd place for an unemployed twenty-three-year-old bloke to take a girl, thought Bella and Jonathan simultaneously. Boz thought nothing. He just felt a prat for picking up a bird who might know something about the murder without him even realising. Mind you, he couldn't be expected to question every damn girl he met, could he?

Jonathan looked at Bella and put a surreptitious finger to his lips. Butt out of this; I'll do the talking, his eyes warned silently.

Naturally, Bella ignored him – and also a warning kick from the now sharper Boz. 'Did Carla come to the golf club alone, Kayleigh?' she asked.

'Yeah. She was waiting for someone. She started talking to me 'cos she said she felt stupid standing there on her own. She spoke good English but she had a funny accent.'

Bella could feel the blue eyes positively burning into her now but risked one more question anyway: 'Do you know who she was waiting for?'

'Nah. He didn't turn up. She gave up after a little while and went. He was an older bloke though 'cos I remember

148

her saying he was old enough to know better than to let a girl down. I dunno why but I thought it was probably the bloke she worked for. Au pairs always knock off their bosses, don't they?'

Bella's mouth was open to ask the next question when Jonathan sprang out of his chair and put a gentle hand on the girl's shoulder. 'Kayleigh, I'm DS Wright and I am very interested in what you are saying. I would like it very much if you would come and see me at the police station on Monday morning and we'll talk about this a bit more. Would that be all right with you?'

Kayleigh's chest, already threatening to explode out of her black sequinned dress, puffed up with pride. 'Ooh – I'd love to!' she said.

'In the meantime,' said Jonathan firmly, 'I would hate to spoil your ball. I will see you on Monday.' He patted the girl on the shoulder. She was dismissed and so was Boz, who, rather sheepishly, led his new conquest back to their table.

The long-haired lead guitarist of the 'Go with a Swing' dance band looked at his watch and heaved a sigh because there were still fifteen minutes of boring waltzes and quicksteps to get through until they could get on to the real foot-tapping good stuff. Why the hell the organisers of balls always insisted on this slow, formal start to the entertainment he never knew. It was not as though anyone knew these out of the ark dances any more and there was only the police Superintendent and that Councillor Hanson bloke on the dance floor, shuffling and twirling away with their wives. All the other people were either slumped in their chairs, stuffed with too much food and too much wine or else fidgeting away because they wanted a good old bop to Abba.

Suzy was one of the fidgeters. But she didn't want to bop to Abba – well not yet anyway; she wanted to be swept onto the dance floor in the strong capable arms of Cecil to dance a romantic waltz.

'I'll lead. I always used to be the man at school anyway. All you have to do is follow my feet and go one two three, one two three,' she begged him.

'You are not going to get me up there doing a waltz!' laughed Cecil, folding his arms across his chest. He was starting to get a little bit irritated with Suzy, who had hardly stopped prattling on all evening and kept gazing up at him with an almost bovine expression of adoration. He didn't like his women too easy – the chase was the fun bit. He liked more of a challenge. Like that Madeleine. Now she would be a hard one to crack.

'Suze,' said Roger timidly. 'I will waltz with you if you like.'

Suzy turned to him in astonishment. 'Roger – I didn't know you could dance!' she said.

'I went to ballroom dancing lessons once,' he explained with a slight blush. He had thought it would be a way to meet a nice young lady, but in fact the class was full of terrifying middle-aged women who pressed him to their ample bosoms and marched him around the floor. He'd liked the dancing bit though, just not the bosoms.

How well they dance together, thought Bella, watching her friends glide around the polished mahogany floor. Roger looks quite handsome in that dim light and Suze, the way she's smiling up at him, looks gorgeous. So, unfortunately, did the Bombshell, who, out of the corner of Bella's eye, looked suspiciously like she was running a seductive tongue up and down the detective's earlobe. Yuk! She shifted her gaze surreptitiously to see whether Jonathan was caressing her too – only to meet that black-browed gaze full on.

One eyebrow lifted quizzically. 'You're uncharacteristically quiet, Miss Smart. Are you having trouble speaking again?'

Bella shot him her most dazzling smile: 'Not all at, DS Wright. I'm just saving my tongue for something worthwhile, that's all.'

The blue eyes flashed and Bella reached for her glass with a smug smile. Now her tongue seemed to be working again perhaps she could have another little drink?

'Bottoms up!' said Cecil, handing her a double vodka and orange a few minutes later. 'We're all hitting the hard stuff now before we get on that dance floor. Come on, drink up!'

Bella swigged obediently. Hmm, quite nice. You couldn't really taste the vodka. A couple of police officers had joined their table, Mr and Mrs Weasel having decamped to join some fellow housing committee members, and Jonathan was engaged in football banter, one arm slung casually around Madeleine.

The band burst into 'It's Raining Men' and Bella, the alcohol hitting her system, felt her feet start tapping.

'Shall we dance?' She prodded Roger, who was folding a foil wrapper from an after dinner mint into meticulous little squares. 'This was Suzy's,' he said, following Bella's gaze. 'I put mine in my pocket for Emily.'

Bella planted a kiss on his forehead and dragged him to his feet. 'Let's boogie, handsome,' she said.

Jonathan watched them laughing and gyrating on the floor and wondered how such an innocent, almost old-fashioned sort of dress could look so sexy on a girl like Bella. He was a man, so he'd never heard of bodice rippers. He had also had a fair amount of alcohol and felt a restless energy. He squeezed Madeleine's shoulder. 'Dance?'

'Oh darling, it's a bit *common* to take to the dance floor so soon. Shall we wait until they play something a little more sedate?' she drawled.

'I'll dance with you!' said Suzy like a shot. Bloody Cecil couldn't seem to shift off his backside and was busy making cow's eyes at that snooty Madeleine anyway. Sod him, she'd get up there and wriggle provocatively in her red dress and he'd soon realise what he was missing.

'OK,' grinned Jonathan, pushing back his chair.

One party song flowed into another and it was half an hour before the foursome returned to the table, flushed, panting and gasping for a drink. Bella, whose hair was rapidly shedding its clips and tumbling into little ringlets around her face, drained her glass in one. 'Anyone want another?' she cried.

'I'll get these,' said Jonathan firmly. 'Same again?'

The second vodka went down like a dream and so, after another bout on the dance floor, did the third. During the fourth Bella developed a violent case of hiccups but they made her giggle so much that she did not care.

'So why aren't you dancing, Madeleine?' she said. 'Doesn't it, hic, burn off the calories?'

The model surveyed her coolly and sipped her white wine spritzer. 'Are you saying I *need* to burn off calories?'

'God! Hic! No! I just thought you must think about calories a lot because you're so slim. There's nothing of you – stand sideways and you wouldn't, hic, see you.'

'Thank you,' said Madeleine. 'But I'm not sure whether that is a compliment. As a leading model, I think I would prefer it if people *did* see me. Fortunately, however, I have never had a weight problem but I do, of course, ensure that I eat healthily at all times. Do *you* have to watch the calories, Bella, or do you prefer the more rounded look?'

Bitch, thought Suzy, opening her mouth to defend her friend. But the insult flew over Bella's head.

'Oh I watch them all the time. But usually when they're disappearing down my throat. Hic! Oh excuse me, I can't seem to shake off these shilly hiccups. I mean hilly shiccups,' she giggled.

Jonathan stood up suddenly. 'You need some mineral water. Come to the bar.' It was an order, not a request, and Bella followed meekly, feeling as though her legs did not quite belong to her as he steered her through the room, one hand on her arm. She was grateful when Jonathan guided her to a comfortable-looking sofa in the corner of the much quieter bar area and flopped down far more heavily than she had intended to. She studied his broad back as he ordered her drink at the bar, chatting pleasantly to the barmaid, and her mind immediately flew to the conversation with Boz's girlfriend. Thus, when Jonathan returned, the question was on her lips.

'So, do you think Carla was knocking off the husband then – Mr Williams?'

'No. And I'm off duty, Bella. And so are you.'

'Well, I think she was and I think you should be looking for his fr ... forenshics ... stuff on her body and checking for his DNA. In fact, I think you should arresht him at once. He could have, hic, killed her because he didn't want his wife to find out. She *was* pretty shcary. Hic!'

Ah ha, thought Jonathan. Been sniffing round there too, have you? 'There is no forensic evidence on the body, Bella,' he explained patiently. 'I got the results today. There's nothing but a few grey carpet fibres. And we have no idea who Carla was waiting for at the golf club. There is no evidence whatsoever that it was Ian Williams – that is merely speculation from a silly young girl.' *Just like your theory*, his tone seemed to say. 'We will, however, continue to make enquiries to ascertain who the mystery person was,' he continued.

Bella gazed at him. 'Why are you talking to me like a policeman's pocket book?' she asked politely.

Jonathan couldn't help a smile. 'Policemen's pocket books don't talk, Bella.'

'Oh yeah.' Bella wriggled back comfortably into the sofa. 'Good answer.' She gave a huge yawn.

Oh dear, thought Jonathan. Here we go again.

Chapter Fourteen

To the strains of Will Young's 'Evergreen', Bella nuzzled her head in Jonathan's chest, feeling his heart beating steadily under the stiff, white shirt. They swayed together to the music, lost in their own little world, until Jonathan stopped and gently cupped one hand under Bella's chin, tilting her face to his while running the other one teasingly down her spine. His blue eyes bore into hers for what seemed like an eternity before he moved his face down to hers. 'I can't resist you a moment longer,' he whispered huskily, bringing those perfect lips closer and closer. Bella felt a wave of something that could only be desire sweep through her body and, closing her eyes, tilted her face upwards, preparing for the electric shock sensation when her lips finally touched his. 'Kiss me ... kiss me,' she murmured.

'Are you absolutely sure about this?' said a matter-of-fact voice in her ear.

Bella jumped out of her skin and her eyes snapped open. Jonathan was lounging on the sofa next to her in the now empty bar, a huge grin on his face and one hand clutching a pint. Her head was on his shoulder and, what was worst of all, there was a patch of something looking suspiciously like dribble on his dinner jacket where her mouth had been.

'Fuck!' shouted Bella, who did not usually say that word.

'What? So soon after our first kiss?' said Jonathan.

'Did I just ask you to...? What did I just say?'

'I believe it was "fuck".'

155

'No. Before that.'

'You said "kiss me, kiss me". And then I asked you if you were sure,' said Jonathan helpfully, his face deadpan.

'I didn't mean *you* to kiss me! I was asleep. I've had too much to drink. I was dreaming and I thought you were … you were … Will Young!' prattled Bella, hearing indeed the strains of 'Evergreen' from the ballroom.

'Isn't he gay?'

Dumbly Bella nodded. 'Yes, I forgot.'

'But he must have something – he made your hiccups go.'

'Yes.' Bella's face brightened. Then it clouded again. 'Did I snore?'

'Not at all,' replied Jonathan gallantly.

'Did I … er … dribble?'

'Not in the slightest,' he lied, smothering a smile. She had, dribble aside, actually looked quite cute slumbering peacefully on his shoulder. He had welcomed the chance to sit peacefully for a few minutes, thinking his own thoughts away from the endless small talk and false, almost frenzied, gaiety of his fellow guests who were determined to squeeze every ounce of enjoyment out of their big night out. They'd better return to the throng now though. The band was playing Robbie Williams' 'Angel' – a sure sign the evening was about to end.

'Do you like Robbie Williams?' he asked Bella.

'Oh yes.' Is this our first conventional conversation? she wondered.

'That's a shame.'

'Why?'

'I was going to ask you to dance. But you might get confused again and ask for a kiss.'

The blue eyes locked with the grey and, if it had been a scene from that very corny dream, one might have almost been able to see the sparks shooting between the two suddenly serious faces. But if it had been a dream, then a very beautiful but irate woman in a £1,000 cream dress would not have walked elegantly into the bar at that very moment.

'*There* you are darling. I've been looking everywhere for you. Come and have the last dance with me,' said Madeleine, extending her long, tapered fingers.

Bella sat on her own stubby nails and watched Jonathan heave himself to his feet. I didn't want to dance with you anyway, she thought childishly. And I certainly wouldn't have kissed you. Suddenly she felt very sober, slightly headachy and just a tiny bit empty. Perhaps I need a Kit Kat, she thought.

At 6am, just as watery dawn was beginning to break, Bella woke up with a crippling thirst, a pounding head and a realisation that she knew exactly who had murdered Carla Kapochkin.

Running through her head was her conversation with Caroline Williams, the selfish, slightly nasal voice droning on about the hassle of losing her au pair and having police officers troop through her house with their great muddy boots. 'We'd only just had the new carpet laid in the lounge,' she had whined.

Then Bella heard Jonathan's voice, as clear as if he was in her bedroom – which, of course, she was very glad he wasn't. 'There's nothing but a few carpet fibres.'

So, there it was. Vital evidence that Ricky Thomas had not murdered Carla and Mr Ian Williams had! So he had been the mysterious man Carla was waiting for at the golf club, the man old enough to know better than to let a girl down. Bella pictured poor Carla, a newcomer to the country, allowing herself to be flattered and seduced by her older, self-assured employer, perhaps creeping

157

downstairs to join him for a coffee after his wife had gone to bed.

He would start slowly, she thought – a touch here, a compliment there. Maybe he might even slip her an extra fiver or two, a fortune to a girl who was carefully counting the pennies to send home to her family. Then he would build up to a kiss and stroke her hair and tell her he was falling in love with her before removing her clothes and taking her hastily, there and then, one ear listening for movement upstairs from his sleeping wife and children.

Afterwards, when Carla was gazing up at him adoringly, he would tell her he loved her and wanted to see more of her but it was not right that they should meet in the marital home. He would suggest taking her out for a drink one night; he would meet her in secret, on his way home from work. Carla would jump at the chance. Then, once he had got her nicely warmed up with one or two glasses of wine, he would pop her in the car and drive to a dark, remote spot – a place where he could enjoy the firm young body without the fear of interruption.

The golf club bar would be the perfect place for such clandestine meetings. It was a ten-minute drive out of town, nicely secluded and, compared to the gossipy pubs of Haybridge, relatively anonymous. But Mr Williams hadn't turned up one night. Perhaps he had been genuinely delayed or perhaps he had experienced a twinge of conscience. Carla was cross, humiliated and hurt. She had probably had to spend £5 of her wages getting a cab to the golf club and then the same again to get home.

Later, back at home, she had tried to carry on as normal and refused to notice the little changes that were taking place in her body. But then she had done a pregnancy test – Bella knew only too well about that – and had the shock of seeing those two blue lines appear. Now she was desperate – she needed help. She'd plucked up courage

158

and told her employer but he had got angry and said the baby could not be his. He gave her money and told her to have an abortion. Bella knew about that too.

Carla had complied, but afterwards, when she wanted cuddles and sympathy, Mr Williams was cold and patronising and brushed her aside. The poor heartbroken au pair would use the only tool she had: she would threaten to tell his wife all that had happened between them.

What happened next was a bit blurry in Bella's mind. She had never seen anyone strangle another person so it was hard to imagine, but she suspected Mr Williams had lost his temper and put his hands round the girl's throat – maybe to stop her making a noise and waking his wife. Whatever happened, though, he killed her, right there in his living room, on his new carpet. Then, thought Bella triumphantly, he wrapped the body in a spare piece of carpet the fitters had left behind – people were always wrapping bodies in carpets on television programmes – and took it to the allotment hut. Probably, she thought, in the boot of his big, posh car.

Now she had solved the murder she wondered what to do next. Should she call the police? Or Jonathan Wright, to be precise. She knew she had to act fast or poor Ricky Thomas could be charged with something he did not do. He was an innocent man – just like his friends had said.

Dialling 999 was a bit drastic, she decided. She could call the incident room except that her still-befuddled brain could not remember the number. It was in the *Gazette* though and she had a copy in the living room. Bella sprang out of bed. Ouch, that hurt like hell. Urgh, her tummy felt all churning and horrible too and her head was spinning slightly. Maybe she should have a few mouthfuls of water from the bathroom tap and then lie down again until she felt a bit better. After all, with Emily not about she could enjoy the luxury of a lie-in for once...

Bella woke at 1pm to a pounding on the door and a cheerful 'coo-ee' through the letterbox. Only Suzy, who had the constitution of an ox, could be that bright and breezy after a night out, she thought, tottering to answer the door with her duvet wrapped round her.

'Oh dear,' laughed Suzy, who looked ravishing in a new pink jacket. 'You look like something the cat threw up.'

Bella tried to answer but her tongue was gummed to the roof of her mouth. One eye seemed to be gummed firmly shut too.

'I'll put the kettle on,' announced Suzy briskly. 'And,' she said, producing a bag from behind her back, 'I've bought us some double chocolate muffins.'

Bella's stomach gave a lurch, then a growl, then righted itself. Yes, I can do chocolate muffins, it decided.

By 2pm, after a blissfully long, uninterrupted bath while Suzy watched the cartoon channel, Bella felt almost normal again. She phoned her mother to apologise for not picking up Em that morning only to learn from her father that the pair of them had gone out to the church Craft Fair.

'They said they'd pick up a few Christmas presents and Mum will drop Emily back to you on the way home,' he said.

'Christmas!' said Bella, when she replaced the handset. 'Why is it that the older people get the earlier they start their Christmas shopping? I haven't got over fireworks night yet!' And had she imagined it or were there a few sparks – of a slightly lustful nature – flying last night between her and a certain detective? Well, he would certainly be proud of her when she told him she'd nailed his murderer.

Maybe, though, in the cold light of day, her theory wasn't so watertight after all? Why would Carla be knocking off Mr Williams and seeing Ricky too? Whose baby had she been carrying? Maybe Bella ought to do just a little bit more legwork herself, just so Jonathan couldn't shoot her down in flames and make her look a fool – again. She could pay Mr Williams a little visit, to suss out whether he looked guilty when Carla's name was mentioned. But he would be at work during the day so it would mean an evening call. Not so good – she'd have to find a babysitter for Em.

But, she realised with a flash of inspiration, she could start at the other end of the scale: by proving Ricky Thomas was totally innocent, thus paving the way for Jonathan to accept Mr Williams' guilt. Ricky was unemployed, would be about during the day *and* she had his address. She could give Sean's press releases the slip and sneak out on Monday morning.

'Hey, dreamer.' Suzy interrupted her thoughts. 'Are you in a fit state to give me the gossip about last night then? Where did you disappear to for ages? We tried to get it out of you on the way home but all you could talk about was how you almost kissed Robbie Williams! Honestly Bel, you are hopeless with alcohol.'

Within minutes the pair were in fits of giggles as Bella recounted how once again she had nodded off on Jonathan's shoulder. She even – because she knew her friend would adore it – described the little patch of dribble on the plush, dark jacket.

'What is it with that man? Is he slipping that date rape drug in your drinks or something? When I meet a new man I'm so excited I can't sleep for days but you just nod off all over them in a great pool of dribble!'

It was only a little pool, thought Bella. And he is not my new man. He is that Madeleine's man, as she made quite clear last night.

'I didn't think much to his girlfriend though,' said Suzy

suddenly. 'Every time I got close to persuading Cecil to dance with me she'd butt in and distract him. She kept whispering in his ear and patting his knee. It was bloody rude, I thought, and I'm sure it was annoying Cecil. He didn't even want to share my cab at the end of the evening.'

Actually, thought Bella sadly, Cecil looked as though he was lapping up Madeleine's attention and really hadn't seemed that interested in Suzy. She waited for her friend's usual speech about how her latest suitor was the man of her dreams but he'd just not had time to realise it yet. To her amazement, though, Suzy changed the subject.

'I thought Roger was really sweet. He kissed me when I got out of the cab,' she said, with a slight blush.

Bella's eyebrows shot up. She hadn't seen Suze blush since she had written that sexy email to Steve, the new sports assistant in the office, and then pressed the wrong button and sent it to Sean the news editor instead. It was something about biting bottoms, if she recalled correctly.

'I saw him get out of the cab to open the door for you. But why shouldn't he give you a peck on the cheek?'

'It wasn't my cheek, Bel.'

'No! Not on the lips? How embarrassing! Did he slobber? What did you do?'

'I just stood there. It was quite nice actually – it was all soft and gentle and he sort of slid his hand to the back of my head and stroked my hair. And, no, he didn't slobber at all.'

'God. How come I missed it?'

'You were still prattling on to the taxi driver about kissing Robbie Williams.'

'Oh,' said Bella, still trying to get her head around the concept of her vivacious friend snogging her very shy neighbour. Or vice versa. 'So what are you going to do about Roger now? I mean, are you going to let him kiss you again?'

'I think,' said Suzy slowly, 'I'll just pretend that last night did not happen.'

Me too, thought Bella. Oh me too.

By the time Emily arrived home it was indeed easy to forget about the previous night, especially when the little girl's first words were: 'Hello Mum. My head itches. I think I've got nits.'

Good timing, Em, thought Bella, watching her mother take a hasty step backwards and Suzy shriek with horror.

'I'm sure you haven't, darling, but we'll check with the nit comb later just to be on the safe side,' she murmured in as placatory a tone as she could manage.

'It's nothing these days,' she assured her mum over a cup of tea a few minutes later. 'It's not like years ago when it was a real stigma – all the children get head lice now. And, of course,' Bella paused to give dramatic effect to the words every modern mum has uttered for reassurance, 'nits only go to the *cleanest* heads.'

Suzy and Mrs Smart continued to sip their tea in silence, each raising one hand to scratch their respective heads in perfect unison. Both, minutes later, made a hasty exit.

'Oh dear, Em, you do seem to have a nit or two,' said Bella, squinting at the fine-toothed comb she had just dragged through her daughter's wet hair.

'Let me see, Mum, let me see!' Em jumped around with excitement. 'Oh look, that one's huge! And there's a baby one! Find some more – please Mum!'

Bella cleaned the comb with a tissue and continued her nit hunt. Soon mother and daughter were surveying a dozen of the creatures, neatly lined up against the white surface. Even Thomas sat enthralled, giving the tissue an occasional interested bat with his paw.

'Look, that one's wriggling. It's still *alive*, Mum. Oh look, it's waving its cute little legs at me.'

Bella saw her daughter's eyes grow large and pleading. 'Oh no, Em, you needn't think you're going to keep it as a pet. No way.' She splatted the creature firmly with her forefinger.

'Oh look, Mum. It's got *blood*. Wow – cool!' said her gory little daughter.

Much later, the excitement caused by delousing having blown the calming bedtime routine out of the window, Bella slumped in the armchair and gloomily surveyed her pile of ironing in the corner. Then she got up, went to the sideboard drawer and took out her one and only decent white tablecloth, which she proceeded to drape artfully over the pile.

'That's better,' she said as she slid *Dirty Dancing* into the DVD player. Scooping a purring Thomas up onto her lap, she settled down to drool over Patrick Swayze, idly scratching her head as she did so.

Jonathan had done an hour on the running machine at the gym followed by half an hour of hard weights. He had sweated it out in the sauna and then completed fifty lengths of the swimming pool. He felt fit, virtuous, full of energy and ... still bloody irritable. It was probably due to the fact that Madeleine had dragged him round bloody houses all afternoon, oohing and aahing over the décor and the granite worktops and the south facing drawing rooms. Why the hell did they need a drawing room, for God's sake?

When Jonathan had suggested the houses were rather large and rather, well, *expensive*, just for the two of them to live in for just a few months, she had gone all petulant and then, God forbid, tearful. Sniffing delicately and dabbing at her eyes with a little lacy handkerchief, she had explained how much she wanted the pair of them to have a nice home, a proper house with a proper kitchen where she could cook lovely meals for Jonathan when he came home from work. And, she sniffed, they needed a nicely decorated drawing room where they could relax together in the evenings and a nice study so Jonathan could spread out all his work papers. Oh, and a couple of smart spare bedrooms for when they had friends down to stay from London.

Jonathan didn't think they had any mutual friends who would come and stay. Madeleine's friends were all those namby pamby fashion types who only stayed in five-star hotels, and his mates were all coppers who, if they got too drunk to stagger home after watching the football, were quite happy to crash on the sofa.

'I know we're only here for a short time, darling, but we still deserve a proper home. Staying in a hotel room is not doing our relationship any good at all,' insisted Madeleine. 'Besides,' she added, 'it will be good practice for when we get back to London. There are some lovely new penthouse apartments near Docklands.'

I don't want to live in a penthouse apartment, thought Jonathan.

'Or,' said Madeleine, 'we could buy a house in the country – just a short commute away.'

I don't think I want a house in the country. I don't want to commute. In fact, I don't know what I want to do apart from being a police officer, Jonathan had thought, suddenly surprised he had reached the grand old age of thirty-five without, seemingly, knowing what he wanted to do with the rest of his personal life.

Bored with traipsing round houses, he had eventually

capitulated and signed a short-term lease on a four-bedroom furnished house on a new development five miles from Haybridge. To celebrate, Madeleine had booked a table for 8pm at a smart new bistro in Weatherford. She had even promised to drive. It was all rather wasted on Jonathan though, who, after the excesses of the ball, would have much preferred to slump down on the sofa with an Indian takeaway and his new Coldplay CD. He wanted to scan through those responses from the carpet manufacturers too – there could be an important lead there. And he needed to digest the new evidence from that girl of Boz's. That could put a whole new dimension on things.

But most importantly, he needed to work out exactly what mischief a certain red-haired *Gazette* reporter was planning to get up to next. Because Jonathan was positive Bella's sharp little brain would be buzzing after Kayleigh's revelation and she would, without a doubt, be planning to shoot off on one of her wild tangents, acting all wide-eyed and innocent while trying to give him the slip. A slow smile slid over Jonathan's face as he remembered Bella's slumbering face on his shoulder. Come on, my Belle of the Ball, it's time you hit me with your next trick, he thought, savouring the pleasurable surge of anticipation.

Chapter Fifteen

A fine drizzle was falling and a biting wind was blowing across Hilltops estate, causing a sheet of newspaper to flap soggily around Bella's ankles as she picked her way along the front path to number 92 Crispin Drive.

She was just noting that someone had made an effort and planted a tub of winter pansies by the doorstep when the door was flung open by a large black woman wearing a lime green tracksuit and a huge smile. 'Oh,' she said. 'I thought you were my catalogue lady come to take my order.'

'Actually, I'm from the *Haybridge Gazette*. I'm a reporter and I'm really sorry to bother you but –'

'Come in, my love. You look perished out there.' The woman moved her bulk to usher her through the door.

Bloody hell, thought Bella. That was easy.

The shabby but spotlessly clean kitchen was filled with the aroma of something spicily sweet and delicious baking in the oven and Bella, who had had no time for breakfast, felt her tastebuds spring to attention.

'Sit down there at the table. I've got some buns in the oven and they'll be ready in a minute. Cup of tea while we're waiting?' said Maria Thomas chattily, going to fill the kettle. She walked, Bella noticed, with a slight limp and occasionally rubbed one side of her hip as though it was painful. When she had made the tea she lowered herself carefully onto the kitchen chair, wincing as she got halfway.

'Ow, the old hip's playing up today. It's the damp

weather you know – always gives me gyp when it rains. I'm waiting for one of those hip replacement operations, but it will take two years on the national health. Two years! It's a disgrace.'

'I'm sorry,' said Bella genuinely. 'It must be horrible for you.'

'But,' said Mrs Thomas, her face breaking out into another huge smile. 'My Ricky says he's going to save up for me to have my op at that new Viking clinic – the private one – and it doesn't take any time at all there for them to fit you in. He's such a good boy, my Ricky. There's only ever been just me and him, you know, and it's been a struggle at times – I'm not too proud to admit that. But it's worth it when they grow up and they're still good to their old mum –'

'Mrs Thomas,' interrupted Bella gently. 'I hope you don't find this too upsetting but I'm here to talk about the trouble with the –'

'The murder. I know. That's why I want you to know what a good boy my Ricky is before you go putting anything in your paper. Because he didn't do it, my love. You do know that, don't you? You do believe us?' The large, dark eyes looked across the table pleadingly.

'I certainly would like to hear Ricky's story,' smiled Bella, who had taken an instant liking to this rotund and friendly lady. Never in a million years could someone as nice as her produce a murderer, she thought. A teenage tearaway perhaps, someone who got into bad company occasionally and committed the odd petty offence – but not a *murderer*.

She explained gently that the *Gazette* was not allowed to name Ricky because the police had made no charges yet. But, she said, she wanted to gather as much background information as possible to ensure that justice was being done. If the police failed to gather enough evidence for a charge, she promised she would personally write a story about Mrs Thomas's 'weeks of hell' while her son was under investigation – and she would tell the whole of Haybridge what a nice boy he was.

'You'd better talk to him then,' said his mum simply. 'I'll get the buns out then I'll get him out of bed for you. He had a late night last night so he's lying in, the little monkey!'

Several minutes later, biting into a warm currant bun liberally spread with butter and home-made strawberry jam, Bella surveyed the sleepy-eyed young man across the table and wondered if she was, for the first time in her life, sharing a feast with a murderer. No, she thought, watching his mother ruffle his hair affectionately and him pretend to be irritated, he could never have killed Carla. He simply hasn't got it in him.

'I didn't kill her, you know,' said Ricky at that moment, through a mouthful of bun.

'Do you think the police believe you?' asked Bella.

'I don't know. Some of 'em look at me like I'm a piece of shit. That tall one, the geezer with dark hair that asks all the questions, he talks to me OK but then he just looks at me like he knows something I don't and I can't tell what he's thinking.'

Tell me about it, thought Bella. 'What did you and Carla row about in the pub that night, Ricky?

'God knows. She was in a right strop. I wasn't rowing at all – she just started shouting and hollering at me for no reason.'

'But what was she saying? Us women may get a bit over emotional sometimes but we don't start shouting for no reason. Had you said something to upset her and maybe not realised it?'

'I didn't say nothing. I was sitting there drinking my pint and she just walked in and went right into a strop.'

169

'What did she say, Ricky? Think hard,' urged Bella.

Ricky narrowed his eyes and put one hand on his chin, the gesture of a thinking man. 'I think,' he said after a long pause. 'I think she said she'd had a really bad day and she was sick of men.'

'Sick of men in general or just you?'

'Men. She said men. And – I remember now – she said all men did was let you down and they made promises but they didn't keep them. Oh and then – it's all coming back now – then she started going on about how she had to get away from Haybridge and she wanted me to take her back to Poland. When I told her I didn't want to go to bleedin' Poland she started really stropping at me again.'

It's all fitting the Mr Williams theory, thought Bella. No wonder the poor kid wanted to get away. 'Had you ever said you would go to Poland with her?' she asked, guessing Ricky had probably pillow-talked a false promise or two.

'Well, yeah, I might have done once or twice, like. But I didn't mean it – I wouldn't leave my mum,' he mumbled, suddenly looking about twelve years old.

Maria Thomas, who had been hovering anxiously behind her son during the conversation, planted a smacker of a kiss on the top of his head. 'See! I told you he was a good boy,' she said triumphantly, ruffling his hair again. 'And I've been telling this young lady all about how you're going to save up for me to have my hip done at that private place. She knows you've got a good heart.'

'Gerroff mum,' said Ricky, looking sheepish.

Bella suppressed a smile. 'You must be good at saving your benefit money. It will cost thousands, won't it?' Even the NHS could do the operation three times over by the time he could save that much in dole cheques, bless him.

Ricky cleared his throat and looked away, suddenly

seeming twitchy. 'I'm ... er ... I'm doing a bit of work on the quiet, like ... I ... um ... don't want people to know about it though.'

'Oh, that's okay. I wouldn't dream of telling the benefits agency,' Bella reassured him. And jolly good luck to you too, she thought, conveniently forgetting the story she had written only three weeks ago urging people to shop benefit fraudsters.

'So,' she said, wanting to bring the interview to a close before Sean started missing her at the office. 'So, do you have any idea who did kill Carla, Ricky?'

'Nah.'

'Do you think she was seeing anyone else while she was going out with you?'

'Ugh – I bloody hope not. I don't like two-timing – it spreads them sexual diseases about. God, I'm glad I was careful, if she was sleeping around,' said Ricky, with a visible shudder.

'See! He's a good boy,' repeated Mrs Thomas with another massive grin. 'And he's a careful boy too. I have always told him to use those ... what are they called?'

'Condoms, Mum,' supplied Ricky helpfully. 'And I always make bloody well sure I do! I've got a real phobia about catching something off some bird. Ugh!' He shuddered again and put down his second currant bun.

He's genuine, thought Bella. Unlikely it was his baby then. She stood up to say her goodbyes, which were prolonged by Mrs Thomas lumbering off to find a paper bag, into which she insisted on putting the few remaining buns. 'Just in case you get peckish later, my love. I'll soon knock up some more.'

Bella felt an urge to kiss her on the cheek but thought it wouldn't be professional, so she shook her plump hand instead. 'It's been a pleasure meeting you,' she said.

Ricky mumbled a goodbye, adding gruffly: 'You'll tell those coppers I didn't do it, won't you?'

'I'll do my best,' promised Bella, wishing him luck.

Back at the office she fought back an urge to ring Jonathan Wright immediately and tell him he was questioning the wrong man entirely. Instead she tried to immerse herself in a story about a really cute three-legged cat that had found by the RSPCA and needed a good home. Bella was tempted herself but thought she probably had enough mouths to feed. Then she remembered the currant buns and dished them out to her fellow reporters, taking the opportunity – as Sean was out at an inquest – to lean back in her chair, put her feet on the desk and catch up with the editorial gossip.

Young Pete, still desperate for a scoop he could sell on to the nationals, had them in stitches when he described how he had rushed out first thing to see a woman in Duke Street who had given birth to sextuplets.

'She came to the door with a baby in her arms and I said, 'Congratulations, where's the other five?' But she just looked at me really weird, like I was a nutter or something.'

Pete flicked through the *Gazette* and showed his colleagues the small ad in the birth announcement section. 'Love and congratulations to Dan and Paula Wesley, proud parents of Daisy Margaret Jessica May Amelia Rose, love and kisses, Mum and Dad Worthington.'

'Oh Pete! Didn't you wonder where the commas had gone?' laughed Bella.

'No. I thought it was a coincidence that they were all girls though,' said Pete ruefully. 'But the woman was OK in the end and we had a bit of a laugh about it. She said she might drop a couple of the names actually because it'll be a bit of a mouthful for the poor kid when she gets to school. Mind you,' he added. 'She said she was lucky to have even one baby. Been trying to get up the duff for years apparently and in the end her sister did something – some host womb thingy – but I didn't really listen because it was women's stuff.'

'Pete!' yelled Bella and Suzy in unison. 'You've got your scoop! Now get back there and get the details.'

'And take a photographer,' they called as he shot out of the office, grabbing Black's Medical Directory on the way to look up surrogate pregnancies.

'Well, that's the front page sorted,' laughed Bella. 'What have you got, Suze?'

'The usual boring rubbish. Illegal fly tipping on the grass verges, someone complaining about dog crap on the Common and a break-in at Ryan's Estate Agents, not much stolen. Then, what joy, I have to do a picture caption for the pensioners' club bazaar. I don't think I can stand the excitement, Bel!'

'You could ring Jonathan about the break-in. He might beef it up a bit with a few quotes.'

'I can't be bothered,' yawned Suzy. 'It's hardly news these days, is it?' She looked up sharply. 'Unless you want talk to him?'

'Good lord no,' said Bella. 'I don't have anything to say to him ... yet.'

She would have to confront him soon, she thought with a shiver of something between anticipation and trepidation. But she would leave it until later that afternoon when he was coming to the end of his shift and his brain might be a little less sharp and not so likely to tear her theory apart. The guy just had to admit he was wrong – it was obvious. He had to accept he couldn't be Mr Bloody Perfect all the time.

She drifted into a nice little daydream about Mr Williams

standing in the dock being sentenced to life imprisonment by a stern-faced judge. Jonathan, sitting next to Bella in court, would wring her hand in gratitude. 'If it had not been for your persistence, I would have charged the wrong man,' he would tell her with a wobble of emotion in his voice. Hmm, perhaps the choked with emotion bit was pushing it. But the rest was cool.

'Miss Bella?' a tentative voice interrupted her. 'I wonder if I could talk to you?'

'Ron!' Bella, as always, was pleased to see the old man. 'How are you? I haven't seen you for ages.'

'I had a couple of days off to go and see my sister. Picked up some lovely new seed catalogues from her and I was all ready to order all my spring planting bits. But then ... then I got another letter from them BestBuys people.'

'What does it say, Ron?'

'Well it's in this funny business language, all long words. I think it's something about planning permission.'

'They've probably lodged an application now. We'll be sent the latest lot soon from the council – next week sometime, I think,' said Bella, remembering her conversation with the bumptious press officer. 'I'll tell you what, Ron, I'll pop round after work if I may and have a quick look at the letter. Oh – and I absolutely promise not to find any dead bodies this time!'

'That will be grand,' smiled the old man. 'And you'll be bringing young Emily?'

'No,' Suzy interrupted hastily. 'I'll baby-sit Em. It's ... er ... it's a bit cold for her to go out at night. I'm sure she had a bit of a sniffle on Saturday.'

'Suze!' said Bella, when Ron had shuffled off. 'Em had nits, not a cold. Why are you so desperate to look after her all of a sudden? Not that you're not always obliging, but why...? Ah, hang on – this wouldn't have anything to do with a certain neighbour of mine, would it?'

'Of course not. I just can't go a couple of days without seeing my Emily, that's all,' said Suzy indignantly.

'OK,' said Bella. 'I'll pick her up from after school club and meet you at the flat at about six. I'll stick a chicken in the oven and we'll all eat when I get back. I shouldn't be very long.'

'I'll bring the dessert,' said Suzy, a complacent smile on her face.

Bella waited until two minutes past five before she dialled the direct line into the CID office. A pleasant-sounding female answered the call and said she was very sorry but DS Wright was tied up in a meeting at that moment. 'May I give him a message?'

'Yes please. Could you ask him to phone Bella Smart.'

'Is it urgent, Miss Smart? Do you want him to call tonight?'

Bella considered, scratching her head. 'Um, yes. That would be great. Thank you.' Might as well get it over and done with, she thought.

The pleasant-sounding girl, who was in fact tennis-playing Jen of the good body fame, was an efficient employee and she immediately wrote out on a Post-It note, in big black capital letters, 'Call Bella Smart. Urgent!!' Then she tidied her already neat desk, switched off her computer and clocked off duty, looking forward to the healthy, low fat pasta bake she had prepared for her supper.

Jonathan, stuck in Superintendent Raymond Nixon's office listening to a string of excuses as to why he could not have his extra burglary patrol officers for another week, was tapping his foot impatiently on the floor and trying to ignore the growling in his stomach. He had been in there for half an hour and the guy was still ranting on about budgets and government allowances.

He'd had no lunch – no breakfast either, come to think of it – and he was ravenous. All he wanted to do was grab a roll or two before the canteen closed for the evening and settle at his desk to tackle another huge mound of paperwork, which included yet more reports from carpet manufacturers and yet another burglary. But the Superintendent droned on and on – and now he was talking about bloody golf, for God's sake.

'So what do you think?' he asked.

Shit, thought Jonathan, who hadn't been listening. 'I think I need to hear the outline of that again, Sir,' he said.

'I just think, given my status as president of the golf club and superintendent of the police, it may be a little *conflicting* if I were to be photographed receiving the cheque for the Carla Kapochkin fund? The members have done terribly well, of course – raised £1,000 I believe. Ted Hanson has had them running around organising all sorts. He plays a good game, does Ted, but he does have that little bit of trouble at the ninth hole. I've won my last three rounds with him, actually.' The Superintendent's chest puffed out slightly with pride. 'But,' he continued, 'I'm just not sure whether I should get *involved* on a public level and receive this cheque. The public might just find it a little confusing.'

'They might also ask if you've caught the murderer yet,' said Jonathan dryly.

'Goodness – so they might! In the circumstances then, you will be the obvious person to receive the cheque on my behalf. Friday. 8.30 sharp – Haybridge and District Golf Club.'

Bloody marvellous, sighed Jonathan, who had planned to watch the England rugby match.

'Sir,' he said, 'just one question: do you have to be a member to drink at the golf club?'

'Absolutely. It's in the constitution. And we don't allow just *anyone* to join, if you understand what I am saying. But I'll get you a pass for Friday and if you're interested in becoming a member I could certainly get you in – we could do with some more young blood. And those barmaids mix a mean gin and tonic!' The superintendent winked.

'Thank you, Sir, but I'm more of a football and pint of lager man actually,' said Jonathan, standing up to make his exit

Striding back into the CID office he almost dropped his ham roll when he saw the note on his computer screen. 'Call Bella Smart. Urgent!!' The big black letters looked almost foreboding and Jonathan felt his stomach give a peculiar little lurch. Urgent. And two exclamation marks. It wasn't like Bella at all to demand attention; prickly independence was more her scene. Perhaps she needed help. Urgent help.

'Who wrote this note?' he demanded of Boz, who was taking his meal break with his feet up on the desk doing the *Sun* crossword.

'Dunno guv. Could have been Jen. Or Lou. Before they left.'

Jonathan opened his telephone book and punched out Bella's number. 'This mobile phone may be switched off,' a robotic voice told him. He slammed down the handset and frowned, trying to combat the uneasy flutter of panic in his gut – not a feeling he usually experienced at all. He waited a couple of minutes then said, as casually as he could: 'Where does that reporter live, Boz? The red-headed one ... I can't remember her name.'

You bloody well can, thought Boz, suppressing a grin. 'Holland Avenue. In the flats – bottom flat on the right.'

Jonathan stood up, giving an elaborate stretch and yawn.

'I'm just going to take a break to blow the cobwebs away. Hold the fort here for a bit, will you?'

Boz watched his boss's retreating back. 'Give her one for me, guv!' he murmured.

Chapter Sixteen

Bella spooned three sugars into her mug to disguise the taste of Ron's dark brown tea and contemplated the letter from BestBuys supermarkets.

'They *have* lodged an official planning application, as we thought. They say there will be a statutory period of consultation, starting after Christmas. They also say that if the application is granted, the allotment tenants will be given three months' notice to leave.'

'So I'll be able to plant my spring peas?' said Ron eagerly.

Yes, but I don't think you'll get to eat them, thought Bella, feeling a sharp stab of sympathy for the old man.

'I think we'll start writing a letter of objection now, Ron. It wouldn't hurt for the councillors to get it as soon as they receive the planning application. And in a couple of weeks I'll do a story about you all facing eviction to whip up some public sympathy. You need to talk to the other allotment holders and make sure they write in too,' she told him.

'Cyril's really upset. He said we should do one of those protest things – a sit-in, I think they're called – when the builders want to start work.'

'You tell him that's a good idea – and another good story. But I really hope it doesn't get that far.' Bella patted the old man's hand.

'I'm sorry you couldn't bring the little 'un, Miss Bella. I saved her some flower pictures from my seed catalogues to cut out. She loves doing that.'

'I'll bring her another time, Ron. It's just that Suzy is up to something. She wanted an excuse to be in my flat because she –' Bella cupped her hand against her mouth and continued in a stage whisper. 'She has a bit of a crush on my neighbour!'

'Ooh,' said Ron, who loved a bit of gossip. 'Is she courting him then? I'll pour you another cup of tea and you can tell me about it.'

Once Ron had been regaled for ten minutes with the antics of Suzy and Roger, causing the twinkle to return to his watery eyes, Bella felt she could go. Besides she was in urgent need of a pee after all that tea and did not fancy using the old man's draughty outside loo, which was linked by a leaky corrugated iron roof to the kitchen.

She sped home, wriggling with increased desperation as she clutched Daisy's steering wheel with one hand and scratched an irritating itch behind her ear with the other. She was eternally grateful when she found a parking space right outside the flat, though it was a bit touch and go when she fumbled to get her key in the lock. 'Make way Suze – it's URGENT!' she yelled as she ran through the kitchen and into the adjacent bathroom, unzipping her jeans on the way.

Every weak-bladdered woman knows the bliss of finally reaching that destination and Bella was no exception. She sat, in utter contentment and pure relief, for a couple of minutes before she realised she had not even said hello to her daughter. She washed her hands and walked across the tiny hallway to the living room. 'That,' she announced, 'is *so* much better.'

'Is it?' said a voice belonging to a totally strange figure which was on its hands and knees next to her sofa. Bella's heart skipped a beat and she felt a huge, prickly hot flush creep up the back of her neck, over her head and finally settle onto her cheeks.

'What the f-flipping hell are you doing here?' she cried, her hands flying up to her mouth.

'I am playing blow football with your daughter, who, incidentally, is a very good shot,' said Jonathan, calmly holding out a straw and a ping pong ball. 'She also has an excellent pair of lungs – which I am sure she has inherited from her mother.'

'Yeah!' agreed Em, flinging up one hand. 'Gimme five, Jonny!'

Jonny? Bella, probably for the first time in her life, was speechless. Her mouth formed a perfect 'O' as her eyes flew from Jonathan to Emily and then from Emily back to Jonathan. Then they darted across to Suzy, who was standing in the doorway wringing a tea towel between her hands.

'So,' said Jonathan. 'What was urgent?'

'I ... er ... needed a pee.'

'Right,' said Jonathan patiently.

'Badly.'

'Right.'

'And how could I have helped?'

'Helped what?'

'Helped you have a pee, as you so delicately put it.'

That diverted Em's attention from blowing her ping pong ball into the shoebox goal. 'Why do you need Jonny to help you have a wee, Mummy? I've been going on my own for *years*.'

Bella stood in the midst of this increasingly surreal little exchange and scratched her head. 'Could we possibly start this conversation again?' she asked weakly.

Suzy took a deep breath. 'Jonathan came round because you left him a message to call you very urgently. When you weren't here he decided to wait and played with Em while I got on with the dinner. Then you came flying in with your trousers undone and shouted it was urgent.

Then...' she shrugged her shoulders. 'Then you had a pee.'

'Ah,' said Bella. Well, put like that... She addressed Jonathan, who had just completed another high five with Em after shooting a blistering goal into the shoebox. Or she spoke to his backside, to be precise, because that was the most visible bit of him while he was in his goal defence position. 'I did indeed call you before I left work. It was no great emergency. I just wanted to tell you something.'

'Can it wait until we've finished this game?' said Jonathan.

'Sure,' said Bella. She walked calmly to the kitchen where she checked the chicken, turned down the potatoes and fed the cat. Then, flinging her arms in the air, she threw back her head, opened her mouth and let out a very long, very silent scream. Why, whenever she was near this man, did she turn into a complete and utter idiot? Every other part of her life was normal, to the extent of being boring; she managed to talk nicely to people without turning into a gibbering wreck, she could sit next to them without falling asleep and slobbering on their shoulder and she could spend time in their company without feeling like she wanted to throttle them.

Why was bloody Jonathan so bloody different?

And now he'd met Em, whom she had tried, God knows why, to keep a secret from him. At least that seemed to be a success though – they were getting on like a house on fire. Probably because they were the same mental age, thought Bella, hurling some green beans in a pan.

Suzy came bustling through. 'What could I do, Bel?' she said, spreading her hands. 'He insisted on coming in to wait. But Em's had a great time. And...' she squinted across the hallway, 'and he's got a lovely bum!'

Bella sidled a bit closer to have a crafty peek. Em spotted her immediately. 'I'm starving, Mum. Is dinner nearly ready?' she piped up.

Two pairs of eyes, one greeny-grey and one startling blue, surveyed Bella expectantly.

'Yes,' she said. 'Er, would you like to eat with us, Jonathan?'

Jonathan wolfed down a plate of roast chicken, mashed potato, vegetables and gravy as if he was a starving man and, even though he protested he never ate desserts, he managed a respectable two helpings of home-made apple crumble – courtesy of Suzy's mum's freezer.

'That the best meal I've had for ages. It was more than worth me dashing over here for your non-emergency, Bella.'

'Was I worth it too?' asked Em, engrossed in making rivers of custard in her crumble.

'You, young lady, were absolutely worth it. Even if you did just slaughter me on that last penalty. You're very good, you know. Do you play football too – proper football?'

'Yep. I'm in the school under-sevens. We're playing on Saturday – Downside Juniors at home – and we are going to kick their butts!'

'EMILY!' shouted Bella and Suzy in unison while Jonathan let out a great snort of laughter.

'Good girl,' he said approvingly.

Em cocked her head on one side and considered him for a long moment. Jonathan met her gaze steadily.

'Would you like to come and watch me play?' she asked.

'I would be honoured to,' replied the detective courteously.

Hello! Excuse me! I'm here, thought Bella. I'm this child's mother and I don't think I want to spend my Saturday with you at a children's football match. Do I get a say in this?

Jonathan turned to her. 'Would that be OK – if I watched her play?'

Bella looked at Em's ecstatic little face. 'Of course,' she said. 'But wear thick clothes. It's freezing on that football field.'

'Yes Mum,' quipped Jonathan. It was funny to think Bella was a mum, actually. How very different she was from his own efficient but unaffectionate mother, he thought, watching her hug her daughter as she wiped the sticky little face with damp kitchen roll. He had misjudged her at first, thinking she was a pleasure-seeking girl about town who breezed through life leaving a trail of broken-hearted men in her wake. But all the time she was stuck at home looking after a child. She's done a good job though – the kid seemed very well mannered. And very cute.

It didn't look as if there was much money about though, he thought, his sharp eyes taking in the old-fashioned cooker, the worn but clean lino on the floor and the chipped paintwork around the window. But he liked the way she had jumbled all those brightly coloured plates on that old dresser and pinned up her daughter's paintings of rainbows and funny stick-limbed people on the wall – it made it look like home, somehow. Well, like a home *ought* to be, he thought, remembering the gleaming and sterile stainless steel and granite kitchen in the house he had just signed up to rent.

As if in defiance at the mere thought of anything sterile, Thomas did his usual post-dinner trick of jumping up onto the table to sniff the empty dishes and Bella scooped him off in one single, practised movement that told Jonathan she had done it a thousand times before. Tail bristling, the cat gave an indignant mew and jumped up onto the worktop instead. Bella left him and flicked the kettle on. 'Coffee?'

'That would be great. Then I really must go.'

Back to the beautiful blonde bombshell, thought Bella.

Who would doubtless be reclining on an elegant sofa, immaculately dressed and made up, sipping a gin and tonic while she waited for her lover to return.

'I hope your girlfriend won't have cooked for you,' she said, unable to resist just a tiny little prod.

'Madeleine? God, you must be joking! She couldn't cook to save her life!'

Hah! Bella felt a warm glow of victory but didn't quite understand why. 'Shall we have coffee in the living room?' she asked rather primly, feeling like her mother.

Em slid off her chair and scooted off to her bedroom to find her Barbie footballers to show her new friend. Bella, Suzy and Jonathan followed more sedately. Oh dear, I wish I'd tidied up, thought Bella, surveying the jumbled, suddenly shabby-looking room. She saw Em's books strewn across the coffee table, a nit comb on the floor, a dog-eared teddy on the armchair, a green felt-tip pen mark on the wall and a pair of pink, age 6 knickers sitting, somewhat incongruously, on top of the television.

This room feels like home too, thought Jonathan approvingly. He saw the warm terracotta walls that had taken Bella five whole evenings to paint, the soft cream throw draped over the sofa, the cosy jumble of cushions, the bright reddish rug on the floor and the warm glow emitted by the old-fashioned gas fire. He leaned back in the armchair and gave a contented sigh, closing his eyes for a couple of seconds.

'Do you like Barbies?' said Em, suddenly hitching herself up onto his lap with a little backward wriggle. Jonathan had never had a child on his lap before. It felt strange, all warm and heavy but somehow light and fragile at the same time. She smelled of soap and wax crayons and her hair tickled his nose.

'What's a Barbie?' he said.

Em thrust a naked plastic page three girl under his

nose. It had mud on its face, a sickly pink smile and grubby blonde hair that stood up in spiky tufts. Jonathan considered it carefully. 'No,' he said, 'I don't think I do.'

'Nor do I,' confided Em, wriggling back comfortably into his chest. 'But I pretend this one is Emmanuel Eboue.'

'But Emmanuel Eboue is black.'

'I did say *pretend*. He doesn't have boobies either.'

'No,' agreed Jonathan, 'he doesn't.'

Suzy giggled. 'Em's a big Arsenal fan, I'm afraid. She re-enacts their matches with her Barbies, but her ambition is to go and see them play for real.'

'Right,' said Jonathan, shooting a sudden glance at Bella, who had the grace to blush and lower her head. Little brother indeed! Why had she been so reluctant to tell him she had a kid?

'Well, I think you've got great taste, Em. Arsenal's a good team.' He tightened his arms round the skinny little body in an instinctive hug. Oh God – where did that come from? Why was he suddenly doing this hugging stuff? Was it all right to go around cuddling other people's kids? Bloody hell – what was wrong with him? One freckled-faced little kid and he'd gone all soft and ga-ga. Time to beat a retreat.

He lifted Emily gently off his lap, drained his coffee in three big gulps and stood up. 'Goodness is that the time? I must go. I'll be late. Loads of work to get through...'

'OK,' said Bella, breathing a sigh of relief.

Outside the flat, with Emily's plea for him to come and visit again soon still echoing in his head, Jonathan took a long deep breath and slowly scratched his head. Well, that had certainly been a new experience. He jumped in his car and drove uncharacteristically slowly back to the station, his mind racing with images of mashed potatoes, fat tabby cats, freckle-faced kids and rosy-cheeked women bearing apple crumbles. When he reached his destination he gave himself a mental shake. Get a grip, you big wussy, he told himself sternly. Get down that pub with the lads and have a pint.

While Jonathan was in the King's Arms, steadily downing pints of best bitter with Boz, who had needed no persuading to abandon his paperwork, Madeleine was trying to apply her new siren-red lipstick to a mouth that was set in a pursed, angry line. Once again it was 8.30pm, she had been on her own in this godforsaken dump all day and there was no sign of Jonathan coming home to entertain her. Not that he was entertaining lately; he was downright boring in fact.

The bedroom action was non-existent too. She had planned a big seduction scene on Saturday night, to celebrate signing for the new house, but even that hadn't worked. She had put on her new purple dress, booked a romantic table for two, and made sizzling, sparkly conversation so vivaciously that it gave her a headache. But when they got back to the hotel Jonathan had brushed her aside, grabbed one of his boring textbooks and mumbled something about fingerprints on plastics. Talk about a damp squib.

Then there was that red-haired girl at the ball – the one in that funny green retro dress. Madeleine narrowed her eyes as she remembered the touching little scene she had interrupted in the bar, the pair of them gazing intently at each other like something huge and unspoken was hanging between them. She was no fool; she could practically feel the electricity crackling in the air. When she had questioned Jonathan in the cab on the way home he'd said they had been talking about pop stars. Pop stars! He wouldn't know a pop star from his elbow ... *She* was the one who mingled with the rich and famous pop stars. Why, she had stood just two feet away from Elton John at that *Hello!* magazine charity auction.

Madeleine pursed her lips even tighter. She was simply not the kind of girl to fritter her life away in a three-star hotel in Haybridge, waiting for a man who seemed to prefer the company of his loose-moralled, beer-swigging colleagues to his chic and cultured partner.

Yet he was so damn attractive and there was something so sexy and *caveman* about him when he came in from work with his hair all rumpled, his jaw stubbly and the top button of his shirt open. She wished he would let her wax all that chest hair off though – hairy chests were so passé these days. She bet Cecil waxed his chest.

Madeleine wondered why she suddenly thought of Cecil, the smooth, good-looking PR manager who had paid her so much attention at the ball. He had his own public relations firm, he told her, and he spent half his life socialising at some glitzy function or other. Now there was a man who would appreciate her new £35 lipstick and pink Gucci bag.

The thought of handbags made Madeleine remember her little cream beaded evening bag – and the business card Cecil had slipped into it while Jonathan was having one of his silly gossips with that frumpy little reporter. 'It has my mobile number on – just in case you're bored one evening. I'm sure I could find something to amuse you,' he had said with a wink. The wink was rather common, Madeleine had thought at the time. But the offer was a good one. And she *was* very bored indeed. It would be good to have a man gaze at her adoringly again. And, best of all, Jonathan would be furious and realise exactly what he was missing. He wouldn't dare push her away a second time!

Madeleine, already imagining the tender reconciliation

scene with her jealous caveman, tottered off in her four-inch heels to find her beaded bag.

Suzy was rummaging through her own bag, looking for her lipstick and face powder.

'Why are you putting make-up on, Auntie Suze? Are you going to another ball?' asked a pyjama-clad Em.

'No darling. I just ... just wanted to look nice for you.'

'But I'm going to bed now. I won't see it. That's a waste of lipstick. Mummy gets cross when I waste her lipstick.'

'Well, I wanted you to think of me looking nice when you're all tucked up in bed. Goodnight sweetheart.' Suzy gave the little girl's bottom a firm shove in the direction of her bedroom.

When Bella returned after reading two bedtime stories, Suzy had applied two coats of mascara and was combing her hair amid a cloud of Diorissimo perfume.

'OK Suze. Presumably you are not tarting yourself up in order to spend an evening in my well groomed company.' Bella looked ruefully down at her jeans and baggy polo-neck jumper. 'So what the hell is going on?'

'Nothing. Absolutely nothing. I just thought you could go and see if Roger wanted to come and eat that left-over apple crumble, that's all.'

'*Me?*'

'Yes.'

'Can't you go?'

'No.'

Bella sighed. Her tiny flat was like Piccadilly Circus tonight. First that bloody Jonathan, who couldn't seem to get away fast enough after he'd eaten his food and now Roger, whom Suzy probably planned to seduce right there on her sofa.

'All right,' she said, stomping to the door. 'I'll go and invite him down. Just as long as I don't have to play bloody gooseberry all night.'

'You're certainly prickly enough,' muttered Suzy, blotting her lipstick.

Halfway up the stairs, Bella stopped, scratched her head and cursed loudly. Damn! She had been so busy playing Miss Perfect Hostess she had totally forgotten to tell Jonathan who the murderer was. Bugger!

Chapter Seventeen

'So we've got the wrong bloke, guv?' said Boz the next morning as he and Jonathan bent over a report from the fingerprint department.

'Probably not. Just because we haven't found Ricky Thomas's prints on a library card doesn't necessarily rule him out from the scene.'

'And there's no prints on the key and lipstick?'

'No – nothing distinct enough to compare, anyway.'

Boz frowned. 'Could he have worn gloves?'

'No. There's no evidence of glove prints and there were no glove fibres round the neck. He wouldn't take them off to strangle her and put them back on to chuck her possessions over the hedge.'

'Good point,' said Boz. 'Could he have tipped the things out of the bag without touching them?'

'No. I saw them in position and they were too far apart. They were thrown, probably separately.'

'Thrown like someone was in a temper?'

'Yes,' said Jonathan, imagining the killer's lips set in a snarl, his arm raised back over his head, preparing to hurl away the evidence into the darkness.

Could mummy's boy Ricky Thomas, with his skinny wrists, puny build and pathetically fake gangster's accent really have worked himself up into such a lethal temper? Jonathan had an appointment in a few minutes with some leftie social workers who ran the Anger Management Classes. He would soon find out.

It was the other prints on the plastic laminated library

card that were a worry, he mused as he drove to Haybridge Social Services Department. A distinct thumb print on one side and a forefinger print on the other, like someone had grasped it firmly – as if they were going to throw it. But the police fingerprint database had come up with no known match. They were certainly nothing like Carla's and neither did they match the prints of the four Haybridge librarian ladies, with whom Jonathan had spent a pleasant hour or so doing his little roll, pad, press routine a few days previously. But two strange prints on a much-handled library card were not enough to let Ricky Thomas off the hook at this stage.

Besides, Jonathan was positive the young Jamaican was lying about something – and he was determined to find out exactly what it was.

The two social workers introduced themselves as Kate Spencer, head of the department, and Jane Grimsby, Anger Management therapy co-ordinator. And very solemn young ladies they were too, thought Jonathan, eyeing their flat shoes and frumpy calf-length skirts as they led the way along endless corridors to the interview room. That Jane one had quite a nice bottom though; shame it was half covered up with that bulky cardigan thing.

The interview room walls were covered in brightly coloured posters which, amid a liberal scattering of user-friendly exclamation marks, urged the reader to use condoms, quit drugs, say no to sexual diseases, beat bullying and avoid crime. By the window there was a huge notice board giving details of rehab centres, STI clinics, teenage mums drop-in centres and victim support helplines. They're fighting a losing battle, thought Jonathan, with a stab of sympathy.

'So, tell me about Ricky Thomas. What sort of kid is he?' he said.

'He is a fairly average representation of the young persons we deal with in today's angry youth culture and consumer society,' answered Jane.

Oh dear, I should have brought an interpreter, thought Jonathan dismally.

'Young people like Ricky have low self-esteem,' said Kate helpfully. 'They want to make something of themselves and they want to feel good about themselves but they don't know how to go about doing it, usually because no one shows them how. They fail at school, they find it difficult to get a job and then they get angry with themselves and resort to violent behaviour. Or crime. Or drugs – sometimes all three. Then they get into trouble with the police and authorities and then they lose even more self-esteem and people start treating them like a criminal – so they behave even more like one. It is a vicious circle, I'm afraid, but we do the best that we can to break that circle.'

You are a very caring young lady, thought Jonathan, thinking back to the wise old cop who had nipped his own rebellious little vicious circle in the bud all those years ago.

Ricky, said the social workers, was not an extreme case. He had been surly at first when the magistrates ordered him to attend the Anger Management classes, but as the course went on he opened up more and more.

'Much of his anger was directed, rather unusually, towards the National Health Service, because his mother was in so much pain waiting for a hip operation,' explained Kate.

'But that could have been a deferred anger from another more deep-seated issue such as early childhood negativity,' chipped in Jane.

Both Kate and Jonathan ignored her.

'How did he feel about his relationship with Carla Kapochkin?' asked Jonathan.

Jane took a deep breath. 'It seemed inconsequential. There were no apparent relevant issues about it. He made spasmodic references to her, using the machismo terminology typically adopted by young persons of his age and background. But she seemed to neither aggravate nor enhance his behavioural pattern.'

'So he wasn't that fired up about her then?'

'No,' said Kate with a smile.

They chatted on about the classes, Ricky's behaviour and his previous convictions.

'He told us during his assessment interview that he didn't keep the goods he stole on the theft charges. He sold them and gave the money to his mother because her hip was playing up and she couldn't work. So he can't be all bad,' said kind-hearted Kate.

Even murderers love their mothers, thought Jonathan.

Walking back along the corridors, Kate put a tentative hand on his arm. 'I think you know a friend of mine. Bella Smart. She ... she mentioned your name.'

Ah, thought Jonathan. So that's how the little devil got to Ricky before me – she had a mole in social services. Who doesn't that girl know in this town?

'Yes, I know Bella. And her daughter.'

'Ah, Emily! She's a lovely child. Although she does need a little bit of work on her gender issues. Sometimes she imagines she is not a female.'

'She thinks she's a boy?'

'Well, she does sometimes assume the male role...'

'What's wrong with that? I think she's great just the way she is!' said Jonathan defensively and, for him, rather hotly.

Well, thought Kate. That's an interesting reaction. Wait until she told Bella!

*　*　*

Bella was having a good day. She deserved it after the lousy night she'd had, tossing and turning until the small hours while thoughts of murderers, ghostly white bodies and grinning Jamaican faces whirled feverishly through her mind. It happened like that – just when she thought the image of poor dead Carla was beginning to fade it would pop up and hit her again with renewed horror.

It hadn't helped that the evening had been so strange. First there was the shock of Jonathan appearing larger than life, on his hands and knees in her living room, then she had had to sit through almost two hours of Roger and Suzy behaving like blushing, tongue-tied adolescents on her sofa.

Inexplicably they had hardly been able to talk to each other but had communicated through Bella, as if she was some kind of safe, neutral interpreter. Normally they would slouch around, watch the television and make idle chit-chat but last night Roger had been determined to maintain a stilted, almost formal conversation.

'I had a good time at the ball,' he said politely.

'Good,' Bella replied.

'I had a good time too.' That was Suze, sounding almost coy.

 'Good,' Bella repeated.

'I enjoyed the dancing,' Roger persisted.

'Good.'

'I enjoyed the dancing too,' said Suze.

The evening had carried on in that vein. For God's sake, what was wrong with the pair of them? Perhaps Bella should have just walked out and left them to it but every time she tried to sidle off Suzy shot her a desperate glance from the sofa. Finally, at 11pm, just when Bella was dreading the next awkward silence and wondering whether she could keep her eyes open any longer, her two friends had stood up to leave, carefully inching around each other in the tiny hallway. Bella had closed the door gratefully behind them. Part of her itched to peep out and see if Roger plucked up the courage to repeat his uncharacteristic snogging act on the pavement but most of her just wanted to collapse in bed and sleep for ever.

Sleep had eluded her though and she woke up from her final fitful doze just before 6am. On the plus side, this meant she had time to wash and blow-dry her hair and make herself look passably decent for once. She had ironed her best cream trousers and teamed them with a dainty camisole top and a soft pale pink cardigan. Even her stomach looked obediently flat – it must be all those calories she had burned up tossing and turning. Having once again failed miserably on her Monday morning diet resolution, she decided to give it another shot today; perhaps a Tuesday was a better day. She would try that new all protein, no carbohydrate thing that all the celebrities were raving on about. She could eat as much meat, cheese and eggs as she liked and she would be at least three pounds lighter by the end of the week!

At work she nobly refused the mid-morning doughnuts Mick, the sports editor, had bought to celebrate his team's win at the weekend and concentrated on rattling out a story about a shortage of bed space at the local hospital instead. Then Sean had actually *congratulated* her on a tight, factual story – meaning of course that she usually overwrote chronically – and sent her out on another decent little story about a pensioner fighting off a mugger in Dower Grove.

By now Bella's thoughts were taken up by her stomach, which was rumbling loudly after her toast-less boiled egg for breakfast and badly missing its 11am sugar and carb fix. She tried to ignore it as she steered Daisy to Dower Grove and almost missed the fact that Trent Drive was right opposite. She slowed down, straining to see number

196

36, and suddenly felt her heart beat a little tattoo of triumph. Yes! Emerging from the door, struggling to get a large blue buggy down the step with one hand and hold on to a small girl with the other, was a tall, frowning man with wispy fair hair. It could only be the sinister Mr Williams! Without hesitation, Bella parked up a few yards down the road and, grabbing her bag just in case she needed her nail file for self-defence, walked eagerly to meet her murderer.

'Hi, let me help you!' she cried, seizing the buggy from the front and manoeuvring it efficiently down the step. Little George Williams looked up at her solemnly, one moist thumb stuck in his mouth.

'Hello gorgeous,' Bella stooped to address Amelia, whose big brown eyes responded with a vacant stare of non-recognition. 'I met you and your mummy at the Halloween party. I'm Bella.' The brown eyes did not change their expression. Oops, perhaps she'd better try her luck with Mr Williams before she made a total fool of herself, Bella thought. Quick ... think of a plausible excuse to be here. She straightened up and smiled her most professional smile.

'I was coming round to see your wife, actually. I spoke to her, as I said, at the Halloween party the week before last. I'm from the *Haybridge Gazette* and your wife was very kindly helping me with my investigations about Carla.' She dropped her voice to a whisper for the last word.

'My wife is at work today. She says it is my turn to look after the children,' said Mr Williams curtly.

'Ah. Perhaps you could help me instead. I just want to clarify a few points,' Like whether you seduced your au pair then strangled her.

Ian Williams was not a stupid man. He recognised the skill with which Bella had dealt with the cumbersome buggy and the practised, easy way she had spoken to his daughter. Here was a woman who clearly knew about small children and maybe here was a woman who could make his job easier for the next half an hour or so. God knows he needed a hand with the little monsters, who had been running him ragged all morning with their incessant whining and demands for drinks, potties, biscuits and nose wipes. He narrowed his eyes and surveyed the red curls and curvy figure. Hmm, not a bad looker too.

'We're just on our way to the burger bar down the road for lunch. Why don't you join us and we can talk there?' he said.

Bella blinked. This was the second time in two days she would be eating with a suspected murderer. She contemplated whether the burger bar would sell her a cheeseburger with the roll. 'OK,' she said. 'I'd like that.'

Instinctively she took Amelia's hand when they crossed the road and was touched when the child looked up with a shy smile and left her tiny hand trustingly in Bella's larger one as they walked along the leaf-strewn street. Mr Williams was occupied with steering the buggy straight and did not speak until they reached the burger bar and he was bending down wrestling with George's straps. 'Bloody things,' he cursed. 'Why is everything to do with children so damn fiddly?'

'I thought you were getting a new au pair to look after them,' ventured Bella.

'We did. And she legged it back to the agency after two days. Said her room wasn't big enough and the TV wasn't a colour one. They expect the world, these girls.'

'Let me help,' offered Bella, clipping open the straps and scooping up George, holding the chunky little body comfortably against her hip.

Ian Williams strode off to order, bluntly refusing Bella's offer to pay for her own meal. 'Chips with your burger?' he asked.

198

'No thanks,' she replied, thinking wistfully of the golden, crispy fries, glistening with fat and a little scattering of salt. Oh, to hell with this stupid diet – the press is always saying celebrities are too thin, anyway. 'Actually, yes please,' she said.

Only when Amelia and George had finished toying with their respective lunches and Bella had mopped the ketchup from their faces and steered them in the direction of a nearby plastic Wendy House, did she dare to bring up the subject of the murdered au pair again. 'So, did you get on well with Carla?'

Ian Williams looked up in surprise. 'Get on well? Well, I suppose so. I didn't take much notice of her really. But she seemed an efficient enough girl. Damned nuisance when she disappeared like that though.'

'Did you talk much to her? In the evenings?'

'Good lord no. I exchanged the usual pleasantries, naturally. A couple of times she asked me about college courses and got me to sign some sort of application form.'

'College courses? Was she going to college?'

'She said she wanted to study computers at some fancy college or something. I'm in the computer business myself. But I wasn't really paying much attention, to be honest. I don't have time to chat much with childminders. Anyway, usually she stayed in her room in the evenings – or she went out with that young bloke who killed her.'

'We don't know that he killed her yet. He hasn't been charged,' said Bella, who suddenly felt quite defensive of Ricky Thomas.

'Nasty piece of work though. I reckon he gave her a hard time. I remember she came back in tears one night when I was just going to bed and I asked if she'd had a row with him.'

'What did she say?'

'Something about man trouble – how you couldn't trust

them. I told her she ought to find a proper man, not some runt of a kid.'

'What did she say?'

'Nothing, actually. She just started crying again and bolted off up the stairs... I probably said the wrong thing but I'm not very good at dealing with this female stuff.'

Bella changed tack: 'Your wife was saying how much hassle it was dealing with all the police after Carla was found.'

'They were everywhere. I thought we'd never get rid of them. And you'd never believe the questions they ask – anyone would think it was me that killed her!'

Bella bit her lip. 'Your wife was cross because they trampled mud into her new carpet...'

'Yes. She wasn't too pleased, I remember.'

'Did it stain? It does on some colour carpets. What colour is yours?'

'Uh? A greeny sort of colour I think. And I think Caroline managed to get it off.' He sounded mildly surprised at the sudden domestic turn.

Bella steered the conversation back to slightly more normal ground. 'The police say some clothes and personal items were missing from Carla's room – which was why you weren't too worried at first when she disappeared.'

'Yes, we thought she'd packed a bag and gone off for the weekend or something. Her washing stuff and some clothes had gone apparently. My wife dealt with that side of things though – that's women's stuff.'

'Good,' said Bella abruptly. 'Shall I help you get George back in his buggy now?'

She also helped zip the children into their coats, steered the buggy safely home and heaved it back over the doorstep before she bid Ian Williams goodbye, and, with a special little wave to Amelia, made her way back to her car.

Everyone knew men were hopeless with colours, she

thought, as she drove the short distance to the pensioner's house in Dower Grove. Green, grey, greenish, greyish – it was all the same to blokes, she thought as she knocked on the door of an old stone cottage.

A grey-haired, apple-cheeked old lady answered, wiping her floury hands on a pristine white apron. This couldn't be better, thought Bella – she was everybody's granny epitomised and the readers would adore her. Gently she explained she was from the *Gazette* and wanted to do a story about her being so brave with that horrible mugger.

'Cheeky little git!' cackled the granny in a broad cockney accent. 'Tried to grab my bleedin' bag, he did. There was no way he was going to nick my flippin' pension so I kicked 'im in the wotsits!'

Bella blinked, then gave a broad grin. 'Can I come in Mrs ...?'

'Bugger off!' came an even louder cackle from inside. The old lady ignored it.

'Mrs Vapolluci. Italian blood, my Freddie was. And nice little backside he had on 'im too.' Mrs Vapolluci gave a broad wink.

'Freddie was my third 'usband. The one before him, Del, was one of them karate nuts. Fifteen years younger than me 'e was. He legged it with a barmaid, a right little tart, but he taught me a couple of them karate moves before 'e went,' she informed Bella as they made their way to an airy kitchen, where a round blob of pastry was waiting to be rolled out on a generously floured table.

Mrs Vapolluci hitched up her lilac skirt. 'I lifted me leg like this!' She stuck out one plump stockinged leg. 'And I went WHAM – right in the little bugger's privates.' She shot out a foot, causing her blue, fluffy slipper to fly across the room. Ignoring it, she seized the rolling pin. 'Then I went WHACK on 'is 'ead with me shopping bag.' She smashed the rolling pin against the edge of the table with a resounding thwack. 'And I had two tins of kidney beans in it. 'E let out a right old squawk,' she added proudly.

Bella winced. 'Good for you,' she said, moving to pick up the slipper. 'Do you mind if I take some notes?'

'Bugger off!' went the cackle, louder this time, from a room opposite.

'Shut up Alfie!' shouted the old lady. 'You go ahead, me duck.'

Bella, slightly worried about the temperamental Alfie in the other room, rummaged for her notepad and flew through her interview. 'Could I send a photographer round to get a picture of you, Mrs Vapolluci?' she asked at the end.

'Ooh yes. That would be lovely. You could get our Alfie in the picture too. Come and take a look at 'im.'

She led the way into a tiny sitting room, where a row of china dogs sat proudly on the mantelpiece, flanked by two overstuffed floral armchairs. In the corner was a large cage, in which was perched a massive red and blue parrot, one leg daintily poised in mid air while it contemplated its visitor with two beady eyes.

'Well, hello,' smiled Bella. 'Aren't you cute?' It was no surprise when she was promptly told, in no uncertain terms, to bugger off again. 'Does he say anything else?' she asked.

As if on cue Alfie shuffled on his perch and declared: 'Get 'em off gorgeous!'

'Oops, sorry. 'E got that from Freddie,' giggled Mrs Vapolluci.

'I'd better let you get back to your pastry,' said Bella reluctantly. 'Are you making a pie?'

'I am, me duck. I'm trying to use up them windfall apples from me garden. Don't like to see 'em go to waste.

Perhaps you'd like to take some 'ome with you?' She shuffled off to find a carrier bag.

'This is a lovely garden,' said Bella, helping to pick up the Bramleys. But obviously far too big for you to cope with alone, she thought, surveying the weeds and brambles.

'Yes. My Freddie was the gardener. I 'ate it. Breaks me nails something rotten,' said the old lady, extending one liver spotted but beautifully manicured hand.

Bella grinned, hoping she would be like Mrs Vapolluci when she was seventy-eight. Clutching her bag of apples, she said her goodbyes and, still smiling, drove back to the office. That was what she loved about this job, she decided: you got to meet some real characters.

Chapter Eighteen

Jonathan drew himself up to his full height, squared his shoulders and looked his Superintendent straight in the eye. 'Well, if you can't get me any extra officers I will do the bloody burglary patrols myself. Starting tonight. Sir.' The last word was an afterthought.

Superintendent Nixon folded his hands together and leaned back in his leather chair. 'We have deployed two officers in the incident room for the murder, DS Wright, as well as two extra civilians to deal with the paperwork. We cannot justify any more. And neither can I justify you taking time off from a murder enquiry to ride around looking for burglars – which is a uniform job anyway. We will have to be patient and we have to think of our budget,' he continued. 'As soon as that Ricky Thomas chappie is charged then we can reshuffle our men and concentrate on the burglaries.'

'Then I will do the patrols in my off-duty time. Sir.' Again that pause. But maybe it was time to put the squeeze on. 'I fear that if we are not seen by the public to be doing anything proactive about this situation then we could be in for some bad press. I understand from my contacts in the media that the people of Haybridge are becoming somewhat impatient and they need to see their police force is tackling the problem.'

Superintendent Nixon frowned. Oh dear, he couldn't afford a bout of bad publicity now, of all times. Not when he had just filed his application for that Chief Super-intendent's post at the other side of the county. Public image was everything these days. And if this rather arrogant young officer was offering to do extra patrols without clocking up overtime and affecting his end of year budget... Perhaps there could even be an *advantage* or two here?

'You have my permission to go ahead, on a trial run, for one evening. Oh, and you may want to arrange to take one of your contacts from the media with you. They could write a little feature – just to show our public how proactive our policing can be.'

'Thank you. Sir,' said Jonathan, making a dignified exit, already rehearsing in his head the speech he would make to his media contact.

'Tonight?' said Bella. It was Wednesday. She had been writing boring council reports all day and she had arranged for Kate and Suzy to come round for a girlie night at 8pm. She'd already bought the chocolate.

'Is it going to be a problem getting a baby-sitter? asked Jonathan. 'We wouldn't start until about 11pm and I only need you for a couple of hours.'

Need? Now that was a new concept. 'Er ... no. I could arrange a sitter.' Well Suzy and Kate would be there anyway. And Suzy, given her current little obsession with Roger, would probably be only too willing to stay until late.

'So I'll pick you up at quarter to eleven? From your flat?'

'OK,' said Bella weakly. It was all in the line of duty.

'What are you going to wear?' asked Suzy, as soon as she got in the door, clutching a bottle of wine, a packet of chicken breasts and a jar of pasta sauce.

'I hadn't thought about that,' said Bella, who had indeed been thinking about nothing else ever since Jonathan had phoned.

'Let me do the supper and amuse Em while you go and have a soak in the bath. Then we'll go through your wardrobe,' offered her friend. 'Kate can help us choose your clothes.' She frowned. 'Or perhaps not.'

Bella kissed her on the cheek and sped off. An uninterrupted bath was too good an offer to refuse. She might even have a chance to shave her legs.

Lying back luxuriously amid a cloud of bubbles – courtesy of Emily's new Bob the Builder bubble bath – she played back the conversation with Ian Williams in her mind and silently rehearsed how she would break the news to Jonathan that he was questioning the wrong man. Even he couldn't ignore the evidence. All he needed to do was pop into Trent Drive, get a sample from the living room carpet and the case would be solved. She lay back complacently imagining Mr Williams cracking and confessing all... 'I knew my time was up when that reporter started questioning me,' he would admit.

Bella's daydream was interrupted by the sound of Kate arriving and Suzy and Em going into raptures over the pudding she had brought with her. She could also smell those chicken breasts sizzling away in the pan and suddenly felt starving. She reached for a towel.

After supper, which Bella ate in her somewhat threadbare white bathrobe, they decamped to the bedroom, where Emily perched on the bed between Suzy and Kate.

'Jeans,' said Suze decisively. 'Preferably tight black ones – and a black jumper like those sassy female private eyes wear on telly.'

'I've only got one pair of black jeans and they have a hole in the knee,' said Bella, producing the dog-eared specimens.

'How about those white ones then?' said Suzy, pouncing on a pair of skin-tight jeans Bella had bought half price in the summer sales on a thin day.

'God, I can hardly sit down in those. And I have to sort of tuck my tummy in because it hangs over the waistband.'

'Try them on.' It was an order.

Bella struggled into the jeans, wishing she had not eaten quite so much pasta and strawberry Pavlova.

Sure enough there was a half-inch gap where the zip ought to do up.

'Lie down on the bed,' said Suze. 'Right girls – *heave...*' The zip groaned into place and Bella, feeling as if she had a straitjacket around her abdomen, stood up gingerly.

'Does my bum look huge?' she said.

'No, it looks good. It holds it all in. Quite sexy, in fact,' declared Suze, causing Emily to dance around the bedroom in fits of giggles shouting 'Sexy bum! Sexy bum!'

'Sweetheart, everyone has bottoms. It is only a part of the female anatomy,' said Kate with a frown. Em ignored her.

'Now a top. How about this?' Suzy rummaged through Bella's drawer and produced a black Lycra, long-sleeved T-shirt with a scoop neckline.

'That makes my boobs look like two wobbly blancmange mountains,' said Bella, who had bought the top also in a half-price sale.

'Try it on.'

Suzy stood back and surveyed the result, her arms folded across her chest. 'Put your shoulders back. Hmm, it looks good. Sassy yet sexy. Just like something out of an American cop programme.'

'Are you sure you wouldn't be more comfortable in something less *fitted*?' asked Kate anxiously.

'No, this will have to do,' said Bella. 'Though Christ knows where I'll put my gun...'

* * *

The evening wore on, painfully slowly as far as Bella was concerned. Even a bout of not-so-gentle prodding about Suzy's feelings for Roger – met with a stubborn refusal to admit anything – failed to provide much of a distraction from the funny jittery feeling she had in her tummy. At 10.45pm sharp the doorbell rang. 'Your date awaits,' quipped Suze.

'He is *not* my date!' Bella flounced to answer the door. She thought Jonathan looked surprisingly sexy in a tight white T-shirt which outlined his chest, a battered brown leather jacket which emphasised the width of his shoulders and comfortably worn-in jeans which emphasised ... well, she didn't want to think about that. His hair was slightly ruffled and he had a two-day stubble on his jaw. Unlike Bella, Jonathan had given no thought whatsoever about what he was going to wear, simply flinging off his formal work suit and grabbing the nearest clean items. But he had an inkling he looked good because Madeleine was pawing all over him before he left, making those irritating little purring noises in his ear. She had been acting really strange lately, he thought – ever since he had got back from the pub late the other night and she wasn't in.

He had been quite relieved actually. It was the night he had stayed to supper with Bella and met Emily. It had thrown him off guard a bit and, after the boys' talk in the pub, he had fancied a quiet half an hour of contemplation to gather his thoughts. But Madeleine had returned a few minutes later, dressed up to the nines, and announced she had been out.

'Right,' he'd said. Well it was obvious she had, wasn't it? Then she said she'd had a lovely time in the wine bar with some friends.

'That's nice,' he'd said.

'One of them was a man. Cecil – from the ball.'

Jonathan had smirked. He couldn't help it. 'Oh, Theshhill! I remember him!'

Then Madeleine had given a great tut and stomped off into the bedroom, where she spent the next hour sighing theatrically while he tried to get some sleep. He had obviously done something wrong but he couldn't understand what. Surely she hadn't expected him to get all jealous and possessive over some ineffectual wimp called Cecil? Bloody women. They were all mad if you asked him...

Bella looked good tonight though. Nice jeans. He motioned gallantly for her to go through the living room door. 'After you,' he said.

Nice gesture, thought Bella with a little glow.

Nice arse, thought Jonathan, with a grin.

He shook Kate's hand and told her it was lovely to see her again. Then he shook Suzy's hand and said he hoped she didn't mind babysitting. Then Bella shrugged on a denim jacket, grabbed her bag and a notebook from the coffee table and they were ready to drive off in Jonathan's surprisingly ordinary-looking and slightly grubby Ford Escort.

'So, we'll hover around the town centre area keeping a nice, low profile for an hour or so and then we'll park up and take a little wander round the back of the shops. Finally we'll find a dark spot where we can sit in the car, with the lights off, and watch quietly for a while. The aim is to stay inconspicuous but if we are noticed, we have to look natural – as though we have a reason to be there. That, Bella, is the art of surveillance.'

I know *that*. I was fine doing my own surveillance until you barged in, thought Bella. She resisted the urge to tell him so and chatted neutrally about the buildings they were passing instead.

'That's the old water tower over there.' She pointed to

a crumbling round tower set in its own gated field. 'The water board got permission to knock it down and build apartments but the local historical society members chained themselves to the gatepost and refused to let the bulldozers through. It was a great story!'

'Did they win?'

'Yes. The members went to the Secretary of State and persuaded him to make it a listed building. The water board, sensing bad publicity, withdrew the application and apologised. We had a pic of everyone shaking hands and making up – "Water Under the Bridge" was the headline.'

Jonathan chuckled. 'You know the town well. You've obviously been here a long time.'

'All my life. That's where I went to school.' Bella pointed. 'And over there on the right is the sweet shop where I committed my first – and last – crime when I was twelve. I stole a packet of bubble gum but I felt so guilty I couldn't eat it. The next day I crept back and put it back on the shelf!'

Jonathan laughed again, imagining the cocky, flame-haired schoolgirl pocketing the gum and then looking at it in horror afterwards.

'I stole something once,' he said.

He had never told a soul before about his teenage brush with the law but he found himself relating the story to Bella, repeating the old Sergeant's lecture word for word. Then he talked briefly about his emotionless relationship with his parents and how desperate he was to get away to police college.

'Do you see your parents much now?' Bella asked, finding it hard to imagine life without her own family.

'Only the odd duty visit really. I never really know what to say to them,' said Jonathan.

How terribly, terribly sad, thought Bella, picturing the three tight-lipped Wrights sitting around a silent lunch table on Christmas Day, politely asking each other to pass the salt. How different from her own chaotic Christmases, where her parents' already cluttered house was filled to bursting with laughing, chattering bodies wearing stupid hats, exchanging joke presents and playing endless games of noisy charades. 'Are you going home for Christmas this year?'

'No. I'll be spending it with Madeleine. In our new house,' said Jonathan curtly.

Oh, thought Bella. A second picture sprang into her mind. She saw Jonathan and Madeleine entwined lovingly on their expensive sofa next to a twinkling designer tree bedecked with carefully colour-schemed decorations. They would raise their champagne glasses to each other as classical music tinkled in the background and Jonathan would hand Madeleine a tiny, beautifully wrapped box. She would open it and gasp with pleasure at the huge, sparkling diamond within and slowly, with that sexy smile, Jonathan would lower himself down onto one knee...

She swallowed hard and vowed not to ask any more questions.

'So what did you want to talk to me about?' said Jonathan suddenly. 'When you phoned and left a message which wasn't urgent after all?' He took his eyes off the road and smiled across at her.

'Ah,' said Bella. 'I wanted to tell you I've been doing a bit of ... a bit of investigative work about the murder.'

'Why am I not surprised to hear that?'

He was still smiling. That was good. 'I don't think Ricky Thomas did it. I think Ian Williams did.'

'Right.'

The smile had gone. But in for a penny... 'Do you want to hear my theory?'

'Absolutely.'

It came out in a bit of a jumbled rush at first: the

carpet fibres, the new greeny carpet that could so easily be grey, the date with the older man at the golf club, the change in Carla's behaviour, the enforced abortion and finally the terrible, fatal argument. 'And I just know Ian Williams is not a very nice person – he couldn't seem to care less about those two lovely children!' she concluded indignantly.

'Right,' said Jonathan calmly.

Bella kept quiet for as long as she could, waiting for him to comment further. 'Right' – was that all he could bloody say? How dare he 'right' her carefully thought-out theory? She wriggled in her seat until the silence became unbearable. 'So what do you think?'

'I think,' said Jonathan slowly, 'that you did very well. But there are just one or two minor points which may need a little more attention.'

Bella scratched her head and looked at him expectantly.

'Firstly,' he said. 'Ian Williams is not a member of Haybridge and District Golf Club. I checked. Therefore he would not be permitted to drink on the premises himself, let alone arrange a rendezvous with a young girl there.'

Damn, thought Bella.

'Secondly, the new carpet in the Williamses living room is a very definite green. I checked that too. Thirdly, on the night Carla was murdered Ian Williams was away on a computer programming convention in a Leeds hotel with approximately forty other computer geeks who can account for his movements at all times.' Jonathan paused. 'But apart from that, it's a really great theory.'

Don't you patronise me, thought Bella. 'But you obviously thought he could be the murderer too? Or you wouldn't have checked out the carpet and the golf club.' Perhaps she could save a bit of face here.

'I'm a detective. It is my job to check everything.'

'And I'm a reporter and it's my job to write about things – not poke my nose in them,' she said ruefully.

To her surprise Jonathan shot her a playful grin. 'I'm getting kind of accustomed to your nose now,' he said.

Bella had a sudden thought. 'If the golf club is so strictly members only, how did Carla get in?'

Jonathan looked serious. 'That's the big puzzle. She must have been an invited guest of a member. On function nights someone is on the door and the member would have to sign her in. But Kayleigh's sighting, unfortunately, was on an exceptionally quiet and ordinary Tuesday night. I've spoken to the manager and I'm currently ploughing through a list of all 200 members. But only one of them so far has admitted he knew Carla, and that was only as a slight acquaintance.'

'Who is he?'

'Your surveillance buddy. Councillor Hanson.'

'Oh my God! Are you saying Ted Hanson did it?' Bella felt the colour drain from her cheeks. 'But –'

'No buts. Because he didn't do it. On the Tuesday night of the failed rendezvous he was at a planning committee meeting. It had been scheduled for weeks so he never would have arranged a date on that night, would he?'

Bella shook her head dumbly.

'And then there is the small but significant point that, while Carla was being murdered, Councillor Hanson had the best alibi I've ever heard. He was at the golf club, in the function room, presiding over a charity dinner and dance until 2am.' Jonathan paused for dramatic effect. 'And he was sitting two seats away from the Haybridge Superintendent of Police!'

'That's a pretty good alibi,' said Bella. She smiled then suddenly looked serious. 'So do you think Ricky Thomas did kill her, Jonathan?'

I like the way she says my name, thought the detective, who gave the question some serious thought.

'Do *you*?' he said finally.

'No. But I don't suppose my opinion counts much, considering my cock-up with the Ian Williams theory.'

'I'd still like to hear it.' The tone was surprisingly gentle.

'Well, I think he's far too nice,' obliged Bella. Jonathan's eyebrow shot skywards. She continued: 'And I also think he was not emotionally involved enough with Carla to be fired up enough to kill her. He had no motive and the only thing in life he seems to feel passionate about is his mum's hip operation. I believe he knew nothing about the pregnancy and I think it is highly unlikely the baby was his because he is always so scrupulous – to the point of being paranoid – about using condoms.'

'Bloody hell – you didn't have to get to know him *that* well!' said Jonathan in mock awe. 'You must have one hell of a chat-up technique!'

Bella ignored him. 'I think Carla was two-timing Ricky with another man, who got her pregnant. This man persuaded her to have an abortion and probably offered to pay for it. She sent most of her wages home to her family, did you know? Then, when she kept getting upset about it afterwards, he killed her.'

'She hardly had time to get that upset,' said Jonathan gently. 'She had the pregnancy terminated only a few hours before she died, Bella. It was a professional job, with an anaesthetic, but no private clinic or hospital within a hundred mile radius has any record of her.'

'Oh.' Bella felt a tell-tale prickle behind her eyes. ' That's really odd. And so very, very sad. The whole thing is sad, particularly when she was a girl with so much to look forward to... She'd even got her college course sorted out.'

Jonathan suddenly looked interested. 'Tell me about this college course, my little super sleuth,' he said.

214

Chapter Nineteen

After an hour of cruising around town in Jonathan's car, Bella was beginning to wish she had not worn such tight trousers. No matter how much she fidgeted she couldn't get comfortable. Surreptitiously she placed her handbag on her lap and popped open the button on the waistband. Ah, bliss...

'Better?' grinned eagle-eyed Jonathan, who had always wondered why women didn't just buy bigger sizes. Not that he was complaining about the rear view, of course. And he quite liked the effect all that wriggling had on her top half too.

But apart from Bella's body, there was no movement at all in Haybridge High Street. Not a burglar in sight. It was midnight now – time to park up and take a stroll around. He swung into a secluded spot behind the post office at the bottom of the street and jumped out to hold the passenger door open.

'Shall we walk?' he asked, holding out a hand. Bella took it instinctively before she wondered what the hell she was doing holding hands with a copper in a pitch-dark alleyway in the middle of a feature about burglaries. She dropped it hastily and shoved both hands in her pockets.

'Right. Let's go,' she said briskly and rather louder than she had intended.

'Shh,' said Jonathan, whose hand felt strangely cold and empty now.

'Oh. Sorry,' whispered Bella, promptly walking into a milk crate with a loud clatter.

'I think it's best I guide you until you get your night vision,' said Jonathan, grabbing her hand.

Was Bella imagining it or was his hand sending little electrical charges through her fingers? She tried to ignore it and let her hand relax into his warm, dry palm. A sudden movement made her jump. 'Cat,' whispered Jonathan, pointing to a large ginger tom in a doorway and squeezing her hand.

Together they roamed the back of the shops, Bella averting her eyes when they passed the door of Hanson's newsagents. One side completed, they crossed the road, passing a solitary drunk weaving his way along the white lines, clutching a can of lager and singing 'Roll Out The Barrel' in a gruff monotone. Bella giggled and felt the hand squeeze hers in response.

Half an hour later her teeth were chattering with cold and her feet were hurting. They had checked out each side of the High Street several times and a biting wind had started to blow down the narrow alleyways. Any burglar with any sense would be tucked up in his nice warm bed with a cup of hot chocolate. Bella sighed longingly at the thought of the hot chocolate. Or any chocolate at all actually.

'Time to watch from the car,' said Jonathan, who noticed the sigh.

He decided the post office spot was as good as any, and nicely out of the way.

'We can't risk starting the engine and having the heater on, I'm afraid, but have this if you're cold.' He shrugged out of his leather jacket and placed it around Bella's shoulders.

'Won't you be cold?'

'I'm tough. Cold's for wimps.'

Bella snuggled gratefully into the soft jacket, leaned back comfortably against the seat and tried to suppress a yawn.

'Don't you dare fall asleep on me again!' said Jonathan, as quick as a flash. 'Talk to me to stay awake. Tell me about yourself. And Emily. How do you manage to hold down a job and bring up a child on your own?'

It was, after all, a mystery to him, all this child-rearing stuff. And he was strangely interested – and impressed – with the way this funny little pair seemed to cope. Bella told him briefly about after-school clubs and babysitters and explained how her kindly editor would allow her to make up the hours at home in the evening if she absolutely had to take time off for Emily's school plays or important events. 'I feel guilty that I can't meet her out of school every day like most of the other mums, and it's difficult for her to have her friends home to play during the week. But I try to make up for that in the holidays and weekends. Often I have a flat full of kids. You can probably hear all the noise from the police station!' She pulled a face.

She's a good mum, thought Jonathan. I was never allowed friends home to tea. I could never make a noise.

'I was really very lucky to get the job though,' continued Bella. 'Not many editors would employ a young single mum when there's so many other people out there desperate to be journalists.'

'Do you have any help from Emily's father?' Jonathan asked.

'No.' The tone was guarded.

'Do you want to tell me about him?'

'No.' The tone was defiant – but hurt.

The bastard, thought Jonathan, feeling a sudden surge of anger. He hurt her! He wanted to thump Emily's nameless father there and then. Right on the nose. He was just contemplating whether he should give him a right hook or a left hook when there was a sudden noise outside. Footsteps. Shuffling footsteps. He squinted out of the window. An elderly man was walking a very small white dog – and he was coming right towards them.

'Quick,' he said, 'come over here.' He shot an arm around Bella's shoulder and pulled her firmly towards his chest. 'Pretend we're a couple,' he hissed in her ear.

Bella went rigid and jerked her head away. 'I can't,' she bleated.

Jonathan cupped his hand round the side of her face and lowered his mouth to a little soft spot just at the bottom of her left ear. 'If you don't hurry up and act just a little bit more convincing about this you might find yourself reported as a burglar – again,' he whispered.

The old man walked a few more paces towards the car, stopped and dithered, peering at the windscreen.

'Shit!' said Bella, promptly flopping her head down onto Jonathan's chest. She lay there, hearing his heartbeat thump steadily in her ear and feeling his arm warm and heavy around her shoulder. This wasn't so bad actually – and he smelt gorgeous. She moved her nose, just a fraction, to savour that musky, yet citrusy scent. Jonathan responded by putting his other hand on her head, and stroked her hair very slightly. 'He's still looking,' he whispered.

'Please don't let us be arrested. It's so *embarrassing*,' groaned Bella. She felt Jonathan's grip tighten around her.

'Kiss me then,' he ordered.

Bella's head shot up. Her chin was level with his. 'You're joking. Aren't you?'

In response Jonathan ran one finger very gently down her cheek and then tilted her chin slowly upwards, holding it until her eyes met his. 'Actually I wasn't,' he murmured, cupping his other hand around the nape of her neck, causing delicious shivers to run up and down her spine.

Once again the grey eyes stared at the blue eyes and the blue eyes stared back unblinkingly. Bella felt her lips tremble and heard Jonathan's breathing start to quicken. Her heart raced out of control then missed a beat completely as he slowly moved his face towards her until his lips brushed slowly, gently against her mouth.

He drew back slightly and looked into her eyes. 'Now that wasn't so bad, was it?' he whispered. Running his fingers through her hair, he lowered his face towards her again. This time Bella's lips moved to meet his – open, eager, expectant...

SMASH! There was the sound of breaking glass.

'What the hell...?' Jonathan sprang back, instinctively shielding Bella against his chest. 'Christ – it's a window.'

He pushed Bella away and leapt out of the car in one swift movement, reaching in his pocket for his phone. Some fifty metres away a security alarm screamed and wailed and a slight, shadowy figure sped off silently into the darkness. 'Stay there!' barked Jonathan, before he turned and gave chase.

Bella had no intention of staying there. She grabbed her bag, leapt out of the car and pelted after Jonathan as fast as her three-inch heels would allow. She panted along, her ankles twisting on the uneven surface, hearing Jonathan shouting instructions for back-up and tracker dogs into his phone. The old man and his dog, now two tiny specks in the distance, squinted in puzzlement at the antics of the courting couple, who now appeared to be chasing each other down the alleyway. And he was sure he could hear a funny noise; perhaps he ought to turn up his hearing aid.

Jonathan stopped outside a white painted brick building, where the noise was deafening. A sign on the back door said 'Perry and Sons Butchers' and a small frosted glass window, five feet from the ground, bore a large, jagged hole. Bella skidded to a halt beside him, panting. He turned to grip her by the shoulders. 'He's gone. I'm going after him. Bella – I'm telling you – go back to the car,' he shouted above the wails. With that he was off, pounding along the rest of the alleyway towards the top of the High Street.

Bella, who had no intention of missing the action, waited until he was out of sight and then tried to peer through the window. She couldn't see a thing. She fumbled in her bag for the key-ring torch and shone it though the jagged hole, standing on tiptoe. Instantly her hand flew to her mouth and she let out a strangled scream – for there, a couple of feet away from her eyes was a ghostly white torso, swinging gently from a hook on the ceiling. She could make out a faint marbling on the pallid flesh and a few red streaks slashing along the curve of its back. Bella felt her stomach lurch and took a deep breath. Then she wished she hadn't as a sweet, musty smell hit her nose. It smelt like ... like raw meat.

The realisation dawned halfway through a very long, very loud scream. Meat. Butcher's shop. Carcass. Thank God. Thank you God. It was a dead animal – not another dead Carla. Her heartbeat slowed, just a fraction.

Above the shriek of the alarm came the wail of a different siren and Bella could see the flash of blue lights and hear the squeal of tyres. Car doors slammed then footsteps came thundering towards her and three uniformed officers surrounded her. One shone a powerful torch in her face while another clamped a powerful hand on her shoulder.

'Can you tell me what you're doing here, Miss?' he boomed.

Bella opened her mouth, wondering where to begin to explain, when there was another thunder of footsteps and Jonathan appeared, panting, in front of her. 'She's with me,' he said.

'What?' The boomer cupped his hand to his ear.

'I said she's with me!' bellowed Jonathan. 'And will someone switch that fucking alarm off.'

'Oh, right... OK guv,' said the one with the booming voice, hastily removing his hand from Bella's shoulder. His colleague heaved his shoulder against the door. There was the crunch of splintering wood and he stepped inside, almost colliding with the ghostly carcass.

'Were you at the scene, guv? Did you see anything?' said the officer with the torch.

'Yes I was. And no I didn't,' said Jonathan shortly. 'I heard the smash and saw the figure running off. The alarm obviously disturbed him. I tried to chase him but he's disappeared.'

'The dogs are on their way and three more cars are out looking. We might still find him, guv.'

Jonathan scowled. 'I'll run Miss Smart home then I'll come back and help. Can you get the fingerprint guys out to that window?' He turned and strode back towards the car. Bella followed, seething. Miss Smart indeed. He'd just been going to snog the lips off her and now he was calling her Miss!

An awkward silence hung between them almost palpably on the journey home. Jonathan pulled up outside the flat and said a curt goodnight, without even looking at her. Bella jumped out, biting back the urge to say good riddance.

She watched the car drive away with a funny sinking feeling in her tummy, then put her key in the lock and tiptoed into the house. On the sofa, illuminated in the dusky glow of the lamp, were Suzy and Roger, curled up together like two Babes in the Wood. Both were fast asleep, Roger emitting tiny grunting snores as his arms cradled the blonde head.

'Huh! I'm glad someone got lucky,' grunted Bella, as she tossed a throw over their legs and stomped off to bed.

* * *

By 8am on Thursday morning the news had spread like wildfire around Haybridge police station and even the civilian clerk at the front desk greeted Jonathan with a hastily-disguised titter. Boz and his colleagues, who had been planning to greet their boss with a rousing chorus of 'Secret Lovers', took one look at the dark, brooding brows and wisely decided to keep their mouths shut.

Everyone had heard the gossip from the uniformed patrol officers about the elderly, rather deaf old man they had seen shuffling along with his dog just after midnight several hundred yards away from the burglary. They had stopped to question him.

'I couldn't sleep. Had too long a nap this afternoon, officer. So I decided to give Snowy a little walk.'

Yes, he had walked past the back of the butcher's shop but no, he hadn't seen any burglars. He had only seen a courting couple – kissing and canoodling they were in the front of a blue Ford Escort. She was a redhead. She reminded him of his Gladys, who sometimes let him kiss her like that in the back of his old Austin Seven all those years ago… No, the couple hadn't seen him walk past – the windows were all steamed up by then. He thought he might have heard a noise though…

Luckily the officers were loyal men who had built up a respect for their new Detective Sergeant. So they wished the old man goodnight and decided against putting his observations into an official report, a report that would have landed on the desk of Superintendent Nixon. But they couldn't resist telling Bill in fingerprints, who told Dave in traffic, who told Edna in the canteen…

'OK you lot.' Jonathan stood by his desk. 'I cocked up. You probably all know the details so we don't need to discuss it. But I'm sorry I missed our burglar and I hope I can rely on you now, more than ever, to help me catch the little bastard.'

His colleagues nodded, impressed. They appreciated a man who could take it on the chin. Boz cleared his throat: 'We have some news on the carpet fibres, guv.'

'I hope it's good,' said Jonathan.

'We've traced it to a company in Yorkshire which specialises in making carpets for cars. They supply the German car manufacturers – Volkswagen, Audi, Mercedes and BMW – but they cannot say which of those four makes these fibres came from. They can say, however, that it was a top of the range model.'

'So,' said Jonathan, 'we know Carla was carried in a top of the range German car?'

'Yes, guv.'

'That's good then. We've narrowed it down to only about a million car owners nationally?'

'Er ... yes guv.'

'OK,' said Jonathan. 'I want a list of every top of the range German car that was stolen from anywhere within a fifty-mile radius on or around the night of Carla's death – October 24th. I would like the information on my desk when I get back – after lunch.' He walked out of the office.

Ian Williams looked up in annoyance from his computer as the tall, dark-haired police officer walked into his office but he instinctively shook the outstretched hand. 'I hope this isn't going to take long,' he said irritably.

'Not necessarily,' said Jonathan, settling himself comfortably in a swivel chair.

'I've already told you everything I know about Carla. I really don't know why you think I can help you any more.'

Jonathan swivelled round to look out of the office window, out to the car park down below where around thirty smart-looking cars were parked in neat lines. 'There's some nice cars out there. Which one do you drive, Mr Williams?'

'The Audi estate. The red one.' Ian frowned. Why the hell was this copper disturbing him at work to talk about cars?

'Top of the range?'

'Yes, of course.'

'Good,' said Jonathan. He paused to scratch his head. 'Tell me about the application form you filled in for Carla to go to college.' He smiled encouragingly.

'It was a standard form, as far as I could tell. For a computer course. But it must have been up to quite an advanced level because it lasted for a year. I remember thinking she could learn quite a lot in that time.

'A year? How could she have got all that time off?' asked Jonathan.

'Oh, it was in the evenings. A couple of evenings a week. You can study at any time at these private places.'

'Private?'

'Yes. That college just outside Weatherford. Peerfields, I think it's called. All the rich kids go there to pick up a qualification. Our friend's daughter did a cookery course.'

'It must be expensive. How could Carla have afforded to go there?'

'I don't know. I never really thought about it. She'd save up out of her wages, I suppose.'

Bella's words suddenly echoed in Jonathan's head: 'She sent most of her wages home to her family, did you know?' How could this girl from a poor background afford to go to a rich kids' college? Why didn't she apply for a government-subsidised course at the local tech? Had someone offered to pay the fees for her? Someone affluent ... a rich lover?

He stood up. 'Thank you for your time, Mr Williams. I will leave you to get on with your work.'

* * *

Peerfields College was an imposing Edwardian building with large stone windows and two massive pillars flanking the heavy oak door. The reception hall smelled of furniture polish and fresh flowers and the receptionist was a heavily made-up woman in her thirties with dark hair cut in a shoulder length bob. Jonathan gave her his most charming smile. 'Now, you look as though you are *just* the person I need to help me,' he drawled.

The brunette flicked her hair and gave a simpering smile. That was easy, thought Jonathan.

He leaned over the desk towards her. 'I'm a police officer,' he said confidentially.

'Oooh,' said the brunette.

'And, as part of a very special investigation, I need a list of all the people who have applied to do a computer course here in the past three months. Do you think you could do that for me?' He gave her another smile and looked her full in the face.

What lovely blue eyes, thought the brunette, who was already reaching for her applications file marked 'confidential'.

' Perhaps I could have a look?' smiled Jonathan, reaching out. The brunette leaned over and handed him the file, wishing she was wearing her new low-cut top. He flicked through the alphabetical forms ... Johannson, Jones, Judson, Karman ... no Kapochkin. Damn!

'Are all the people who applied in this file?'

'All the people who were accepted, yes.' The brunette flicked her hair again.

'Were any applicants refused?'

'No. They take anyone here – well, anyone who can afford to pay the fees. Ha ha.'

Jonathan chuckled obligingly. 'How much would it cost to do a twelve-month computer course, two nights each week?

The brunette scanned a list on her desk. 'Advanced Computing, Evenings. £3,000.'

'So what if someone made an application for that course but then they couldn't afford to pay the fees?'

'We might, in special cases, perhaps to fill the disabled quota, help them get some sort of grant. But otherwise we have to file their details and contact them again a few months later to see if their financial situation has improved. Sometimes it has, you know.'

'And where would you file these details?'

The brunette frowned slightly. Jonathan flashed her a smile. 'Please – if you could just take a little look...'

She melted immediately and groped under the desk for a red folder marked 'Losers' file'. 'I didn't write that – it was my colleague's idea of a joke,' she explained hastily. Jonathan forced another chuckle and thumbed quickly through the forms, surprised at how many poor losers there were. H, I, J, K ... Yes! Carla Kapochkin. He scanned the piece of paper, noting Ian Williams' name and address under 'employer's details'.

'It would help me considerably if I could borrow this form,' he said.

'Well ... I shouldn't really. But...'

'Thank you,' Jonathan deftly folded and pocketed the form. 'You have been a great help.' He turned to go.

'Wait,' said the brunette, scribbling on the back of an envelope. 'Here's my phone number – just in case you need me to help again.' She gave him a full-on, dazzling smile.

'Goodbye,' said Jonathan, walking out of the door.

Chapter Twenty

It was Friday the thirteenth. And Bella, who never walked under ladders and always touched wood, woke with an ominous jittery feeling somewhere between her chest and her tummy. She knew it was actually nothing to do with the date because she'd had this funny feeling ever since Wednesday night when Jonathan had kissed her, ever so gently, on the lips. It was as though that one little kiss, a real butterfly wing of a kiss, had blown away all the rock-solid defences she had painstakingly built up ever since ... ever since Hugo.

Just like Hugo, though, Jonathan had let her down. He had stripped down those defences and then brushed her aside, leaving her feeling exposed, vulnerable, almost raw. As if that wasn't enough, she felt cheap. She had given in so easily – and he'd gone off her so quickly. He had not even been able to look her in the eye afterwards, for God's sake. And she hadn't heard a single word from him since. He was probably too busy having mad, passionate sex with Madeleine. Bella shuddered. She couldn't believe she had even contemplated kissing a man who was living with someone else – practically *married* to her probably. Whatever had she been thinking of?

Over breakfast, Em made matters decidedly worse by asking incessantly if 'Jonny' was coming to watch her football match the following day. 'But he promised, Mummy,' she said, her little brow wrinkling as she picked up Bella's reluctance to confirm it.

'He's very busy, Em. He may not be able to make it.

If he can't we'll ask Grandad to come and watch instead – that would be lovely, wouldn't it?'

'I want Jonny. He knows about football,' said Emily, her bottom lip trembling. 'You could ring him and ask him – couldn't you, Mummy?'

'We'll see,' replied Bella, suddenly hating Jonathan Wright and his stupid promises and his stupid kisses. How dare he do this to her daughter?

The envelope was propped against her computer keyboard when she got to work. It was a thick, white, hand-delivered envelope addressed simply to 'Bella Smart' in firm, definite handwriting that she just knew was Jonathan's. Here come the excuses, she thought, ripping it open.

'Dear Bella, I am looking forward to watching your daughter kick some butt on the football pitch tomorrow. Could you call and tell me what time the match starts and where it is. Does she have shin pads? Regards, Jonathan.'

A mobile phone number was printed neatly at the bottom of the page.

Bella felt a ridiculous surge of gratitude. Thank God, he wasn't going to let Emily down. He was obviously going to be mature about that silly kissing business and forget that it happened. Perhaps they could treat it as a little blip and just be friends – well, working acquaintances might be better. Working acquaintances with a shared interest in Emily's football. She still didn't fancy talking to him though. With a bit of luck his mobile would be switched off and she could leave a voice message.

It may have been Friday the thirteenth but Bella's luck was in. The phone clicked straight into a recorded voice that told her to leave her message after the tone. 'Hi, it's Bella,' she gabbled. 'Thank you for your note. The match is at 10am on St Peter's School playing field. Um, she doesn't have shin pads but I don't think they really need them in children's football. Thanks again. Em will be thrilled you're coming. Bye. Thank you.'

Oh dear, she'd babbled on a bit and she'd thanked him three times. She hoped she didn't sound like a piteously grateful old spinster. She sighed.

'Chocolate biscuit?' Suzy held out a packet. 'This guy is really getting to you, isn't he?'

'Absolutely not!' said Bella, jutting out her chin.

'You're not your usual chirpy self, Bel. You've been odd ever since Wednesday when you went out with him.' Suzy paused and bit her lip. 'It's nothing to do with finding Roger and me asleep on your sofa, is it?'

'Suze – I've told you, I think that's great! I thoroughly approve of you and Roger.'

'Good. But don't get too excited. It's early days yet and my great romances usually fizzle out after a couple of weeks.' Suzy smiled ruefully. 'Anyway, I still can't help thinking he's not my type.'

'He's millions nicer than the posers you normally go for,' said Bella, feeling suddenly defensive of poor Roger.

'So, it's the Jonathan thing that's making you depressed then?'

'I'm not depressed.'

'Just a little bit down maybe?'

'Maybe.'

'One chocolate biscuit down or two chocolate biscuits down?' said Suzy, holding out the Hob Nobs again.

'Give me three,' said Bella through gritted teeth.

Jonathan had switched off his mobile phone because he had just had a row with Madeleine and he had pretended his signal failed in the middle off it. He knew from experience that women always liked to have the last word so he decided to stay peacefully incommunicado for a bit.

She had phoned while he was in the car to tell him they were going curtain and accessory shopping in London tomorrow. She had suggested they travelled down tonight and stay at her apartment.

'Do you want me to book some theatre tickets? It's so long since we've had a civilised night out, darling.'

'I'm busy tonight. I have a job at the golf club – for the Superintendent,' Jonathan had said shortly.

'Oh,' said Madeleine. 'Well we'll just have to travel down in the morning then. What a nuisance.'

'I'm busy in the morning too.'

'But you told me you had the day off!'

'I did have. But ... er ... something cropped up.'

'What?' Madeleine had demanded.

Jonathan, who was a truthful man, told her he had to watch a football match in Haybridge.

'A football match! For God's sake, Jonathan, you can watch football any time. It may have escaped your notice but we happen to be moving into our new house in seven days' time and we do not have a single pair of curtains or anything to put our stamp on the place.'

Jonathan, who indeed had shoved the new house to the back of his mind and had not given a single thought to curtains and accessories, gave a sigh. 'The bloody place is furnished, Madeleine and we're only there for a short time. Do we need them?'

'We do. So you can cancel this silly football match.'

'I can't.' A picture of Emily's earnest little face sprang into his mind. He smiled. He was looking forward to seeing the kid play.

'Who is it anyway?'

'What?'

'Who is playing football?'

'Oh. A kids' team. Local kids.'

'Christ Jonathan!' Madeleine's voice rose an octave. 'I

don't believe you!' She launched into a monologue of all his faults, ending with: 'So you would rather watch some little brats kick a ball around than come to London to spend the weekend with me?'

'Yes,' he had replied simply. That was when he pretended the signal was breaking up.

Jonathan gave himself a mental shake and pulled up outside the Swan pub. Friday lunchtime. It could be a good time to catch Ricky Thomas's little drinking pals. And he fancied a pint after all that hassle with Madeleine.

Ms Amazonian was washing glasses at the bar and her formidable brow crinkled into a frown as she broke off to pump Jonathan's pint of draught lager. 'You're not old bill, are you?' she asked, viewing his smart suit and tie.

'Good lord, no,' said Jonathan, carrying his pint to a quiet table by the window, from where he had an excellent view of the car park.

He tried to ignore the harsh lights and pounding music as he sipped his pint, wondering whether he fancied a ham roll or not. He was getting sick of living off ham rolls actually – and even more sick of eating that fancy restaurant stuff in the evenings. His mind wandered back to Bella's kitchen and mashed potatoes and roast chicken. Then he saw Bella's face, laughing as she teased little Emily about having custard on her nose. Then he saw the same face, tilted towards him in the darkness, eyes huge and expectant and lips slightly parted as his mouth moved towards hers. He felt a sudden whoosh of desire somewhere deep in his abdomen. He took another hearty swig of lager.

God, he'd got a bit carried away there, trying to get rid of that old man. He hadn't meant to. Just a pretend cuddle would have been enough but for some reason he'd

231

had this all-consuming urge to kiss her. He hadn't banked on his reaction when his lips touched hers though. He had wanted to shower her with kisses ... her face, her nose, to run his hands down her body and kiss that tiny little tender spot, just at the base of her throat, where he could see her pulse fluttering so wildly. It was lucky that burglar came when he did, he thought wryly. Or God knows what may have happened.

He really had to pull himself together though. He had a lot of respect for Bella, the way she was holding down that job and bringing up the kid. But, for all her reporting skills and her feistiness, she had something just a little bit vulnerable about her. The last thing Jonathan wanted to do was hurt her, and he knew, if he did succumb to this strange, chemical attraction, that it *would* end in disaster. She needed stability and security – not a five minute wonder with a guy who avoided commitment like the plague. He couldn't bear to hurt Emily either – he really liked that kid. But there was no way he was equipped to play daddy; he just did not have it in him. Watching her play football was okay though. Wasn't it?

He sighed, scratched behind his ear and looked out of the window. Two cars were pulling into the car park, each bearing a couple of young men who looked around Ricky's age. Jonathan squinted and recognised, clambering out of a shabby grey car, the good-looking black guy with whom Bella had been in conversation round the dart board. Good, he thought – the ringleader. The car, he clocked immediately, was a slightly rusty BMW – old but top of the range. So Ricky may have had access to a vehicle that night, he mused.

The young men spilled into the pub, laughing and bantering. They even managed to get a reluctant smile out of Ms Amazonian as she flipped the tops off their bottled lager.

It obviously wasn't macho to sit at a table so the men stood at the bar and Jonathan strained to hear their conversation. He found himself listening mainly to expletives, which they seemed to use every third or fourth word, interspersed with the occasional, and totally unnecessary, 'innit'. He listened to a long discussion about football, a heated debate about whether a rap artist he'd never heard of was crap or not and a little bit of attempted banter with the muscle-bound landlady – who shot them straight down in flames. Finally he was rewarded with a mention of the name he had been waiting for: Ricky Thomas.

'Is Killer Rick coming tonight then, Jay?' said one lanky, fair-haired lad.

'Nah. He don't come out much now. Says he's saving his money in case he gets put inside. He didn't even come to that gig on Wednesday. Said he was busy,' said the ringleader.

'He told me his mum was going in hospital – that private place – and he's doing some work to pay for it. He's a right mummy's boy, innit?' said another thickset, mixed-race lad.

'Where's he working then?'

'Dunno. Somewhere on the quiet. He's still getting his dole.'

'Good job. He won't get much in the nick. They've had a whip round for that Carla bird – thousands of pounds, the *Gazette* says they've got – but no one will give a toss about poor bleedin' Rick. And he didn't even kill the silly cow. Or so he says.' Jay went to spit emphatically on the floor then shuffled his feet and changed his mind as the landlady shot him a warning glance.

'Fucking birds! They're just not worth it,' sighed the mixed-race lad. He held out his empty bottle. 'Anyone for another?'

Jonathan drained his own pint and slipped quietly out

of the pub, glancing inside the rusty BMW as he passed it. Navy blue carpet – no good. But it was still a possibility Ricky had borrowed a car from another mate. Maybe he had a vehicle for this job he was doing. Jonathan frowned. It was time he did a spot of totally unauthorised surveillance on poor dole-fiddling 'Killer Rick'. But first he'd better check his phone.

Ten minutes later he was in a small sports shop just off the High Street. 'She's about this big,' he told the middle-aged assistant, gesturing somewhere about his hips with one hand and scratching his head with the other.

'Small then,' said the lady, pulling a selection of shin pads out of a drawer. 'We have the economy range for £6.99, standard for £9.99 and deluxe, extra padded, for £15.50.'

'I'll take the best,' said Jonathan, reaching for his wallet and wincing at the thought of some lout kicking his great boot into Emily's skinny little shins.

'Is Jonny coming?' was Emily's first question when Bella collected her from the after-school club.

'Yes, darling, he is,' said Bella, stooping to give her daughter a hug. 'And,' she said, 'I'm taking you to McDonalds tonight for a pre-match treat!'

Emily let out a whoop. 'Cool!' she said. Her friend Megan, who had gone to after-school club so her non-working mum could do an early and leisurely Christmas shop in Weatherford, was looking decidedly wistful as the do-gooding Sharon was buttoning her into her sensible duffel coat. 'Would you like to come too, Meggie?' said Bella.

Megan's solemn little face lit up. 'Can I, Mummy?'

Sharon considered. She didn't really approve of Megan eating junk food but then it would give her time to get her Christmas presents all wrapped and labelled. And there was a jolly interesting programme about organic gardening on television...

'You may. You little girls will have a super duper time! Shall Mummy pop round and pick you up at –'

'I'll drop her home,' said Bella, hastening off in case Sharon offered to join them. It was a Friday evening and she was knackered. She couldn't face all that hearty enthusiasm right now.

Two little girls are often easier than one little girl for tired, jaded parents, and Emily and Megan amused themselves, chattering away while seeing who could cram the most chips into their mouth at once. Bella just smiled at them occasionally, mopped up the ketchup, put together the amazingly complicated free Happy Meal toys and helped them judge the longest chip contest. Apart from that she was free to have a blissful read through the newspapers the fast food restaurant so thoughtfully provided.

She looked in her purse. She had a £20 note – a miracle at the end of the week. Enough to buy a chocolate sundae each and to rent a Disney video for her and Em to snuggle up and watch tonight. For the first time in forty-eight hours, Bella gave a contented sigh. Life was good again. Who needed men?

Half a mile away, sitting at the old family kitchen table, Kate Spencer looked at Paul and Rita Smart's anxious faces and felt her stomach sink.

'I hope you didn't mind us asking you to pop round after work,' said Rita, fidgeting anxiously with her teacup. 'It's just ... just that we don't know what to do. It was all a bit of a shock when this letter came.'

'May I take a look?' said kind-hearted Kate gently.

Paul Smart reached into his trouser pocket and produced a folded piece of paper which, in the few hours since he'd received it, he must have read thirty times. He could recite it almost off by heart. It was from a firm of solicitors in London.

Dear Sir,

We are writing on behalf of our client, Mr Hugo Copeland, who is the biological father of your granddaughter, Miss Emily May Smart.

Our client understands this letter may come as a shock, which is the reason he has requested we write to you, rather than directly to the child's mother, Ms Bella Smart.

Mr Copeland has asked us to convey the fact that he deeply regrets not having had contact with his daughter in the past. Recently he underwent an experience which made him realise how wrong this action was and he is now extremely keen to rectify the situation.

He also wishes to take financial responsibility for the child and has requested us to enclose this cheque for £10,000 as a goodwill gesture for Ms Bella Smart until a formal maintenance agreement can be drawn up.

Mr Copeland has further requested us to implement legal proceedings immediately to allow him official access to Emily May Smart. He hopes, most sincerely, that this application will not be contested.

In the meantime, our client has asked us to forward his telephone number, which is printed above, should Ms Smart wish to contact him directly to discuss matters further.

We look forward to your reply.
Yours faithfully
Edward Billingdon-Hunt.
Grimthorpe, Ashley and Hunt Solicitors.

'Oh dear,' said Kate, chewing her thumbnail. 'And you haven't told Bella yet?'

'No,' said Mrs Smart, her eyes filling with tears. 'How could we tell her, dear? After all she went through because of this man. He couldn't...' A fat tear rolled down her cheek and she fumbled for her handkerchief to wipe it away. 'He couldn't take our little Emily away, could he?'

'No, he most definitely could not,' said Kate in her most authoritative social worker voice. 'Bella is an excellent mother; she has coped splendidly for almost seven years and the courts would have no grounds whatsoever to grant Hugo custody.' She paused, and lowered her tone to a more gentle one. 'But they could well rule that he can have regular access to Emily, particularly as he is clearly willing to pay towards her upkeep.'

Paul Smart got up and paced the kitchen floor, feeling his fists clench in his pockets as he experienced an uncharacteristic surge of aggression.

'Bastard!' he growled, prompting his wife to almost choke on her tea in surprise. 'Sorry, my love.' He put a hand on her shoulder. 'But the man has such a bloody cheek – ignoring our Bella and little Em for all this time then demanding to waltz back into her life without so much as an explanation. And sending that great fat cheque thinking it makes up for it all. As if we want his money – he must be joking!'

His wife wiped her eyes again. 'Ten thousand pounds is a lot of money, Paul. Maybe Bella–'

'She won't touch it. I know my daughter – she won't be bought.' Paul Smart almost spat the words out.

Kate agreed with him. She could picture Bella tearing up the cheque in disgust, her eyes blazing with fury. Her mind flashed back to the day, over seven years ago in this very house, where her friend had sobbed her heart out when Hugo left her in the lurch. She had coped so amazingly well over the years and Emily was a happy, well-adjusted child. She was a real credit to Bella. But years of social work training had taught Kate that problems cannot be shelved forever and fathers cannot be pushed into the background as if they do not exist. Even if Hugo had not made a move to see his daughter, Emily would, in time, demand to see him. And she had every right to; he may have been an utter bastard, but he was still her father.

Hugo had been young and stupid when Bella had announced her pregnancy. It hadn't even been a proper relationship, Kate recalled. He had been honest about not wanting the child and Bella had decided to go ahead alone. But why was he suddenly showing an interest after all this time? What was this 'recent experience' the solicitor referred to? Maybe he really had changed? Maybe he really could play a part in the life of little Emily? But what if he hurt her or let her down? Kate felt an unprofessional surge of anger. If he hurt that child, she personally would rip his bloody head off! She took a deep breath and addressed the Smarts: 'You have to tell Bella about the letter. You realise that, don't you?'

The couple nodded seriously.

'But not in front of Emily. Bella needs time on her own to think about this. It's going to be a terrible shock.'

'Perhaps we could have her round tomorrow night. We'll ask Toby to come and take Emily out or something,' said Rita.

'That's a good idea,' said Kate. And she would be waiting anxiously by the phone – ready to mop up the tears.

Fifty miles away, in a loft apartment overlooking the Thames, Hugo Copeland was pouring champagne into glasses and trying to control the intense wave of craving running through his body. He handed a glass to each of his dozen guests and reached discreetly for his own sparkling mineral water.

'Cheers,' he said. 'To my new apartment.' He raised his glass.

'And to your new life,' said a striking blonde girl, coming forward to kiss his cheek. 'Poor Hugo. Was it absolutely dreadful in that place?' she said, pushing back the floppy fringe from his eyes.

'Bloody awful,' grinned Hugo. 'But it's done the trick, my angel. No more booze for me!'

'Well, we are all terribly proud of you,' said another long-haired blonde called Annabel. 'Jamie Halsworth went to one of those drying-out clinics and said it was absolutely awful. He climbed over the fence one night to buy a bottle of whisky from the local off-licence. He got into terrible trouble, you know – they threw him out after a few weeks.'

'I was tempted to break out at times,' confessed Hugo, remembering with a shudder the days he had spent almost climbing the walls, crippled with nausea, headaches and bodily tremors so violent he could hardly stand. 'But the doctors were very good – they provided masses of distractions.' Particularly in the form of nubile little nurses in those cute, white uniforms, he recalled with a smile.

'Which clinic did you go to, Hugo?' asked one of the men, who was admiring an original Victorian hunting scene on the wall.

'The Royal. In Geneva. Costs a thousand pounds a day apparently, but the parents coughed up.'

'Golly. A thousand pounds just to sit around all day and not drink. That's amazing,' said Annabel, wide-eyed.

'Well, we weren't allowed to sit around all day actually. We had counselling, group therapy, one to one therapy … we spent most of the time talking.'

'Goodness! What about?'

Hugo closed his eyes for a split second, remembering the endless probing questions about his childhood, his teenage years and his escapades as a young adult with a large, private income from his doting parents. After a few weeks in that place he found himself pouring his heart out to anyone in a white coat, telling them about the wild parties, the constant social drinking, the cocaine and the fast cars. He explained how the parties gradually blurred into one until life became one long celebration, one non-stop round of drink and drugs. It was only when he woke up one day, literally in the gutter, covered in vomit, and unable to remember a thing about the previous forty-eight hours, that he realised he needed help and called his parents in France.

The psychologists told him he had become alcohol and drug dependant because he had never had a purpose or structure to his life. They talked about his views on jobs and relationships and marriage – and children.

'Actually I have a child – a daughter,' Hugo had blurted out. The words had sounded strange on his lips because he had never said them before.

'What's she like?' one white-coated woman had asked.

Hugo, who could barely remember what the child's mother looked like – though he seemed to recall she had red hair – could only shrug and confess that he'd never seen her. 'But I know her name – Emily. We went to live in France before she was born but my parents still pick up a bit of gossip from their home town, I think,' he told the woman.

They asked if he had ever thought about contacting his daughter and taking responsibility for her. It might be just what he needed in his life, they told him. Hugo hadn't, until then, given it a single thought. But somehow, once the idea was planted in his head, it grew and grew...

He wondered what Emily looked like, whether she had his blonde hair, or his green eyes. He wondered whether her mother could afford to bring her up properly – give her nice clothes, toys and perhaps a little pony or two to ride. He seemed to remember his sisters were mad about horses when they were small. He hoped she didn't go to the local school in Haybridge. He really didn't want any daughter of his speaking with a local accent.

Soon, night after night, Hugo was lying awake, fighting the urge to slip out and buy a bottle of vodka by thinking about his daughter instead. As soon as he got out of the clinic and had his new apartment sorted, he made an appointment to see the family's solicitor near Knightsbridge. 'Money's no object. I just want to see her – and I want to support her,' he had told the grey-haired old lawyer earnestly.

Now, today, he knew the solicitor's letter would have reached Bella's parents. By this time next week he could be seeing his daughter for the very first time. He took a gulp of his sparkling water and put one arm round Annabel. 'My new life is looking good, angel,' he grinned.

Chapter Twenty-One

Bella dressed carefully on Saturday morning. She put on a thermal vest, a long-sleeved T-shirt, a thick baggy sweater, some jogging bottoms and two pairs of socks. To finish off the ensemble she slung on a navy blue fleece jacket and wound a bright pink scarf round her neck. So what if she was so bundled up she could scarcely move her arms? At least she would be warm – and no one could accuse her of dressing to impress a certain Detective Sergeant, could they?

Bella then stood in front of the mirror and studied her reflection from three different angles. She was horrified; she would rather freeze than look like a Michelin man with no waist at all, a very saggy bottom and two distinct saddle bags on its thighs. She promptly peeled off the fleece, the scarf, the baggy jumper, the T-shirt and the vest, kicked the jogging bottoms across the room in disgust and stood in her bra, knickers and two pairs of socks while she contemplated the contents of her wardrobe.

Bella then dressed very carefully again in a pair of jeans and the same long sleeved T-shirt, topped with a tailored black jacket and the scarf. She peered in the mirror again, then swept her hair back in a pony tail and slicked on some mascara and lipstick. Not that she was doing any of this for Jonathan, of course: she just wanted to look good for Em. And she could always jiggle about a bit if she got chilly. Didn't you burn off more calories in the cold anyway?

Emily had gone past the almost hysterical chatter stage

and sat silently in the car on the way to the school, clutching her football boots on her lap, the expression on her small face wavering between grim determination and absolute terror. She was the only girl playing among fourteen boys and this was her very first local school league match. It was a big event for a six-year-old and Bella felt a small stab of anxiety. She leaned across and squeezed her daughter's hand. 'Just do your best Em, and I'll be proud of you,' she said.

Jonathan was already waiting at the side of the field, sensibly dressed in jeans, chunky boots and a warm jacket. He was frowning across at a huddle of boys, all of whom were at least a head taller and half as wide again as Emily.

'Jonny!' Emily ran up to greet him, throwing herself round his legs. He gave her a quick, embarrassed hug, then gestured across to the boys. 'They're huge compared to her,' he whispered.

'She'll be fine,' said Bella, bending to peel off Emily's trousers and jacket. Underneath the little girl was wearing a regulation school blue and white football shirt so big that the sleeves dropped almost down to her bony wrists and the bottom hung only a fraction of an inch above her baggy shorts. From out of the shorts poked two skinny white legs, each sporting a blue football sock firmly pulled up to a tiny knobbly knee. Jonathan felt a sudden surge of protectiveness towards those little stick limbs and frowned again at the group of boys. He reached into his jacket pocket. 'Here – you'll need these,' he said gruffly, thrusting the pair of shin pads into her hand.

Em's eyes shone, just like her mother's did sometimes. 'Wow! Thank you! I was going to ask Father Christmas for shin pads but I never thought I'd get them *now*! These are well good ones.' She hugged Jonathan's knees again.

'Let me put them on. I'll tie your boots properly as well,' he said, squatting down.

This child was just like her mother – can't keep still for a minute, he thought as Em wriggled excitedly, itching to join her teammates. 'Go on then,' he said, tugging the final lace firmly. 'Go and kick some butt, gorgeous.'

'That was so kind of you to buy her the shin pads,' ventured Bella, as Emily took her striker's position on the pitch.

'Shh,' said Jonathan. 'They're starting. God, I hope she's going to be okay.'

Hang on a minute, thought Bella. Am I not the one who's supposed to play the anxious mother? She glanced across at Jonathan, whose eyes were avidly following the game as though it was a World Cup final. 'Yes!' he shouted as Emily deftly tackled a chunky ginger-haired boy to win the ball.

'Go Em, GO!' he yelled as the skinny little legs flew with all their might, dribbling the ball down the pitch.

'You BASTARD!' he screamed as the ginger kid hurled himself at the little body and neatly reclaimed the ball.

'Er, Jonathan – these are only children,' said Bella, worried the headmaster might complain about the language.

'Sorry... Look – she's got it again. Go Em. Show the bastards what you can do!'

Bella giggled, then joined Jonathan in an almighty cheer as St Peter's scored a goal. Ten minutes later they were yelling themselves hoarse again after a well-judged corner pass from Em resulted in another goal headed into the net.

At half-time it was St Peter's two and Downside Juniors nil. Jonathan rushed straight to a panting Emily, who had not stopped running for one split second. 'You're doing brilliantly,' he said. 'Now – let's talk tactics for the second half.'

A few minutes later, the child ran out with renewed vigour and a big grin, only to scowl fiercely when seconds later Downside shot the ball into the net. After that she was like a little whirlwind, running after the bigger players and tackling ferociously for the ball. When, on several occasions, she was knocked to the ground in her efforts, Jonathan and Bella took a simultaneous sharp intake of breath – only to let it out in a relieved whoosh as a mud-covered Em immediately sprang up and resumed her chase.

'She's a good little player – she's fearless!' said Jonathan proudly, turning to Bella. Unfortunately, at that moment Downside neatly knocked in a second goal. 'Shit! Two all,' he groaned.

Five minutes before the end Jonathan's jaw was clenched and his hands formed tight fists in his pockets. Emily had taken possession of the ball from a particularly robust kid in the centre of the pitch and, ponytail flying behind her, she was speeding up towards the goal, well ahead of the Downside defenders and the puffing referee.

'Yes! You can do it, Em. Go for it – go girl!' shouted Jonathan as she reached the box. A second later the ginger-haired boy sped in from the wing and made an undisguised grab at the baggy shirt. Emily fell sideways, the ball rolling from her feet.

'REF!' screamed Jonathan. 'Are you bloody *blind*? He pulled her. That's a *penalty*!'

'OK, OK – calm down, mate. Penalty to St Peter's,' announced the ref, who was, after all, only a willing dad who gave up his Saturdays so the kids could have a bit of fun.

Both Bella and Jonathan stopped breathing as Emily lined up the ball, her small brow furrowed with concentration. They hardly dared watch as she walked calmly backwards, squared her shoulders and then ran towards the ball, shooting out one skinny leg...

'YES! YES! YES!' cried Jonathan as the ball shot past the outstretched keeper and firmly into the back of the

245

net. 'She did it!' Without thinking, he flung his arms around Bella and swung her off the ground, his feet jumping a little dance of victory on the ground.

Bella, who had gone just a little bit tearful with the emotion of it all, felt her face once again resting in what was rapidly becoming its own little place on Jonathan's chest. She inhaled the now familiar scent and felt a tingle down her spine. Bloody hell, she thought, here we go again.

'This calls for a celebration,' announced Jonathan, as they made their way back to the car park, with Em chattering incessantly and re-enacting the match second by second. 'Let me take you both out to lunch.'

Em stopped in her tracks and considered Jonathan with her cocked head gaze. 'Chips?' she said.

'Yep.'

'Cheeseburger?'

'Yep.'

A grin was spreading over the freckled face. 'Ice cream with lots of chocolate sauce?'

'You bet,' said Jonathan.

'Wicked!' pronounced Em, grabbing his hand and swinging on his arm.

Her hand felt like a delicate little bird. Jonathan was scared to close his fingers around it in case he broke those tiny little bones or something. Then he remembered the ruthless tackles on the football pitch and grinned – this kid was tougher than she looked.

'She's very grubby to go out to lunch,' said Bella with a slight frown. Jonathan glanced at the mud-streaked face, the ragged hair hanging down from its ponytail, the black little knees and the filthy blue and white shirt.

'She looks fine to me,' he said. 'Shall we go in my car?'

In McDonalds – for the second time in less than twenty-four hours – Bella and Emily tucked into burgers and chips with identical gusto, taking it in well-rehearsed turns to dip into the little pot of ketchup. When the ice creams arrived they both picked up their spoons with identical groans of pleasure, Emily matching her mother mouthful for mouthful. How can something so small pack so much food away? wondered Jonathan. And how can one ice cream make so much *mess*? He chuckled as Emily wiped her mouth with a hand already covered in chocolate sauce, spreading the sticky brown mess right across one cheek. He reached for a paper napkin and leaned across the table. 'Come here, chocolate face,' he said.

Bella had a tiny blob of chocolate on her nose. 'And you,' he grinned, dabbing at it with the napkin.

'Right, ladies. If you've quite finished smearing your lunch over your faces, what would you like to do now?'

Two pairs of huge eyes regarded him. One pair blazed with defiance and one with excitement. Go away, thought Bella. Leave us alone. Go and do civilised Saturday afternoon things with your posh girlfriend and stop playing happy families with us... The second pair of eyes, more green than grey, lowered their lashes shyly. 'We could go to the cinema... But it does cost a lot,' said Em. The eyes flashed open. 'I promise I won't whinge for popcorn, so it wouldn't cost *that* much!'

In the car again, driving to Weatherford with Em happily singing to herself in the back, Bella was still mildly irritated. 'You don't have to do this, you know,' she hissed. 'Just because ... just because...'

'We kissed?' whispered Jonathan, putting a hand on her knee.

'Just because Em scored a goal. Actually. And you need to change gear,' retorted Bella, firmly removing the hand.

'*Actually* it's an automatic,' grinned Jonathan.

'Oh.' Bella swallowed and fumbled for a safer subject to keep the hand at bay. 'How's work? Any new leads on the murder?'

'Not much at all, unfortunately. We've identified the grey carpet fibres on the body.' He stressed the word grey. 'But only enough to tell us they came from a top of the range German car. No such cars were reported stolen that night though, so Ricky must have borrowed one from someone. Oh, and I've also found proof that Carla had been planning to do an expensive private computer course at Peerfields College but pulled out at the last minute – probably due to lack of finance.'

'But she must have known she'd never have that kind of money,' said Bella. 'I reckon someone must have promised to pay for her then let her down.' She frowned. 'Probably the same man who let her down at the golf club.'

Jonathan nodded. 'Talking of which, I spent an extremely boring hour at the golf club last night receiving another £1,000 cheque for your Carla Fund on behalf of the Superintendent – who just happens to be the club president.' He raised one eyebrow.

'It's not my fund. I'm just the messenger here. It's all down to Councillor Hanson,' murmured Bella.

'He was there, hobnobbing with the Superintendent. He insisted on introducing me to his golfing buddies.'

'Councillors?' asked Bella, who knew most of them.

'No. Far more influential than that,' said Jonathan, thinking back to the polished, well-groomed men he had been forced to greet politely. 'There was a barrister, an accountant, a consultant – private, of course, not NHS – and some guy who had his own city finance firm.' And they were all mind-numbingly boring and pompous. I'd much rather eat McDonalds with you and Em than make inane small talk with a group of stuffed shirts, he thought.

'Does he work for Viking Clinic?' asked Bella.

'Who?'

'The consultant. That's the private clinic just outside town – where Ricky Thomas wants to send his mum for her hip operation.' She grinned. 'If he did I thought you might have been able to negotiate a discount. You have to look after your murder suspects, you know.'

Jonathan gave her a playful squeeze under her ribs. 'I think that's taking proactive policing just a bit *too* far, young lady!'

Oh dear, thought Bella. He just squeezed my fat bit.

But Jonathan didn't seem to mind. He let his hand rest, once again, companionably on her thigh. This time Bella left it there.

Madeleine was perched on the bed, surrounded by carrier bags, when Jonathan ambled back to the hotel around 6pm, full of popcorn, fizzy orange juice and images of cartoon animals saying really quite clever things in human voices. He had been surprised how much the silly little kids' film had made him laugh actually, though most of his pleasure had come from sitting between Emily and her mother as they giggled at exactly the same bits. The funniest part though was when the film was in the final stages, launching into one of those slushy, sentimental endings that kids obviously love. He heard Bella give a little strangled sniff beside him.

Em nudged him. 'Mum will start crying now,' she hissed in a stage whisper.

'Why?' Jonathan whispered back.

'Dunno,' Emily shrugged. 'She always does.'

'Do you cry too?' whispered Jonathan.

'No way! Crying's for *girls*.'

'Right,' said Jonathan.

A second later there was a whisper in his other ear. 'I wasn't crying actually.'

'Are you sure?'

'Yes.'

Jonathan reached out an arm, pulled Bella's face towards him and ran the tip of his finger under her bottom lashes, all in one swift, gentle movement. 'Then why are your eyes wet?' he whispered into her ear.

'My mascara has liquidated. It's hot in here.'

'Do women always wear mascara to football matches?'

'Shh! I'm trying to watch the film.'

Jonathan felt in his pocket, brought out a clean, folded handkerchief and passed it to Bella. 'Just in case your mascara spontaneously liquidates again,' he whispered kindly.

'Thank you,' said Bella, mopping her eyes.

Jonathan gave an involuntary chuckle as he remembered Bella's embarrassment. Then he hastily smothered it because Madeleine was looking at him strangely.

'Would you like to see what I've bought for our house today?' she said.

'Absolutely,' said Jonathan, who couldn't think of anything more boring than looking at someone else's shopping. But he sat down on the bed and tried to show willing as Madeleine rummaged through the carrier bags.

'Look at this sweet little embroidered cushion – I thought it would go beautifully in the spare room – and I love this little pottery dish. Looks like it's hand painted. How sweet is that?' She rabbited on happily while Jonathan lay back against the pillows, arms stretched behind his head, thinking of football and penalties.

Madeleine looked at the prone figure, studied the way his T-shirt was stretched tight across his chest and the muscles bulged on his upper arms, then gently removed the carrier bags from the bed. She lay down beside him and ran one manicured finger slowly down his taut abdomen. 'I bought some new lingerie too,' she purred, undoing the buttons of her blouse.

Afterwards, lying with Madeleine curled against him, Jonathan tried to analyse the totally alien feeling he had somewhere deep in his gut. In the spot where he usually felt a pleasant post-coital glow he was feeling ... a funny sort of guilt. But why should he be feeling guilty. He hadn't done anything wrong, had he? And, as always, he had been the perfect gentleman.

He shifted slightly. He found the weight of Madeleine's head on his shoulder irritating and he didn't like the way her hair was all stiff with hairspray. The smell made his nose tickle too. In fact, he felt an overwhelming urge to shrug her head off his shoulder, get dressed and walk out of the room. But he didn't know why. Madeleine was running her fingers through his hair now and her long nails were scratching his head. Normally he found that soothing but today it was just making him cranky... He scratched his head in irritation, then scratched again behind his ear.

'Stop scratching, honey,' murmured Madeleine.

'I'm not.'

'You are. You've been scratching your head, on and off, ever since you walked in. It's annoying.'

'Have I?' said Jonathan, scratching an itch behind his other ear.

'You have. You even started scratching when you were...'

'Oh. Sorry about that,' said Jonathan, scratching the nape of his neck.

'Oh, for God's sake, this is getting beyond a joke. Let me have a look. Perhaps you need one of my scalp treatments.' Madeleine elegantly uncurled her naked body and raked her nails through Jonathan's dark hair, peering closely at his scalp. He closed his eyes – and then almost jumped out of his skin when Madeleine let out a piercing scream and leapt off the bed.

'Aargh!' she cried, running wildly round the room, clutching her own head. 'Aargh ... Aargh ... Aargh!' she screamed as she ran into the bathroom and turned on the shower.

Jonathan heaved himself off the bed, wrapped a towel round his waist and watched quizzically as Madeleine frantically shampooed her lovely long hair. 'Do I have dandruff?' he said. 'Isn't this a bit of an overreaction?'

Madeleine stared at him with wild eyes, clutching the shampoo bottle with trembling hands. 'You have ... you have *creatures* in your hair,' she sobbed. 'I can see them crawling about and ... and they may have crawled on to *me*!' She let out another huge, racking sob. 'I think they must be *head lice*!'

Jonathan went to the mirror and peered at his head with interest. Bloody hell, he thought. I've got nits. His detective's brain slowly assimilated the information. Nits; kids; an article in *The Times* about head lice being rife in schools; a funny, fine-toothed white comb lying on Bella's living room floor and Emily's hair brushing against his as she sat on his knee.

'Oh dear,' he said.

'Is that all you can say? Oh dear?' shrieked Madeleine, who was now emerging from the shower with a towel wrapped round her head. 'You walk in here and infest me with head lice – probably caught from those common little children you insisted upon watching play football this morning – and all you can say is "oh dear"? Have you any idea how *embarrassing* this will be for me to explain to my hair stylist next week? In fact...' she clutched Jonathan's wrist and looked at his watch. 'Couldn't we call someone now – a doctor or someone – who can give us something to treat them?'

Jonathan was gripping the washbasin with knuckles that had gone white in the middle of this speech. He squared his shoulders and turned to face Madeleine. 'Emily is *not* a common little child,' he said, ominously slowly.

'And who the hell is this Emily?'

'Emily is the daughter of Bella, the journalist you met at the ball.' The tone was carefully neutral now.

Madeleine's eyes narrowed. 'And where, may I ask, is Emily's father?'

'Bella is a single parent.'

'Hah!' stormed Madeleine. 'So not only has she got nits but she's a tart too!' She spat the words out but regretted them as soon as she saw Jonathan's face. His expression was like thunder.

Jonathan regarded her silently, his blue eyes blazing and a muscle twitching in his jaw. Finally he spoke: 'Those, Madeleine, are probably the most inaccurate words you have ever spoken.'

He turned away, pulled on his clothes, and walked out of the door.

Bella and Emily were also hurriedly getting dressed after a quick and companionable bath together and the little girl could not believe her luck.

'So I won my football, I went out to lunch, I went to the cinema and now Uncle Toby's taking me out to dinner! That's a lot of treats, Mmmy!'

'I think you've had three months' worth of treats in one day, darling. Just don't expect every Saturday to be like this,' smiled Bella, kissing her daughter's forehead. 'It will be back to trudging round the supermarket and helping me with the dusting next week.'

Today had certainly been busy, she mused, as she drove across Haybridge. And it had been strange too. It was odd how easily Jonathan slotted in with her and Em and even more odd that he seemed to enjoy it so much. Maybe he was practising for when he and Madeleine had children. Not that he needed to practise – he was a natural. Bella imagined Jonathan and Madeleine strolling through the park hand in hand laughing together as two stunning-looking children gambolled ahead of them. One would probably be very dark like him and the other very fair, like her.

Bella found that thought wasn't a very nice one after all, so she concentrated on the evening ahead instead. It would be lovely to spend some quality time with her parents, catching up on the Haybridge gossip while Toby and his girlfriend entertained Em. It was odd they were so insistent on taking her out though; Em would have been quite happy staying in and talking football. She hoped she wasn't going to get spoilt with all these treats. Still, it meant she would have a rare couple of hours of peace and she couldn't complain about that.

Holding Emily's hand, Bella walked up her parents' garden path, a smile of pleasant anticipation already on her face at the thought of the cosy and uncomplicated evening ahead.

Chapter Twenty-Two

'Oh God,' said Bella, the colour draining from her face. 'Please tell me this is a bad dream.' She looked pleadingly from one parent to another and clutched the solicitor's letter and Hugo's cheque in her hand.

'Bella, I'm afraid it's real. He does want to see Emily and he does want to give you some money.' Mrs Smart reached for her daughter's hand. 'You have to decide what you're going to do and whatever you do we will be behind you.'

Bella continued to sit absolutely still on her parents' sofa, staring down at the letter, for several long minutes. Paul and Rita looked at each other, waiting for the outburst. They'd expected tears; they'd expected tantrums and hysteria – but they had never expected this terrible, painful silence. Wisely though, they waited for Bella to speak. When she did, it was in a voice that was scarcely above a whisper: 'I suppose I always knew, deep down, that this would happen one day.'

Her parents waited for more. Again there was silence. They watched as their daughter's eyes filled with tears.

Paul Smart could bear the agony no longer: 'What are you going to do, love?' he said gently.

Bella looked up and rubbed her hand across her eyes. 'There's only one thing I can do, Dad. And that is ask the one person who really matters in all this – Emily. I have to tell her the truth, as best as I can, about what happened and let her decide whether she wants to see her father.' She paused, rubbed her eyes again, and jutted

255

out her chin. 'But I don't want his money though and I certainly don't want Emily dragged through the courts. He can stuff his legal action and stuff his cheque.'

With that Bella ripped the cheque firmly into two. 'He can stuff his maintenance payments too. We've managed so far and we'll continue to do so.'

'You could fight it, love. Go through the courts and stop him seeing her. If you're worried about the legal costs, we'd find the money somehow,' said her father.

'I know. Thank you, Dad.' Bella gave him a watery smile, 'But do you not think I've rehearsed this scenario a million times in my head? And I know if I stopped Em seeing her father now she could track him down herself as soon as she's old enough – and blame me for keeping them apart. I've tried to bring her up to be honest and now it's time for me to be honest with her. The questions were starting to come anyway. Only the other day she asked where her daddy was. And the older she gets the more complicated the questions will become. In a funny sort of way, it will be almost a relief to get it over with.' Bella jutted out her chin again and took a deep breath. 'Now, how about we put the kettle on, Mum? And you can wipe away those tears too. We'll be fine and so will Emily.'

She continued to sit and stare at the letter as her parents bustled out to the kitchen. She intended to go out and help but she didn't think she could stand up yet – her legs were trembling and the room was swimming slightly. She needed to talk to Kate – thank God for dear sensible Kate – but she knew instinctively that she had handled this the right way. No drama, no courts, no rows … just keep calm and think of Em … think of Em.

She had imagined this moment so often. When Emily was a tiny baby she would hold her in her arms and daydream about Hugo returning, repentant and tearful, begging to be allowed to see his beautiful daughter. She had pictured herself victorious, telling him he had been an utter bastard and that he didn't deserve Emily. Then she would clutch the baby to her breast and order Hugo to leave at once – and never set foot near her or her daughter again.

It was a good daydream. In fact Bella still indulged herself with it sometimes. But hours of earnest discussion with Kate over the years had taught her that this was not the right way to deal with the situation at all. She knew the courts would probably view a repentant father in a favourable light, no matter how much of a bastard he had been. And she also knew that she had made a choice to go ahead with the pregnancy against Hugo's will. She had kept Emily to herself for over six years. Now she had to learn to share her with a part-time father – even if the very thought of it made her feel like someone was sticking a knife in her chest and twisting it very slowly. A tear slid down her cheek.

Sleep eluded Bella completely that night. At 2am she gave up trying and crept into the living room where she curled up in the armchair and tried to watch television as a distraction. When that failed she tiptoed into Emily's room and stared at the little sleeping face, watching the eyelids twitch and the legs give tiny, occasional jerks as the little girl dreamed her football dreams. That made her want to cry so she went to the kitchen and searched for a chocolate biscuit – only to put it back in the tin, uneaten. Even chocolate could not help this time.

Eventually Bella just sat, deep in thought, remembering every sentence of the lengthy telephone conversation she had had with Kate as soon as she had got Em to bed. 'You're doing the right thing, Bella. Your relationship with Em is so solid that nothing can affect it. Hugo will be an addition to her life – not a replacement for you. You must remember that.'

But what if Hugo wasn't an addition? What if he was a replacement? What if he showered Em with toys and presents and took her to all the places Bella could never afford? What if Emily grew to love him more than she loved Bella? What if she demanded to live with her daddy one day? What if she lost her daughter?

Cold tendrils of fear curled through Bella's stomach and, clutching a cushion to her chest for comfort, she finally gave in to the tears, sobbing as she had never sobbed before.

At 5am, when the sobs finally abated, she got the letter out of her handbag, read it slowly, then refolded it neatly. She had decided exactly what she was going to do and, for the next two hours, she literally counted the minutes until she could do it.

Hugo also had been awake most of the night but, unlike Bella, his state of mind was excellent. He had been to the opening of a new art gallery and had met a very interesting girl called Sofia. She was a pretty little thing, all big brown eyes and dark curls, and terribly keen to point out all the finer details of the paintings to Hugo. He had been impressed with her knowledge but even more impressed with her little pert bottom. When the gallery closed he had gone back to Sofia's flat for coffee and, within half an hour, she had allowed him to reveal a few finer details of her own.

He returned to his apartment as dawn was breaking, unable to face a cosy breakfast with Sofia, and was currently sipping a fresh orange juice and wondering whether to go to bed for a few hours before his lunch date with Annabel at noon.

The phone trilled. Hugo glanced at his watch – 7am. Oh dear, he hadn't given Sofia his mobile phone number, had he? He picked up the handset. 'Hi, Hugo here.'

'Hello. This is Bella Smart. I think we need to talk.'

Shit, thought Hugo. This is the mother of my child. This is weird. What do I say? He said the first thing that came into his head: 'Please let me see my daughter.' It came out almost pathetically pleading.

'Or, if I can't see her, then please could I see a photograph?' he gabbled. 'I just need to see what she looks like, whether she has my eyes, or my hair...'

'She has your eyes and your mouth. And she has sandy-coloured hair,' said Bella. 'And you can see her – but only if she wishes to see you. I am going to ask her today. But first I would like to get a couple of things straight...'

She then launched into a lecture so severe that Hugo almost believed he was back at prep school, quaking in front of the headmaster's desk. There would be no solicitors, she said, no cheques and no court applications. Hugo could see Emily – if the child agreed – for one or two hours at a time initially and only when Bella herself was present. This would continue for as long as it took to build up a good relationship. After that he could take her out, by himself, at agreed times and return her at agreed times. But there would be no overnight stays unless Emily herself requested them. Finally Hugo had to be aware he was making a huge commitment as Emily's father and it was a job for life, not a passing whim. If he let her down, failed to keep a promise, failed to show up at an agreed time, or hurt one tiny hair of her daughter's head then Bella would personally ensure he spent the rest of his life a very, very miserable man indeed.

It was a fine speech and Hugo was impressed. Christ, he thought, whatever happened to that timid little red-headed thing I took to bed that night? His heart was thumping as he gratefully agreed to every single proviso. 'I'll do anything, anything. I give you my word, Bella. But can I see her soon?'

'I'll be in touch,' said Bella firmly, ringing off.

Afterwards, still clutching her cushion, she trembled from head to foot and contemplated having another cry. Then she gave herself a mental shake and headed for the shower. Em would be up soon – and they had a busy day.

Hugo, a huge, soppy grin on his face, picked up the handset again and dialled Annabel's number. 'Wake up, angel – we're going shopping. To Hamleys!'

Bella decided to take Emily for a walk to break the news. She let her swing on her hand, feed the ducks on the pond by the Common and generally let off steam for about half an hour before she broached the dreaded subject.

'Em, do you remember we were talking about daddies the other day?'

'Yes,' said Em, picking up a rotting conker shell. 'Mine is busy.'

'That's right. He has been very busy. But he wrote a letter the other day to say he isn't so busy any more.'

'How do conkers get inside the shell, Mum?'

'They grow from little seeds.' Ah, this could be handy, actually. 'Just like you did in my tummy.'

Em burst out laughing. 'But you don't have *prickles* on your tummy!'

'No,' said Bella. Perhaps she should steer clear of the birds and the bees then. And conkers. 'Anyway, your daddy wrote a letter –'

'What a shot!' yelled Em, who had hurled her conker and hit a tree trunk.

'Emily. Would you like your daddy to visit you?' There! She'd done it. Bella held her breath.

The little girl cocked her head to one side and considered. 'Does he like football?'

'I don't know, darling. Because he's been so busy I haven't seen him either – well, not for a very long time. So I don't know what he likes. We'll both have to find out.'

'Will he take me to Disneyland like Tom's daddy? Tom's mummy and daddy don't live together either.'

'Probably not,' said Bella.

'So he'll just come round and drink tea and stuff?'

'Probably. And, of course he'll want to get to know you and talk to you.'

'It sounds a bit boring.'

'Well, it's up to you. You can give it a try if you want to.'

'OK,' said Emily, looking up at her mother with Hugo's eyes. 'Tell my daddy he can come to tea tomorrow. And could we have shepherd's pie?'

I am in a supermarket buying mince to make a shepherd's pie for a one-night stand whom I have not seen for over seven years and who is the father of my daughter. This, thought Bella, must be about as weird as it gets.

She had decided to drive to the new BestBuys, just outside Weatherford, to do a major food shop, partly as a much-needed distraction and partly because her cupboards and her freezer were almost empty of standby provisions. Em was swinging on and off the trolley, making frequent pleas for items that were far too expensive or far too bad for her.

Bella surreptitiously removed a packet of lurid orange Cheezy Treatzies from the trolley and glanced around her

261

with interest. It was a huge supermarket and amazingly busy for a Sunday afternoon. But it was an ugly-looking place – just a large rectangle built out of what looked like giant squares of white plastic adorned with the green and white BestBuys logo. It would stick out like a sore thumb on the old allotments, spilling out onto the pretty little Common. Surely in this environment-conscious day and age the councillors couldn't grant planning permission for a monstrosity like this?

But the produce inside the plastic walls was, despite Ron's tales, of seemingly excellent quality. There was a massive selection of fruit and vegetables and even Bella, tempted by the dewy fresh grapes and gleaming apples, found herself buying far more than she and Emily could realistically eat. Other people obviously had the same problem, she thought, watching a couple of middle-aged women come in with a basket and then scurry off to get a trolley.

In the sweet section she dithered over the 'finest' Swiss chocolate bars on a 'buy one get one free' offer. She flung two in the trolley; calories don't count when they're a bargain. Emily was looking wistfully at a chocolate selection box with pictures of footballers on it. 'You can have just one little thing, Em,' said Bella, steering her towards the small sweets. What a hypocritical parent I am, she thought.

Bella was just pushing her loaded trolley towards the checkout when she noticed three dark-suited men walking towards a door marked 'office'. Something about the burly shoulders and ruddy face of one of them looked familiar. The men came closer, chatting animatedly, the middle holding out his hands as if to emphasise a point. Oh! She *did* know him! It was Councillor Hanson! Damn – he'd recognised her. Bella gave a little wave.

'Bella – my ace reporter! Nice to see you here.' Ted

came striding over. 'And this must be your daughter. What a lovely little girl. Are you doing your shopping?'

Well that's pretty obvious, thought Bella but flashed him a smile. 'Yes. There's so much to choose from here. We've spent far more than we meant to!'

'That's what we like to hear,' said one of Ted's companions, a tall, balding man in his fifties, who bore a badge saying 'Paul Davison. Regional Manager' on his lapel.

'You have an excellent selection,' simpered Bella. But you can still keep your hands off our allotments, she added silently.

'I'm delighted you think so,' said Mr Davison.

The other man, who didn't have a badge, did not seem too amused by this casual chit-chat and was fidgeting, glancing at his watch.

'We'd better go,' said Councillor Hanson. 'I'm just having a meeting with these two gentlemen about the planning application. I expect you'll be writing a story about that soon, Bella.' He winked. 'And you must give me a call next week and we'll do a follow-up about the Carla Fund – it's still growing!'

'I will,' promised Bella.

The councillor bent down to address Emily. 'And you, young lass, are the prettiest thing I've seen all afternoon. I think you deserve a little present.' He reached out to the display rack near the checkout and took a packet of Smarties. 'Here – don't eat them all at once.'

'Thanks!' grinned Em, delighted.

'Thank you, Councillor Hanson. I'll talk to you soon.' Bella joined the checkout queue. Ah, that was sweet. But she didn't like that hard-faced fidgety-looking man who was looking at his watch. She bet he was the one who wanted to build on their allotments.

She unpacked her shopping, her thoughts flying back to Hugo, and the jitters immediately returning to her tummy. She'd better hurry home and make that bloody shepherd's pie.

Jonathan had spent a pleasant Sunday alone, Madeleine having driven back to London in disgust to make urgent appointments with her hair advisors on Monday morning. She had been pale but quiet when Jonathan had returned late on Saturday evening, slurring slightly after the effects of six pints of bitter in the King's Arms. She had made up a makeshift bed on the small sofa in their suite so Jonathan bedded down there obligingly, his head stuck at an awkward angle one end and his feet hanging over the edge at the other.

He spent Sunday catching up on paperwork and flicking through the papers. After lunch he drove quietly to Hilltops and parked his car behind a convenient transit van close to Ricky Thomas's house.

He watched for three hours before Ricky suddenly stepped out of his front door carrying a black sports bag. In the loping gait peculiar to idle young men he walked down the road, turning left into Truman Drive then right into Wordsworth Place. Here he rapped smartly on the door of number 37 and greeted a burly, middle-aged man.

Jonathan, who had followed on foot, spent a chilly hour loitering behind a ramshackle row of garages before he saw Ricky emerge – minus the bag – and lope back home. There, Jonathan saw the front room curtains close and the bluish light of a television glow through a crack in the middle. Looked like he was settled for the evening, he thought, making a mental note to do an electoral roll check on number 37 Wordsworth Place.

An idea formed in his brain. He frowned, then scrabbled in his glove compartment for a pen and a piece of paper to write himself a list of questions he wanted to check first thing in the morning. At the bottom of the list he wrote 'HAIR' in big black capitals, and underlined it twice.

Now Jonathan was back in his hotel room trying to watch a rugby match on television, scratching his head idly and imagining his nits crawling busily about his scalp. He obviously needed one of those white comb things but he hadn't a clue where to get one in Haybridge – and it was hardly the kind of thing he could ask his CID colleagues.

Bella would know what to do though. He would give her a call in the morning.

Chapter Twenty-Three

'We are feeding the information through the database right now,' said Dr Peter Marsh, who was not too pleased to be called so urgently at one minute past 9am – before he even had time to set up his coffee percolator – by this urgent-sounding Detective Sergeant. The chap had been so well mannered and patient before. What had got into him?

'I think I can help you speed things up,' said Jonathan. 'I am going to give you a name. Write it down carefully and I would like it checked at once.'

Dr Marsh wrote down the name with an irritated tut and then firmly replaced his handset. He knew all about these detectives with their fancy theories that rarely amounted to anything at all. This one could wait until he'd had his coffee; he had rather a nice Brazilian blend he wanted to try out.

Jonathan tapped his pen on his desk and consulted his list. He switched on his computer and clicked on to the electoral roll search, keying in 37 Wordsworth Place, Hilltops. The names Edward and Helen Robertson flashed on to his screen. Jonathan swiftly fed the former name into the Police National Computer. Hmm – interesting… He picked up his phone, intending to summon Boz on his mobile but at that moment the young detective burst into the office, clutching two sheets of paper.

'Burglaries, guv – just got them from the control room. Two of them, reported a few minutes ago.'

'Two?' Shit, that's bad.

'Yeah, looks like things are hotting up, guv. First time we've had two the same night.'

Jonathan reached for the report forms and scanned them quickly. Bessie Muggeridge from Bessie's Bargain Basement had opened up as usual at 8.55am to find her back window smashed, a locked drawer forced and her petty cash tin missing. She estimated it contained about £80, mostly in coins. The intruder had also rifled through her stock and stolen several pairs of training shoes and a few dozen packs of batteries.

Four doors away at Greens and Co Greengrocers, Mr Brian Green also opened up to a floor covered in broken glass. His charity collection tin and a locked cash box were missing, the latter containing £250 he had been planning to pay to his potato delivery man that very morning. No fruit or vegetables appeared to be stolen.

'We'd better get down there, guv,' sighed Boz. 'I can't believe these people still persist in leaving cash around after all our warnings. And they haven't even fitted burglar alarms. I bet it's the age old excuse – "I was just getting round to it, officer".' He sighed again. He had been up half the night with a tearful Kayleigh, who had somehow found out he had a steady girlfriend. The last thing he wanted was more bloody burglaries.

'Let's go,' said Jonathan. 'We'll take Gazza. But we'll go in two cars.'

'Why?' asked Boz.

'I was just getting round to having an alarm fitted – honestly, officer,' said Brian Green, a rotund man in his early sixties with cheeks like shiny red apples.

'We were offered a good deal from the Chamber of Commerce, you see. They sent a letter round recommending this security company who could supply and fit for a 40 per cent discount. I even phoned them but they were booked up till next month. I reckoned it would be worth the wait.'

Mr Green scowled at his broken window. 'It wasn't worth this, though,' he sighed.

'It could have been worse – they haven't touched your stock,' said Boz reassuringly.

'No lad, but they've still beaten me. It's not like the old days any more when you could leave your door open all day and trust folk. I reckon it's time for me to sell up and retire now; take up golf or something a bit safer.'

'That's a shame,' said Jonathan sincerely. He had just heard almost identical words of gloom from Bessie Muggeridge, a slight, middle-aged lady who had been pale and trembling after the shock of the break-in. She gratefully sipped the tea Jonathan had made her in the tiny little kitchen at the rear and confided her plans to sell up and buy a small villa in Spain.

'It's knocked our confidence, all these break-ins – especially when we know the burglars are still on the loose... I'm sure you're doing your best to catch them, officer, but it's going to come too late for people like us,' she said sadly. 'It's costing us a fortune too. My insurance premium has gone up by 30 per cent because of all this hassle – they say we're in a high risk area now. It's going to go up even more now, I bet.' Bessie shook her head. 'It's not even as though we're taking the money to cover it. Takings are going down every year and if that new supermarket place comes it will knock us for six. No, officer – it's time for me to head for that sunshine. I think.' She managed a watery smile.

Jonathan had handed Bessie over to Gazza to give her statement and walked to the greengrocers. As Boz started taking a statement from Mr Green, Jonathan went to inspect the window, bending down to examine the broken shards of glass on the floor. Pulling on a clear plastic glove from his pocket, he carefully picked up one piece. 'Boz – could you bring me an exhibit bag?' he called.

Jonathan pocketed the plastic bag and went to sit on an old stool near the till, tapping his feet and glancing repeatedly at his watch. 10.06am. Any time now, he thought.

As if on cue his mobile phone rang. He gave an abrupt greeting then listened carefully for 30 seconds. 'Thank you,' he said, clicking the off button and walking towards Mr Green.

'I am afraid something has cropped up and my colleague and I have to leave. But another Detective Constable will be with you in a few minutes to finish your statement. I am sorry for the inconvenience.'

Wisely Boz kept quiet until they were in Jonathan's car. 'What the hell is going on, guv?' he said.

'We are going to arrest our burglar,' said Jonathan simply. 'You'll find some handcuffs in the glove compartment.'

'What?'

'We are going to arrest Ricky Thomas, who, through DNA analysis of the hairs found at the scene of the Spar shop burglary two weeks ago, is undoubtedly the little shit who has been causing havoc in Haybridge.' He paused for one second. 'And yes, before you say it – this has completely buggered my theory on a professional gang!'

'But the DNA result wasn't due for another week!' said an amazed Boz.

'I had a little theory,' said Jonathan, 'so I gave Ricky's name to Dr Marsh an hour or so ago. He compared the details and bingo – we had a 99 per cent certainty match. And could you possibly shut your mouth, Boz, I am worried you might catch a fly.' Or a nit, he thought, scratching his head.

The detective shut his mouth obligingly. 'Christ, guv – you've got the murderer *and* the burglar in one fell swoop. That's a pretty good clean-up rate!'

'Is it?' said Jonathan.

Mrs Maria Thomas, thank goodness, was out when Jonathan rapped at the front door of 92 Crispin Drive, having first arranged for two uniformed officers to cover the back entrance. He didn't think he could have stood the inevitable hysterics as he carted away her precious 'good boy'.

Ricky answered the door himself, his eyes dull with sleep and his short black hair sticking up in tufts from his head. He took an involuntary step back when he saw Jonathan and Boz, then held out his hands, palms outwards. 'I haven't done nothing!' he protested.

Jonathan took advantage of the outstretched arms and swiftly snapped a handcuff on one wrist. 'Ricky Thomas, I am arresting you on suspicion of burglary. I am warning you that anything you have to say...'

He repeated the usual warnings and then asked if Ricky wanted to collect anything before he was taken to the police station.

'Er ... can I get my fags?'

Snapping the other cuff onto his own wrist, Jonathan followed Ricky through the kitchen into the front room, where he noted a duvet and pillow heaped on the sofa. You and me both, mate, he thought.

In the car Ricky was silent and Jonathan could feel the young man's hand trembling through the metal cuff.

'Where's your mum, Ricky?'

'In hospital. Having her hip done.'

'Right,' said Jonathan. 'How much did it cost?'

'Ten grand,' said Ricky automatically, then bit his lip. 'Right.'

'I haven't done nothing. I don't know why you're arresting me.'

'Don't you?' said Jonathan.

Back at the police station Ricky refused the offer of legal advice from the duty solicitor and sat alone, hunched miserably over the table in the now familiar interview room. Jonathan plonked an ashtray in front of him and clicked on the tape machine.

'Can you tell me what you were doing last night, Ricky?'

'I was at home. Watching telly. Then I went to bed.'

'On the sofa?'

'Yeah.'

'Why?'

'Why what?'

'Why did you sleep on the sofa. Did you come in very late and you were too tired to go to bed?'

'No.'

'Did you break into Greens and Co Greengrocers last night, Ricky?'

'NO! Honest – I didn't.'

'Did you go anywhere near Greens and Co Greengrocers last night, Ricky?' Jonathan sounded almost bored.

'No – I told you.'

'Then perhaps you could explain why this piece of broken glass, found inside Greens and Co, is stained with blood which we can prove came from your hand.' He put the evidence bag on the table.

'What?' said Ricky, suddenly shifting in his seat.

'You have a small cut at the side of your right hand. Show me.'

Ricky's hand was trembling visibly when he held it out. 'I did it at home – with a knife. I was making a sandwich,' he said.

Jonathan ignored him. 'Our scenes of crime people will find footprints outside Bessie's Bargain Basement store and they will match footprints found at Greens and Co. So you committed two burglaries last night, didn't you, Ricky?' It was a bit of improvisation about the footprints but it *could* happen.

Ricky hung his head. Jonathan continued, this time sticking to facts. 'You also broke into the Spar shop in Green Street late on the night of the third of November.'

'I didn't.' The head was raised a fraction.

'And you left behind two hairs, snagged in the broken glass. Those hairs have been scientifically proven to be yours by DNA testing.'

Ricky hung his head again.

'I put it to you that you are responsible for a spate of burglaries of shops, businesses and trade premises in various locations in Haybridge between June and November this year. Am I correct?'

Ricky said nothing.

'You kept the cash and sold the other goods to third parties, including a Mr Edward Robertson of 37 Wordsworth Place. Is that right?' said Jonathan, hoping the uniformed officers had obtained an emergency warrant as instructed and were searching that address at that very moment.

Ricky stayed silent, but gripped the side of the table.

Jonathan waited for a full minute before speaking, in a tone that was suddenly gentle: 'You did it for your mum, didn't you, Ricky? So that she could have her hip operation – to stop her being in pain all the time. You didn't like seeing your mum in pain, did you?'

The young man put his face in his hands and Jonathan could see his shoulders shaking. He made a low, guttural noise somewhere between a sob and a groan, then suddenly raised his head and looked Jonathan straight in the eye.

'But I didn't murder Carla,' he said.

* * *

When the tape was switched off and Boz had been dispatched to bring Ricky a cup of tea, Jonathan asked the young man how his mother was.

'She's doing good. The doctor bloke says she'll be out by Wednesday. But she's got to take it easy.' Ricky bit his lip. 'Will I be allowed bail – to help her, like?'

'I don't know,' said Jonathan. 'They do operations on Saturdays then, that Viking Clinic?'

'Yeah – in the mornings. Any chance to make money, the greedy bastards.'

'And it cost ten thousand pounds?'

Ricky nodded and suddenly looked wary.

'When I added up the value of everything stolen in the thirty-seven burglaries it came to well over twenty thousand pounds. What did you do with the rest of the money, Ricky?'

There was no reply, but the brown eyes darted all over the room.

'Did you give it to someone else? Was someone taking a cut? One of your mates?'

'My mates knew nothing about it. You keep them out of it.' The tone was aggressive – or was it scared?

Jonathan changed tack. 'There was a break-in at Adams hardware shop and some tools were stolen on the night Carla was killed. Was that you, Ricky? Did you lie about going home and watching the football?'

Ricky nodded and, for the first time, smiled. 'So you believe I didn't kill her?'

'Not yet,' said Jonathan firmly.

At that moment Boz burst in with the tray of tea and a paper plate of biscuits. Jonathan's stomach gave a growl – when the hell had he last eaten? He had bought a sandwich from a garage yesterday lunchtime but he couldn't remember eating it. God, he'd kill for a King's Arms pie.

'There's some bloke downstairs who says he's from that fancy solicitor's firm, Watkins and Ellis. He says he's been sent to see Ricky,' Boz announced.

That's strange, thought Jonathan. The boy had only made his one permitted phone call and that was to the Viking Clinic – to get a message to his mum that he wouldn't be visiting that afternoon. 'Do you know anything about this, Ricky?'

Ricky shook his head and looked genuinely puzzled.

'You'd better send him up then. All two hundred pounds an hour of him,' said Jonathan with a sigh.

It was 3pm before Jonathan finished dealing with the arrogant Rufus Liddlington and his pompous objections to Ricky being held overnight for further questioning. The solicitor had refused point-blank to answer any questions about who was paying his bill, saying it was not something police officers should concern themselves about. He had, however, dropped numerous veiled threats about the Human Rights Act and insisted upon talking to his client alone and at length.

It was 6pm before Jonathan finished with the paperwork from the statements and reports, including one from the search warrant officers detailing the nice little stash of stolen goods they had found at 37 Wordsworth Place. The householder, a Mr Edward Robertson, had been arrested on suspicion of handling stolen goods and was currently being questioned by Boz and Gazza.

Jonathan rubbed his eyes and contemplated putting his head down on the desk for a quick nap. Then he shook his head, stood up and went to his locker for his gym bag. He would do a quick session on the running machine, lift some weights, and then have a swim. Then, he thought, scratching his head, he would sort out these bloody nits before they drove him crazy.

Back at the hotel, Madeleine was acting Lady Bountiful, pressing a £5 note into the hand of a wide-eyed young waiter who thought he'd never seen anything so beautiful as this vision in that flowing white silky thing and sparkly diamond earings.

'So I want the very best room service. I want you to light the candles, serve the champagne – do make sure it's properly chilled – and bring all the food in silver dishes, do you understand?'

The waiter nodded dumbly and Madeleine ran through the menu, ticking off the dishes on her fingers.

'Wild mushroom pâté served with baby spinach garnish, fillet of Dover sole with buttered vegetables, and baby strawberries in sorbet nests. Have you got all that?'

The waiter swallowed and nodded again.

'I will see you at 8.30pm. Do not be late.'

The waiter scurried out of the room. Madeleine walked to the mirror to check her reflection and gave a small, satisfied smile. She looked good. Jonathan would not be able to resist her tonight, especially when she fed him those baby strawberries. Maybe she should have ordered some whipped cream?

Madeleine, after two days of sulking, was anxious now to make amends. Her stylist in London had assured her she had not a trace of a head louse and she realised now she may have overreacted just a teeny little bit to the whole situation. And if Jonathan *was* getting a bit too interested in that Bella girl then it wouldn't do any good at all for Madeleine to be off the scene for too long. She had to put some effort into this, it would be worth it in the long run. Tonight he would come home to a surprise candlelit welcome, a champagne meal and a passionate reunion. That would soon woo him away from that little tart...

Bella was desperately trying to act normal but knew she wasn't quite pulling it off.

'You've just put my school shoes in the fridge, Mummy,' said Em, who was drinking a glass of milk at the kitchen table.

'Oops, sorry,' said Bella, putting the butter in the fridge instead.

'And your face looks all red and funny.'

'Oh dear,' said Bella, flying out to the hallway to look in the mirror. Em was right. She did look funny – it was the combination of frizzy hair, bright red cheeks and wild eyes flanked by huge dark circles that did it, she thought. She ran to the bedroom, where she frantically applied mousse to her hair, and powder to her cheeks. Just for good measure she slicked on some lip-gloss. She couldn't understand why she was bothering though – what did it matter how she looked to Hugo? He was here to see Emily, not to judge her.

Bella had just checked the shepherd's pie in the oven and was wiping off Emily's milk moustache when the knock came at the door. For a long moment she stood there, clutching the wad of kitchen roll, feeling her heart thumping wildly in her chest.

'Is that my daddy?' whispered Emily, suddenly looking apprehensive.

'Yes,' whispered Bella. 'Shall we go and let him in?'

Hand in hand they tiptoed to the door. 'Why are we whispering?' whispered Em.

'I don't know,' whispered back Bella.

Mother and daughter surveyed each other solemnly,

then suddenly burst out laughing as they both realised how silly they were being.

It was that sight that greeted Hugo when the door was flung open. A pretty, red-haired woman with the sparkle of suppressed laughter in her big, grey eyes and an amused smile on her wide, generous lips. Next to her was a child with a huge grin on her little sharp, freckled face and an identical spark of laughter in her eyes. His eyes. His chin. His daughter. His heart missed a beat. Inanely he started babbling about his journey here ... the traffic ... . how much Haybridge had changed since he was last there ... how they'd built a new road in to the town... Shut up you idiot, he told himself. Say something to your daughter.

The child was regarding him solemnly now. 'Do you want to come in?' she said. The mother jumped back, flustered and then she started babbling inanely too. Yes, Haybridge had changed ... there had been dozens of new houses built ... they were building a new road out to Weatherford soon ... had the journey from London taken him long?

Hugo followed her retreating back and tried to remember that curvy little figure in bed beside him, the night his daughter was conceived. He couldn't. All the women he'd had back in those wild days had merged into one big grey blur. He could remember the hair though – and there was something about those eyes. He followed Bella into the living room and sat down, as invited, on the armchair. Mother and daughter perched opposite him on the sofa, staring expectantly.

God, he's handsome, thought Bella, taking in the floppy blond hair, perfect aquiline nose, the chiselled jaw and the tall, lean body in its perfectly cut chinos and shirt.

Hugo reached into the huge carrier bag he had carried in with him and drew out a large pink box. 'I bought you a present, Emily.'

Inside was a blonde, curly-haired doll with vivid blue eyes and bright pink lips. 'I walk, I talk, I ask for my potty. I am your very own little girl', the box proclaimed.

Emily took the doll, which was almost as big as her, and thanked Hugo politely then stared at the toy with interest. 'Does she kick?' she said.

'Good lord, I hope not,' said Hugo with a nervous, over loud laugh. 'Shall I help you get her out of the box?'

'Yes please,' said Em.

Father and daughter bent over the box, undoing endless loops of the plastic-covered wire which held the doll in place. Em picked up the doll and, holding it awkwardly on her lap, resumed her place on the sofa. She sat in silence.

'Well, how lovely!' trilled Bella. She jumped up and clapped her hands. 'Now – who would like some nice shepherd's pie?'

Emily stifled a giggle. 'You sound like Megan's mum!' she said.

Hugo seized the opportunity. 'Is Megan your little friend, Emily?'

'Yep. I have three friends. Megan is my best friend, Grace is my second best friend and Jennifer is my third best friend. Grace plays football with me sometimes but Megan and Jennifer don't like it.'

'Ah – you play football?'

'Yep.' Em gave a grin. 'I scored a goal on Saturday. A penalty.'

That's my girl, thought Hugo, with a strange glow of pleasure.

Once father and daughter had found common ground they chatted quite happily, Hugo relating tales of his soccer matches at school and Emily regaling him with every detail of her Saturday match. Bella bustled around setting the table and serving up supper. She found it hard to look at Hugo without blushing for some reason but on the whole it wasn't as bad as she had thought. He certainly didn't seem as though he was going to snatch Emily up from under her nose and whisk her off forever – in fact he seemed almost *scared* of the child. He seemed to appreciate the shepherd's pie too, though he refused seconds. Bella had trouble swallowing more than a few mouthfuls but Em, as usual, tucked in heartily, chattering with her mouth full to both her parents.

After the meal, when Emily slipped off to wash her face, Bella and Hugo faced each other across the kitchen table. Suddenly they both started to talk at the same time.

'You first!' laughed Hugo.

Bella looked at him shyly. 'I was going to say this wasn't as bad as I'd expected – and Emily seems to be fine.'

'And I was going to say what a thoroughly excellent job you have done of bringing up that little girl. She is a real credit to you,' drawled Hugo charmingly.

Bella felt her heart do a funny little flip and a rush of pride swept through her body. God, she'd forgotten how smooth this bloke could be; no wonder she'd been swept off her feet all those years ago. She was wondering how to answer the compliment when two things happened simultaneously: Emily came bursting back into the kitchen and the doorbell rang. 'Excuse me,' she said, rising from her seat.

Jonathan stood at the door clutching a bunch of rather wilted yellow chrysanthemums. 'Hello,' he said. 'I have a little problem. I need your help.'

Chapter Twenty-Four

'Nits?' gasped Bella. 'You have nits?'

'Yes,' said Jonathan, peering into the kitchen and suddenly realising Bella had company. A mini tornado flew through the door and launched itself at his legs.

'Jonny!' The tornado hugged just above his kneecaps and Jonathan gave a slight stagger. 'My daddy's come to see me, Jonny. He's not busy any more! And he calls football "soccer"!'

'Oh,' said Jonathan.

Bella was leaning against the wall, her shoulders slumped. 'You need a nit comb,' she said weakly.

Jonathan took in the moussed hair and the faint shine of lip-gloss on her lips. 'This isn't really the best time, is it?' He suddenly remembered the flowers and shoved them in Bella's hand. Her face lit up.

'Thank you,' she said. 'I'll put them in water – and then I'll find you a nit comb.'

'Come and say hello to my daddy,' said Em, grabbing Jonathan's hand and dragging him into the kitchen.

Hugo, who had perfect manners, jumped up from his chair. 'Hugo Copeland. Pleased to meet you,' he said, extending his hand.

'Jonathan Wright. Likewise.' Jonathan shook the hand firmly.

'I see you know Emily.' Hugo's voice was even but his mind was racing. Who is this bloke? He can get his hands off my daughter. I haven't waited six years for some cranky-looking bloke to muscle in on my little girl.

I bet you're shagging her mum. Well I got there first, *mate.*

'Yes. She's a great kid.' And you don't fucking deserve her, you bastard. How dare you show up here after ignoring her for six years – letting Bella struggle all that time? If you think you're going to charm her into bed again you can get your feet out from under that table and sod off now, *mate.*

Well, at least they seem to be getting on all right, thought Bella, slipping out to find the nit comb. The whole evening was taking on a totally surreal aspect now. She felt a yearning to go into her bedroom, fling herself down on the bed and leave them all to it. Instead she rummaged through the sideboard drawer for the nit comb and thrust it discreetly into Jonathan's hand.

The two men stood silently, facing each other. Just *go* – both of you, thought Bella. She looked at her watch pointedly. 'Er, it's Emily's bedtime now...'

Hugo turned to her with a charming smile. 'I guess my time is up then. Can I come next week – as we agreed? Perhaps,' he said, shooting a glance at Jonathan, 'perhaps you would allow me to take you and Emily out to dinner next time, to repay you for your hospitality.'

'That would be lovely,' squeaked Bella. 'Emily, come and say goodbye to your ... to Hugo.'

'Goodbye Hugo,' said Emily solemnly. Thank you for my dolly.'

Hugo felt an irresistible urge to sweep the little girl up in his arms and kiss her. Instead he patted her tentatively on the head. 'Goodnight angel. Daddy will come to see you again soon.'

At the door Hugo thanked Bella profusely. 'You don't know what this means to me,' he whispered. 'I wish I could turn the clock back, Bella, and start all over again. I know I've been a complete bastard but I'll make it up to you – I promise I will.' He leaned forward and gave her a smooth kiss on the cheek. 'And if it's any consolation, you are even more beautiful than I remembered.'

He walked out, leaving Bella with one hand touching her cheek in the spot where his kiss had landed. That's probably the nicest thing anyone has ever said to me, she thought, misty-eyed.

Jonathan was still standing in the middle of the kitchen, eyeing the remains of the shepherd's pie wistfully. He looks starving, thought Bella. 'Do me a favour – finish that up,' she said, plonking a plate and knife and fork on the table. 'There's some vegetables here. You can heat them in the microwave. I'm going to bath Em.' She walked wearily out of the kitchen.

Jonathan was scraping the last crispy bits of potato off the edge of the pie dish when Bella returned with a pyjama-clad Emily dancing ahead of her, demanding to say goodnight to Jonny. The child clambered onto his lap and put one arm round his neck.

'Night, butt-kicker,' grinned Jonny.

Em giggled. 'Night, naughty mouth.'

'Night, baggy shorts.'

Em rubbed her face against Jonathan's. 'Night, scratchy face.'

'Goodnight, my champion football player,' smiled Jonathan, lifting Emily to the floor. 'Bed now.'

'Goodnight,' said Emily, walking slowly to the door. In the doorway she paused, and addressed Jonathan. 'I think my daddy's okay. But I wish *you* were my daddy instead.'

Fuck! thought Bella, grabbing her daughter's hand and leading her to the bedroom.

Fuck! thought Jonathan, sinking his head into his hands.

He was still in that position when Bella returned several

minutes later after reading the bedtime story. She sat quietly opposite him and surveyed his scalp through his parting, noticing a few tell-tale tiny white eggs among the dark hairs. 'Sorry about the nits,' she said.

Jonathan raised his head slowly. 'That's OK.'

'Do you know what to do with the comb?'

'Er, run it though my hair and hope the little buggers jump out?'

Bella smiled. 'You have to wash it first and put loads of conditioner on it. Then you comb them out. If that doesn't work we can get some stuff from the chemist to kill them.'

'We? You have them too then?'

'I certainly do not.' Bella sounded offended. 'Why should you say that?'

'It's just that you scratched your head once when you greeted me at the door and twice while you were saying goodbye to that ... to Hugo.'

'Oh,' said Bella, suddenly feeling an urge to scratch behind her ear. She sat on her hands.

'Lean forward. I'll check,' ordered Jonathan.

She obliged and he parted the red curls and peered at her scalp. He moved her head to the side, parted and peered again, massaging the side of her head slightly with his fingers as he did so. Umm, thought Bella, that feels lovely. She let her shoulders slump and relaxed into the soothing little movements...

'Hah!' cried Jonathan, making her jump. 'I saw one!' He raised her head, put a hand either side of her face and looked her triumphantly in the eyes. 'So we're *both* nit infested!' he said with distinct glee.

'And that's a cause for celebration?' Bella returned his gaze steadily.

'No, sweetheart. It's a cause for you and I to do some serious communal nit combing,' grinned Jonathan. 'Do you want to go first or shall I?'

Sweetheart? Gosh, thought Bella, he's never called me that before. Two men saying nice things in one night – now that's a first. She stared blankly at Jonathan.

'OK,' he said, standing up and hauling her to her feet. 'I think it's a case of ladies first!'

'Um, how's work going?' she muttered a short while later. It was hard to think of anything more original to say when a burly police officer was sitting next to you on the sofa and raking through your wet hair with a nit comb.

'Very well, thank you,' replied Jonathan politely, conscious of the slight pressure of her thigh against his.

Bella raised one eyebrow. Hey, that's my trick, thought Jonathan. 'We arrested Ricky Thomas today – for the burglaries. We're hoping to charge him tomorrow morning.' And we would have done it today had not that fancy solicitor turned up and caused such a bloody fuss, he thought.

'No!' cried Bella, jerking her head round to face Jonathan. 'Ow!' she cried, putting one hand to her head.

'I told you to keep still.' Jonathan gently untangled the comb from a damp, curly lock. 'He's more or less confessed that he did it to raise money for his mum's operation.' He silently counted to three.

'Oh,' said Bella, her eyes misting over.

I knew it, thought Jonathan with a smile. 'Don't feel sorry for him. He's a burglar – and perhaps a murderer too,' he said firmly.

'Perhaps?'

'He's still denying it, more strongly than ever in fact. He says he was committing a burglary when Carla was killed.'

Bella waited expectantly. 'But,' Jonathan continued, 'there would actually have been plenty of time to do both.'

284

'So he lost his temper with Carla, told her to hang on for a moment while he committed a quick break-in, then went back and killed her? And she waited obligingly for him to do so?' Bella sounded indignant.

'That,' said Jonathan slowly, 'is exactly the problem I'm having with that little theory too.' He paused. 'But at least we'll get the burglaries wrapped up – and not before time too. I feel quite guilty after talking to the latest two victims today.'

'Why? You should be pleased you've helped them by catching the burglar.'

'Because it's too late for them, Bella. Some of them are thinking of closing down. It's knocked their confidence and when the new supermarket comes they're worried they won't be able to survive.'

Bella's mind flashed back to the laden shelves of the huge BestBuys store. 'They'll certainly find it hard to compete – the place is massive.' She related the story about her visit to the store, finishing with her encounter with Ted Hanson and his kindness with the Smarties.

'I think I might go and talk to some traders tomorrow and do an emotive, human interest story. That won't interfere with your investigation, will it?' she said.

'Not at all,' smiled Jonathan. 'You go ahead, super scoop.'

Twenty minutes later, Bella's plump nits having been flushed down the loo, it was Jonathan's turn to wash his hair over the bath and surrender to the comb. If Bella had trouble thinking what to say before she was finding it almost impossible now – at least he'd had his shirt on while he was delousing her.

She tried to avert her eyes from the muscular brown chest and taut, six-pack stomach. It was incredible how

he could sit in this position with barely a crinkle, let alone
a roll, she marvelled. She sneaked a quick glance at the
dark hair that curled across his chest and down his
abdomen and suppressed a giggle. It would be funny if
he got nits in that!

Jonathan caught the glance and put one hand up to
his chest. 'Er, you don't think...?'

'Good lord, no!' said Bella, letting the giggle spill into
a laugh.

Jonathan's shoulders started to shake. 'I've spent some
crazy evenings in my time but never one like this!' He
too started to laugh – deep, rumbling chuckles that made
Bella's giggles even worse. 'Ow! Ouch! You're pulling!' He
gave another huge guffaw, setting Bella off into a couple
of unladylike snorts because she couldn't get her breath.

'You are such a wimp!' she gasped, slumping weakly
against his shoulder.

Quick as a flash, Jonathan's arm shot round her neck,
flipping Bella's head onto the perfect little cavity that was
waiting for it on his chest. He tightened his grip on her
shoulders. 'Wimp?' he growled. 'We'll see about that!'

Bella, still giggling, put up a struggle and aimed a
playful pinch at Jonathan's side. Immediately his hand
clamped down on hers. Oops, she thought, I'm stuck now.
But maybe it wasn't such a bad place to be stuck – and
there was that smell again... She breathed in deeply and
her head relaxed just a fraction.

'So you surrender?' laughed Jonathan, sweeping her hair
off her shoulder and intending to playfully bite the little
ear lobe that suddenly looked so exposed and lonely. Instead
his lips found her neck. Suddenly he was kissing it and his
hands were cradling her head, tilting it backwards as his
mouth moved round to her throat. His breathing quickened
as he heard a small moan escape from Bella's lips. His
hands slid down her back and the kisses became more

urgent, travelling up her throat, onto her face, and onto each closed eyelid, then down towards the mouth... The eyes fluttered open and the lips were clamped closed. 'No ... no, we mustn't,' panted Bella, her breathing ragged and her hands pushing ineffectually against Jonathan's chest.

He sprang back, trying to control his own breathing. 'I'm so sorry ... I...'

'No,' said Bella, trying to control the tears suddenly pricking at the back of her eyes. 'It's me. It's my fault. It's just ... with ... Hugo and everything.' One tear spilled down. She had been going to say Madeleine but the word just wouldn't come out somehow. Why had she said Hugo? Oh God, she was so confused. And she felt all cold and empty now Jonathan's arms had gone. Another tear spilled down her cheek.

Jonathan viewed her wretched face with horror and a horrible sinking feeling in his stomach. Christ, what had he been thinking of? The poor little devil was obviously hung up on that bastard – having a loving reunion and all that – and he'd waded in with his size eleven boots. What the hell was wrong with him? Where was his self-control? She looked so wretched, staring at him like that with her bottom lip trembling.

He reached out and very gently touched the tip of her nose. 'Bella. I am so sorry. I didn't mean to make things difficult for you, and I wish you the best of luck with that ... with Hugo,' he said. Then he reached for his shirt and quickly shrugged it on. 'It won't happen again,' he said, almost curtly, as he walked out of the door.

Bella stayed put, watching him go. But I *want* it to, she thought, totally irrationally.

'Surprise!' trilled Madeleine the second that Jonathan walked in the door. She eyed his still damp hair. 'You've been a naughty boy and stayed late at that gym, haven't you? But don't worry, honey – I've kept your surprise warm.'

With that she pulled off the belt of her white silk negligee to reveal her naked breasts and a pair of tiny lace panties. Then she stepped over to a table and lifted the lid off a heated silver serving dish. 'Dover sole, darling, with wild mushroom pâté to start and baby strawberries for dessert.' She ran her tongue over her lips. 'With whipped cream.'

Jonathan's stomach gave a lurch of protest. Bloody hell, he was still full of shepherd's pie. 'Er ... how lovely,' he said politely.

Madeleine walked over to him and flung her arms around his neck. Then she looked at his hair and took a slight step backwards. 'I take it you got rid of the –?'

'The nits have gone,' said Jonathan firmly, taking his place at the candlelit table.

'Eat up, darling,' coaxed Madeleine twenty minutes later, holding a forkful of Dover sole to his lips.

Jonathan gently pushed her hand away. This was heavy going – both the meal and the conversation. His stomach felt uncomfortably full and his head was aching. It didn't help that Madeleine was prattling on about some fashion shoot she'd attended in London, going into minute detail about every single bloody dress. He also felt a nagging sense of guilt about Bella but he didn't know why. It wasn't as though anything had happened. But something would have happened if ... he pushed the thought firmly away. God, his head hurt.

Jonathan interrupted Madeleine while she was in full flow about some green Chinese silk number and stood up from the table, pushing his plate away. 'I'm not very hungry actually. If you don't mind I think I'll go to bed.'

'But honey, you haven't had your dessert!' cried Madeleine running into the bedroom after him, her breasts bobbing.

'I'll have it for breakfast,' he sighed, pulling his shirt over his head.

Madeleine watched the muscles ripple on his back and felt a huge urge to grab one of the silver serving dishes and hurl it at his head. Instead she took a deep breath and clenched her fists. 'Okay honey. I'll be with you in a minute. I just have to cleanse my face,' she trilled, through teeth that were gritted.

Suzy and Roger sat side by side on Bella's sofa, gripping each other's hands in excitement as they listened to her account of her evening. They had been hovering on the stairs, on and off, ever since they had heard Hugo arrive, desperate to know how the rendezvous was going.

Bella assured them Emily seemed to have taken it all in her stride and that Hugo had been the perfect gentleman. Both breathed a visible sigh of relief.

'Then when we saw Jonathan turn up we nearly *died!*' laughed Suzy, who was looking very pretty but understated tonight in an ordinary blue T-shirt and no make-up. 'And when he didn't come out for ages we wondered what on earth you were doing, didn't we, Rodge Podge?'

'We did, Pooh Bear,' said Roger, gazing at her adoringly.

'I must admit, we did try to listen a teeny bit, outside the door, didn't we, Rodge Podge?'

'You did, Pooh Bear. I was too much of a gentleman!' he laughed.

Roger, who seemed to have adopted his spiky hairstyle from the ball as permanent, looked quite cool tonight, thought Bella. He was wearing a new pair of jeans that actually fitted round his bottom for once and a deliberately faded blue T-shirt with a trendy logo on the front. He had abandoned his usual shiny black lace up shoes for a pair of Timberland boots.

In fact her friends both looked relaxed and happy ... and sort of *different*, she mused. Roger was far more confident and Suzy was just like Suzy when no men were around – kind and funny and sweet instead of over-vivacious and clingy. Perhaps this unlikely partnership really could work. How wonderful that would be. The Pooh Bear and Rodge Podge bit was a bit dodgy though.

Bella knew she would be interrogated next about Jonathan, so she swiftly steered the subject to work, strangely reluctant to talk about the passionate little interlude. She told Suzy about Ricky Thomas and the burglaries, enjoying watching her eyebrows shoot up in surprise.

'That's a hell of a story, Bel – "murder suspect charged with dozens of burglaries". It's almost too good to be true!'

So were Jonathan's kisses, thought Bella ruefully.

Chapter Twenty-Five

Bella and Suzy were having a working lunch, which meant they were stuffing Rolos from the vending machine in their respective mouths while they frantically tapped away at their computers.

'How's the court report going, Suze?' asked Bella, her mouth full of chocolate.

'It's a bitch,' declared Suzy, who had been covering a Crown Court case in Weatherford about four Haybridge men charged with armed robbery of a petrol station. 'There are four defendants, each with a different barrister and I'm getting all the names muddled up. One of them was gorgeous though – he looked so sexy in his wig.' She paused. 'But his bum wasn't half as cute as Roger's.'

'So, um, have you seen it with, you know, with no clothes on?' It was no good; Bella just had to know.

'The barrister's bum? Nah,' grinned Suzy. 'Funnily enough, he kept his clothes on in court.'

Bella giggled and held out the last Rolo. 'Just give me a yes or a no and this is yours.'

'Then it's a very definite yes,' said Suzy, shoving the Rolo in her mouth.

Bella let out a shriek of excitement, causing Sean to shoot her a warning frown. She lowered her voice: 'Out of ten?'

'Eleven,' said Suzy firmly.

Bella shrieked again and this time Sean got up from his desk and walked across to her. 'Just because your spelling is at a comparable level to a small child there is no need to behave like one, Bella.'

I can spell bugger off, thought Bella, trying to smother a giggle. My best friend is having passionate sex with my neighbour – that's momentous! Instead she gave the news editor a disarming smile and asked what she had spelt wrong.

'Believe, appealing, apparent and committee,' snapped Sean immediately, counting off each word on his bony fingers.

'Oh, that's all right then – only the usual,' said Bella, returning to her computer. Conveniently, at that moment her phone rang and Sean stomped off with a theatrical sigh.

'We've charged him,' announced Jonathan, with no preamble.

'With how many?' said Bella, who had clicked straight back into work mode.

'Thirty-seven. Involving goods to a total value of £20,000. He'll be going before the magistrates in the morning and we'll be applying to remand him in custody until the case gets to Crown Court.'

Bella, scribbling frantically, felt a sudden stab of sympathy for the doting Mrs Thomas.

'And before you ask,' continued Jonathan, 'I have made arrangements with social services to provide home care for the mother, who is coming out of hospital tomorrow. Your friend Kate has been very helpful, actually.'

Stop reading my mind, thought Bella. It's too spooky. 'That's really sweet of you to think of his mum,' she said.

'I am not *sweet*. I am a police officer.' Jonathan sounded indignant and Bella could hear a snort of laughter in the background. Boz, probably, she guessed.

She lowered her voice. 'You were very sweet last night.' She just couldn't resist it.

Jonathan lowered his voice too. 'I was off duty.' Bloody hell – was she *flirting* with him? That was a first. Wasn't she meant to be saving the flirting for that wimpy Hugo? Or was she just teasing him? Well, if that was what she wanted, he could out-flirt her any day. 'And *you* were irresistible,' he whispered sexily.

Bella felt a shiver run down her spine and clutched the phone closer to her ear, just above the spot where Jonathan's lips had been. 'Was I?' It came out as a squeak.

'Yes,' said Jonathan. He glanced quickly around the CID office. Boz and Gazza were quibbling over whose turn it was to make the coffee. He lowered his voice again. 'You were so irresistible that I wanted to kiss you ... all over.'

Bella felt little beads of sweat break out on her upper lip. She clutched the phone even tighter and let out a small, involuntary moan. 'Oh my God – are we having phone sex?' She couldn't help it; the words just came spilling out.

There was a chuckle at the other end of the line. 'Probably, sweetheart. It's just a shame we can't seem to make it in real life!' With that the receiver was replaced with a gentle click.

Bella leaned back weakly in her chair, knowing her cheeks were flushing scarlet. I guess that's Round Two to him, she thought with a sigh.

Jonathan, still chuckling gently to himself, had wandered down to the custody suite to see Ricky, who was huddled forlornly on the wooden bench, staring at the floor of his cell.

'So who is it then, mate?' said Jonathan, plonking himself down beside him.

'Uh?' said Ricky, looking up swiftly.

'Who were you working for? Who told you to do the burglaries? And who took half the proceeds?'

'No one. Nobody did.' The eyes were suddenly shifty.

'Listen, Ricky. I wasn't born yesterday and you're crap at lying. Tell me who was giving you the orders. And why did they tell you to avoid the big stuff – to leave the valuable stuff behind in some of the shops?'

Ricky stood up and shoved his hands in his pockets. He looked defiantly at Jonathan. 'My solicitor told me not to talk to you without him there. He said it's against my human rights,' he paused. 'Innit?'

'But it's your human right to take all the flack for someone else? *Innit* Ricky?'

'I dunno what you're talking about.' The eyes slipped back to the floor.

'Who's paying for your solicitor, Ricky? Is it someone who knew Carla?' Jonathan launched his long shot without really realising why he did. A vague, vague idea was forming somewhere at the back of his brain but it was so blurred he couldn't even process it into a proper thought yet.

Ricky's head shot up. 'No. No mate – he didn't know Carla! He'd never even . . .' He stopped abruptly and chewed his lip. 'Oh fuck,' he said quietly.

Back in the office Jonathan took a sheet of A4 paper and folded it into three sections. At the top of the first section he wrote 'Ricky', on the second 'Carla' and on the third 'Ricky and Carla.' He chewed his pen thoughtfully. The third column was probably the easiest to start with. Now, how many people could he think of who knew both Ricky and Carla?

He wrote down the lads he had seen in the Swan, giving descriptions where he did not have the names. He chewed his pen again. 'Boz, what's the name of that bird you took to the ball?' he called across the office.

'Kayleigh, guv,' shouted Boz obligingly. Jonathan wrote it down. Then he reached for the pile of statements in the tray marked 'Murder' and flicked through them. He scribbled down the name of a local GP who had once treated Carla for an irritating cough and the name of a couple of women who said they had spoken to her at the local playgroup.

After an hour of racking his brains and leafing through statements, Jonathan had ten names under the first heading, ten under Carla and only five – Ricky's mates and Ricky's mum – under people who knew them both. He tapped his fingers on the desk and doodled aimlessly at the top of his paper. The problem was, he knew so few people in Haybridge. It wasn't his patch. He needed someone with solid local knowledge.

He stared blankly at the sheet of paper. Oh dear, he'd doodled a little heart shape. Bloody hell, he was turning into a right nancy. Jonathan hastily scribbled the heart out with bold, black strokes. At the same instant he thought of exactly the person who could help him.

'Lunch? But it's ten to four.' Bella frowned. This wasn't some code for more of that phone sex stuff, was it?

'Is it?' Jonathan glanced at his watch in surprise. 'Afternoon tea then?'

'I have to pick up Emily in ten minutes. We finish early on Tuesdays.'

'Oh.'

'Why did you want to talk to me?'

Jonathan explained about Ricky's admission and his three little columns. 'So I'm looking for the Mr Big behind the burglaries – a person who knew Ricky but didn't know Carla,' he concluded.

'Oh,' said Bella. 'I've got some friends of Em's coming back for tea so I won't have time to think for a few hours.' She paused. 'Shall I call you tonight if I think of any more names?'

'That would be great,' said Jonathan, feeling slightly disappointed that she hadn't suggested he pop round to see her. It would have been nice to see Em again too. She could have shown her friends how she could hammer him at blow football. She would love that. I bet that bastard Hugo never plays blow football with her, he thought. He'd be too worried about creasing his poncy designer trousers.

He wandered off to the canteen to grab his belated lunch, wondering what Bella would be cooking for the children's tea. Suddenly, for the first time for at least twenty years, he had a huge craving for fish fingers and chips, with a blob of tomato ketchup on the side. He could almost feel his teeth biting into the crispy, golden coating and sinking through to the deliciously pappy white fish underneath. His mouth watered.

'The usual?' asked Edna, holding out a stale-looking cheese roll.

'Thank you. Unless ... er, I don't suppose you –' Jonathan glanced around furtively. 'I don't suppose you have any fish fingers, do you?'

'GLADYS!' roared Edna, turning to the open kitchen door. 'The boss wants FISH FINGERS. Can you cook 'im some?'

'NO!' came the answering yell. 'Tell the boss I've got a nice bit of plaice in batter but I ain't never heard of a copper wanting *fish fingers*!'

Jonathan winced and grabbed the cheese roll, flinging a handful of change on the counter. 'Don't worry, this will be fine,' he muttered, hastening out of the canteen, trying to ignore the two uniform sergeants who were dunking biscuits in their tea and humming, 'Oh I do like to be beside the seaside, Oh I *do* like to be beside the sea.'

At 9pm Jonathan was still at his desk, where, chin propped on one hand, he had been deep in thought for at least an hour. He was still trying to bring into focus this niggling little notion at the back of his brain but every time he got close, it swirled irritatingly out of his mental grasp.

His mobile trilled. 'Hi, sorry it's so late.' Bella sounded breathless. 'Em's been a little horror about going to bed.'

Jonathan grinned. 'Why? What's she done?'

'Oh ... the usual six-year-old stuff,' sighed Bella. 'Threw the soap down the loo when she had her bath and tried to say it slipped out of her hands.'

'Well, it probably did!'

'Rubbish,' said Bella. 'She was pretending to be Jonny Wilkinson at the time.'

'Rugby hey? Good *girl*!' said Jonathan approvingly.

'Then she refused to get dry and made me chase after her with a towel.'

'Good exercise,' nodded Jonathan.

'Then she tried to dive-bomb onto my bed but bounced off and bumped her head on the dressing table.'

'Oh my God! Is she okay?'

'She's fine. But she managed to knock over a bottle of my best perfume when she fell. And the lid wasn't on properly,' said Bella ruefully. She only possessed one bottle of scent and now most of it was over her bedroom carpet.

'I hate perfume anyway. It makes me sneeze,' said Jonathan.

'Oh,' said Bella, wondering then why Madeleine had reeked of Chanel at the ball. 'Anyway, I thought of some people for your lists.'

She rattled off the names of several people who would

have known Carla, including the leader at the local playgroup, where Amelia would probably attend three or four mornings a week, the volunteer mums who ran a nearby toddler group and Mr Benson at the post office who would have dealt with her regular letters to her parents. 'Then of course there's Boz's Kayleigh.'

'I've got her,' said Jonathan. 'Though from what Boz was saying today she's not *his* Kayleigh any more. She gave him the elbow.'

Bella laughed. 'When will he ever learn? Is he on to the next one yet?'

'Funny you should say that. He went into the little Italian place, Luigi's Pasta, the other day – Kayleigh works there the odd lunchtime apparently – with the sole intention of wooing her back and promising to dump his regular girlfriend. But,' Jonathan paused, 'he got talking to her fellow waitress, a little blonde, and disappeared with her instead!'

'That boy needs a government health warning,' said Bella, suddenly feeling very old. She moved on to Ricky, but apart from Kate and her social services colleagues, and maybe the youth and community workers on Hilltops, she could not think of anyone who he would have associated with. 'I don't really know much about the young trendy scene,' she confessed. 'But I can certainly ask around.'

Thinking of people who knew both Carla and Ricky was a real problem. 'You've obviously got his mates from the pub – did you get the landlady? She may have seen them in there together.'

'Good one,' said Jonathan, writing down Ms Amazonian. With those muscles she would certainly be capable of murdering someone but he couldn't for the life of him think of a motive.

'Mrs Thomas?'

'Got her.'

'The Williamses? Ah, no – they never met him, did they?'

'No,' said Jonathan.

Bella yawned. It had been a busy day and her brain was tired. Jonathan yawned too, suddenly imagining her snuggled up next to him on the sofa, her head on his chest. 'We'll think about it some more in the morning,' he said. 'It sounds like you need to be in bed now.'

The word bed seemed to jump out over the phone lines and reverberate between them, hanging in the air amidst an awkward silence. Both simultaneously cleared their throats and started talking briskly about needing early nights.

'Goodnight then,' said Bella.

'Goodnight. Sweet dreams,' said Jonathan, feeling an irresistable urge to see that red hair splayed out on a pillow.

He put down the phone and picked up his pen. *Work, you silly old fool*, he told himself.

Chapter Twenty-Six

Wednesday morning saw Jonathan summoned to Superintendent Nixon's office and Ricky summonsed to court.

Ricky received a remand in custody for seven days. Jonathan, expecting praise for the burglary result, received a rocketing about the lack of an arrest for the murder instead.

'This does not do our reputation any good at all – our public expect an arrest and they expect it quickly. It's obvious this Thomas chappie is a bad apple and I cannot understand what is holding you back,' barked the Superintendent, scratching his balding head.

Bloody hell – not you too! Jonathan thought, wondering if head lice could leap across desks. He peered at his boss's wispy grey hair, looking for telltale little white eggs. Hmm ... perhaps it was just dandruff.

'Are you listening, officer?'

'Absolutely, sir,' said Jonathan. 'I was just weighing up the evidence in my mind but I'm afraid my conclusion is the same. We do not have enough to get a murder charge past the Crown Prosecution Service. But this will change – very soon.' He wished he felt as confident as he sounded.

'You have a week, DS Wright. Just one week. After that, we may need to have another little talk to consider whether we can justify the expense of having you here in our little Haybridge family.' The tone was pleasant but the threat was obvious: pull your finger out or you're sent back to the Met with a great big 'Failed' on your personal record. Jonathan considered telling him where to stuff his personal record but flashed him a false smile instead.

'I'll do it … sir,' he said.

Bella's face was also frozen in a smile so false it was making her jaw ache. 'It's nice to see you, but I don't know why you are here,' she said. 'Emily's at school and anyway you're not due to see her until Monday.'

'I came to see you.' Hugo pushed back his hair from his forehead and lowered his eyes, revealing those irresistibly long lashes. 'I want to talk to you; I want you to tell me everything about Emily and all those years I've missed. I want to get to know my daughter. I don't want to bring her a doll when she'd prefer a football; I don't want to not know what her favourite colour is… Please Bella, I need you to help me.'

Bella felt her heart do a funny little flip. 'But the *Gazette* car park is hardly the place for me to give you Emily's life history, Hugo.'

Hugo smiled. 'Of course not, angel, and that's why I'm asking you out to dinner. Just you and me – tonight. I thought I'd catch you as you went into work so you'd have time to arrange a babysitter.'

Bella stared and Hugo continued. 'How about the Queen Elizabeth Hotel at eight? You could meet me there if you prefer me not to come to the flat before my Emily day.' He smiled his most charming smile and pushed back that cute little floppy bit of hair again.

Bella had never been treated to dinner at the Queen Elizabeth in her life. But she had heard about the legendary sweet trolley, which apparently groaned with no less than two dozen desserts, many of them liberally laced with cream and chocolate. The thought of dressing up and spending an evening in sophisticated male company was appealing, she had to admit. And it was good she and Hugo could be so grown up and *sensible* about all this, wasn't it? They had to set a good example to Em, after all. She pushed back a nagging worry about what her parents would say and another little niggle about how Jonathan would react. She told herself not to be silly – she was a grown woman and Jonathan had a steady girlfriend anyway.

She told Hugo it was a lovely idea and that she would meet him at the hotel at eight. She could bring some photographs if he liked.

Hugo's smile became dazzling and he kissed her on the cheek. 'I'd love that. Thank you, angel,' he said, before walking off to his shiny, low-slung red car.

Ron, dusting the desk in reception, looked out at Bella standing in a daze in the car park, rubbing her cheek where Hugo had kissed it, and he wrinkled his leathery old brow in a frown. He didn't know who that man was but he didn't like him. He looked far too much of a flash Harry for Miss Bella.

The 'flash Harry' drove off with a self-satisfied smile. His sentiments about his daughter were entirely genuine and he really did want to get to know her mother. But ever since he had seen Bella bending over to get the shepherd's pie out of the oven on Monday he hadn't been able to stop thinking about that curvy little body. Annabel, Sofia and all the other Sloane Rangers in his little London harem suddenly seemed very insubstantial compared to Bella – mentally as well as physically.

He hummed to himself as he drove to meet an old school friend at the other side of town, allowing himself a little daydream about him and Bella running through the park, swinging Emily between them, before returning ravenous and rosy-cheeked to a cosy little house somewhere and a hearty home-cooked meal prepared by Bella's fair hand.

He might have a bit of competition of course – that tall, dark guy had seemed distinctly miffed to see him. But Hugo, weaned on the highly competitive atmosphere of public school, didn't mind competition at all. In fact, he relished it. He knew he would always win.

Bella, still dazed, was sitting at her desk. 'Suze,' she hissed to her friend. 'I need your help ... I need you to babysit and I need something to wear tonight.'

Suzy's eyes shone. 'He's taking you out then?'

Bella nodded.

'That's brilliant, Bel! Roger and I were only saying last night how fantastic you were together!'

'Were you?' Bella frowned.

'And he is so good with Em. Honestly Bel, you'd be hard pushed to find another man who's as good with her. I'm just so glad the pair of you have come to your senses and stopped all this silly squabbling.'

'Uh?'

'Squabbling. You and Jonathan are always doing this bickering thing – trying to score off each other when it's obvious you've both met your match and neither of you will win. Rodge was only saying the other day –'

'Suze,' said Bella gently, 'I'm going out with Hugo tonight.'

'Oh dear,' said Suzy. She racked her brains for something to say. 'Um, perhaps we'd better have a doughnut.'

Bella was in the Ladies, splashing cold water on her face to cool her flushed cheeks and focus her brain, which was still fuzzy after Hugo's invitation. She stared at her reflection in the mirror. Hmm, she needed to pile on the make-up tonight. Perhaps she could wear her smart trousers and her camisole top with her black jacket. Would that be smart enough for the Queen Elizabeth? She could put her hair up to look a bit more dressy. Experimentally she piled her hair on top of her head and fumbled in her bag for some hairpins. Her mobile rang, making her jump, and she answered it with one hand holding up her hair and a mouthful of grips.

'Bella?'

'Hmmm.'

'What have you got in your mouth?'

Bella spat the grips gently into the washbasin. 'God, Jonathan, you don't miss a thing, do you?'

'No. And what have you just spat out in such a ladylike fashion?'

'Hairpins.'

'Why?'

'Why what?'

'Why are you fiddling about with hairpins? That's not like you. That's the sort of thing –' Jonathan stopped.

'The sort of thing Madeleine does?' supplied Bella. Jonathan grunted. 'How is Madeleine?' she continued sweetly.

'Er, she's fine.' Well, as far as Jonathan knew she was fine. She had hardly spoken a word to him since he had refused her bloody dinner on Monday. He had gone on to refuse her body as well – the sight of those naked breasts bobbing about over the slimy Dover sole had turned him right off. That rejection hadn't gone down too well at all... But she had thawed slightly this morning and was spending the day shopping again, faffing about buying things for the new house – the new house they were moving into in just two days' time. Jonathan's heart sank.

'When are you moving into your new house?' Still the sweet tone.

Jonathan wished Bella wouldn't read his mind like that.

It was spooky. 'On Friday,' he said, wondering whether to add the word 'unfortunately'.

'Oh, how super!' trilled Bella. You two-timing, teasing bastard, she added silently. 'Gosh, we both have an exciting week, don't we?'

'Why?'

'I have an important engagement tonight. I'm dining at the Queen Elizabeth Hotel with Hugo.' Oh dear, she'd gone from sounding like Enid Blyton to the Queen in just one sentence. But it would show him she wasn't going to sit at home twiddling her thumbs while he played happy homes with Madeleine.

'How nice for you,' said Jonathan with gritted teeth. 'Now, if we could get on to business... Did you manage to come up with any more names for the list? Only I'm under a bit of pressure to crack this murder now.'

'No,' admitted Bella. 'Who's putting you under pressure?'

Jonathan gave her a précis of the Superintendent's little speech and repeated his veiled threat. 'He says he wants a result for his public but he really means his cronies at the golf club.'

'Golf club?' Bella's mind raced. 'Um ... what sort of –?'

'A Mercedes. Blue. Top of the range,' grinned Jonathan, who knew exactly how her mind was working. 'I have to go – I'll talk to you later.' He replaced his handset and laughed out loud. Now Bella would go off on one of her flights of fancy and think Superintendent Nixon was the murderer. He loved her little theories – they were so entertaining. He didn't like the thought of her with that bastard Hugo though. That wasn't entertaining at all.

Hugo leaned across the table and gently brushed a tendril of hair away from Bella's cheek. 'You look very lovely tonight,' he murmured.

Bella's mouth was full of the last chunk of duck in cherry sauce so she could only give a funny little grunt. She chewed hastily and swallowed, taking a sip of wine to wash it down. It was nice wine actually, all fizzy like lemonade.

'Did you bring some photographs?' said Hugo.

'I did,' Bella fished in her bag and produced a wallet of photos showing Emily from a newborn baby to her sixth birthday. It was strange handing them to Hugo one by one, explaining the story behind them. 'That was when she had her very first bath – she yelled like crazy!' 'That was when she took her first steps.' 'Oh, she had chicken pox there – she was covered in spots!' 'That was her third birthday party. I made her a fairy castle cake.'

Hugo's eyes devoured them all, then he laid them down gently. 'I have missed so much. Am I ever going to make it up to her, Bella?'

'I don't know,' said Bella honestly. 'But to be fair, Emily herself doesn't really know what she's missed.'

Hugo laid his hand gently over hers on the table. 'And you, Bella? Can I make it up to you? It must have been such a struggle on your own. And all because of my selfishness.' He lowered those lashes again.

God, he's handsome, thought Bella, feeling the colour rise to her cheeks. His hand felt nice on hers, warm and comforting. She smiled. 'You could start making it up to me by … by ordering the dessert trolley so I can choose one of those wonderful puddings!' she joked.

Hugo laughed. What a wonderful, uncomplicated female. How different she was from all the rather spoilt and attention-seeking women in the London set. And how good it was to see a girl tuck in too – instead of picking at her food like an anorexic sparrow. 'Angel, you can have all the puddings on the trolley if you wish,' he said gently.

Now *that's* my kind of guy, thought Bella with a rapturous grin.

At 10.50pm Jonathan, who rarely smoked, felt a sudden urge for a cigarette. He decided to walk to the 24-hour garage across town, not, of course, because it happened to be a few doors away from the Queen Elizabeth Hotel but because he felt the need to stretch his legs. He also felt the need to get away from Madeleine's prattle about a house-warming party.

He bought his cigarettes, lit one, looked across at the hotel then looked at his watch. 11.10pm. Jonathan, who had wined and dined a fair few women in his time, estimated Bella and Hugo would be drinking coffee and eating after-dinner mints by now. He decided to stand on the street corner for a while – not because he wanted to spy on them but because he wanted to enjoy his cigarette in peace.

Three cigarettes later, Jonathan's feet were freezing. He was just contemplating leaving when he heard a familiar trill of laughter coming from the doorway of the hotel. It was Bella – in full canary mode, he thought with a frown.

Two figures stepped on to the pavement, one with its arm slung round the other. 'Mind the step, angel,' he heard Hugo say protectively. 'I'd hate you to hurt yourself.'

Yuk, thought Jonathan, his fist clenching into a tight ball in his jacket pocket.

The figures disappeared round the corner to the car park and Jonathan could just make out a faint giggle from Bella, then the slam of a car door. He pictured them driving home together, Hugo's hand possessively on Bella's knee, then walking into the flat, hand in hand, then him leading her to the bedroom... That was enough! Jonathan thrust his hands deeper in his pockets and stomped off towards his own hotel, wondering why he felt quite so angry – and sort of empty.

At 3am Bella, who had driven herself home full of chocolate mousse and given Hugo a polite goodbye peck on the cheek in the car park, suddenly woke up, sat bolt upright in bed and thought not of Hugo, not of Jonathan, but of Superintendent Raymond Nixon. A thought had been niggling her all day but now it came back with a vengeance.

She racked her brains to conjure up a picture of the Superintendent, whom she had met at police presentations or press conferences three or four times over the years. He was in his fifties, probably mid-fifties, she recalled, and was tall and lean with balding hair and a great beak of a nose. She seemed to remember he was married – yes, his wife was at the ball, a thin, rather severe-looking woman with her grey hair in a tight bun.

Would Carla be attracted to a man like Raymond Nixon, a married man well past his prime? Could he be the mystery lover? Bella found it hard to imagine but knew some girls were attracted to power and authority rather than looks. Perhaps he had been a father figure, a substitute for the dad she had left behind in Poland? It was an incredible theory but, Bella mused, not a totally ridiculous one and it would certainly explain the Superintendent's keenness to see Ricky Thomas charged with murder. How dare he threaten Jonathan in that way!

The man played golf, he drove a Mercedes. So he could have arranged to meet Carla in the golf club on that Tuesday night – a quiet night when no fellow members would notice him – and he could have carried her body in his car a few weeks later, safe in the knowledge that no police officer was going to nick his own Superintendent to have his boot forensically tested. Anyway he was a highly trained police officer; if anyone could commit the perfect, clueless murder, he could.

Ah, Bella suddenly remembered a vital fact. Raymond Nixon had been at a charity dinner dance at the golf club on the night Carla was killed. He had alibis all night, until around 2am, if she recalled correctly. That could be a problem. She went to get a drink of water and carried it back to bed, where she sipped it thoughtfully.

What if he had slipped out during the dinner? Or perhaps after the dinner, when he couldn't be missed? What if he had met Carla, rowed with her, strangled her, bundled her body in his Mercedes and dumped it in the hut – then calmly returned to the golf club? He was a police officer and he was trained not to show emotions, to keep calm in the face of adversity. It would be a doddle for him.

Suddenly Bella knew exactly what she had to do. She had to find out if Superintendent Ray Nixon had disappeared at any stage during the evening. And she knew one person who may just be able to give her that information: Boz's Kayleigh. Bella mentally calculated how much money she had left in her purse. She was sure she had a £10 note and that meant she could afford a nice lunch at that little Italian restaurant Jonathan had mentioned last night. Bella looked at her bedside clock. Actually it had been the night before last. She yawned and stretched luxuriously. It was time for this ace detective to get some much needed beauty sleep.

Bella slept for another three hours but it was neither beautifying nor relaxing. She dreamt vividly and disturbingly of Jonathan and Madeleine entwined on the sofa of their beautiful new house while she hammered on the windows, begging them to let her in because Superintendent Nixon, wearing a black balaclava and wielding an axe, was chasing her round the garden threatening to kill her and chop her into tiny pieces. But Jonathan and Madeleine ignored her screams and continued to gaze lovingly into each other's eyes. Every so often Jonathan would lean forward and shower kisses on the elegant white neck and Madeleine would moan in ecstasy.

Bella, in her dream, cowered in the porch and punched out Hugo's number on her mobile. 'Help me! Come and help me!' she cried. But Hugo simply gave a cackling, eerie laugh and told her: 'I can't, angel – I'm busy.' Then the Superintendent loomed closer, holding out a huge white pillow. He shoved it into Bella's face, and pressed and pressed...

She woke up bathed in sweat and gasping for breath. Thomas was sitting serenely on her head, purring loudly and kneading the pillow with his claws and Em was gazing at her quizzically, her hands on her hips. 'You look all hot, Mummy. What's for breakfast?' Bella, with her heart still thumping and remnants of her dream still dancing before her eyes, reached out for her daughter and pulled her towards her, inhaling the comforting, little girl smell until the panic died down and her heartbeat slowed to normal.

Oh dear, she thought, God knows what a dream analyst would make of that one. If that's what rich food does to you I'd rather live off fish and chips.

Chapter Twenty-Seven

' 'Ello,' came the voice down the phone, 'I want to speak to that nice young reporter called Bella.'

'Speaking,' said Bella politely. At the same moment someone squawked, 'Get 'em off gorgeous!' in the background.

'Hello, Mrs Vapolluci. And good morning, Alfie,' smiled Bella, thinking how nice it was to hear from the colourful old lady again. 'How are you both?'

'I'm fine, me duck. I'm busy making a bleedin' great batch of chutney from all them apples and some green tomatoes. Twenty jars I've got but I don't know what the 'ell I'm going to do with them all. Now my Freddie, 'e were a devil for a bit of chutney. Loved it, did my Freddie. 'E used to eat it on his toast in the mornings like jam.'

'Was Freddie the one that did karate?'

'Oh no, me duck. That were Del – the one that legged it with the tarty barmaid. My Freddie was the one with the nice bum.'

'Oh yes, of course,' said Bella.

'Anyways, I'm ringing to thank you for that lovely story you done on me. It came out great, didn't it? The pensioners at me Friday club cut it out and stuck it on the wall – I was right proud, I was. Do you think I should of 'ad a bit more lipstick on though? I thought me lips looked a bit scraggy but it's probably me age. I've bin thinking about getting some of that cellulite stuff – to plump 'em up a bit and make 'em all kissable.'

'I think you mean collagen actually,' said Bella. 'All the celebrities have it. They call it the trout pout.'

'Bugger me – I'd be an old trout with a young pout then, wouldn't I?' laughed Mrs Vapolluci, quick as a flash. In the background Alfie shrieked, 'Give us a snog, babe.'

'That's a new one,' said Bella.

'Yeah. That were Del taught 'im that... Or was it Freddie?' mused the old lady. 'Anyways, I was wondering if you could do me a bit of a favour, me duck?'

'Of course.'

'Do you think you could put one of them advertisements in your paper for me? For someone to do me garden? Only it looks such a bleedin' mess, I've got to do summat with it. I thought I could pay someone a few quid a week to get it looking nice and maybe grow some veg and a few chrysanths. I'm not short of a bob or two – my Freddie saw me proud, 'e did, bless him – and I might as well spend it before I pop me old clogs, mightn't I, me duck?'

'I think that's a very good idea. I'll tell you what – shall I pop round later and collect the advert?'

'That would be bloody marvellous, me duck. And you can take a couple of jars of this bleedin' chutney with you when you go.'

Bella put the phone down and pondered for a while, watching old Ron trying to fix a squeaky drawer across the office. Now, wouldn't that be just a perfect plan? If he had a large back garden to fuss over and plant his precious seeds in, it would soften the blow of BestBuys seizing his allotment. He could grow his produce to his heart's content, Mrs Vapolluci could cook it to her heart's content, and everyone would be happy. And Ron's cottage was only a couple of minutes' walk away from the old lady – he could wheel his barrow there. It would be perfect! With a little glow of pleasure, Bella beckoned Ron over.

* * *

Jonathan and Boz were leafing through a series of leaflets about silicon breast implants and waiting for the Head of Clinical Services to emerge from his office at the Viking Clinic.

'Do you reckon you can feel the difference then, guv?' asked Boz, squinting at a 36DD 'after' picture.

'Um, definitely,' said Jonathan distractedly. He was engrossed in the section about patient aftercare following a general anaesthetic.

'Has, er ... Madeleine had them then?' Boz was interested now.

'Yes, a year or so ago. Most models do apparently.'

'So ... er ... how do they feel then, guv?' Boz made crab-like pincer movements with his hands.

Jonathan, who much preferred his women natural, suddenly realised this conversation wasn't entirely appropriate and that he probably wasn't being much of a gentleman. He ignored the question and changed the subject, leaving Boz with a disappointed expression and his hands suspended in mid-air.

'So you phoned every single hospital and abortion clinic within a hundred mile radius, Boz?'

'Yep. None had a record of Carla.'

'What if she used a different name?'

'I asked if anyone of her age and description was admitted for a termination that day ... I'm not stupid, guv! They all said no. It was pretty easy actually because as I told you, a lot of them don't do operations on a Saturday.'

'This place does though. Ricky Thomas's mum had her hip operation here last Saturday.'

'Yeah, but when I phoned they said it was exceptionally quiet on the day Carla died. They had a couple of nose jobs and a boob job apparently but no terminations at all. I don't really understand why we're here, guv – not

313

that I'm complaining, of course.' Boz gestured towards the breast implant leaflets.

'Ah, here's our man,' said Jonathan, standing up and hastily tucking his breast leaflet out of sight.

Dr Alex Patterson was a friendly-looking, upright man in his sixties, smartly dressed in a navy blue suit and matching tie. A crisp white handkerchief protruded neatly from his top pocket and his black shoes gleamed with polish. Ex-military, I bet, thought Jonathan.

'How can I help you, gentlemen?' he asked once he had ushered them into his tidy office, where pictures of several fresh-faced youngsters, obviously grandchildren, adorned his desk. Jonathan explained their problem and Dr Patterson's brow wrinkled with concern. 'It would be impossible for a young lady to have a pregnancy termination without there being a comprehensive record of it somewhere. The days of backstreet abortionists are, thank goodness, long gone.'

'It was a definitely a professional job, according to the pathologist,' said Jonathan. 'Could a clinic perhaps lose a patient's record?'

'No. There is always a back-up system and anyway a copy would be sent to her GP, who would have referred her to the clinic in the first place. Presumably you checked with the GP, gentlemen?'

Boz nodded. 'That was our first call. He knew nothing.'

'Tell me how your clinic works, Dr Patterson,' said Jonathan. 'Are the surgeons employed by yourselves?'

The doctor explained that Viking only employed one full-time general surgeon but had a comprehensive team of anaesthetists, surgical assistants and nurses who could be hired out to other consultant surgeons using the clinic's equipment and rooms.

'So effectively you hire out your facilities to other consultants?' said Jonathan. Dr Patterson nodded.

314

'And the consultant can carry out his own operations but borrow your theatre?'

The doctor nodded again. 'That's right. It works well for both of us. We get the revenue – particularly on the aftercare side – and it does the consultant a favour. Often he or she will work part of the week for the NHS in an ordinary hospital and part of the week running his own private practice,' he explained.

'I see,' said Jonathan. 'So patients do come here for private pregnancy terminations?'

'Indeed they do. We have virtually no waiting lists here. And terminations can, of course, be immensely stressful if the patient has to wait for any length of time under the NHS. Our care is excellent too, even though it is usually only a day-surgery case. We even offer post-termination counselling,' said Dr Patterson proudly.

'May I have a list of consultants who perform pregnancy terminations here?' asked Jonathan.

'Of course. If you ask the receptionist as you go out she will give you their details.' This was a cue for the police officers to leave and they stood up obediently.

'I'm sorry I can't help you further,' said Dr Patterson, shaking their hands. 'I hope you solve your mystery.'

We will, thought Jonathan – given time. He prepared to charm the receptionist. He was good at that.

Bella, having eaten two jam doughnuts, felt a bit full for lunch, but looked up the number of Luigi's Pasta to call and enquire if Kayleigh was working that day. 'I'm her friend and I was hoping to pop in and surprise her,' she lied.

A female with a heavy Italian accent told her Kayleigh was working every lunchtime that week. 'She saving up for Christmas presents. She good girl, she is. She works hard for us.'

When Bella arrived at the tiny family restaurant an hour later, Kayleigh was indeed working very hard, scrubbing the tops of the red Formica tables, her plump arms pumping energetically. She was wearing a short black skirt and her ample breasts spilled out of the top of a tight, white tee shirt. She looked up blankly when Bella greeted her.

'I met you at the police ball. You were with Boz,' Bella explained.

Kayleigh's lips compressed into a thin line and she folded her arms across her chest. 'Yeah, and a right prick 'e turned out to be too! You're the reporter what found Carla's body, aren't you? Bella – isn't it?'

Bella nodded. 'I wanted to have a little chat with you about the golf club actually.' She glanced towards the short, stocky Italian man who was counting small change into the till. 'But I don't want to get you into trouble with your boss. Could you talk while you serve me with lunch perhaps?'

'Oh, Luigi – he's no trouble.' Kayleigh beckoned the man over. 'Luigi. This is my friend, Bella. She's come to have 'er dinner here.'

Luigi hastened over, wiping his hands on his large, slightly stained white apron, and promptly went into raptures. 'Ah, Bella! Such a pretty name – and such a pretty hair! I cook you special dinner – special for my Bella!' He planted a great moist kiss on Bella's cheek then drew himself up to his full 5ft 2ins and shouted at the top of his voice: 'Mamma! You come here! You come and see our Bella!'

Out of the kitchen bustled an even shorter, very plump Italian woman, with an identical stained apron straining over her voluminous stomach. Gosh, she must be as round as she is wide, thought Bella in awe. The woman broke into a trot and skidded to a panting halt next to Bella, where she flung out her arms as though she was going to launch into an opera refrain. 'You is friend of Kayleigh?' she asked, her chins wobbling and her eyes moist with emotion.

Bella nodded, only to find herself suddenly pressed against the most massive bosom she had ever experienced. 'Then we cook for you special. Luigi – come! We cook for beautiful Bella!' With that the pair hurried away, babbling excitedly in Italian.

Kayleigh grinned. 'They get a bit excited, like, what with being Italian and all that. I only 'ope you're nice and 'ungry, love.'

'They're lovely,' smiled Bella.

'What did you want to know about the golf club then?' said Kayleigh, plonking herself down on a chair.

Bella sat down next to her and explained she wanted her to think back carefully to the night of the charity dinner dance in October.

'Yeah – I remember that. I was doing the bar for a bit and then I helped serve the dinner. They 'ad roast lamb in red wine stuff – it were well nice. And they had raspberries in this meringue stuff afterwards.'

Great, thought Bella. The girl has a good memory. 'Do you remember seeing Mr Nixon there? The police superintendent?'

'Yeah. Ray Nixon. 'E's the president. I knew 'e were a copper as well but I didn't realise 'e were such a bigwig.' Kayleigh looked impressed. ''E sat on the top table, with all the VIP people – I had to serve the top table 'cos the other waitresses kept spilling stuff.'

Bella let the girl ramble on about the evening, listening to her describe how many bottles of wine were drunk, how they held a charity auction before the dancing started and how much money was flying about as the guests tried to outbid each other to look impressive.

'Was Ray Nixon there for every single minute?'

'Nah – 'e's a right bugger is Mr Nixon. 'E's always droning on about how busy 'e is and how much work 'e does for the club but he gets everyone else running around doing it all for him really.' Kayleigh pushed her hair out of her eyes and grinned. 'But I've caught him sitting in his office on some of these dos – 'e's sneaked off to have forty winks or read the paper, the crafty old sod!'

'Did he sneak off on the night of the dinner dance?' Bella could feel her heart rate accelerating.

'Yeah. I remember 'e did one of his disappearing acts after the auction, 'cos I was looking for him to ask if he'd got an extension lead for the band. There weren't enough plugs for their gear, you see.'

'I don't suppose you remember how long he was gone for?' Bella's heart was pounding now.

'I do!' said Kayleigh proudly. 'I had me timetable, you see. I had to get the last coffee served by 10.30pm and I done that on the dot. He was there then because 'e pinched my bum when I served him.'

'He pinched your bum?' Dirty old goat, thought Bella indignantly.

'Yeah, they all do that,' said Kayleigh dismissively. 'Then the band came and asked about the plug thing, so I went back say, five minutes later, and 'e were gone. In fact half his table had gone – there was only a couple of women left.'

'Had he finished his coffee?'

'No, he hadn't. I remember being cross 'cos he'd made all that fuss about me serving it on time and then he didn't even drink it, the old bugger.'

'When did he come back? When did you next see him?'

'I remember that too. It were about one minute past eleven. I was just starting to panic 'cos the band were meant to be starting at eleven and up 'e popped. He went off to get an extension lead and then the dancing started.'

318

'Thank you,' said Bella, 'you've been very helpful.' She was suddenly conscious of delicious smells wafting from the kitchen, and a moment later Luigi appeared, bearing a huge plate of pasta in a thick red sauce, flecked with basil. 'You try this, Bella *cara* ... Is Luigi's special ... you like?' He hovered anxiously as Bella took her first mouthful. She let out a groan of ecstasy... 'Ummm, Luigi – it's delicious!'

'Mamma – is delicious! Bella say it is delicious!' Luigi bellowed. Mamma came scurrying out of the kitchen, standing at his side and watching while Bella took another mouthful. Several minutes later the pair were still watching, their hands folded across their ample stomachs and their eyes following every laden forkful. Each time the fork got to Bella's mouth, they would open their own mouths, very slightly, then close them when the pasta reached its destination.

Bella, who had been struggling slightly towards the end, pushed away her empty plate with a blissful sigh and wiped her mouth on the napkin. 'That,' she said, 'was the best pasta I've ever had.'

Luigi and Mamma did a funny little dance. 'Is the best! Is the best!' cried Luigi. He held one hand up authoritatively. 'Wait,' he said, then disappeared into the kitchen. Mamma followed. Almost immediately they reappeared, holding aloft a large plate of chicken in a creamy sauce. Bella looked at Kayleigh in horror. 'The pasta was the starter – now you've got the main course,' the girl giggled.

'And the vegetables?' Mamma held out a tureen crammed with buttered carrots, sugar snap peas and baby new potatoes. Bella helped herself to a modest portion. 'Ah Bella *cara*, don't be shy. You eat some more. You get some meat on those bones!' said Mamma, promptly ladling on a huge pile.

Again the two pairs of eyes watched the fork journey

from plate to mouth and again two mouths opened, ever so slightly, at the same moment as Bella's. The creamy, garlicky chicken was amazing but halfway through Bella could feel her stomach growling in protest at the thought of another mouthful. But conscious of the eyes upon her and desperate not to disappoint her anxious hosts, she surreptitiously popped open her trouser button and ploughed on ... and on...

By the final few forkfuls, beads of sweat had broken out on Bella's brow and her stomach felt like it was going to explode. She hid the last lump of chicken under a couple of sugar snaps and a new potato, leaned back in her seat and gave a gentle belch. 'Luigi, Mamma, that was magnificent!' she said. 'But you must tell me how much I owe you now. I have to go back to work.'

Luigi flapped his arms in protest. 'Oh no ... no Bella. You have no dessert! Mamma she made tiramisu – special for Bella!'

Bella shook her head weakly and planted a kiss on the man's cheek. 'I really have to go,' she said. Mamma shoved Luigi away and engulfed her in a crushing hug. 'I pack it up for you – you take it to work,' she murmured, holding Bella against those massive breasts. Don't squeeze me, begged Bella silently, feeling her stomach lurch.

Several minutes later, after more hugs and kisses all round, numerous promises to return another day and a lengthy protest to Luigi, who insisted on only taking £5 for all that food, Bella finally managed to get out of the door. She staggered along the pavement, one hand clutching her stomach and the other a plastic container of tiramisu, wishing she had brought her car. She longed to undo her trousers, flop down on her bed and not move for the rest of the day. Instead though, she had another three hours' work to do in the office...

A beep of a car horn made Bella jump suddenly. She

turned to see a familiar-looking silver vehicle draw up beside her and a figure inside lean across to open the passenger door. 'Looks like you need a lift,' said an amused voice.

A pair of very blue eyes looked at her face, travelled to the pot of tiramisu, then rested on her stomach straining over her trousers. 'You're not going to throw up in my car, are you?'

Bella shook her head and flopped on the seat beside Jonathan. 'No, but don't expect me to talk. I'm too full up.' She gave a large, unladylike belch and then her hand flew up to her mouth in horror. 'Oops, sorry.'

Jonathan leaned over and fastened her seat belt then drove away gently. 'Office?' Bella nodded. 'I won't swing round any corners,' he said with a grin. As requested, he kept silent until they reached the *Gazette* car park. Bella had leaned her head back on the headrest and was sitting with her eyes closed, breathing deeply and emitting the odd small belch.

Jonathan turned off the engine and turned to face her. 'Perhaps,' he said mildly, 'perhaps this has proved you don't quite have the stomach for playing private detective.'

Bella's eyes flew open. 'What do you mean?' The cogs in her brain slowly ground back to life. 'You followed me, you ... you...'

'Bastard? Yes, I did,' said Jonathan simply. 'I enjoyed watching you through the window when you were forcing the last of that chicken down!'

'How did you know...?'

Jonathan sighed. 'Bella, I don't have to be Einstein to work out that you think Raymond Nixon is the murderer and you were going to talk to Kayleigh.' He grinned. 'I even let slip where she worked for you.'

'So you think this is just another of my silly little theories?' Bella was angry.

'You took the words right out of my mouth. Talking of which...' Jonathan planted a quick kiss next to her lips, which were still open with surprise. 'Your breath stinks of garlic!'

Bella shut her mouth hurriedly, snapped off her seatbelt and flounced out of the car. 'I hate you,' she said, through gritted teeth.

'Love you too, sweetheart,' retorted Jonathan, driving off.

It was a subdued and still slightly uncomfortable Bella who whisked Ron away from the office at 5pm and drove to Mrs Vapolluci's house in Dower Grove. 'I don't know whether I'm good enough to be a proper gardener, Miss Bella,' the old man protested.

Bella patted his leathery hand. 'You're the best, Ron – and she's a lovely lady. Don't worry.'

A few minutes later she was leaning back in Mrs Vapolluci's comfortable armchair with a smug, self-satisfied smile on her face. She had been right – the pair were getting on like a house on fire, Ron's hesitant tones mingling with the old lady's more raucous cockney ones as they sat side by side on the sofa, leafing through seed catalogues.

'How about parsnips?' suggested Ron.

'Ooh yes, me duck! I make a lovely parsnip soup. You can't beat a nice bit of home-made soup these cold evenings, can you?'

'I have that tinned stuff. I get it from the Spar shop,' said Ron.

'Oh dear. Oh dear. You can't go eating that tinned rubbish, me duck. That won't put 'airs on your chest. I'll boil you up a nice pot or two. My Freddie used to love my home-made soup. 'E was my hubby, but 'e's dead now.'

'I never married, myself. Never found the right woman somehow,' confessed Ron.

'Didn't you, dear? That's a shame,' said Mrs Vapolluci, fixing him with a beady eye.

Bella chuckled and interrupted them to say she had to go and pick up Emily. Mrs Vapolluci immediately clamped her hand down on Ron's bony knee. 'You can stay here, me duck, and walk 'ome later. I'll fix you a bit of tea and we'll talk about me garden.'

A silly grin spread across Ron's face, only to waver slightly when Alfie shrieked his instruction to 'Get 'em off gorgeous'. Mrs Vapolluci patted his knee. 'Don't you worry about our Alfie – 'e only says that to people he likes.'

Bella blew the pair of them a kiss and made her exit, clutching two jars of home-made chutney. She may be a rubbish private detective but she certainly knew how to make two old people happy, she thought.

Chapter Twenty-Eight

The call came a couple of minutes before 5.30pm and at first Jonathan did not have a clue as to the identity of this man who was telling him that he had some very bad news indeed. He had been engrossed in staring at the three business cards laid out in a straight line on his desk, each bearing the words 'Gynaecological Consultant' in expensive-looking embossed letters, and he had only given the caller half his attention at first.

'Sorry – *who* are you?' he said. The caller repeated his name and spoke at length. Jonathan listened quietly, his face impassive. 'Thank you for letting me know so promptly,' he finally said. There was another pause, then Jonathan spoke again. 'No. In the circumstances I don't think that will be necessary. But thank you anyway.' Then he replaced the handset thoughtfully, stood up and announced to his colleagues he was going off duty.

'What's he up to then?' said Boz, who was perched on Bolter's desk reading the latest email jokes on his computer.

'Dunno – you never know with him,' said Bolter. 'Did you read this one about the clubbers in Yorkshire rubbing ecstasy powder in their mouths?' He gave a chortle. 'E by gum, they call it! That's bloody brilliant!'

'Not as good as that one about the Welshman and the sheep,' said Boz, chuckling at the memory. 'Shall we pop out for a pint then, as the boss has gone? I'll tell you all about his bird's breast implants.'

Bolter's eyes widened. 'You expect me to listen to scurrilous gossip about our Detective Sergeant?' he drained his cup of police station tea and leapt to his feet. 'Your round, mate...'

Madeleine, whose implants were looking particularly impressive that evening in a push-up bra and black, low cut top, was busy packing her carefully co-ordinated wardrobe into matching Louis Vuitton suitcases. 'Honey, you're early! What a lovely surprise!' she said when Jonathan walked into the room.

There was no preamble. 'Madeleine, I have something to tell you and it is not very good news, I'm afraid.'

Approximately twenty seconds later Jonathan's eardrums were ringing with Madeleine's shrieks. 'What do you mean, it *flooded*? How dare they? We're due to move in first thing tomorrow and they have the cheek to tell us it's flooded! Do something, honey – just *do* something! Surely we can sue them – quick, let's call a solicitor!'

'It's not the agent's fault the house flooded, Madeleine, and neither is it the landlord's. A pipe burst upstairs in the bathroom and it was only when the agent went to do the final inventory this afternoon that it was noticed. The place is three inches deep in water and it's going to be a long insurance job to put it right.' Jonathan tried hard to keep his tone level and gentle.

Madeleine's eyes filled with tears. 'But the agent can find us somewhere else, can't he, darling? He must have lots of other houses and we've paid him all that deposit.' A tear slid down her cheek, and she hastily dabbed at it with a tissue to prevent her mascara from running.

Jonathan put one hand on her shoulder and looked her in the eye. Suddenly he felt the biggest bastard in the world. He studied the symmetrical features, the glossy lips and the flawless chin and felt an overwhelming surge of guilt that he was about to make this face crumble. Because he knew he could never fall in love with its owner.

But, as much as he hated to hurt her, he owed it to her to be truthful. Even if that truth was going to be unpalatable. 'Madeleine,' he said gently. 'I'm really sorry but I think it's probably best that we don't find anywhere else.'

He held his breath and waited for the shrieks. None came. Madeleine sat down on the bed and watched him silently with narrowed eyes and pursed lips. Hating himself, Jonathan continued: 'I think it's best you return to your apartment in London and I find somewhere smaller to rent up here for myself.' He took a deep breath and floundered for the decent thing to say. 'You're a wonderful person and you deserve better than me – you deserve someone who can make you the happiest woman in the world,' he announced finally and truthfully. Again he waited for the shrieks. 'I'm so, so sorry,' he repeated, to fill the silence.

Madeleine, still sitting on the bed, contemplated screaming. She contemplated moving her right hand slightly to grab her porcelain pot of designer face cream and hurl it at Jonathan's head; she even imagined it smashing into several razor-sharp pieces while the white goo dripped over his hair and face. Then she imagined herself running to his wardrobe, armed with her nail scissors, and slashing maniacally at his crisp, tailored shirts and smart suit jackets until they hung in satisfying ribbons.

But in reality she continued to sit, perfectly still and poised, slowly seeing her house in the country, her witty dinner parties and her whole perfectly elegant future, crumble away into nothingness. She studied the tired, slightly craggy face looking down at her. Her eyes slipped down to the broad shoulders more suited to a faded T-shirt than a pin-striped suit; the strong hands that preferred to hold a pint than a crystal cut glass of champagne and the taut stomach that craved for steak and chips instead of caviar and canapés, and suddenly Madeleine knew that she had probably been a very stupid woman indeed. He was right. She was a woman who needed far more than just an overworked, unromantic and rather *ordinary* detective to make her truly happy.

Her thoughts flew to the distinctly more glamorous Cecil, with whom she had she enjoyed a witty and gossipy lunch only a few hours previously. How silly she had been to keep him at arm's length while she continued her losing battle for Jonathan's affection and attention. Now Cecil was a man who appreciated her for her true worth. He would *never* have the audacity to push her away! Why, Cecil would move to a house in the country with her tomorrow.

Madeleine paused in her thoughts and crinkled her brow – then swiftly smoothed her expression in case she got wrinkles and needed more Botox. Cecil wouldn't appreciate a girl with wrinkles and she had a big impression to make – and a very speedy one. She reached for a particularly nice lacy blouse and folded it carefully into her suitcase.

'Er, are you all right? Aren't you going to say anything?' asked Jonathan, totally perplexed by this seemingly calm reaction.

'Only two words,' snapped Madeleine. 'Fuck off.'

Bella, still too full-up to face food, was chopping a chicken breast for a stir-fry for Em, who was sitting beside her on the worktop, chatting companionably and swinging her legs.

'So why are we going for a ride in the car after dinner, Mummy? We don't usually go out after dinner. Is it really an adventure?'

'Sort of, darling. It's a little adventure to do with Mummy's work.'

'How can we have an adventure without getting out of the car?' Emily wrinkled her nose.

'Well, we're timing something – seeing how long it takes to drive somewhere.'

'That's boring!'

'You could hold the watch for me.'

'But I can't tell the time,' wailed Emily. 'I get the big hand muddled up with the little hand and the numbers are stupid.'

'I think we'll have to practise that,' frowned Bella. 'I'm sure you should be telling the time by now.'

'That's what my teacher says,' grinned Em. 'I've got a wobbly tooth though – look!' She opened her mouth wide and prodded a front tooth.

'Hey, that is *so* grown up! You'll be all gappy soon.' Bella felt quite emotional at the thought of the first lost baby tooth. 'You'll have to show daddy on Monday.'

'Yeah! And Jonny,' Emily held out her arms. 'Can you lift me down so I can watch *The Simpsons* now?'

Bella obliged and tossed the chicken strips into the pan with a sigh. This campaign to get Emily all joyful about her long-lost father wasn't really working. The child accepted Hugo with a polite but pragmatic interest and while she was clearly not disturbed by his sudden materialisation, she wasn't unduly enthusiastic about it either. Bella herself had been pleasantly surprised at the new, caring, humbled Hugo and had reassured both her parents and her friend Kate at length that she was coping just fine. But she still hadn't told them about the dinner date – they might have thought that meant she was coping just a bit too well.

She smiled as she remembered Hugo telling her how lovely she looked – that's more than Jonathan had ever said to her. Mind you, how could she possibly look lovely to him when he was used to gazing at Madeleine's face and body every night? What was that saying about silk purses and sow's ears? Well, Madeleine was definitely the silk purse in this instance.

Bella chopped a mushroom particularly savagely and looked at her watch. Better get a move on if they were going to make this little outing.

Thirty minutes later Emily was sitting behind her in Daisy, frowning in concentration at Bella's watch. 'It's seven past two,' she announced. Bella squinted at the car clock. Ten past seven. She drove for four minutes to the entrance of the allotments. 'Are we going to see Ron, Mummy?' cried Emily excitedly.

'Not tonight, darling. I think he's busy,' said Bella, smiling at the memory of Mrs Vapolluci's hand on the old man's knee. 'What's the time?'

Emily squinted. 'Nearly three past seven.' Bella glanced at the clock – fourteen minutes past seven. She did a not-so-neat three-point turn and headed out of Haybridge. There was only one road leading to the golf club, a long, winding country lane, and Bella drove more quickly than usual, steering carefully round the bends, until she saw the large, black-lettered sign – 'Haybridge and District Golf Club. Members Only'. She pulled into the car park and lined up Daisy to face the entrance of the building. 'Time, Em?'

'Just past five.' She said it with great authority. Damn, thought Bella. Twenty six minutes past seven. The trip had taken twelve minutes. Superintendent Nixon's flash Mercedes could probably go a little bit faster than her Mini Cooper but even he couldn't do a minimum twenty-minute round trip, commit a murder, load a body in his boot and then carry it across an allotment and be back at his table in less than half an hour. Or could he?

Bella sat in silence for a moment, while she checked and re-checked her sometimes dodgy maths and recalled her conversation with Kayleigh. No, for once she was right – according to the girl's impressively precise timings he'd been missing for between twenty-six and thirty minutes. And that was allowing for him to get in and out of the club itself. Bella gazed at the front of the brick-built building for inspiration. Shit! What was that little round lens she could see, illuminated by the light from a window? Was it a CCTV camera?

Bella obeyed her initial instinct – to turn Daisy round and drive quickly out of the car park before Big Brother caught her snooping once again. Then it dawned on her: Superintendent Nixon would have been captured on camera too, getting into his car just after 10.30pm on that fateful night! Now how easy it would be to prove her theory was not just a flight of fancy.

Bella was so busy congratulating herself and imagining Jonathan being forced to admit how clever she was that she failed to notice Emily had fallen sound asleep in the back of the car, her little head slumped towards the window and her hand still clutching the watch. When she did notice, it was with a sharp pang of guilt. She may be brilliant at solving murders but she was a crap mother, she thought.

When Bella had carried her dead-weight daughter into the flat, tucked her up in bed and finished worrying about whether the child's teeth would rot after one night without cleaning them, she sat down in the armchair with a pad of paper and a pen. She wrote the heading 'Evidence' and underlined it carefully. Then she wriggled and undid the top button of her trousers. She wriggled again, then undid the zip, watching in alarm at the way the flesh underneath bulged its way to freedom. She sighed, walked to the bedroom and substituted her clothes for her baggiest, softest and tattiest pair of flannelette pyjamas. Ah, bliss.

Bella's pen flew across the paper as she meticulously detailed how Superintendent Nixon would have wooed Carla, persuaded her to embark upon an affair, promised to buy her a place at college and then finally got her pregnant – then panicked when she threatened to blow the whistle and destroy his reputation. The girl, distraught and woozy from her termination, would have called him, probably from a phone box, in the middle of the charity do, begging him to meet her or she would turn up at the club and cause a scene. 'Check Superintendent's incoming calls with mobile phone company,' Bella underlined. He would have been in the middle of drinking his coffee. He had pushed the cup aside, made a polite excuse and hastened out – desperate to protect his precious reputation at any cost.

The whole thing probably only took a couple of minutes. It was easy for a tall strong man to overpower a sobbing girl who was still woozy from an operation. Afterwards Nixon had lifted the body into the boot of his car – 'Check boot carpet with forensics,' Bella wrote and underlined – then sped to the allotments before finally hot-footing it back to the golf club.

She scanned what she had written. It was perfect – all apart from the timing element, which was, she had to admit, almost impossibly tight. But she was relying on the memory of just one waitress, a girl who had been rushed off her feet that night and may just have got her timings a little bit muddled. Bella needed a second account, a second eyewitness who saw Nixon slip away from his table. She tapped her pen on the paper and gave a slow smile … she knew just the person.

In capital letters she wrote 'GET TED HANSON TALKING ABOUT GOLF CLUB DO' and she underlined it – twice. She would call Ted on some pretext about the BestBuys application and she would somehow steer the subject round to the golf club and his golfing buddy. It would be easy. She knew she could do it.

Bella leaned back with a self-satisfied smile, feeling better now her course of action was clear. Her tummy felt better too now – almost empty in fact. She could almost fancy a chocolate biscuit or two actually. Well, she deserved a little treat, didn't she? It wasn't every day you proved a police chief was a murderer.

Chapter Twenty-Nine

Jonathan woke early on Friday morning to a blissfully peaceful and slightly bare hotel room, which bore not a single trace of Madeleine's presence. He sniffed the pillow next to him and decided there was maybe a faint whiff of Chanel, but that would go when the maid changed the bed later that day. He stretched luxuriantly and felt a deep sense of relief flood through his body. It was over! No more treading on eggshells around Madeleine's fragile ego; no more tears and tantrums when he got back from work late and no more guilt when he simply couldn't be the person she wanted him to be.

He had helped her load her cases into her car the previous evening and genuinely wished her the very best. 'If there's anything at all I can do to help...' he had offered, coming out with the lame old cliché that he hoped they could be friends. Madeleine had answered coldly that she would be fine, and made her exit with her head held high and her beautiful hair cascading down her back. Jonathan had seen a trace of the old Madeleine, the quietly dignified and coolly self-sufficient woman he had first met, and he had felt just the tiniest little pang of regret as he watched the sporty little car disappear down the road. But the pang quickly disappeared. He had been deluding himself that this relationship could ever work. And, more seriously, he had been deluding Madeleine too. She needed someone to make a fuss of her twenty-four hours a day and he didn't have the time or the inclination. He was a detective and he had work to do.

Jonathan jumped out of bed and within forty minutes was showered, shaved, smartly-dressed and at his desk, where the three business cards were still neatly lined up awaiting him. He picked up the middle one: Mr James E Rutherford, consultant obstetrician and gynaecologist. That was the one. He was positive – his memory for names was excellent. Jonathan picked up the phone and dialled the number on the card. A female answered: 'Mr Rutherford's secretary. Can I help you?'

'Yes,' said Jonathan firmly. 'I need to make an urgent appointment to see Mr Rutherford – today if possible.'

The secretary, once she had been assured the caller was a police officer and not a weird man with gynaecological problems, told him Mr Rutherford had a ten minute 'window' between appointments at 12.30pm that day, just before he was due at the Surgeons' Annual Lunch. That would be perfect, Jonathan told her politely.

He looked at his watch and made another quick phone call. Five minutes later he was in his car and on his way to Springfields, a small Category C prison built in late Victorian times just outside Weatherford. He parked his car in the visitors' car park and walked through the heavy, foreboding doors to reception, where he endured the usual search and frisking procedures with mild impatience.

'Pockets please, sir,' instructed a uniformed prison officer, holding out a small plastic bowl. Jonathan rummaged in his trousers and jacket, finally producing a mobile phone, a wallet, a handful of change, a handkerchief and a packet of football stickers he had bought for Emily in the newsagent's on the way over. He also held out a pack of cigarettes and a box of matches he had bought at the same time. 'Can I hang on to these? They're for my personal use,' he asked. The officer nodded and peered at the stickers with interest. 'Arsenal, eh?'

'The best,' said Jonathan firmly, allowing himself to be escorted to the remand block.

Ricky Thomas was sitting at a plastic table in a tiny, windowless interview room. He looked tired and drawn and his shoulders were slumped. 'How are you coping?' said Jonathan, pulling up a chair beside him and putting the cigarettes and matches on the table.

Ricky's eyes lit up. 'A lot better now thanks,' he said, swiftly opening the packet.

'The cigarettes are strictly between you and me, Ricky. As is this conversation.' The tone was firm.

Ricky took a long drag than held out his hands. 'Look, I know what you want and I can't tell you. It's more than my life is worth. You don't understand.'

'I understand perfectly. I can see that the person who put you up to these burglaries obviously has some kind of hold on you. But you're safe here, Ricky. He can't get you in here. And if you just give me a name then we can act quickly and put him away – lock him up where he can't reach you.'

'Yeah – but he could hurt my mum though, couldn't he?' The voice was a mumble.

'Has he threatened that?'

'No, not in so many words,' admitted Ricky. 'But he would – I know he would. He's capable of anything, this bloke. He's not your ordinary geezer – he's ... he's...' He groped for the right word. 'Powerful. That's what he is – powerful.'

'In what way. Is he big? Strong? A fighter?'

Ricky looked down. 'Not powerful in that way. It's more that he's ... he's *important*. He knows people in the right places and stuff.' He stubbed out the cigarette in the tin foil ashtray and looked Jonathan in the eye. 'Look, you're wasting your time, mate. I'm not going to tell you. I can't.'

Jonathan, realising the boy could be pushed no further,

changed the subject. He talked about prison life, warning Ricky to avoid the bad crowd, the ringleaders who would cause trouble. 'The best thing you can do is keep your head down and do what the prison officers say,' he told him.

'Yeah. I'm doing that. I'm getting loads of books out of the library here and read most of the time. I'm thinking of doing one of them courses actually – learn something useful for when I get out.'

'Good man,' said Jonathan, patting him on the shoulder. 'You do that and I'll make sure the judge knows about it when you get to court.' He smiled sympathetically. 'This could be a chance to make something of your life, Ricky. You could learn a trade and earn good money.'

'Yeah, that's just what me mum said in her letter,' mumbled the lad.

'Good. And you make sure you write back to her.' Jonathan fumbled in a tiny pocket at the back of his trousers and flung a strip of postage stamps on the table. 'Here – you'll need these.'

'Hey thanks, mate. Thanks!' Ricky's face lit up.

It was as though he'd given the boy the earth, thought Jonathan as he walked out of the prison with a smile. Sometimes it was worth bending the rules a bit – even if you were a respectable police officer.

James Edward Rutherford was an athletic-looking but prematurely grey man of around forty and he spoke in the clipped accent of a good public school education. 'Do I know you from somewhere?' he said, shaking Jonathan's hand politely.

'We met briefly at Haybridge Golf Club last Friday evening. I was receiving a cheque on behalf of the police,' Jonathan explained.

'Ah, of course! It was for that fund for the poor young murdered girl... What was her name again?'

'Carla Kapochkin,' said Jonathan slowly.

'You must forgive me, old chap. The old memory's not quite what it used to be. I blame it on my workload.' He gestured to the pile of papers on his desk.

'Are those patient records?' asked Jonathan.

'Yes.' James Rutherford looked puzzled. 'Was it help about a patient you wanted? Only it could be a bit tricky – patient confidentially and all that.'

'Was Carla Kapochkin your patient, Mr Rutherford?'

'Good lord no. I didn't do her op! I don't think she could have afforded our prices on her wages, poor girl.' The consultant smiled and looked Jonathan in the eyes. 'You're more than welcome to look through my files to check if you like – as long as you don't go reading my patients' private details.'

'That won't be necessary. But thank you anyway.' Jonathan returned the smile and leaned back casually in his chair. 'So how long have you known my Superintendent?'

'Oh several years now. I met him through the Rotary Club and he invited me to join the golf club a couple of years ago.' He looked at Jonathan. 'Do you play?'

'No. Maybe I should take it up though. It seems a very sociable sport.'

The consultant nodded. 'It certainly is. They're a friendly crowd at Haybridge. I'll recommend you if you like.' He glanced at his watch. 'I'm afraid I must go now though – I have a luncheon to attend.'

Jonathan rose. 'Thank you. You have been a great help,' he said, his face expressionless.

James Rutherford watched him leave and ran his hands through his hair, suddenly perplexed. 'Have I?' he muttered to himself.

*   *   *

Bella was annoyed. Sean had sent her to the magistrates' court to cover a story about nine people being fined for not possessing a television licence. Bloody marvellous, she thought. She was inches away from catching her murderer and forced to sit in a draughty old court all morning, listening to a string of boring drinks licence applications until her equally boring case finally came up. Her feet were freezing after sitting still for all that time and she was starving hungry. She could murder one of Luigi's pastas right now, she thought, her mouth watering at the memory of that rich, garlicky tomato sauce.

Instead, as soon as the case was heard, Bella drove to the nearest garage to grab a sandwich, remembering to switch on her phone as she returned to her car. She had an important call to make. The screen flashed up 'message received'. She had a text. She pulled up by the car wash, took a mouthful of slightly stale brown bread and ham and clicked on to 'read message'.

'Hello beautiful Bella. Can't stop thinking about you. Love to Emily. X'

Bella's heart did a flip and the sandwich turned to sawdust in her mouth. Frantically she scrolled down to 'sender'. Oh – it was Hugo. Oh. She gave herself a mental shake. How stupid. For a moment she had thought it was Jonathan. But why would she expect Jonathan to send her a romantic text like that? And, even more stupid, why did she have that funny little pang of disappointment when it was Hugo instead?

Bella decided it was all far too complicated to analyse and concentrated on her sandwich, forcing her thoughts to return to murder and Superintendent Nixon. She glanced at her watch. Jonathan should have finished moving into his love nest by now. She punched in his number.

'You need to do something really important,' she said, through half a mouthful.

'Hairpins again?'

'Ham sandwich. Listen – can you check some CCTV film?'

'Possibly,' said Jonathan slowly. 'Where's the camera?'

Bella told him. Then she explained her theory, so quickly that she was panting slightly at the end of it. 'So we need to know exactly when he slipped out. We know he did because Kayleigh remembers going to find him and the table was almost empty,' she concluded.

'Empty?' Jonathan frowned.

'Well, apart from a couple of the wives... But we need to check those timings as quickly as we can. Can you get the CCTV film or not?' said Bella impatiently.

'It will probably be a tape. Most small establishments use a standard camera which is fed with a VHS video tape every 24 hours.'

'Do they keep the tapes?'

'Usually for about a month. Then they might recycle them on a rotating basis for the next month – otherwise they end up with hundreds of tapes to store.'

'So we're in time then? Aren't we?'

'It will be a month next Saturday since Carla was murdered,' said Jonathan, sounding slightly distracted. 'Bella –'

Bella interrupted. They could not afford to lose a minute. 'You'll do it then? You'll check the tapes?'

'I will do it this afternoon,' promised Jonathan. 'And I will call you this evening.' He held his breath.

Bella's voice dropped. 'You could ... er ... you could...'

'I could pop round if you want,' said Jonathan. 'Maybe play with Em for a bit then go through some case files with you. There's some stuff I want your opinion on.'

Bella beamed and swelled with pride. He wasn't dismissing her theory – and he wanted her *opinion*. 'That would be great. See you later – and good luck!' she said.

The smile remained on her face as she drove back to the office. She had some pork chops in the freezer. She could make some onion gravy and roast some potatoes. Oh, and she still had Mrs Vapolluci's windfall apples – she and Em could make a pie if they were quick. Of course, this feast would not be for Jonathan's benefit. No, not at all. The food needed using up, that was all.

'Something smells wonderful,' said Jonathan, when he walked into Bella's rather steamy and untidy kitchen a few hours later. He sniffed appreciatively at the tantalising mix of roasting pork, onions, apple and cinnamon.

'You're welcome to stay for dinner,' said Bella almost shyly. 'But you might have to get back for...'

'Madeleine. No. I –'

Bella, who hated talking about Madeleine, interrupted swiftly and started fussing about the flour on the table instead. 'It gets a bit messy when Em makes pastry. Mind your suit.' She dabbed at the table with a cloth, feeling like a 1950s housewife.

Jonathan threw off his jacket, undid his tie and plonked himself down at the table. 'I couldn't give a toss about a bit of flour,' he said. He raised his voice. 'Now – where is my champion butt-kicker?'

A flour-covered apparition rushed through the doorway and launched itself into his lap. 'I was setting up the blow football but Thomas has run off with my ball. He won't give it back,' it wailed.

Jonathan stood up, squared his shoulders and rolled up his shirt sleeves. 'That's theft, babe. And this is a job for Catman, ' he said in a mock growl. 'Lead me to the villain.'

Twenty minutes later the cat burglar was weaving himself around Bella's legs, purring loudly as she dished up the pork chops and roasted vegetables in her best – and only

– serving dishes. 'Dinner!' she yelled to the giggling pair in the living room. They emerged, both streaked slightly with flour, and both squabbling happily about whether the final goal should have been allowed or not.

'This looks wonderful,' said Jonathan, sitting himself down at the same instant as Thomas jumped onto the table. He put out an arm to scoop him down then retracted it hastily as the cat gave a shudder, then a cough, then a lurch.

'Oh dear. He's going to...' At that moment Thomas made a strangled gagging noise, shook himself, then jumped off the table, his tail bristling in indignation. Bella and Jonathan stared in equal horror at the small, brown, slimy-looking ball he had left behind, deposited neatly between the pork chops in gravy and the dish of roast potatoes.

'Oh my God. It's ... it's not what you think,' gabbled Bella. 'It's a fur ball. He's a long-haired cat. They sometimes swallow fur and cough it up... Honestly, it's a fur ball.' She was blushing scarlet.

'I think that's probably the best scenario we can hope for,' said Jonathan, one eyebrow arched.

'Looks like poo to me,' said Emily nonchalantly from her doorway, where she was standing, hand on hip, surveying the little domestic drama with mild interest.

Jonathan looked at Bella's face and felt a familiar bubble rise up into his chest and a chuckle escaped through his lips, then a louder guffaw. Bella, experiencing identical symptoms, managed to snatch up the dubious little ball in a piece of kitchen roll and squirt the table with antibacterial spray before she collapsed onto a chair in a helpless fit of giggles. The pair of them snorted and wheezed merrily, occasionally managing to regain control only for one to look at the face of the other and start up all over again.

Emily, who had helped herself messily to a pork chop, banged her fork on the table bossily. ' Will you guys stop being silly please – your dinner's getting cold.'

'Sorry sweetheart,' said Jonathan weakly, mopping his eyes and leaning over to cut up her meat. 'Your mother and I will behave now – I promise.'

It might be hard to keep that promise, mused Jonathan, when Emily was fast asleep in bed and he was sitting just half an inch away from Bella on her sofa with his police files spread out on the coffee table.

He felt warm, full and contented and she smelled so lovely, like flowery soap and apple pie. He had an urge to pull her onto his lap and wind one of those funny little curls around his finger while he closed his eyes and had a little nap. He pulled himself together. They had unfinished business to get through. He smiled at his choice of expression – how well that summed them up!

Bella was looking at him quizzically. He cleared his throat. 'First the CCTV tape.'

'Yes?' said Bella eagerly. 'What did it show? Did you see...?'

Jonathan's eyes met hers. 'There was no tape, Bella.' He watched her mouth open in surprise. 'They retain the tapes for a month, as I guessed, and they are numbered one to thirty one for each day of the month. So I was looking for tape 24 – for October 24th.'

'But it wasn't there?'

'No. There was number 23 and number 25 but no 24. The club steward looked everywhere. He was really apologetic. He could only assume it had been thrown away by mistake.'

'Do you think it was? A mistake, I mean?' Bella's eyes were wide.

'No. I don't. All the tapes were clearly marked with "CCTV – Do Not Destroy".'

'So someone could have taken it? To hide the evidence perhaps?'

'Perhaps,' agreed Jonathan.

Bella sat in silence, digesting the information. 'So what do we do now?' she asked finally.

Jonathan absent-mindedly rubbed away a streak of flour from below her cheekbone. '*We* don't do anything, Bella.' He was suddenly very serious. 'I know I've told you to back off before and it's even become a bit of a joke between us but I am deadly serious now. This investigation is closing in and there's some important, perhaps dangerous work to be done. I need you to promise you will not talk to anyone else or see anyone else about these latest developments. I need a few days, Bella, that's all, and then I promise I will explain everything. You will be the first person to know when it is all over.'

It was a long speech and Bella had paled visibly in the middle of it. She suddenly longed to feel Jonathan's arms around her, all strong and safe, and she looked longingly at that place on his chest where her head seemed to fit so well. She contemplated throwing herself onto him but then jutted out her chin instead. 'I don't want to know when it's all over. I want to help.'

'You sound like Em,' smiled Jonathan, fighting an urge to throw his arms round her and hold her tight against his chest. 'You can help me in two ways. Firstly, I want you to answer one question – did you ever write anything about Carla having a pregnancy termination in any of your stories?'

'Absolutely not!' Bella shook her head. 'You told me not to mention that.'

Jonathan frowned. 'OK. The other way you can help is by writing me a story…'

Bella listened carefully and scribbled notes on her pad as Jonathan outlined the story he wanted her to write for Tuesday's *Gazette*. 'I want you to recap all the burglaries and hint that the police have not quite finished their investigation. Perhaps you could say we are thinking of going back to the scene of every single one for more detailed forensic tests. I want to spook this Mr Big – to get him worried that we know someone else is involved and we're on the trail. It's a long shot but it might just make him do or say something stupid,' he explained.

'OK,' said Bella.

'I've brought you the list of all the burglaries, going right back to June. It will save you looking them up in your files. It says what was stolen too, and the value.'

'Thanks,' said Bella, reaching for the sheet. 'God, it looks a lot when you see them all together, doesn't it?' She looked carefully down the list. 'They speeded up towards the end though, didn't they? The last few were really close together.'

Jonathan nodded and Bella continued to look at the list, studying the last batch of shops. She frowned.

'What's up?' said Jonathan.

Bella shook her head, as if to clear it. 'Nothing – just a vague sense of déjà vu, really. But I suppose it's because I've written about them all before, one by one.' She shook her head again. Something was really niggling her – something deep in her sub-conscious. She would probably wake up at 3am and remember it, right out of the blue. That was always happening to her these days. She turned her attention back to Jonathan.

'How's Hugo?' he was saying.

'Hugo? Oh, he's fine! It's all going really well actually. I'd been dreading him showing up for so many years, then when he finally did it wasn't anywhere near as bad as I imagined.' Bella prattled about the solicitor's letter, her subsequent phone call and how Hugo seemed to genuinely care about his daughter now. Jonathan listened patiently, wondering why he felt so annoyed when it was obviously good news for Bella – and for little Em.

'Have you seen him since Monday then?' he asked suddenly.

Bella lowered her eyes, blushed slightly and fidgeted with the pen she was holding. 'No,' she said quietly.

Oh sweetheart, thought Jonathan. You are such a rotten liar. I don't think I can listen to this any longer.

He stood up and gathered his files off the table. 'Sorry, I have to dash now.' He kissed Bella softly on the cheek. 'Don't get up. I'll see myself out.'

Chapter Thirty

Bella felt unaccountably down all weekend. The adrenaline rush she had experienced while chasing to solve the murder had vanished, leaving a kind of numb disappointment in its place. It was obvious Jonathan was going to do this alone and Bella was sure he was exaggerating about the danger aspect. All he had to do was step into the next office and arrest his boss, for God's sake. The guy was hardly going to pull a knife on him in the middle of the police station, was he?

It was the story of a lifetime though, and although Bella was miffed to be kept out of it, she still relished the prospect of writing about it. A few days, Jonathan had said. She wondered if it would make Tuesday's edition. She hoped so – the national press would be calling the *Gazette* and begging for the story by Wednesday. 'Police chief arrested for murder' – what a scoop!

In the light of this potentially huge event, Bella was mystified as to why Jonathan kept going back to the much less dramatic story about the Haybridge burglaries. She had a feeling he was hiding something from her – as if there was a missing link somewhere he was not telling her about. She felt a surge of irritation towards the secretive detective, who was confiding in her one minute then tight-lipped the next. He was also all over her one minute, showering her with kisses and finding her 'irresistible', then cool as a cucumber the next, thought Bella, who had felt a ridiculous disappointment when Jonathan had left so abruptly on Friday night. He obviously couldn't wait to get back to his big, flash house and his posh, skinny lover.

Her unsettled, slightly resentful, mood dragged on throughout the weekend. On Sunday Bella spent the day at her parents' house, catching up with the gossip from her sister Sophie, who was home from university, and Toby and his girlfriend had called in – much to Emily's delight. It was just the sort of day that Bella usually loved but she had felt strangely detached and ill at ease in the happy family atmosphere.

Something was still niggling her at the back of her brain and the niggle was getting worse and worse. If only she could think what it was. Perhaps it was to do with a story she had written. She mentally scanned through her main stories over the past few weeks: BestBuys and the allotments, Carla and the murder, Ricky and the burglaries, the Haybridge traders, the response to the Carla Fund. She arranged them all in an orderly file in her mind, and flipped through them, backwards and forwards. But that one little thought continued to remain elusive.

Jonathan also spent a restless weekend, alternatively sitting at his desk in the office spreading pieces of paper out in front of him, frowning at them and occasionally shuffling them around almost as though he was playing a game of Patience. This murder hunt *was* like a game of Patience, he thought wryly, except it was hard to be patient when there was a sense that time was running out and some of your pack of cards was still missing.

When Jonathan was not at his desk he sat in the King's Arms, on the sofa where he and Bella had fallen asleep together on that night which seemed so very long ago now. He smiled at the memory and ate his pie, which didn't seem to taste the same at all without Bella. Old Ed the landlord shot him an occasional sympathetic glance. Poor bloke – it looked like he was missing that pretty young red-haired lass of his.

Jonathan's only change of scene was for an hour on Saturday afternoon when he knocked at the door of a little stone cottage on the other side of the Common from Ron. It was called 'The Retreat' and he had seen it advertised to let in the *Gazette*. A friendly-faced lady answered the door and ushered him inside, explaining that she was going to live with her daughter in Australia and wanted to find a nice, reliable tenant.

'Only you hear so many horror stories, you know. All these youngsters who leave the place trashed – it's a real worry. But you seem a lovely, steady chap.' She eyed Jonathan up and down approvingly.

Jonathan agreed he was a steady chap – so steady I'm boring, he thought with a sigh. He looked around the small, cosy kitchen, where the late winter sun was streaming in through the gingham-curtained windows. It reminded him of Bella's kitchen – sort of warm and homely.

In the living room there was a large inglenook fire-place containing a black wrought iron grate and a wicker basket of logs. The rest of the room was painted white and there was a squashy-looking red sofa, a huge, slightly battered leather armchair and a coffee table. Perfect, thought Jonathan, imagining himself reading the paper in front of a roaring fire on cold, winter evenings. Upstairs there were two small bedrooms, one painted white with a double bed and simple wardrobe and one painted a soft blue with a frieze of football players around the walls.

'Sorry about that,' said the woman. 'It's my young grandson's room when he stays – he's mad about football.'

'Don't be sorry,' said Jonathan. 'It's great. The whole

house is perfect.' He reached in his pocket for his
chequebook.

On Monday morning Bella arrived at work on time, freshly
showered, neatly dressed and determined to tackle this
problem logically. She pulled out copies of the past four
weeks' *Gazettes* and cut out every one of her stories. Then
she went back through her notebooks. On a blank sheet
of paper she wrote a neat heading: 'Other Questions To
Be Asked'.

'What are you doing, Bel?' asked Suzy, realising her
friend had been too busy to even notice the Monday
morning doughnuts, let alone break her diet with one.

'I don't know, Suze. I really don't know,' said Bella,
looking up with a frown.

In the CID office Jonathan was leafing through a telephone
directory when Boz thrust a sheet of blue notepaper under
his nose. 'It's a thank-you letter, guv. Makes a change for
someone to bother to thank us. And a fifty quid cheque
for the Police Federation fund as well – can't be bad.'

Jonathan scanned the handwritten sheet irritably, taking
in the words 'on behalf of the traders in the town',
'excellent and thorough burglary investigation' and
'satisfying result'. It was, he noted, signed by Councillor
Ted Hanson on behalf of the Haybridge Chamber of
Commerce.

'Want me to give it to Superintendent Nixon, guv? It
might get us some Brownie points,' asked Boz.

Jonathan stared at the letter, then at his desk. He
thought so long and so hard that Boz started to get a bit
worried.

'Guv! Shall I give it to –'

Jonathan looked up sharply. 'No, Boz. Leave it on my desk please.' He picked up the phone and dialled a number. ''Ello, can I help you?' said a broad Italian voice.

Bella, after much sighing and pen-chewing, made her first entry under 'Other Questions To Be Asked'. She wrote 'Identity of hard-faced man in BestBuys', followed by a big question mark. She couldn't explain why she was curious about the man, other than the fact that she had taken an instant dislike to him and he hadn't seemed too impressed with her. Therefore he must have been up to no good. And somehow, thinking about the hard-faced man being up to no good made that niggling little thought in the back of her brain stop swirling around quite so much and swim tantalisingly towards her grasp.

Then she leafed through her contacts book and dialled a London number. 'Companies House,' a voice answered. Bella asked to be put through to Kevin Ayres in the press office. She had dealt with Kevin before and he had been helpful – even a bit flirtatious.

'You want the directors and company officials of BestBuys Ltd? Sure, I can do that,' said Kevin obligingly. Bella waited while he keyed the name into his computer and then carefully wrote down the eight names he dictated, checking the spelling of each one. She looked down her list – none of the names rang any bells at all.

'That's it then,' said Kevin. 'There's a note here saying there was a change of company secretary eight weeks ago but that's not very interesting to you, is it? I've given you the current one.'

'Who was the old one?' asked Bella.

'You know I can't tell you that. I'd have to access the private file.'

'Oh Kev,' Bella's tone was wheedling. 'And I was just

telling my friend Suzy here what a helpful press officer you were.' She watched as Suzy looked up from her computer in surprise.

'Bella – I can't!'

'I bet you can. You sound really clever to me. And I wouldn't dream of telling anyone how lovely you've been.' Bella tried not to laugh as Suzy mimed vomiting actions across the desk.

'Oh all right, you smooth-talking lady.' There was a long pause as Kevin accessed another file on his computer. 'A Mrs E. R. Hanson.'

'What does the E stand for?' asked Bella, her heart suddenly starting to pound.

'Elizabeth. Now – no more questions,' said Kevin firmly.

Bella put the handset down, forgetting even to say goodbye, and immediately clicked on to the electoral register service on her computer. Shakily she keyed in a name and town and held her breath as she pressed 'search'. There it was, in Elm Grove. A house called Larchwoods. And the occupants were listed as Hanson, Edward James and Hanson, Elizabeth Rose.

Bella stared at the screen in horror. She had it! She had found her 'other question to be asked'. It was a very big question indeed. And she was going to bloody well ask it right now.

She grabbed her bag and jacket. 'I'm nipping out, Suze.'

'Where?'

Bella looked at her friend for a long moment, debating whether she should tell her. Maybe there was a rational explanation for this. Maybe the Hansons could explain and it was all above board. Bella decided not to spread any scandal until she knew it was true. What a story it would make if it was though!

She hooked her bag on her shoulder, checking her notebook and pen were inside. 'I'm just popping out to

351

check something with Councillor Hanson. Tell Sean I won't be long, if he asks,' she said as casually as she could. Suzy grunted, already bored, and returned to writing her Women's Page feature.

'How quickly can you do it?' barked Jonathan at the poor scenes of crime man, who had taken two steps backwards at the sight of this scowling officer waving a piece of paper at him.

'I told you, sir – two to three hours. We have to soak it in a special solution to get a perfect result.'

Jonathan ran a hand across his brow. 'I just want a result – I don't care about the fucking quality. I'll be back in thirty minutes.' He thrust the paper into the man's hands and almost ran out of the office, muttering to himself as he went.

The SOCO man scratched his head in amazement. Was he muttering about Smarties? He'd heard this new guy was a bit offbeat and there was even some tale circulating about fish fingers in the canteen. But he seemed particularly nutty today...

They'd better be in, thought Bella, who was by now in a slightly confrontational mood as she drove towards Elm Grove. The thought flashed through her mind that she had promised Jonathan she would neither visit nor interview anyone until his investigations were over, but she pushed that thought aside. This was nothing whatsoever to do with his murder investigation, was it? This was, or could be, a case of commercial fraud – and a massive one at that. Ah, that was the councillor's BMW. Good, he was in.

Ted Hanson didn't look like a commercial fraudster

when he answered the door. He looked really rather ordinary in grey flannels and a blue cardigan. He also looked tired, and rubbed his hand across his eyes before he gave Bella an effusive greeting.

'To what do I owe this pleasure, lass?' he said, ushering her into the study.

'Is your wife in?' said Bella.

'No,' said Ted, looking mildly surprised. 'She's away at her sister's in Ireland with the children.'

'Aren't they at school?' Bella didn't know why she was asking – anything to delay the crunch question, she supposed.

'No, lass. They go to private school. They've finished for Christmas.' Ted looked even more puzzled. 'Now, what can I help you with? Is it about the fund?' He looked at his watch. He seems edgy today, thought Bella. And a bit rough round the edges somehow. Perhaps it was because his wife wasn't there to look after him.

She took a deep breath and came straight out with it. 'Was your wife Elizabeth the Company Secretary of BestBuys until eight weeks ago?'

Ted's mouth opened, then closed again and a flush spread slowly across his broad cheeks. 'That is rubbish. I don't know what you're trying to say here, young lady, but you'd better be careful. Your editor won't be too pleased with you making allegations like that,' he snapped, his northern accent suddenly getting stronger.

Shit, thought Bella. He looks a bit angry. 'I did a check with Companies House. They confirmed a Mrs Elizabeth Hanson was –'

'How dare you!' interrupted Ted. 'You've been sticking that nose in right where you shouldn't, young lady!' He was shouting now, and the flush was spreading downwards, towards his neck.

He stood up and loomed over Bella. Suddenly he

seemed very big and very tall. She shrank back in her chair, wondering how best to make a hasty exit. 'And where else have you been snooping round about me, girl? You tell me – what else have you found out?'

'Nothing!' bleated Bella. 'Honestly, I was just doing a follow-up about the planning application and I–'

'You can't kid me.' The councillor's face was going slightly purple now. He did not look well. He raised his voice slightly: 'I've seen you skulking about with that police officer, pretending you're so clever. It's not good for young girls to get clever with me. Makes me look a bloody fool, it does.' He clenched his large fists at his side. Beads of sweat were glistening on the purple brow. He was getting out of control now and Bella felt her heart thumping. Who would have thought he'd be so easily riled? The Mr Good Guy of Haybridge was turning into a monster before her eyes. She ought to get out of here.

She groped for her bag on the floor and stood up. But two hands gripped her shoulders and shoved her down roughly onto the chair. 'I think you'd better sit there and answer my questions!' Ted was literally spitting the words as he leaned over her, saliva flying from those thick red lips on to Bella's face.

She gave a whimper. 'Please, Councillor Hanson, I didn't mean to upset you. Please...' The words came out as a barely audible whisper and Bella half rose. 'I'll go now.'

'SIT!' The hands clamped her shoulders painfully and pushed her down. Bella winced and opened her mouth to plead some more. Something was wrong with her voice – she couldn't talk. Talk. Phone. Help. This man was dangerous. He was hurting her. She could dial the office, ask for David Ryan to come out and explain – calm down this strange, angry outburst. Quickly she groped into her bag, her trembling hand closing round the reassuring bulk of her phone.

354

'Oh no you don't!' screamed Ted, grabbing the phone out of her hand and hurling it across the room. 'You want to fuck with the big boys then you don't go crying to the cops. I'm sick of your questions – you can answer mine for a change.' He hauled her to her feet like a rag doll and gripped her shoulders again. He shook her once, grunting with the effort and causing Bella's head to fly back and crack violently against the wooden shelf of the bookcase. 'Aargh,' she screamed, feeling the searing pain.

Ted shook her again. 'Now perhaps you'll tell me. First question; what were you doing at Ricky Thomas's house?' His grip tightened.

Bella could hardly see his face any more. The room was spinning round and hundreds of black dots were dancing in front of her eyes. His words sounded echoey in her ears. But somewhere in the recesses of her brain she realised he was talking about Ricky Thomas. Why? This was about BestBuys.

'You know Ricky?' It didn't sound like her voice. It was all floaty.

Smash! Her head smashed against the bookcase again. 'You know damn well I do. And it was fine until the stupid little fool got himself nicked – thanks to *your* copper.' A great blob of saliva landed on Bella's forehead. She felt her stomach lurch – she was going to be sick … She tried to wriggle free from Ted's grasp.

'Oh no you don't!' bellowed Ted, aiming a fist at her stomach. Bella bent double, gasping for air, and Ted seized the back of her hair, yanking her head upright. For a terrifying moment she stared into his eyes, which were red-rimmed and blazing with pure hatred.

Suddenly the elusive thought that had been bothering her all weekend exploded up to the surface. Ricky. Burglaries. List! She could picture the neatly written list she had found in the newsagent's desk: Ryans Estate

Agents, Perry and Sons Butchers, Bessie's Bargain Basement and Greens and Co Greengrocers. Then an image of Jonathan's list of burglaries flew before her eyes – the identical shops in the identical order.

Bella's shoulders went limp as the realisation dawned. 'You told Ricky to do the burglaries, didn't you? You gave him a list of shops to rob.' Everything suddenly fell into place, crystal clear in her poor throbbing brain. 'You wanted to scare the traders away, so they wouldn't object to BestBuys – so you and your wife could make lots of money. That's right, isn't it?' she whispered.

She felt Ted's hands creep round her neck and he lowered his face until it was an inch away from hers.

'Clever little slut, aren't you? It doesn't do for little sluts to get too cocky. Look what happened to that crazy au pair girl when she tried to get all clever with me.'

Bella could smell his rancid breath now and could see the saliva and sweat drooling down his chin. She could feel something warm trickling down the back of her neck and wondered whether it was blood or whether she was sweating too. Her stomach gave another lurch. She felt the hands tighten their grip just a fraction. No! Surely he wasn't going to... 'NO!' screamed Bella at the top of her voice. 'NO!' An image of her daughter's little freckled face flew into her brain. 'NO ... EMILY!' she screamed. 'EMILEEEE'.

Ted's hands tightened, his fat fingers meeting around Bella's throat. He lowered his voice to a whisper, which was somehow far more sinister than his previous bellows. 'You're just like that fucking Carla. She thought she knew it all too. And look where that got her!' Sweat was streaming freely down Ted's face now and his hands were trembling violently as they pressed on her throat. Bella's lungs were burning, searing with pain, and desperately she tried to suck in air through her mouth. The hands tightened again.

The room swam and a huge whooshing noise filled Bella's ears, so loud it was blocking out Ted's words as he ranted about sluts and bitches. Images of Carla's dead body kept floating before her eyes – Carla's mottled legs, Carla's bulging eyes and poor, strangled neck. But only one word kept drumming through Bella's brain, over and over again: Emily, Emily, Emily.

Her last conscious thought was that she had promised Emily fish fingers for tea. Then the room went black, the whooshing noise stopped and there was a huge crash instead. Bella felt herself fall, in almost graceful, floating slow motion, to somewhere far more warm and soft and welcoming than the hell she had been in for the past ten minutes . She allowed herself to float peacefully away, her lips poised to call her daughter's name one last time: Emily, Emily.

Right at the final second she added another name – Jonathan ... where are you, Jonathan?

Chapter Thirty-One

'I'm here... I'm here...' The voice kept whispering on
and on and it was irritating. Bella flapped a hand to push
it away but something was stopping her moving properly.
There was a tube thing coming out of the back of her
hand and it was attached to something. She didn't know
what it was or indeed where she was but it wasn't very
comfortable at all. The lights were too bright and her
head hurt. It was too quiet as well. There was no little
girl chattering... Emily! Where was Emily? She had to
pick her up from school – she would be late. She had to
go. Quick – Em! She tried to struggle up from her prone
position.

'Shh,' said the voice and a gentle hand pushed her
back. 'Emily is fine. Roger and Suzy are looking after her
at your flat. Your mum is there and they're all eating a
huge chicken casserole that she brought with her.'

Bella relaxed back against a hard lumpy pillow, while
the hand gently stroked her brow. Oh, that was all right
then – just as long as Em was having a proper dinner.
It was quite a nice feeling, this hand stroking her face.
She gave a little sigh and allowed herself to relax. She
felt a soft pair of lips brush her cheek. 'That's right,
sweetheart, you have a little sleep. I'm not going anywhere.
I'm staying right here.'

In the morning Bella opened her eyes, sat bolt upright,
clutched her head – which seemed to be swathed in

bandages – and said very loudly: 'What the fuck...?'

The person holding her hand, the hand without the tube coming out of it, gave a deep chuckle. 'Well, your vocabulary certainly doesn't seem to have suffered!'

Bella swivelled her head, then regretted it. 'Ouch.' She stared at the unshaven, exhausted-looking face beside her, taking in the deep, dark circles under the eyes and the anxious lines around the mouth.

'Shit – you look bloody awful!' she cried.

'Bella,' sighed Jonathan. 'You have been fully conscious for about thirty seconds and said less than ten words, three of which happen to be swear words. Is this percentage ratio going to continue? Only there are a couple of elderly ladies over there looking particularly offended.'

'I don't know,' said Bella. 'I'm not very good at percentages.'

'So I recall,' said Jonathan, remembering their very first conversation. He continued, making his voice gentle. 'To answer your first question, you are in hospital, but luckily, apart from a nasty case of concussion and a couple of stitches to the back of your head, there is nothing seriously wrong with you and you should be allowed home later today.'

He gave an involuntary shudder, remembering how he had thought there was something very seriously wrong indeed with Bella – in fact how he had been convinced she was dead – when he had smashed his way into Ted Hanson's study. He clutched her hand tighter, and watched her face, pale against the pillow, crinkle into a frown as her memory gradually returned.

'Do you want to talk about it, Bella? We needn't – not yet. It's enough that you're safe and well,' he said.

'Too bloody right I want to talk about it!' Bella answered. The old lady opposite tutted and Jonathan addressed her politely across the room. 'I am so sorry, Madam. It is occasionally a symptom of concussion that a patient uses rather ... er ... extreme language. I can assure you that she is a very nice young lady really.'

He turned back to Bella. 'I suppose you want to ask the questions?' She nodded.

'Okay. Fire away.'

'Ted Hanson killed Carla, didn't he?'

'Yes. He did. He confessed everything when I arrested him.' And, Jonathan added silently, he almost killed you too – causing me the worst few minutes I have ever experienced in my life.

He continued: 'He had met her two months before she died, when she came to babysit his children one Saturday night. He admits he felt a huge sexual attraction to her and made a pass at her when he drove her home in his car. He found out her dream was to go to college to study computers but her employers refused to give her time off to do the free daytime course at the local place. So Hanson tried to buy her. He promised to pay £4,000 for a private course at Peerfields.'

'So she had sex with him for a college course?' Bella was incredulous.

'Sadly yes. It meant that much to her. She was besotted with Ricky, of course, but it seems she viewed Hanson as a business arrangement – something to secure her future. Hanson said he had sex with her three times over the course of several days, always in the car in a secluded place. Then, it seems, he tired of her. She was asking to be taken out more – she wanted to be wined and dined as well and told him she was sick of meeting in the car. He agreed to take her for a drink and that was when they arranged to meet at the golf club.'

'But he didn't show up?'

'No – he never actually intended to. He had a council meeting scheduled all along. He hoped she'd feel a fool at the club and slink off, never to bother him again. But it didn't work out like that.'

'Because Carla was pregnant?'

'Yes. She phoned Hanson at his house the week before she died. She'd got the number from her employers' address book, he thinks. It threw him into a real panic because his wife could have answered the phone.'

'I can't imagine he's scared of his wife though,' said Bella. 'Unless she's a real battleaxe.'

'That's another story,' said Jonathan, who had been told by his colleagues in Ireland of the relief in Elizabeth Hanson's eyes when they broke the news that her husband had been arrested. 'I think his wife may had been an unwitting pawn in this whole mess for a long time. 'But,' he continued, 'Hanson's biggest worry of all was his reputation. He showed no remorse to us about killing Carla. His only concern was what his colleagues at the council and the golf club would say about it. Oh – and the Chamber of Commerce too, but I'll tell you more about that later.'

'I always thought he was egotistical,' mused Bella. 'He always liked to shout about his good deeds.'

'It's probably a sign of some deep insecurity and a need to be liked,' said Jonathan. 'Well, I expect that's what they'll say on his psychiatric reports anyway.'

'So he was cross when Carla told him she was pregnant?'

'Furious, yes. He tried to say the baby wasn't his then when she insisted it had to be – because Ricky was always so careful – he talked her into having an abortion.' At this point Jonathan gave Bella's hand a sympathetic squeeze and looked anxiously to see if she was upset.

'It's OK. I'm over the Hugo stuff now,' she said. 'Go on.'

'It had to be hushed up. Hanson was scared Carla would start talking if she had to wait for a National Health abortion. He was also worried she'd change her mind and keep the baby – which would ruin his squeaky clean reputation. So he contacted his golfing mate, a consultant called James Rutherford, and persuaded him to do a very quick, very private job at the Viking Clinic the next Saturday afternoon.'

'The chap you met at the cheque presentation?'

'Yes. Well remembered,' said Jonathan approvingly. 'Rutherford gave me a vital clue on Friday when I went to see him. When I asked if Carla was his patient he immediately denied carrying out her operation. But, of course, there was no way he should have known she'd had one. That was when I started putting two and two together – but it was all very jumbled.'

Jonathan explained how the consultant had slipped Carla in the back entrance and performed the surgery single-handed, breaking every law in the surgeon's book. 'He won't ever operate again – in fact he could face prison,' he said grimly.

Hanson had taken Carla to the clinic in his car and then returned a couple of hours later to pick her up. But the young au pair was not happy, he said.

'Of course – she'd lost her baby,' said Bella, her eyes filling with tears.

'Well, actually she was more bothered about the fact that she had phoned the college the day before to check the start date of her course and they told her it hadn't been paid for. Hanson had changed his mind and not sent off the cheque he'd promised – but hadn't even told her. That was what they were rowing about on the way home from the clinic.' Jonathan patted Bella's hand. 'But I'm sure she was terribly upset about the baby too,' he added.

Bella nodded and Jonathan continued: 'Hanson had arranged to drop her near her employers' house and he was going to drive on to the golf club do and meet his wife there. But Carla started getting really upset and angry and was screaming at him. She tried to get out of the car while he was driving along.'

'And Hanson was worried someone would see, I bet. Someone who might recognise him?'

'You got it in one. So when they stopped at the traffic lights just down the road from the Swan he wasn't too bothered when Carla suddenly shot out. She left her holdall in the boot though – the bag she'd packed with spare clothes and bits and pieces to go to the clinic. He dumped that in the canal later.'

'Which is why the police weren't that bothered when she was first reported missing?'

'Exactly,' said Jonathan. 'This concussion doesn't seem to have made your brain any less sharp, by the way. Are you sure you don't want a little rest now though?'

'Don't stop now, for God's sake,' said Bella, through gritted teeth.

'OK. Hanson drove to the golf club where he was having a nice, relaxed evening – until 10.30, when Carla called his mobile.'

'She was still upset?'

'Hysterical. She'd rowed with Ricky. He'd slapped her round the face and left her standing in the street, alone, feeling ill and furious with men in general. She'd been forced to have an abortion, her dream of a college place had gone and her boyfriend had shown her no sympathy whatsoever – not that he knew any of what she'd been through anyway.'

'Poor, poor Carla. So she let rip with Hanson?'

'Not half! She screamed and shouted apparently and threatened to tell his wife. But she also said something which deeply disturbed Hanson – about someone he hadn't realised she even knew.'

'Who?' Bella looked puzzled.

'Ricky Thomas. The guy Hanson was paying to burgle the hell out of Haybridge.' Jonathan paused for effect then continued: 'Carla, who was not a stupid girl by any means, had heard Ricky brag about one or two items he'd stolen and once she'd seen him sell something to his handler down the road. She listened to a phone call one night at his house and heard him address the caller as Councillor. Ricky had hinted to her that he was working for a very influential person so she put two and two together – and hit Hanson with the lot of it during that phone call... She threatened to tell the police he was the Mr Big of the burglaries.'

'Yes, I'd worked that out too,' said Bella, and explained about the list of traders she had seen in Hanson's drawer.

'So your little surveillance exercise paid off after all!' grinned Jonathan.

Bella had the grace to blush and changed the subject. 'I can't help feeling sorry for Ricky. He really was just a pawn in all this. Will he get a lighter sentence now?'

'Without a doubt. Hanson has confessed he was the mastermind behind it all and took half the proceeds. He wanted to put the wind up the traders. He even offered them cheap alarms through the Chamber of Commerce, using a mate of his who he knew couldn't handle the workload. While the traders were waiting for the alarm to be fitted, Hanson got Ricky to burgle their shops. He pocketed half the cash to maintain his affluent lifestyle. So, ironically, the money he gave out in generous donations – including a £50 cheque for the Police Federation incidentally – was money from the proceeds of crime!'

'Great story,' grinned Bella. 'And of course he stood to make loads more money if the BestBuys planning application went through.'

Jonathan looked at her blankly.

364

'His wife was BestBuys company secretary until recently – I did a check. So it was obviously a massive corporate fiddle and her name was probably whipped off at the last minute so the council wouldn't make the connection. But you can bet there would have been big money involved for Hanson.'

'Good girl,' said Jonathan. 'I'll be having a little chat with those BestBuys people then. I think you'll find that planning application may be withdrawn now. And, thank God – that explains something that's been really bugging me.'

Bella raised an eyebrow. Jonathan grinned – the eyebrow was his trick. 'The Smarties!' he said. 'Why would Hanson take a packet of Smarties off the shelf and give them to Em if the shop is nothing to do with him?'

'Oh yes,' said Bella, 'good point. But back to the murder...'

'OK, my bloodthirsty little sleuth. It was exactly as you speculated – except you had the wrong person at the time. Hanson agreed to meet Carla because he was scared of the burglary threat. He drove to the car park of the swimming pool – where there's no CCTV cameras – lost his temper with her and strangled her. But he didn't dump the body there and then – he kept it in his boot until *after* the dinner dance and slipped out after his wife had gone to bed.'

'Ah,' said Bella. 'That explains why my timing was out. So Ted Hanson was missing at the same time as the Superintendent?'

'Yes, but the Superintendent was having a bit of stomach trouble in the loo, it transpires. Too much rich food, he says! It was when you told me the table was half empty though that I first started to suspect Hanson.'

'You didn't tell *me* you bloody well suspected him!' yelled Bella.

Jonathan winked at the old lady opposite. 'Shh ... I didn't know it myself at first. It all started coming together yesterday morning. I couldn't stop thinking about the missing CCTV tape – which Hanson has admitted to destroying, by the way. I was trying to work out who could take it. I'm afraid I never could take your Superintendent theory seriously.' He smiled and continued. 'So I rang Kayleigh and got her to draw me a table plan of the guests. Then I kept thinking about those bloody Smarties – and Hanson's name kept coming up, again and again.' He paused. 'Then the final bit was the letter. He sent a letter to congratulate us on the burglary arrest and it sounded so ... so false somehow. I shot downstairs to SOCO and got them to compare the fingerprints on the letter to the fingerprints on Carla's library card. They did a bit of a rush job but it was obvious it was a match.'

He looked Bella in the eyes. 'Then I rang you – just as I promised I would when I finally got the breakthrough. And Suzy said you weren't there. She said you'd gone to see Ted Hanson...'

Jonathan's heart pounded as he recalled that terrible, breakneck drive across Haybridge, steering the car one-handed as he called for back-up and rang Bella's mobile, time after time, only to get the number unobtainable tone because it was lying broken on Hanson's floor.

'Oh yes,' said Bella. 'I'm sorry I broke my promise. But I didn't know –'

'Hey. It's okay.' Jonathan reached out and stroked her hair. 'I got there just in time, that was the important thing.'

'What happened?' whispered Bella, starting to tremble.

'He had almost strangled you, sweetheart. I broke down the door of the house and rushed in to find him with his hands round your neck. You ... you didn't look good,' said Jonathan, shuddering at the memory of the pale, rag doll-like figure, bleeding from the back of the head. 'So I grabbed the nearest thing – a heavy iron doorstop – and I hit him over the back of the head. He let go, you fell to the ground and I caught you just as the back-up crew arrived. It was pretty perfect timing actually.'

Bella gave a watery smile. 'Thank you,' she said. 'I guess I owe you now.'

'Rubbish,' said Jonathan, trying to be brisk because he felt a little bit emotional himself. Well, quite a lot emotional actually. 'Now, I think you should rest. Your parents and Emily are coming later. I'll stay with you, but is there anything I can get you. Drink? Food?'

'No thanks,' said Bella, with a smile. 'Well, perhaps there's one thing you could do.'

Jonathan cocked an eyebrow.

'Could you just lie down here so I can put my head on your chest – on that little bit, just there?' She pointed. 'Only this pillow is bloody uncomfortable.'

Chapter Thirty-Two

'Wake up, you two,' said the nurse, prodding Jonathan gently in the stomach. 'I need to do your blood pressure now.'

Bella moaned and snuggled deeper into Jonathan's chest. He put a protective arm around her. God, he'd just had the most blissful nap. He hadn't slept so well in months. 'Can't it wait?' he yawned.

'Not really,' smiled the nurse, 'it's nearly visiting time. You've been asleep for hours – sleeping like babies, the pair of you. We've all been watching you, thinking how cute you looked.'

'Cute?' said Jonathan, feeling the curled-up body next to him begin to giggle. 'I don't think I'm a cute sort of person.'

'That's not what your Detective Constable said when he saw you – that young curly-haired chap. He said he'd tell them all back at the station how sweet you looked. Oh, and he said don't worry about the paperwork, he's got it sorted.'

Boz! Oh no, thought Jonathan, feeling Bella's shoulders wobble even more. 'Come on then, Sleeping Beauty,' he said. 'I know you're awake. Roll that sleeve up for the nurse. I'll go and get us some tea.'

Bella's eyes lit up. 'And...'

'Yes – and a bar of chocolate.' Jonathan turned to the nurse. 'I think you'll find she's feeling better if she's fancying chocolate.'

He returned to find Bella in pleasing clinical shape and

minus her tubes and drips but scowling at her appearance in a hand mirror. 'God, why didn't you tell me I looked so awful?' she groaned, surveying her blood-streaked, bandaged head and mascara rimmed eyes.

'You look fine to me,' said Jonathan, popping a square of chocolate into her mouth. 'But I'll get you a cloth to wipe your face if you want – before Em sees you.'

He wandered off to chat up a nurse and returned with a bowl of warm water and a flannel. 'Here, I'll do it,' he said. He dipped the flannel in the water and gently wiped around Bella's cheekbones, then her forehead, under the bandage, then down her nose. Very gently, he rinsed the flannel again and repeated the action on the delicate skin of her throat and under her eyes. Smoothing her hair back off her face, he surveyed the result. 'God, you're beautiful,' he murmured, his eyes suddenly looking very blue.

Bella stared back. Once again the blue eyes met the grey eyes and held their gaze, unblinkingly, for what seemed like forever. Gently, Jonathan put down the bowl of water and flannel, and cupped Bella's face in his hands. She put her hands round his shoulders, feeling the soft, dark hair curling at the nape of his neck and slowly, very slowly pulled his face towards hers until their lips were a fraction of an inch apart.

'I don't care about Madeleine and your house. Just kiss me once,' she begged.

'There is no Madeleine any more, sweetheart. She's gone. There's no house either – just a tiny little bachelor pad of a cottage. A cottage by The Common where a certain beautiful reporter and her wonderful little daughter will be welcome to pop in any time they like – for as long as they like.' He paused. 'When they're not seeing Hugo, that is.'

Bella, enjoying the feel of Jonathan's warm breath on

her lips, felt a delicious shiver run down her spine, through her arms and into her fingertips. 'There is no Hugo either. At least not for me. He'll always be welcome as Emily's dad but that's all,' she said, slightly breathlessly. Then her heart sank as she remembered one important fact. 'How can we pop in for as long as we like when you're going back to the Met soon?' she whispered.

'That's not necessarily a fact,' said Jonathan.

'In that case, then...' Bella stroked the back of his neck. Jonathan moved his lips closer. They brushed against Bella's, gently at first, then just a tiny, tiny bit harder...

Orchestras started to play, waves began to crash against sandy beaches and a ton of fireworks were just about to explode into a great, starry mass in the sky when suddenly: 'Coo-ey! We're here!'

Bella and Jonathan sprang apart. There, standing in a great smiling crowd, clutching gifts in abundance, was a veritable visiting committee. Their eyes took in Emily at the front, holding a home-made card almost as big as herself, then Bella's beaming parents, holding magazines and flowers, then Suzy and Roger with a multi-coloured bunch of get well soon balloons, and finally a dazed-looking Ron with one arm round Mrs Vapolluci's waist and the other holding aloft a bunch of purple sprouting broccoli. He caught Bella's eye. 'I reckon those hospital veg are horrible, Miss Bella. You need your vitamins,' he explained.

Emily put her hands on her hips. 'Were you two *kissing*?' she squeaked, grinning hugely.

Jonathan and Bella blinked in unison, wondering what to say. Their guests waited in silence, holding their breath as one. Suddenly they were saved by a commotion at the rear, and in crashed a red-faced, panting Luigi and, skidding to a halt behind him, an equally breathless Mamma, bearing a massive covered dish. 'My Bella – Bella *caro*!

We heard you were poorly. Poor, poor Bella. We bring you some food,' she cried.

As one, the group of visitors surged forward, suddenly all talking at once, asking what happened, how was Bella's poor head, when was she coming home ... Bella, who had scooped Emily up in her arms and was blissfully inhaling the little girl scent, sat quietly and smiled, happy for Jonathan to answer for her.

'Love you, Mum,' whispered Emily. 'Love you too,' whispered Bella back.

After fifteen minutes, when the food was all gone, the cards read, the flowers put in water and the broccoli carted off to the hospital kitchens, the festive atmosphere was still showing no sign of abating. The visitors were getting on like a house on fire. Jonathan, still sitting on Bella's bed, with Em's legs sprawled across his knees, quietly surveyed the happy faces.

'How the hell can I leave all this and go back to London?' he murmured to Bella, watching her face light up in response.

'But what will you do – about your job?' she whispered.

'Well, there's a nice little permanent vacancy in Haybridge CID I could apply for. And I'm told there's a cracking little Haybridge journalist who could assist on the more tricky cases.' ·

Bella moved to fling her arms around his neck – then stopped abruptly when she remembered her visitors.

Out of the corner of his eye, Jonathan saw a nurse approaching, tapping her watch. Quickly he stood up, scooped Emily under one arm and turned to face the crowd. 'Ladies and gentlemen, I have a request to make and I would like to ask a certain little girl first.'

He turned the child round to face him and looked at her solemnly. 'Emily Smart – do I have your permission to kiss your mother?'

371

Emily cocked her head and looked him squarely back in the eye. Her face broke out into a huge smile. 'You crack on, mate!' she told him firmly, raising one fist in the air.

Behind her the crowd broke out into a huge cheer and even the balloons bobbed in agreement. Jonathan held up one hand. 'I take it that's unanimous then?' The cheer erupted again.

Jonathan plonked Emily down next to her grandparents and swiftly pulled the curtains around the bed. 'If you will excuse me then, we have some unfinished business to attend to,' he told the crowd, before disappearing inside.

This time there was no preamble, no teasing and not a single regret. The lips met, urgently, passionately, exploding into an intensity neither had ever felt before. They kissed on, and on, and on, lost in their own silent little world.

They probably would have kissed for ever had not a skinny little body broken free from its grandmother's clutches and launched itself through the curtain onto the bed – right between them – to beam down at them with an interested, freckled face.

'Yuk!' declared Em. 'Is that how long kissing takes? I'm never going to do *that*!'

Bella and Jonathan took one little hand each and smiled at each other over the top of Emily's head.

'You will, darling – when the time is right,' they said, in absolute unison.